BEFORE WE WERE WICKED

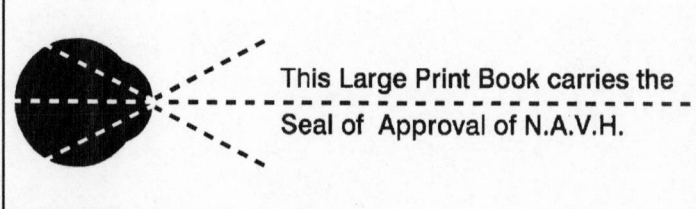

This Large Print Book carries the
Seal of Approval of N.A.V.H.

BEFORE WE WERE WICKED

ERIC JEROME DICKEY

THORNDIKE PRESS

A part of Gale, a Cengage Company

Farmington Hills, Mich • San Francisco • New York • Waterville, Maine
Meriden, Conn • Mason, Ohio • Chicago

Copyright © 2019 by Eric Jerome Dickey.
Thorndike Press, a part of Gale, a Cengage Company.

Thorndike Press® Large Print African-American.
The text of this Large Print edition is unabridged.
Other aspects of the book may vary from the original edition.
Set in 16 pt. Plantin.

LIBRARY OF CONGRESS CIP DATA ON FILE.
CATALOGUING IN PUBLICATION FOR THIS BOOK
IS AVAILABLE FROM THE LIBRARY OF CONGRESS

ISBN-13: 978-1-4328-6238-1 (hardcover alk. paper)

Published in 2019 by arrangement with Dutton, an imprint of Penguin Publishing Group, a division of Penguin Random House LLC

Printed in Mexico
2 3 4 5 6 7 23 22 21 20 19

For Carolyn. For Virginia.
For Lila. For Vardaman.

We are torn between a nostalgia for the familiar and an urge for the foreign and strange. As often as not, we are homesick most for the places we have never known.

— Carson McCullers

Love is an untamed force. When we try to control it, it destroys us.

— Paulo Coelho

Birds born in a cage think flying is an illness.

— Alejandro Jodorowsky

CHAPTER 1

Los Angeles, 1996

That Friday night we'd been sent to Club Fetish by our employer, San Bernardino.

I was a bill collector, a small-time enforcer, and had to talk to a stubborn man about an overdue debt. He was ninety days late with the duckets.

That was the night I met her.

I was driving; had the top down on my convertible Benz, warm air turning cool as we moved through desert county down unforgiving La Cienega Boulevard. *La Cienega* was Spanish for "the swamp" and rightfully so, since it was always inundated with traffic. My coworker and I had rolled north from the edges of Culver City to the overcrowded area up into Hollywood, had left the workingmen's zip codes around ten p.m. and mixed in with the pretenders and tourists rocking BMWs, Lamborghinis, and Maseratis. A couple of DeLorean DMC-

12s were on the road with the luxury and sports cars. A Ghanaian who called himself Jake Ellis was at my side. He was my wingman. We were well dressed, fashionable, as I moved us from Leimert Park to the plastic and pretentious side of Los Angeles, the mile-and-a-half stretch of Sunset between Hollywood and Beverly Hills known worldwide as the Sunset Strip. Bright lights, six lanes of snarling traffic. Hundreds of clubs and bars existed on a snaking street that stretched from the bustle of downtown LA's Garment District and her skid row to the ocean-side mansions of the rich and more-famous-than-rich in Malibu. One end of Sunset was poverty and obscurity, and the opposite end was fame or fortune, or fame and fortune if enough people loved your acting, your directing, or the cocaine you sold. That twenty-two-mile boulevard was a metaphor. It was everyman's journey. Not many made it from Crackland to Cocaineville. Men like me had started in the middle but still had spent all of their lives trying to make it from one end to the other. Women had done the same. I wasn't even halfway. Most days felt like I was still at the starting gate. But I was young. I had time.

As we crawled past the Comedy Store, Jake Ellis asked, "Bruv, we set?"

Checking out droves of foreign women as the club hopped, I nodded. "We set, bro. We set."

"You strapped?"

"Yeah. But I'm leaving it in the stash spot. Security's gonna search us."

Jake Ellis nodded. "Some fine women out tonight."

"Always. From all over the world. Every woman in the world ends up here at some point."

"Women in Ghana and Nigeria still look better."

"I'll bet they do."

"How would you know?"

"You say it over and over."

I cruised the section of West Hollywood bounded by Doheny Drive on the west and Crescent Heights Boulevard on the east, went down a mile and a half of that metaphor called the Sunset Strip, where celebrities went to overdose curbside, hollered at a few honeys from the car, took advantage of rocking a convertible, then turned back around, headed to our official destination. The Strip was in party mode. It was always in party mode.

When the sun set, the lights were brighter than Vegas and the sky was polluted with billboards pimping out the latest up-and-coming Hollywood movie. People sat in traffic, bumper to bumper, from sundown until two in the morning. Headlights for miles; brake lights for days. The mile-and-a-half commercial strip was packed with restaurants and clubs. Sunset Boulevard was drug central, Cocaine University, the Hollywood culture on steroids.

Jake Ellis asked, "Heard from that girl you broke up with?"

"I called Lupita a few times. Left a couple of messages. Left my pager number. Nothing."

"She's got a new dude and she's not looking back this way."

"So it goes."

"Not many women can handle what we do."

"Never should have told her."

"I told you that from jump street."

With Jake Ellis at my side, I stepped into the spotlight of a swank alcohol- and cocaine-filled club near the Boulevard of Broken Dreams, blended with a twenty-one-and-over crowd rocking it out to Biggie Smalls. Mostly white people. White people loved rap music the way people from Memphis loved Beale Street barbecue. Men grabbed their dicks if they loved hip-hop and women rubbed their tits if they loved

Big Poppa.

Jake Ellis said, "Spot is hot."

"Packed like a can of sardines every night and this motherfucker crying broke."

"Boss man will be here tonight?"

"He'll be here. He's back from Cancún, and San Bernardino verified he'd be here."

"How bad we have to hurt this one?"

"Bad enough for him to never miss another payment to San Bernardino."

"Pretty bad."

"Yeah, pretty bad. But not as bad as we did that guy down in San Diego."

With Jake Ellis leading the way, we moved through the controlled madness. Everybody flocked to the most expensive clubs, paid a grip to park, then popped E and did more white lines than were on I-5 going north. I never understood this life. It was a spot where liberals and freaks went to prove how liberal and freaky they were by having a bathroom fling or a ten-minute parking-lot rendezvous with someone from another culture, and some performed as strangers watched the show. There was plenty of girl-on-girl action in the stalls. Hollywood men were in back seats of luxury cars giving other Hollywood men brain too. Or those same men, those male ingénues who were hungry for fame, stood on a powerful man's designated side of a glory hole. Anything to get a movie deal. Or just to get laid.

Jake Ellis said, "Your people are wild."

"Shit, these ain't my people."

"They're Americans. You're American."

"I'm African American."

"No such thing because there is no such country."

"That joke is getting old, bro."

"There is no country called African America on a map. All of you capitalists are Americans."

AIDS had arrived and made people think that getting herpes wasn't such a bad deal after all. Gays died and President Reagan turned a blind eye because he was too busy with his war on drugs, which was really an extension of Nixon's war on hippies and black and brown people. Hypocritical religious leaders were on the air preaching and smiling and laughing that AIDS was the work of God, his way of ridding the world of homosexuals. That was until white men saw masculine men like Rock Hudson catch the virus, wither, and succumb. Then God left the equation. AIDS billboards stood high on every boulevard in West Hollywood and South Central, but the rich and famous and their hangers-on still partied like it was already 1999. Some places, anything goes. Club Fetish was one of those spots. It was a new club, and people loved new things. Our boss, San Bernardino, had fronted an ambitious foreign man part of the money to make the club happen; was owed in the five figures, and the agreed-upon payments hadn't been made since the club opened three months ago. We'd been sent to deliver a message. Not to Cabbage Patch or chat.

But that didn't mean we weren't gonna party a bit and check out the talent.

Jake Ellis was a Ghanaian who could be a boxing contender. He had grown up in abject poverty and used his hands to fight himself out of what would be called his African ghetto. Both of us grew up in boxing gyms, only his had no walls and no roof and his atmosphere was the weather. When we traveled as a team, it was always about the money. It was always for money owed to San Bernardino. We were the last men you wanted to see step in a room looking for you. We had been busting heads and breaking limbs for San Bernardino for three years. That money was being used to put me through college at UCLA. I was a sophomore, in my second year. I had started a year late because of lack of money. I had found a job that paid in cash, and doing a little wrong was going to make my life a lot more right.

I hurt people, but they weren't good people. They always had it coming. There were bad people out there, but I was arrogant enough to think I was the baddest of the bad. There were wicked people, but I could be more wicked if I needed to be. When a man was young and yet to be humbled, hurting people could seem like fun.

I was twenty-one, rocking a convertible, young, dumb, and full of come, and still a man not easily distracted.

But when I saw her standing in the crowd, when my eyes touched hers, that changed.

Long, thick, wavy hair. Brown skin, sweet like agave. Pretty enough for Tom Ford to hire her for his fall Gucci line. White short skirt, red high heels, the right amount of cleavage given up by her red blouse. She should've been on the cover of *Vogue Paris.* There were a lot of fine-ass trust-fund girls in this arena sponsored by Yves Saint Laurent, Dolce & Gabbana, Victoria's Secret, and Louis Vuitton. But she was the one who had my attention. It was more than her looks. It was all about energy. I saw her when Jake Ellis and I crossed the dance floor, saw her tugging on her hungry miniskirt, slowed my stroll and watched her pull it down. Soon as she did, it again tried to rise over the curve of her butt. She tugged. It was a never-ending battle. An erotic battle. I prayed for the miniskirt to win. She caught me looking and I winked at her. She moved her hair from her face.

Then she smiled. All it took to start trouble was a smile. That was how Delilah got Sampson. The cutie with the booty was with a guy who rocked a suit, but she stood out in the crowd of American Express–carrying cokeheads. Cutie had some energy that tugged me her way. Her gravitational pull was a beast. That energy muted the music and made everyone else fade into the background. For a moment, it was just me and her. Adam and Eve. Only my Eve probably wore a headscarf to bed and her hair smelled like coconut oil. And maybe she liked patchouli and burned incense every now and then. The instant I saw her, I was snared, and it took my mind off the reason I was there.

I grabbed his shoulder, told Jake Ellis, "Hold up, bro."

"What's up, bruv?"

The cutie stood next to her date, a well-dressed bro who looked successful. He was holding her hand, but she wasn't holding his hand in return. She looked at me, touched her hair. A man held her hand and with a boldness, she smiled at me. I knew what that smile meant. She wanted to initiate something but didn't know how to get free.

I posted half a smile and told Jake Ellis, "Keep your eye on the target."

"He'll be here all night."

I motioned toward the pretty brown skin. "What you think?"

"She's what we call a *tonga*."

"*Tonga?*"

"That's a Twi expression — a dialect of my country's Akan language."

"Break it down."

"It means she is a gorgeous, overwhelmingly appealing woman."

"No doubt."

"And women like her have the power to lead the strongest of men into hard situations."

"I can handle her."

"The guy with her is looking at you like he's pissed that she's staring at you."

"I can whup his ass, then make him shine my shoes and wash my car."

"Bruv, looks like pretty boy is ready to rip you a new one."

"If a fight breaks out, don't jump in it unless someone else helps pretty boy."

Jake Ellis saw a hot momma on the other side of the club. A Janet Jackson type. She was checking him out and so were at least a half dozen other women. Jake Ellis went to the left and I went to the right.

Body checking people as I strolled, I swam upstream to that white skirt and stood in front of her.

I said, "Whassup?"

She responded, "Hi."

I sized up the guy with her. He was built like a power forward, at least six foot six, weighed two hundred and some change, bigger than me, was a Gregory Abbott type, had the Al B. Sure! complexion that made panties drop, but I could knock the light skin off of that motherfucker. He looked at me, uneasy, and I put my eyes on that white skirt hiding the heaven standing next to him. He had her. I wanted her. It was the primitive part of a man aroused.

Her guy stopped sipping his drink, confused. "What's going on?"

"I'm not talking to you."

"Is there a problem?"

"Yeah. There is a problem. A big problem. You're with my girl."

"Excuse me?"

"You heard me."

19

I told pretty boy that he was talking to my girlfriend and advised him to skedaddle while he could still skedaddle. He stared me down, saw this wasn't a joke. Then the big man backed the fuck away. He was a big man, and I was a solid man. I got in his face, like boxers at the start of a fight. He knew better. He nodded good-bye to White Skirt, said something to her in a foreign language, then nervously vanished into the crowd.

She evaluated me, nodded twice, then said, "So, I'm your girlfriend?"

"Who was that loser?"

"He's my boyfriend."

"Was your boyfriend."

"You're pretty confident."

"He's a coward. Punk-ass boy like him can't protect a pretty woman like you."

"Punk-ass boy? Must you emasculate him without knowing his name?"

"I saved you from a night of misery."

"I'm sorry. Had no idea I was a damsel in distress. Whoever you are."

She was incredibly soft-spoken and elegant, her accent sensual, arousing. And at the same time, that miniskirt and cleavage let me know she was all cayenne and honey, maybe more fire than sweetness.

I introduced myself. "Ken Swift."

She moved her hair from her face, shifted on her heels. "Jimi Lee."

"You have a southern name and an accent that doesn't match."

She tsked. "I know all about you."

"Do you?"

"Your accent, the inflection, the diction, tells me you're black American. Some college, if any at all. You haven't matriculated from a university, not yet. Maybe you grew up middle-class, but definitely not upper-class, and you didn't attend a private school. That edge, that boorishness you have, is public school."

"Good guess."

"Am I on point?"

"You're throwing a lot of stereotypes my way."

She said, "I know I'm right."

I asked, "Where are you from?"

"Ethiopia."

"That guy was talking to you in Ethiopian."

"Amharic. Our language is Amharic." She exhaled like she'd explained it many times before. "*Ethiopian* is a native or inhabitant of Ethiopia, or a person of Ethiopian descent, which we both are. *Ethiopia* is our fatherland."

"Your voice is amazing."

"Is it? How so?"

"The tone and texture. Your diction. You speak like soft music."

"You like this song?"

"Could listen to it all night long."

"That won't be happening."

"You never know."

She grinned. "You have amazing brows and lashes. And those lips. You have nice lips."

She smelled like Dior perfume. "You're pretty hot and tempting yourself."

"Okay. Let's cut to the chase. You have kids?"

"That's a strange question to ask at a club."

"I watch *Jerry Springer.* It's what black American men lie about the most, their flock of baby mommas."

"Flock? A flock of baby mommas? Is that the proper grouping?"

"I just wanted to get that out of the way."

"Sassy."

"If you have kids, even one, and that also considers any you might have on the way, any child you are denying and know might be yours, if any woman is claiming you are the father of her child, pack your drama, then walk away, and let me catch up with my old *punk-ass* ex-boyfriend. That punk ass has a PhD, just so you know."

"No. No baby mommas and no contenders. And most black American men don't have one."

"Oh, we know that is a lie. I watch your movies and talk shows."

"You're watching the wrong movies, and you sound too smart to watch those stupid talk shows."

"Okay, all this talking has me parched. Mr. Single, buy me a drink."

I grinned, guessed I had passed the interview. "What's your poison?"

"Long Island Iced Tea. Since I have no money and you scared my date out of the club."

"You're snarky and bossy. Small and act like you're twelve feet tall."

"You're arrogant and intrusive."

"And I'm your new boyfriend."

She laughed. "Make good use of yourself. A sister is feeling parched."

"You're sexy and flippant, but I don't think one outweighs the other."

"I'm the queen of sarcasm."

"Oh, you're bilingual."

"I speak four languages, and sarcasm is the fifth, and I speak sarcasm both well and often. If you can't handle it, if I am too sassy, now is a good time to walk away from this queen and leave her as you found her."

That made me laugh. "I've been here once or twice. Never seen you here before."

"First time here; never been to a club on the Sunset Strip, and I am here to dance and live life to the fullest."

"Then let's drink and dance and live life to the fullest."

CHAPTER 2

I copped us those drinks, got her a Long Island and I had an old-fashioned.

Jake Ellis was across the room, beer in hand, getting his flirt on. He nodded at me. I nodded at him and went back to Jimi Lee. Jake Ellis continued flirting and watching our prey, kept his eyes on our meal ticket. I kept my eyes on the brown-skinned number in the tight white skirt that loved to ride upward over a mound of joy. Drink in hand, Jimi Lee danced that sweet ass all the way to the spot she wanted. She didn't move like a pole swinger, didn't turn around and offer me her ass to humpty hump to the beat. She was full of rhythm, but she was subtle, had sexy movements that brought sensuality to life. She was just getting warmed up. Jimi Lee finished her Long Island, put her empty glass to the side, broke loose, and became a hair-bouncing hip-hop queen. I finished my old-fashioned and took it to another level. We had a little dance off. The Roger Rabbit. Cabbage Patch. Running man. Butterfly. Hammer. But the Tootsie Roll. Her ass rolled and her breasts bounced. The Bart Simpson. The wop.

I bought us more drinks. Got her another Long Island and I had an Irish Car Bomb. We moved from the Smurf to the Harlem shake and got jiggy with it. We were sweating like we'd run a 10K.

The guy she was with carried a Mount Rushmore–size frown as he left the club. Jimi Lee saw him leave too. He'd stood with his anger, watched us drink and party. I'd scared him. She danced with me like she didn't care.

I said, "Hope homeboy wasn't your ride back home."

"I'm driving. He lives in Hancock Park. We met up here so we could hang out."

"Doesn't seem like your type."

"Intellectually, yes. He has his PhD from Yale. I will be at Harvard after the summer."

"Seriously?"

"Very smart man. Brilliant. But he was boring. Didn't want to dance. This isn't his type of crowd."

"Guess he should have taken you to a museum."

"Why invite me to a dance club and go through all of this trouble if you want to hold up a wall? I'm good. Plus, before you had come over, he was looking at the breasts and ass of every half-naked woman when she walked by."

Jake Ellis was still tracking our target. I saw the club owner across the club by the DJ booth. Women were all over him, begging for his attention. Motherfucker looked like Elmer Fudd but was pulling babes like he was the new Marlon Brando. Money made ugly people overnight superstars. I looked at the crowd of more than three hundred, maybe four, tried to calculate how much money he had made tonight at thirty dollars a head, plus another twenty for everyone to park in his private lot, plus those people who paid thirty to rest their rides at valet parking, plus the money from all the overpriced drinks. The motherfucker was raking in cash. This was why San Bernardino was pissed off. I was in the wrong business. Spots like this made men millionaires in less than a year.

Hot, dank, Jimi Lee led me from the dance floor and asked me, "Where are you from?"

"I was born in Mississippi."

"You don't sound like you're from Mississippi."

"Grew up here."

"Your parents? African or from the islands?"

"My parents and grandparents are originally from Oklahoma."

"No black person in this country has roots that start in America."

"That's as far back as I can trace mine."

"That's tragic, in my opinion. I know my bloodline back to when the Big Bang happened."

"My family is from Mississippi, but it wasn't a straight line to get here. Some of my folks been in Cali for four decades. Came here to run away from southern racism. Before that, some of my people were run out of Oklahoma when the Black Wall Street was burned down. That part of my family lost everything, came west, started over."

"Never heard of a Black Wall Street."

"They kept it out of the papers. It was a conspiracy."

"And this thing was in Oklahoma?"

"Yeah. Black people had homes, were thriving. White people got mad and burned it all down."

"People died?"

"As many as three hundred black people."

"How many white people went to jail?"

"None. But they locked up black people. Jailed all the black men. Black people had to have permission from white men to be able to walk their own streets. Pretty much everybody black was left homeless."

"Why have I never heard of a Black Wall Street?"

"White people own the media. They don't report their own crimes."

"A black town burned down by whites? No way. I don't even hear black people talking about that."

"It happened. Lots of black people don't know about it."

"I will go to the library and look that up."

I asked, "What about you? How did an Ethiopian end up in America?"

"Buy me another drink and I'll tell you."

"I'll buy you two."

"Just one will suffice."

She was born in Debre Marqos, Ethiopia, about two hundred miles from the capital, Addis Ababa, but her family moved to America when she was eight. Before moving to Southern California, she lived up north in Dunsmuir, a town named after a coal baron from British Columbia. Her parents were Ethiopian activists and schol-

29

ars, intellectuals, and she had always been the rebellious daughter driving them mad. She had siblings, but she was the one always getting into trouble.

I said, "Is Jimi Lee a common Ethiopian name?"

"My real name is Adanech Abeylegesse Zenebework."

"Adanech. That's a beautiful name."

"But call me Jimi Lee."

"Why not use your real name?"

"People in America snicker at true African names. If your name is easy to pronounce, people will favor you more. Blacks are treated badly, and Africans are looked down upon, no matter what level of intelligence we possess. White people treat black people badly and it seems that black people love to treat their sisters from Africa worse."

"You've had a couple of bad experiences. But not all black people are that way."

"So, I made up a name to make it easy for stupid Americans. Saves me a lot of anger and explanation."

"Jimi Lee."

"Jimi Hendrix. I took part of my easy-to-say name from him."

"You like his music?"

"Not really. Just like the way he spelled his name. Looked very sexy."

"The Lee part?"

"I like movies by Spike Lee."

"Your favorite?"

"The black-and-white one with Nola Darling."

She's Gotta Have It.

"She was a bold girl. I've always wanted to be bold like that."

One smile led to another. One conversation to another. One drink led to another.

Alcohol did what alcohol was supposed to do, loosened inhibitions. Made men brave. Made women bold.

LA was a horny town, a Sodom like Las Vegas, a Gomorrah like South Beach. When the sun went down, the needs came out to breathe. Everyone pulled off their professional masks and exposed their true selves.

Jimi Lee laughed, tipsy, caught her breath, then asked, "When's your birthday?"

Soft smile on my face, staring into her brown eyes, I told her.

She laughed. "Liar."

"Why would I lie about my birthday?"

"Let me see your ID."

I showed her my license to drive like it was my license to kill.

She said, "This is crazy."

She showed me her Cali ID card.

I said, "We have the same birthday."

"What are the odds?"

She was under twenty-one. The makeup, hair, and body had added five years to her appearance.

I asked, "You're what . . . eighteen?"

She laughed and whispered, "Shhhh. I used a fake ID to get in."

"Wow."

"That turn you off?"

"I'm cool. You're an adult."

"Yes, I am."

"Then I'm good with it."

Tenderoni was eighteen pretending to be twenty-one. Said she spoke Spanish, English, Amharic, and college-level French. This was her gap year, her year off before college. Harvard, Yale, Princeton, and Johns Hopkins wanted her. She had options, at least five million in scholarship offers, but had chosen Harvard. She was a smart girl.

She moved her powerful hair from her face and asked, "Where do you live, *yetewabe*?"

"*Yetewabe?*"

"Means 'handsome' in Amharic."

"Leimert Park."

"With your parents?"

"Haven't lived with them for three or four years."

32

"You have an apartment?"

"Two-bedroom."

"Do you have a roommate?"

"I live alone."

"Two bedrooms?"

"I like to have a little space."

"And no kids?"

"No kids. No pets. No plants."

"You're not nurturing."

"Grew up in a crowded house. Good to have some peace and quiet."

She asked, "What's your name again?"

"Ken Swift." I paused, then asked, "So, where do you live?"

"We now live in Diamond Bar."

"An hour away."

She winked. "It's going to be a long drive after drinking so much."

"I'm a lot closer."

She smiled. "Really?"

"Really."

"Is that an invitation?"

"It's an invitation."

"How close is that Lee Works Park?"

"Leimert Park. Lah-mert. Leimert Park."

"Sounds like it's far away."

"Twenty minutes, tops."

"And you live alone?"

"You can come chill out for a bit."

She grinned. "Yeah?"

"Yeah. Kick your shoes off. Chill."

"You have coffee at your place?"

"I can stop and get some at 7-Eleven."

"Ethiopians and coffee, you know?"

"What about it?"

"We invented it."

"I didn't know that. But that explains why so many are at Starbucks all day long."

"We should leave soon, if you want me to follow you home."

"I'm parked at valet."

"Me too."

"Your date left."

"Dammit."

"I'll pay."

"Thanks so much. Had forgotten about that."

"You have an overnight bag?"

"I can stay at your place about an hour."

"Only an hour?"

"I'm in my parents' car. Have to get back to Diamond Bar."

"You're eighteen."

She waggled a finger. "Tonight, my name is Jimi Lee and I'm twenty-one."

"Same birthday. Same age."

"And I think we both want the same thing. To be bad together. I think this was meant to be."

I smiled, our understanding strong. "Let me tell my friend I'm about to raise up."

CHAPTER 3

I went to Jake Ellis, nodded, and he followed me. We had work to do, work ordered by San Bernardino.

We trailed the Norwegian club owner Jake Ellis had been stalking all evening. We caught Elmer Fudd in the bathroom taking a piss. He didn't see us when we came in. Other cats who did looked at us, felt the energy, and skedaddled. When Norway was done and had shaken his dick three times and washed his hands, we gave him a sudden beat-down. The way we attacked him, getting beaten for thirty seconds felt like twenty years in Tehachapi.

I got down on my haunches, looked the man in his eyes. "San Bernardino."

He tried to crawl away from me, ran into Jake Ellis. "I'll pay."

The African said, "You're delinquent."

"I'll pay."

I kicked the man in the ribs. "I know

you'll pay."

Jake Ellis crashed the lid from a toilet over his head.

I asked, "Why did you do that?"

"To see if it would break."

"Yeah?"

"Yeah."

I took a lid from another toilet, crashed it over the target's head.

We looked at each other, nodded.

Jake Ellis said, "They do break."

"Just like in the movies."

With that message delivered, we left the target unconscious and bloodied. Jake Ellis washed the blood from his hands. I did the same, and we left the bathroom, went back into the nightclub's pandemonium.

Jake Ellis said, "You pulled a hot one tonight."

"She's African."

"She has a bad body and killer legs."

"Come say hi, so she won't think I was off with a chick."

Jake Ellis followed me to Jimi Lee.

He introduced himself. "Kwamena Gamel Nasser."

He rarely used his birth name, but he did that with Africans to show he hadn't lost his roots.

Then my partner in crime added, "But

37

they call me Jake Ellis."

She told him her name, then nodded. "But call me Jimi Lee."

"My friend tells me that you're *African.*"

"Can't you tell I'm Ethiopian?"

"I'm from Ghana."

"And here we are *Africans.*"

They laughed like it was some joke only Africans new to America would understand.

Jake Ellis said, "Yeah, boy. I didn't become *African* until I left Africa."

"You know? Americans lump all of Africa together, like we are one country."

"The entire continent. They talk like the fifty-four countries are one city the size of Atlanta."

Jimi Lee raised a finger. "If the de facto states are included, and the territories, then the number is sixty-six."

Jake Ellis gave her the thumbs-up. "I stand corrected. Sixty-six countries."

It had felt like she was more interested in Jake Ellis than she was in me, which would have been okay — a woman was just a woman and we had the bros-before-hoes code before there was a code — but then Jimi Lee took my hand and left with me. She let me lead her as we headed for the club's exit, moved around heated bodies, half of them floating above the clouds, then made it outside into the cool air, waited on our cars to be pulled up to valet.

Jake Ellis went back to the party, this time to a sister who looked like the singer Tracie Spencer.

He had arrived with me, but he'd find another way home. Or to someone else's home.

Jimi Lee said, "Your friend is from the heart of the slums in Ghana."

"How do you know?"

"I can tell. The scars."

"From boxing. He fought his way out from the slums and out of that part of Africa the same way men here fight their way out of Boyle Heights and East Saint Louis and every other ghetto that tries to hold them back."

"His hands are rough. Like my father's hands."

"Rough life, rough hands."

"Boys like him, my mother and father told us to keep away from."

"Okay. So much for African solidarity."

She paused. Looked at my chest. "Is that blood on your shirt?"

I opened and closed my left hand, the hand I had beat the club owner with.

I said, "Must be ketchup. Had fries at In-N-Out earlier."

"I love In-N-Out."

"I'll get you some in and out when we get to my apartment."

She swayed a little. "Mannish. But appropriate, considering what we are planning."

As we moved upstream against the crowd I said, "You're drunk."

"I'm not."

"Are you sure you can drive?"

"I can manage a twenty-minute drive to get a two-minute ride." She sniggered at her little joke, then nodded. "Can't believe I'm going home with you. A black American I only just met. But you are so damned handsome."

"We'll cruise the speed limit and be at my place in twenty minutes."

She laughed a little. "We'll be done twenty minutes after that."

"Is that right? You said two minutes a moment ago."

"That's all black Americans do, right? Drink, smoke, and have sex?"

"Now who is insulting whom?"

"My observations are based on music and the movies about black people made by black people. Why do black Americans always hold a forty-ounce? I mean, who

40

would want to drink that much alcohol at once?"

"Well, I've heard the same shit about Africans."

"Whatever you heard about Africans came from the mouth of a liar. We are not a single group."

"You can't learn about people watching the crap Hollywood turns out."

"My parents kept me sheltered. They don't allow me to listen to rap music. I have to sneak and listen to Snoop or N.W.A. when I am in Malibu with my friend for a sleepover."

"What are your parents like?"

"My parents are very smart, strict, focused, and political. Tomorrow they will have another secret meeting with at least thirty other Ethiopians. They meet in private and talk about overthrowing their government."

I laughed. "They're in sunny California planning an Ethiopian revolution? You're joking, right?"

She said, "No, I'm serious. They send money back to finance the cause. The wars. They want to solve issues with clean water, economic poverty, many things — too many to mention. They talk American politics, Saudi Arabian politics as well, but mostly, they talk about Ethiopia. The Mengistu government. They go on about the civil war that started in the seventies. Every conversation is about People's Democratic Republic of Ethiopia or Workers' Party of Ethiopia. The battle with Eritrea has left my country landlocked. Too much to talk about, but they go on for hours."

"Had no idea there were so many problems in East Africa. We don't hear about it."

"The bulk of skirmishes are about property and borders between territorialized cultural groups. We fight over the use of our land, water sources. My parents and my uncles and my community, the ones here, strategize over how to gain access to state resources, things like funds, jobs, investments. Go on for hours about cultural policies and prestige, our Ethiopian pride, and the current language policy in education and administration. There are Suri, Dizi, and Me'en battles in the Maji region, Oromo–non-Oromo associations in Wollega, and the Anywaa-Nuer conflict in Gambela. There is more. I can tell by your expression, like most Americans, you have no idea about these political things."

"So, Africans battle over blocks and streets. For ownership. Like the Crips and the Bloods here."

"Enough of this. I am sounding like my parents. The brainwashing is strong."

"You've changed the mood."

"How do we change it back?"

"Any suggestions?"

She came to me, tiptoed, and we kissed. We kissed and I held her ass, pulled her to me, could see wild thoughts in her eyes. She touched me between my legs. I touched her between hers.

She bit the corner of her lip. "Bet you're done in ten minutes."

"Bet you tap out at five."

Her four-door Nissan was pulled up. My convertible Benz was right behind hers.

"That's your car?"

I nodded.

"Impressive."

Before we could get the keys from valet, sirens broke into the night as an ambulance rushed into the lot right behind our cars. Cars driven by the local police came the opposite way up the driveway. Pulled up in front of us, left no room to maneuver around them. Cops jumped out like they were ready to bust some heads.

Sounded like Jimi Lee cursed in Amharic, then huffed, "Now we're blocked in."

"Let me see what the valet can do about this."

43

I knew whom they were coming to get. The club owner was white. This zip code was white man's land. More members of the Hollywood PD pulled up right after the first ones. Like a lynching party ready to make strange fruit.

The valet was powerless. He had brown skin from south of the border. This wasn't his world either.

We had to wait. I took Jimi Lee's hand, watched the drama. She watched it too.

She swayed, moved her hair in that sweet motion, said, "Something bad must've happened inside."

"And we missed it."

A fire-red Corvette came into the small lot, sped in like the driver was the child of a billionaire Wall Street CEO or a Hollywood exec. Jimi Lee sobered up, adjusted her mini, waved at the sports car, then hurried away from me, almost running; left me without saying where she was going. I thought she'd abandoned me for a rich guy, but a sister got out of the ride. Ghirardelli chocolate with legs like stilts. She was maybe five-ten without heels, skin as dark as 11:59. Long straight hair that was as black as her clothing. It was her hair. The way it was parted was the reveal. She wore Corvette-red high heels and a black catsuit, one made to shut it down. Full lips, small nose, full cheeks, small waist that was the gate to an understated bottom being guarded by the sweetest hips. Über-feminine. A mixture of hip-hop and rap music spilled out onto the streets and both of the sensual girls playfully danced the wop for a moment. The closer Little Red Corvette came, the more the winds brought me her scent, Christian Dior J'adore. Everybody had their eyes on the rich black girl who'd crawled out of the little red Corvette. Exotic, dark, and beautiful.

Jimi Lee spoke up over the noise, told her, "This is Ken Swift."

"Swift?" She said that as if she wanted to be sure. "Ken Swift?"

I nodded. "Yeah. That's my name."

Jimi Lee said, "Ken Swift, this is my best friend, Lila."

"Did my girl tell you who she is? Did she not tell you how special she is? She is smart and beautiful. Tell me about yourself, Ken Swift. What career do you have? What are your goals? What are your intentions with my friend?"

"Don't embarrass me," Jimi Lee stopped her friend. "We're just leaving."

"Where are you going?"

"We are going for coffee."

45

"Where will you go to get this coffee?"

"Leimert Park."

"He's taking you to a park? Have some dignity."

"No, that's an area. A nice black area not too far from here."

"A nice black area?"

"I know."

"Oxymoron."

They rode the stereotype train and laughed at the conductor.

Lila asked, "Is it safe there?"

"I have never been there, Gelila."

"All you ever see on television is black people shooting black people out that way."

"I've never heard the news say anything about this Leimert Park area."

Lila turned to me. "That's not like South Central or Watts, is it?"

I said, "It's near Baldwin Hills."

"Never heard of the Baldwin Hills."

"The Black Beverly Hills."

"Black Beverly Hills?"

"Lots of black doctors, lawyers, and entertainers live in that area."

She laughed. "No such thing exists. At least not in my *Thomas Guide.*"

Jimi Lee said, "The moment I met him, he was talking about Black Beverly Hills and a Black Wall Street."

46

"Black Americans be out here making up shit. I've never heard anyone call Beverly Hills the *white* Baldwin Hills. He said that like they are sister cities. I tell you, black people be making up shit left and right."

Jimi Lee laughed. "Be making up shit? Really? *Be making up shit?* You talk like thugs now?"

"Look at you. You can hardly stand up straight. How much have you had to drink?"

"Barely light-headed."

"You need an intervention."

"Don't make me unhappy to see you."

"I don't think you should go for coffee."

I took that to mean that this one-off was about to be canceled. Little Red Corvette was fresh in from Cock Blockville by way of Hater Town and wanted to shut this down before we made it to the District of One-Night Stand.

The friend took her eyes from me, then asked Jimi Lee, "What happened to . . . ?"

"Negasi?"

"Yes. Didn't you come here with Negasi?"

"He left. I will tell you about it."

"And now you're leaving with an American?"

"What is the issue, Lila? Must you show up and be so dramatic?"

Lila poked her lip out. "Are you really

leaving the moment I get here?"

"You said you were on your way three hours ago."

Lila laughed. "Friday-night traffic."

"Oh, please. I know you. You made a detour for some jazz before coming here."

"Are you judging me?"

"I am judging you because you are judging me."

"Because you came with one guy, and now you're about to come with another."

Jimi Lee's eyes widened and she snapped, said something coarse in Amharic.

The tall, dark, and lovely girl shot something back in the same tongue.

Lila and Jimi Lee stepped to the side, not far, but continued fast-talking in Amharic. A girlfriend fight. It looked like Jimi Lee was being scolded, but Jimi Lee wasn't having it. The girl moved Jimi Lee's hair from her face, kissed Jimi Lee on both cheeks, then smiled at me, not a true smile, but a smile. Little Red Corvette evaluated me head to toe. She waved good-bye to Jimi Lee before she did her Naomi Campbell walk toward the club.

Jimi Lee regained my attention and said, "I can trust you, right?"

"You can trust me."

"You won't get weird on me, will you?"

"Is that what your girlfriend said to you?"

"She's jealous. Guy she sneaks to see is older and has a girlfriend, and she judges me."

"How old is she?"

"Eighteen."

"Fake identification."

Jimi Lee bit her lip. Looked like the night air, bright lights, and chat had sobered her up a bit.

She took in my eyes, my brows. "Are you dating someone?"

"Nobody but you."

"Let me rephrase; is someone dating you?"

"Nah. I'm SINRRNW."

"Which means?"

"Single income, no rug rats, no woman."

"What happened to your ex? And don't say you don't have a dozen of those."

"Was dating an Afro-Mexican, but it didn't work out."

"Afro-Mexican? Is there such a thing?"

"There is a whole community of Africans who grew up in Mexico."

"I've never heard of Africans growing up in Mexico."

I nodded. "Afro-Mexicans are real. They get no love, no recognition on any census. Colonial Mexico probably had the highest numbers of African slaves. Mexico used to harbor black fugitive slaves."

"And the breakup with your Afro-Mexican is for real?"

"She moved to Maryland. Scholarship at Johns Hopkins."

She made a face like she was impressed. "Smart girl."

"And she's seeing a smarter man now. Was kind enough to send me a Dear John letter."

She regarded my car. "So no woman will come knocking on your door in the middle of the night."

"Won't be no *Jerry Springer* action at my crib."

She gave me a soft smile. "May I use your mobile phone?"

"Who are you calling?"

"Gelila. The jealous girl I was just talking to. She asked me all of those questions."

"She's in the club and you're going to call her?"

"I don't want to talk to her, only want to leave a message on her home answering machine."

I took out my Nokia, handed it to her. She called her girlfriend's Malibu number and spoke in Amharic. One of the things I recognized was my license plate number. Then she switched back to Amharic, said other things, then changed her language to English, said my name again, and smiled. Jimi Lee had seen my identification in the club. She had done that intentionally, to verify who I was before she went on this adventure. Jimi Lee promised to call Lila again after the coffee was done. Jimi Lee laughed. Was tipsy. Then she gave me my mobile phone back.

She said, "So she won't worry, may I leave her another message when I get to your apartment?"

I nodded. "We'd better get going."

"Lila showed up and ranted my ear off. I'm a girl driving at night in Los Angeles alone, far from home, had a few drinks, leaving with a guy she's never met, a black American I just met, yada yada, so my friend is worried."

Little Red Corvette would have my info, plus my mobile phone number was in her house phone's caller ID.

That meant that when Jimi Lee called her again from my home, she'd have my home number too.

Jimi Lee was more at ease. "Okay. Let's get that coffee."

I looked at the cops, then held Jimi Lee's hand and walked right past the slave catchers, used her, let her be my cover, my alibi, as they looked for a suspect, each badge hungry for a motherfucker to Rodney King at midnight.

Valet finally found room for us to maneuver our rides and leave the madness on the Sunset Strip.

CHAPTER 4

Jimi Lee followed me down La Cienega to a
7-Eleven at the bottom of the hill by Pico
Boulevard, then from the edges of Hollywood south through Culver City, and from
there east to a tree-lined street in LA's Leimert Park area. I took her the long way,
through white areas, then through the edges
of what we called the Black Beverly Hills.

Many didn't know there was a black side
of town that wasn't like *Boyz n the Hood*–
ville.

Leimert Park was a jewel hidden in plain
sight. Spanish Colonial Revival homes. Tree-
lined streets. Up Stocker were the big
houses and the Black Beverly Hills, but east
of the Shaw, down here was a Black Green-
wich Village. The world-famous Comedy
Act Theater was around the corner, in the
same section, with spots for late-night blues
and jazz. There were theaters, poetry hot
spots, museums, and venues for the people

who thrived on hip-hop.

This was Jimi Lee's first time seeing a categorically black area in LA that hadn't been infested by gangs and didn't have graffiti from end to end. She had never driven down the Crenshaw Strip. We found our way down Stocker, then circled the block until we found parking spaces near my crib. This part of zip code 90008 was lush, filled with evergreen trees and palm trees. It was a concrete jungle built on top of a desert, every tree imported from another city or island. This was middle-class and working-class. The area was a village of two-level apartment units, tris, quads, and some with twelve units. Garages were in the back, but most people went for the street parking, and by sundown, hardworking people were home; all the good spots were gone until the next sunrise. Most of the units were larger than condos on the Culver City side. I had a spacious two-bedroom apartment, the size of a small house, and that set me back nine hundred a month, plus utilities. It was one of the nicest spots on the block and worth it. My crib had refinished oak floors, high ceilings, arched doorways, restored 1930s detailing. My rent was more than average because my space was better than average. The kitchen had been redone top to bottom, had new stainless-steel appliances including a dishwasher and built-in microwave. My spot had ceiling fans, beautiful period light fixtures, and wrought-iron curtain rods with plantation shutters throughout.

Jimi Lee had finished her cup of hazelnut coffee by the time we hit Stocker. While I drove, I downed a shot of Yohimbe, an energy drink. I took Jimi Lee's hand and she followed me, taking it all in, her heels clicking on the sidewalk as we made it to my mauve stucco building. I lived on the second floor. We kissed our way up the concrete stairs, her heels announcing each step toward my entry. I tried to suck the hazelnut coffee off her tongue and she kissed me like she loved the way I tasted. She let me free long enough for me to unlock the door; then we stumbled inside like beautiful animals in uncontrollable heat. Lights off, I led her across the wooden floors right to the master bedroom. The other bedroom was a gym/office. I lit a candle, then kissed her again, sucked her neck, and took the queen to the king's bed. White comforter on red sheets. Bed was made up. I was glad I always made my bed up in the morning. Mississippi habit passed down. All of my windows were open, lights down low, cool breeze and moonlight coming through.

I pulled that white skirt away from her toned frame, then pulled away her sexy pink underwear, had her naked from the waist down. She wasn't wearing a bra. Would have loved to have taken that off too. Then I eased her out of her top, went mad for her breasts. Small, yet amazing. She held my head, moaned. I suckled. Her breasts felt brand-new, like she had picked them up at Nordstrom a few hours ago. Erotic and toned. With an ass that wasn't obscene but could bring an army to its knees. A nice ass was about shape, not size. Loved her butt. It was like a Lamborghini, sleek and aerodynamic, not like an eighteen-wheeler hauling more cargo than any one man would ever need.

She said things in a foreign tongue, then moaned, "You suck my breasts so good."

Jimi Lee was on her back, naked, looking so small, like a bird. I was scared to keep going, scared that if I had sex with her, I might hurt her. She tugged at my clothing, wanted me nude. And in two blinks of an eye I was naked, over her, cock in my hand, not wanting to rush, but wanting to be inside her. I put my erection against her dampness, let my rigidness rest on her vaginal lips, moved the hardness up and down over her opening. It felt so good and her face said she felt the same sensation. Fine hairs covering her sex were trimmed low. She rolled her hips into me, did a slow grind until she couldn't stand it.

She panted, "Condoms?"

"Fuck fuck fuck fuck fuck fuck fuck."

"Are you joking? We bought a cup of coffee and forgot condoms?"

"Let me check my stash."

I rolled away from her, opened the drawer on my dresser, looked in the coffee can.

I groaned. "Shit."

"Oh boy."

"Sorry."

"This is not going how I saw it in my head."

She had come here for sex. Only for sex. She had come to test the merchandise. She wanted me inside of her and I wanted to be inside of her so deep we became Siamese twins. Standing in this wildfire, nothing else mattered.

I told her, "I'll eat you out since I can't dig you out. I got this. I'll make you come until you can't no more."

"What should I do?"

"Enjoy."

"What about you?"

"You don't have to do me to get done."

"You sure?"

"I can jack off while I eat you. Make myself come."

"At least let me do that."

"Yeah?"

"Especially if you're going to do oral. I've never had a man do that to me before."

"Never?"

"No, never."

"Tongue virgin."

"Look at that smile on your face."

She was wet, sweet like just-ripe mango, and tasted utterly divine. Jimi Lee tasted like tropical candy. I couldn't stop. Each lick was sweeter than the one before. She squirmed and cooed and held my head, then pulled at her own hair. I had her knees back to her breasts, then put my hands under her ass. She eased her legs down, trembled as she pulled me up to her, panted as she sucked my tongue.

She whispered, "Your tongue. You're good at that. Real good. Jesus, you're amazing doing that."

While we kissed, I gave her two fingers, made that "come here" motion, found that magic bean, massaged it over and over.

She squeezed her thighs against my hand,

moaned things in Amharic. She glowed. I sucked her nipples, kissed her belly.

She whispered, "Go down on me again, please."

She rode my tongue, fucked my face, her hands on my head.

Women were so beautiful when they were aroused.

She looked down at me, licked her lips, contemplated some powerful desire, then pushed my mouth away from her, kissed my neck, my chest, licked across my stomach, held my hardness in her soft hand.

As she shuddered, a little nervous as she whispered, "What if I want to try this with you but don't know how to do this?"

"Really?"

"Will you tell me what to do?"

"I can do that. But do what comes naturally."

She stroked it, kissed around it, took the tip in her mouth, licked the tip, started off easy, then held me with both hands, stroked me with both hands, her hands feeling so small. Then she took the head between her lips, kissed the head, sucked the head, found a rhythm, savored it like she liked the taste, became ravenous, sucked and suckled.

"Am I doing this right?"

I moaned louder, fought the urge to grab

her head and thrust. It was her moment. Jimi Lee came back to me, kissed me, bit my lip, sucked my neck as she stroked me like she couldn't let my cock go.

I sucked her neck. Fingered her until she couldn't control her breathing. I touched between her legs and she held my hand, made me finger her, went back to sighing and mewling. I strummed her clit. She put her face in a pillow for a moment, gave her sounds to that softness, then hid her face in my shoulder, pulled in a lungful of air.

She bit me, bit me hard, her need strong.

She whispered, "Two minutes."

"What?"

"Let me put you inside me."

"You sure you want to go raw?"

"For two minutes. Then we will stop."

"Okay."

"Not there. Not without a condom. Here."

"Here?"

"Just the beginning."

"Just the tip."

She whispered, "Go slow."

"Okay."

She mewled again, sang, "Slow like that."

We kissed and soon she lost it again. She closed her eyes tight, stretched moans into sensual shapes, put nails in my skin, held on like she was falling. Her body contracted.

Ecstasy rose. I was there with her, riding her waves, panting with her, breathing thick and hard with her, watching her squeeze her breasts, watching her shake and pull at her own hair, watching her touch her face, drag her fingers down her face as she simmered, felt her shuddering, unraveling one harsh breath at a time, heard her moans turn into spiritual singing, African singing, and felt her working against me, taking more of me, wanting more of me, grinding, coming like she was going mad.

Soon we were on opposite sides of the bed, strangers with their legs tangled. Orgasms had been strong. Labored breathing rose from both of us. It was a chilly night, but we sweated hard enough to make the bedroom so humid we could swim in it. We cooled down, came down from the marvelous delirium we had felt.

She rubbed her nose. "What's your name again?"

"Ken Swift."

"What's my name?"

"Jimi Lee."

"Lucky guess." She smiled. "My real name?"

"I can't pronounce that."

"Adanech Abeylegesse Zenebework."

"Gesundheit."

She chuckled. "Water, please. My body is damp like the ocean and my throat is as dry as the air in Chino."

When I got up, she asked me where the water closet was located, then asked for soap and a fresh towel. I gave her a towel, told her Dial soap was on the sink, and she went to the bathroom. Heard the faucet whine and come on. Pipes rattled. She was cleaning herself. It took her a few minutes. She would see that my toilet was sparkling white. Looked brand-new. She didn't have to hover if she wanted to take a piss. I knew she had gone into my medicine cabinet. They all did. She probably hunted for pubic hairs, for products for a woman, for a hairpin, found nothing feminine. When she came back, I handed her the bottled water. She thanked me, sat on the edge of the bed, looked around at my belongings, somewhat impressed. I kept a clean house. I did my own cooking. I knew she was looking for the signs that other pussy had been here, trying to figure out if a woman had done the decorating, or was seeing if a woman lived here, was looking for signs that I had a girlfriend. She exhaled, nodded. There were no signs.

Jimi Lee looked out the window and said,

"This is a nice area you live in."

"Told you."

"From what I see, very interesting."

"All black. Well, mostly black."

"Nothing like this out my way. Not even in Moreno Valley."

"Nothing like this until you get to Oakland going north or Atlanta going east."

"So, all the black people around here, where are they from?"

I told her the area was populated with folks from New York, Houston, Florida, and Seattle, and they lived with Barbadians, Trinidadians, Jamaicans, Antiguans, Bahamians, Haitians, Ethiopians, Eritreans, Somalians, and Dominicans. Plenty of Haitians and Africans were in the mix. Within two miles there were people from Costa Rica, Honduras, Guatemala, Belize, Nicaragua, Panama, El Salvador, and almost every country in South America. I let her know that white people were still around as well. They owned a lot of the properties the minorities rented. White flight had sent many running, but most held on to their real estate, were passing it down generation to generation. The area used to be white only, had been designed that way, until the laws were forced to change. The larger number of people of European heritage

63

lived to the west in Culver City, but blacks were there too, along with the Mexicans, Jews, and Asians, the same groups that had been locked out of those areas when Leimert Park was developed and sold as the perfect whites-only, Negro-free, no-Jews, no-Mexicans white haven.

When I was done talking, she said, "Interesting."

"What's popping out your way?"

"I don't know the history of my area, not like that."

"All that land out there was ranches. Diamond Bar would be the name of someone's ranch."

"Makes sense. I live next to Phillips Ranch. Nothing out there but cows. Can smell them in the morning. Chino is to the south, and the wind blows the stink from the cow farms all day. I have seen flies as big as my fist."

I read her body language. It didn't match her conversation. "You okay?"

"It's late. I have a long drive." She nodded. "I should leave soon."

I asked, "Can I get your number?"

"Nope."

"Can I page you or something?"

"Page me? I don't have a beeper. Why would I have one of those things?"

64

"Home number?"

"Oh no. Boys aren't allowed to call me unless their parents have met my father and mother."

"How can I get in touch with you or see you again?"

"You live an hour from me."

"What does that mean?"

"I live in area code 919 and you live all the way out here in area code 213."

"So what?"

"You are geographically undesirable."

"Never been good at geography and I still want to see you."

"You know calling from my phone to your number would cost a lot, and an hour's drive in one direction is out of the question, especially with gas prices as high as they are. I would never date someone in area code 818, 714, 213, 619, 310, 805, or any of those places. It costs more to call those places than to call someone in New York."

"Geographically undesirable."

"Sorry. I didn't mean to mislead you. I thought you understood what we were doing."

She touched my skin. Smiled at my face. Took in the details, added me to her memory.

"So, you're twenty-one and in university."

She hummed. "UCLA, huh?"

"And you're eighteen and going to a big-time Ivy League university."

"After the summer ends. I go home to Ethiopia, come back to America, then to Harvard."

"Only rich people take gap years."

"And exhausted people. Since I was born, this is my first time ever being able to take a breather."

"Must be nice to be able to take a year off as a break."

"Well deserved. The stress. Hard living up to someone else's expectations all the time."

"I understand stress too."

"Ha. Have you not met African parents before?"

"I have heard about African parents."

"But you know nothing about Ethiopian parents. They are on a different level."

I touched her hair. "You're going back to the motherland. Back to the fatherland."

"I go home to Ethiopia for six months, reconnect with family, then come back and go to uni."

"Can't imagine what calling you in that part of Africa would cost."

"International rates? Two minutes are more than a mortgage. Maybe more than two mortgages."

"You exaggerate."

"I've seen my parents' phone bill. It would be cheaper to fly there once a month."

"Definitely geographically undesirable then." I nodded. "Maybe we'll run into each other again."

"Doubt it. When I get back from Ethiopia, I will hit the ground running. I get off the plane, move onto campus, and start classes within a week. I'll be taking a full load, will have labs, too much homework, and be too busy to talk."

She pulled on her white skirt, her top. Her actions told me she had come and was ready to go.

She said, "It's cold outside. Hot as heck out my way. We have to run the air conditioner day and night."

"We're closer to the beach. Seven miles. Cools off when the sun drops. Breeze comes across the Pacific Ocean to kiss us good night. Temperature drops to about seventy. That's why most of us don't have air-conditioning. Most of the buildings were put up before central air-conditioning was a thing. Before it was the latest technology."

"It's almost one hundred during the day where I live. How hot is it during the day out here?"

"Almost eighty."

"That's cool. For me that's cool."

"Hot to me. But with a couple of fans on, it's bearable. If not, mall is two minutes away; can hang there."

"I love this air. I would love to sleep with my windows open for a change. I'm fifty miles from the beach, more or less. Land-locked with the cows and the flies. It is always hot, dry, and no good breeze where I live."

I gave her a Malcolm X hoodie to wear to keep warm until she made it back to hell.

Prada bag in one hand, shoes in the other, she led the way toward my front door. Nighttime in LA. We heard the helicopters in the distance at almost two in the morning, sirens screaming from all directions. That would go on until the next sunrise. And during those drive-by and gangbang hours we stood at her car, kissing like crazy.

She said, "This is very unlike me. I let loose tonight. I released all inhibitions."

"Would love to have been able to make you come the other way."

"I'll bet you would."

"You liked it?"

"You were gentle. And skilled. It was both more and better than I had hoped for."

"Glad you enjoyed it."

"I'm still tingling. You made me come that way."

"You look so sexy when you come."

"I didn't expect that to happen, not with a guy I just met."

"Same birthday."

"That must be the secret."

"The way you came, I think women enjoy sex more than men do but won't admit it."

"Men I know would call them sluts. *African* men. The Nola Darlings of the world are considered a disgrace."

"Did you talk sex with your ex?"

"We talked politics but never about sex. We did it; then it was as if we didn't do it. We didn't talk about it. We never talked about sex before we had sex, didn't talk during sex, and didn't talk about sex after."

"How did you get from point A to point B?"

"We were at his home, kissing; then it was like, he's touching my breast, now he's pulling at my zipper, so I guess he's trying to undress me and have sex with me. He did. All he took off was my bottoms. Still had my bra on. We did it; then he looked guilty, pulled his pants back up. We went back to doing whatever we were doing before we had sex as if we hadn't had sex, went back to politics and the news. I felt like mentioning it was taboo. It was like the sex was for him. Like I was there as a device to please him, and his orgasm should have been enough for me. Not long after, he seemed to be uncomfortable in my presence, or my being there had served its purpose, so I went home, studied until I was tired enough to fall asleep."

"Wow."

"I never had an experience like this. I didn't get naked with him, not like this. I never took my bra off. He kept his underwear on. I never saw him naked. I never saw his thing. He just put it in, humped, and had an orgasm. He didn't look me in my eyes. I looked at his ceiling the whole time. Began looking at designs, imagined horses and flowers. Then my mind drifted and I began thinking of complicated math problems. P versus NP. Hodge conjecture. Riemann hypothesis. That's where my mind was while we did it. He didn't make any sound until the end. He never did anything with my breasts. He didn't kiss my neck. He never nibbled on my ear. We barely kissed a good kiss."

"There was no foreplay?"

"He wasn't passionate. Or very adroit. And no tongue."

"This was different for you."

"I was naked with you. That's a big deal to me. This was a fantasy. I wanted good sex, to know what that was like, and I wanted to experience a foreigner who was a black American."

"Lucky me."

"I saw *The Lover.* So sexy. I have watched that movie at least twenty times. I wanted to feel like she feels with her foreign lover."

"I enjoyed you."

"I enjoyed you too."

"You topped me off real good."

"Was a bit nervous to put your *intinih* into my mouth. That is so personal. And I didn't want to get a bucket of guck shot in my eye. Lila, my friend who lives in Malibu, she warned me about that."

"Little Red Corvette is Lila and she lives in Malibu, just to be clear."

"Yeah. Lila. Or Gelila. She said she was shot in the eye with guck and it was not nice. She said it stings like fire. We were drinking, acting crazy, and she showed me how to give a blow job. With a banana. It's silly, but we practiced with a soft banana."

"Why a soft banana?"

"The phallic shape, for one. You're doing it right if the banana doesn't have teeth marks."

"Damn."

71

"Two years ago, I never would have done any of this."

"You would have been sixteen."

"And a virgin. I thought all of this was gross."

"You came out of your shell."

"Now that I have experienced this, I shall take a deep breath and return to said shell."

"Will you tell your friend in Malibu?"

She chuckled, moved her wild hair from her face. "It will be my turn to brag about being bad."

"You will tell her the things I did."

"I will try not to, but she will ply me with alcohol and pry it out of me."

I nodded. "Well, thanks for letting me get to know Africa."

"Your ex was African."

"Afro-Mexican."

"I am more than Africa."

"I was joking. My ex was born in Mexico. So I guess you can say, in this way, I've never been to Africa before."

"I was your first."

"You said I was your fantasy, so I guess you were mine."

"I'm doing things that would anger my parents. They want me to live in a world with no boys, an intellectual world filled with books until I somehow suddenly end up at the altar getting married after I achieve my PhD."

"You're staying out beyond your curfew."

"Until the very last moment. Tonight, I feel so free. I've never stayed out past one in the morning." She hummed, shifted like she needed to go but was enjoying being on parole too much. "I live under someone else's roof and they have a million rules. My day starts no later than six in the morning. Cooking. Cleaning. Do this; do that. They hate to see me relaxing for one second. They always treat me like I am a damned child."

"I grew up the same way, pretty much. When Mom or Pop woke up long before sunrise, everybody had to get out of bed. If you didn't go to school, you'd better have a job. When they left the house, everybody left the house. They worked if they were sick or well and nobody got to lounge. On weekends, we were busy. You either did work inside the house on Saturday, or you were outside the house doing yard work or fixing up the house in some way."

"Sundays?"

"All day at church. From Sunday school to whatever they had in the evening."

"It is that way for us, only on Saturdays."

"No matter what time you went to bed, you had to wake up at dawn and go to church."

"Same for us. Even if we are sick."

"Yup. If you were too sick for church, you were too sick to leave the house."

"So your parents were strict."

"Strict enough. I got a job at fourteen just to be able to get out of the house and have my own spending money, but once I started working, my old man took half of whatever I made, said that was my way of paying rent. If you were old enough to work and make money, you were old enough to help pay the bills. Nobody got a free ride."

"You went to school and worked and paid bills since you were fourteen?"

"Might have been thirteen. Cut grass, did yard work, painted, fixed cars, tutored, anything that paid."

"That's incredible."

"You don't work?"

"Never had to."

"Not even at a fast-food joint?"

"My parents would never let me do that."

"How'd you get money?"

"Allowance."

"Lucky you."

"My job was to study. And from birth, I have been cooking and cleaning like I am their maid. I would have preferred having a regular job. Don't get me wrong, I am grateful. My parents sacrifice so I can focus on my studies. They want me to be prepared for the rest of my life. They want me to be a good wife to some man one day."

"Are they arranging your wedding?"

"They have a boy in mind, a boy I grew up with, but he has never interested me."

"They've planned your life for you."

"But I still want my independence. I want to be able to have fun, like a normal girl. Like Lila does. Even tonight I had to argue and compromise to be able to get out. I had to threaten to run away and never come back."

"Seriously?"

"I am serious. I have to be home before the new day. They go to bed by nine or ten and get up with the sun. But tonight, I know one of them, if not both, will be waiting for me the second I come inside the door."

"What would your parents do if you disobeyed curfew?"

She tsked, had flashes of what looked like pain in her eyes, then lowered her head. "On that note . . ."

"Will your father beat you?"

"Did your father beat you?"

"My father is from down south."

"And mine is from Africa."

I nodded. Understood we had something

else in common.

She grinned softly. "I had a good time. Everything. The entire evening."

"Me too."

"Especially what we did here. I don't want to go to uni and be naïve about everything. I don't want to be a slut, or as carefree as my friend Lila, but I don't want to be in an Ivy League school and be seen as a dumb African."

"You wanted to practice."

She replied, "I want to be normal."

"You wanted to graduate from bananas."

"You must experience certain things, study at things to become proficient, to be seen as normal."

I nodded. "They say it takes ten thousand hours to become an expert at anything."

"It's not a career move. Maybe something to do to have fun with a boyfriend on the weekends."

"Too bad I wasn't prepared."

"I know."

"Would have been a lot better if we had picked up a condom with that coffee."

"I'll bet it would have been."

"I know it would have been."

"On that note . . . ."

Jimi Lee reached into her Prada bag, took out her chic eyeglasses, slid them on, then

76

pulled her powerful hair into a ponytail. Superwoman became a melanin-drenched, white-skirt-wearing version of Clark Kent. That vulnerability humanized her. Made her that much more gorgeous. Without speaking a word or giving a gesture telling me adios or thanks for the coffee and the Os, the African Cinderella eased into her pumpkin and drove away from my life.

CHAPTER 5

Back in my bedroom, Jimi Lee's scent rose from the disheveled sheets. The perfume she wore was an aphrodisiac. Not for the scent, I would have thought her being here was a dream, that I had imagined her. I'd have to wash my sheets, check for any hair she left behind. I'd do that in the morning. I'd clean my spot tomorrow.

I called Jake Ellis's apartment. He answered on the second ring.

I said, "You home?"

"You called my house. Stupid question, bruv."

"How'd you get back to this side of town?"

"Met a police officer at the club."

"She arrested you?"

"She came after some buster got jacked in the bathroom. Found out it was the club owner. People think he was robbed. We got to talking after they took him away. She was getting off work. One thing led to another.

She's here. She's originally from Liechtenstein. She speaks three languages. Plans on going to law school. She's very interesting. And she is very creative with a pair of handcuffs."

"Sounds like you hit the jackpot."

"Ethiopia gone?"

"She came and went."

"You hit it or was it a dry run?"

"Like Tyson hit Spinks."

Jake Ellis yawned. "Message from the boss was on my machine when I got in."

"Bad news?"

"Good news. San Bernardino is happy with our work tonight. More work coming our way."

"What about the guy up at the pool hall in Sherman Oaks by Jinky's Cafe?"

"The guy from Ecuador?"

"Yeah, that con-man guy."

"I think we can work for him at the same time. They don't have any beef."

"We'd better check with San Bernardino first."

"We can do that. But they all out of the same camp."

"We can make that money while there is money to be made."

"Make that money and get on that plane and follow me to Africa."

"That's the plan."

"When you get to Africa, once you go surfing in Nigeria, once you swim in Ghana, once you see the women over there, you ain't going to want to come back. To them, you will be a rich American. They will be all over you."

I smiled, nodded. "Get back to the cop."

"She's waiting on me so we can take a shower."

"You're making a dirty cop clean."

As soon as I hung up the phone, I turned off the lights, went to my computer, turned it on, fired up America Online. The computer threw its soft glow, lit up the office while AOL connected, took over the phone line. The five-minute dial-up began, started whirring and making electronic sounds, the hissing and crackling of the modem handshake, aggravating sounds that could irritate the most patient of men. I lived alone, so I didn't have to worry about anybody picking up the phone, starting to dial a number, and knocking me offline, killing my connection, and forcing me to have to start this hit-and-miss process all over again. I flipped through a few double-sided, high-density disk drives, forgot what was on half of them. I found two disposable Kodak cameras with film that hadn't been developed. Probably pictures I had taken back when I was dating Lupita. Then I picked up a copy of the *LA Times* that was next to the desktop, glanced at the headlines. Boat people from Haiti turned away. Someone killed at an ATM. Government trying to expel illegal aliens from school and deny them medical coverage in order to save California jobs. I dropped the paper when the Internet was connected.

"Welcome. You've. Got. Mail."

As soon as I was connected, I headed for chat rooms. Was going to see what hot women were hanging out in AOL's cyberworld. As soon as I started to type a message, there was a fast set of taps at my front door.

The only thing that visited a man like me this late was the Ghosts of Christmas.

And it wasn't the right season for those three motherfuckers.

I turned off AOL and the computer told me, "Good-bye."

I pulled on baggy jeans, readied my .38, and tiptoed to see what kind of trouble was at my door. No flashing lights were outside my window. No one announced they were LAPD. The job we'd just done at Club Fetish was hot on my mind. Had to be blowback from that beatdown we gave up on Sunset Boulevard.

In a voice that dared anybody to fuck with me, I called out, "Who the fuck is that at my door?"

"Ken Swift?"

"Try again. Ken Swift is on this side of the door. Who is that?"

"You sound different."

It was Jimi Lee. She had come back. I put the gun away and let her into the darkness.

She kissed me right away, kissed me with passion, then held out her hand. The room was pretty dark and it took me a moment to see what she had in her hand. She had gone by a gas station and bought a box of condoms.

She whispered, "Make me come the other way."

"Yeah?"

"Fuck me. Make me come the other way."

I picked her up and she wrapped her smooth legs around me, that short skirt riding up over her tight ass. I kicked the door shut behind us and carried her. We didn't make it out of the living room. The soft glow from outside made us aroused silhouettes. We were kissing; then she was panting, unbuckling my pants, tugging at her clothing. She didn't take her skirt off, only pulled it up over her ass. I pulled her panties to the side, put on a condom as fast as I could and took her right there, on the plush sofa, my pants dropped to my knees. I took her to Back Shots City, went deeper than Barry White's voice. Her hot spot had become a five-alarm fire. Jimi Lee, the girl I had met only hours ago, the cute girl who looked like the girl next door if you lived in Addis Ababa, was intense. She moved better than she had the first time. Took more of me than she had the first time.

"Fuck me. I want you to fuck me the way you fuck other girls."

It was like I was with a new woman, like she had left and sent her doppelganger for round two. Her vagina had its own life, was alive, and it felt like the lips were holding on to me, like the parts beyond her fleshy folds were massaging and pulling at my cock, trying to suck the baby-making batter from my bouncing balls. The way her muscles contracted, did that thing called tenting, and that sucking sensation drove me mad. I don't know what she did while she was gone, but this felt different than before. Grunts. Moans. Mewls. Hard breathing. Skin slapped skin in slow motion, then with a fury, then again in slow motion. The sofa inched from the wall. It felt too good, and I lost control, showed her no mercy. She queefed and I still didn't slow down. When I did slow down, she told me not to. She wanted it like this, like she had seen in dirty movies, where the black man was the dick of all dicks and gave the fuck of all fucks. Jimi Lee put her face in the cushions, moaned, cursed, moved away from me, disconnected, fell off the sofa, and crawled away from me, moaning, shaking, like I was giving her too much of the Dr. Feelgood, but then she pushed back into me like she couldn't get enough, bounced against me like the fire inside her body burned higher, like she couldn't get the heat to go away. She moved across the floor and I moved with her. We were almost in the kitchen. She quinted over and over, tensed and made her vagina squeeze my dick tighter, almost as tight as a handshake. I had a hard time coming, because the second nut was always the hardest. I stroked her hard, was hard, but couldn't get over the hill, and she didn't complain. We moved across linoleum floors, bumped into the kitchen table. She looked back at me, her expression that of erotic amazement, then moved her leg, twisted until I was on her missionary style, her legs around my back. I was on top, going deep, then shallow, pulling all the way out then easing in to the root of the tree. Her skin was beautiful — smooth, unspoiled. She smelled like heaven. It was damn near three in the morning. I know my downstairs neighbors heard us. And if they didn't hear, they felt us making Leimert Park shake.

Winded, skin dank, her gaze drunken, Jimi Lee stared at me, eyes dreamy.

She whispered, "Wow."

"Wow?"

"Yeah. Wow."

Cool air raked across us. We sweated like we were in a tropical rain forest.

"I don't think my skirt will ever be the same."

"I'll buy you another one."

"It's fine. My mother has no idea I own this one."

"Really?"

"I had to save, then sneak and buy it. She would die if she saw me in this skirt. I have to hide it in my purse, then change clothes after I leave home. Will change back into my other clothes before I get home."

I was on my back, pants at my ankles by then. I tried to kick them off. Couldn't. We scooted backward, out of the kitchen, stopped at the living room floor. She laughed and scooted with me, crawled to me, kissed my chest, sucked my nipples, touched my dick, held it as it lost its hardness, stroked it until it became flaccid.

She whispered, "Bathroom?"

I pointed. "Same place you left it."

Jimi Lee took the condom away from my waning erection, then rose to her feet. Exhausted sexy walk, and at the same time, she moved like she could kick your ass. She flushed the rubber, came back with a damp towel, wiped me down with warmness, then took me into her mouth again, sucked the head while I held her hair.

I hummed, enjoyed the heat.

She smiled. "Do you mind? I want to be able to see you. You have a nice body."

"Go ahead."

She turned on the lights. I closed my eyes, blinked, then opened them slowly. She was disheveled, her clothing wrinkled. The living room looked like someone had broken in and tossed the place. She pulled my pants away from my legs, studied my body, smiled at my nakedness, moved her fingers across my skin, kissed me here and there. She liked what she saw. I did the same to her, undressed her, kissed up and down her spine, kissed her legs until she cringed. I went to the bathroom, found Band-Aids, then put one on each of her knees, covered her wounds. Felt like I had pubic hair in my teeth and she licked the inside of her mouth like she could still taste me.

I got back down on the floor, moved her knees apart, kept my weight on my arms.

I sucked her nipples, kissed her belly, kissed between her thighs. Sex and passion weren't acts of cleanliness. Sex could be weird or gross or embarrassing or everything at once, and it still felt fucking awesome. Nothing felt better. Jimi Lee shifted, looked self-conscious. Sex exposed our darker needs.

She took a breath like she was coming down from her high. "The time . . . I really have to go home now."

She pulled her clothes back on. I did the same with mine. With her makeup halfway wiped away, she frowned, stood at the mirror, touched her hair. Anybody who looked at her would know she'd been ridden hard and put up wet. The moment she walked in her door, her parents would know their good girl had gone bad.

She gave up fixing her clothing and motioned at pictures on the wall. "Your family?"

"Yeah. Mom. Dad. Grandfather. Uncles. Aunts. Cousins. Siblings."

She glanced up. "You have a nice bicycle.

Surfboard, which is surprising."

"A black man with a surfboard surprises a lot of people."

"Nice bookshelves." She walked over, curious. "A lot of books are in here."

"I read a lot."

"Philosophy, engineering, Spanish. Civil rights movement. Books on boxing. Then this shelf. Djmaa el Fna. Sossusvlei Dunes. Spitzkoppe. Pyramids of Giza. Nyika National Park. You have books on a lot of different subjects, and I'm impressed, but over half of them have to do with some part of Africa. What's that all about?"

"My plan is to graduate from UCLA, sell all I own, fill a backpack, then travel to Africa."

"Seriously?"

"I want to start at Ghana."

"There are better places to visit."

"I could swing by Ethiopia and do the Sally Struthers tour."

"Those commercials are disgusting and a source of pain and cruel jokes for my people. That is another reason I use the name Jimi Lee. The moment I say Ethiopia, they start with the jokes about starvation."

"I will see it for myself. I plan to make my rounds and break bread with people. Hit the Ivory Coast. Nigeria. Move around a bit. Visit Johannesburg. Windhoek. Tunis. Nairobi. Dar es Salaam. Cape Town. Kigali. Libreville. Lagos. Asmara. Addis Ababa too. And I've read some fascinating things about Gaborone, Botswana."

"You're very interesting."

"Likewise."

Then we stared at each other.

She said, "When two people make contact, merge the way we have, there is a special reaction, a physical reaction, a chemical reaction. I feel it inside. I feel different. All of a sudden, I don't want to be anywhere but here."

"Stay the night."

"Don't get me in trouble."

"When's your curfew?"

"Sunrise. Before my parents wake."

"Okay."

"But I'm calculating how much time before that happens in my head."

"Sun comes up around six thirty in LA. I think you have the same sun in Diamond Bar."

"Our sun is hotter."

"So I've heard."

"Takes me an hour to get home. To be safe, I have to be on the freeway by four thirty, no later than five. It's already almost four. So to be safe, I have twenty-nine minutes and thirty seconds before I have to be on the freeway."

"If you leave now, you won't have to rush."

"I want you to give me a reason to have to rush."

"Yeah?"

"If you can."

By the time she had twenty-eight minutes left, a condom had been opened and Jimi Lee was naked, heels on, bent over in the bedroom doorframe. I was behind her, long stroking while she dug her nails into the doorframe.

It was an intense, desperate-to-come fuck. We went on like that for a minute, maybe two. I'll bet we woke up half of Leimert Park. She didn't care. This wasn't her zip code. No one knew her. She could be wild, loud, intense.

She moaned. "We have ten minutes."

"More or less."

"Take me to your bed."

I carried her, then eased down on the mattress, made it sigh, then made it rock hard for the next five minutes. Jimi Lee saw the time, then positioned herself doggie style, put me inside her that way, worked that little ass, pistoned back and forth, moaned in her native tongue, clasped the sheets while I held on, while I took sharp breaths.

90

She slammed into me like she was the one in charge of the fucking. She grew tired, collapsed on the bed, then grabbed my pillows, stuffed both under her stomach. That was when I took over, rode her hard as I could.

CHAPTER 6

Jimi Lee's eyes were bloodshot. Face was dry. Makeup removed, she looked sweet sixteen. We grabbed our clothes, moved fast. I dressed, pulled my door up, made sure it was locked, and we pretty much ran to her parents' car. Jimi Lee was dog tired, so I took the keys. I put her in the passenger seat, then crawled into her parents' ride and drove her up Crenshaw to the 10 East, up the 10 East to the 60 East, and took the 60 toward Diamond Bar.

She held my hand, talked, eyes half-open, in a daze. "Half of our bodies come from beyond the Milky Way, from star clusters millions of miles away. You took me back there. Never felt so alive. I saw the Big Bang and I rode solar winds across galaxies. You made me feel like a celestial being. I don't want this night or this feeling to end."

A man would never feel what a woman felt. I envied that as I told her, "I'm glad you came back."

"I was leaving. But I allowed biology to overpower reason. I capitulated."

"I hope you enjoyed me as much as I enjoyed you."

Her eyes were closed, her words softer than cotton. "You made me see the beginning of time, made my body lose control that way again, and I topped you off at the end. Wanted to make you feel the same thing; tried to make you leave your body and be at one with the universe. I wanted you to see God. And I saw God."

Then she was sleeping.

Forty minutes and almost just as many miles later, I exited the Pomona Freeway at Diamond Bar Boulevard. Diamond Bar might've been a two-exit town. The main street was a mix of residential, fast-food joints, and strip malls. It was Crenshaw Strip with cleaner streets, better makeup, and no road acne. It was their Shaw, only this was a nonblack area. No lowriders would be cruising up and down this boulevard on Sundays blocking traffic for miles. This area was non-Hollywood. Non-LA. Same for the cow-town communities in its shadow.

When I touched Jimi Lee, she jumped up,

shocked, looked around. "Where are we?"

"You're back in Kansas, Dorothy."

She realized where we were, then panicked. "Don't park here. Please, go to the Del Taco parking lot. Eritreans own this 7-Eleven. They know my family and if they see me like this, they will start rumors about me."

I put the car in reverse, backed out of the lot, headed toward Del Taco.

"Did they see you driving my parents' car?"

"I don't think so."

"If they see a black American driving me in my parents' car . . . at this hour . . . it's complicated."

I parked, then asked, "Okay. Where do you live? Did I get you close enough to your crib?"

She frowned back at the 7-Eleven. "Diamond Bar Country Estates."

"How many bedrooms?"

"At my parents' home? Just six."

"Just six? You're rich."

"I am broke. My parents have money. They let it be known that they allow me to live with them."

"I stand corrected."

"That will change soon."

"Harvard."

Nervous, she checked the time, then asked, "How will you get back to LA?"

"Bus should be running. Sun will be up in a few minutes."

"Can you catch a taxi?"

"A taxi'll cost way over a hundred dollars."

"If I had the money, I would pay."

"No problem."

"You're a long way from home. I feel so bad."

"I'd feel bad if you didn't make it home."

She looked around, saw no one could see us, then kissed me again. "I enjoyed myself."

"When can I see you again?"

"You know I'm eighteen."

"I want to kick it with you. Hang out. Have fun."

"No. I have to go back to my reality."

"Before you leave for Ethiopia."

"You really want to see me again and are not just saying that?"

"I really want to see you. As soon as I can."

She tapped her lip with a finger. "I may be free later today. If I could stop by, would that work for you?"

"Today. Serious?"

"If Lila helps me, if I can concoct a tale, today may be the only day I can manage to be free again."

"What time? I can drive back out here and meet you, if that helps."

"You have an apartment. In a cooler area. Out here, it's too hot to be outside until the fall comes."

"We'd have to get a hotel or motel room."

"I don't want anyone I know out here seeing my car at a hotel. They would summon my father right away."

"I don't want you to get in trouble."

"If my father found me with a black American . . ."

"It's not like I'm a white boy."

"He would prefer me with a white boy than a black American."

"Really?"

"The way he sees things, the hierarchy is Ethiopians, then whites, then black Americans at the bottom."

"No shit? Why is that?"

"You know nothing about Ethiopians."

"No."

"Let's say that skin does not tell the race. Some Ethiopians are Caucasoid."

"Is that possible?"

"We have a connection to Caucasia. Some Ethiopians are as much as forty percent Caucasoid."

"That's close to half."

"Many prefer to identify with that part of

their heritage."

"So, you don't see yourself as black?"

"There is a joke that is not really a joke to many. Ethiopians were considered black until the year 1896, until the Battle of Adwa. That was when my country smashed the Italians and their army. They laugh and say Italians started the day as whites, but ended it as mixed race. Ethiopians started the day as blacks, but ended it as whites."

"That makes no sense."

"Only whites win. Ethiopia won. The joke is, so that made Ethiopians white. To preserve theories of whiteness being all-powerful, Ethiopians were given the status of being white. It was a promotion from being black."

"Why couldn't you be black, win, and still be seen as black?"

"Let's not get into that Darwinism and theories regarding white supremacy, the Caucasian myth, and such."

"So, you're telling me that you see yourself as being superior to black Americans."

"Which would be hard for blacks to understand, since many think so little of Africa."

"We're all black. Why would we see each other any differently in a white man's country?"

"We are different. Different cultures. Ethiopia was never colonized. We were never enslaved."

"And black Americans are the children of the enslaved. We're the bottom of the totem pole."

"African American history is rooted in slavery, in loss, not in absolute victory."

"Your people defeated the Italians. Then the issue is race."

"And the discussion regarding the concept of race could include biology, history, linguistics, and geography, as well as physical features. Some say we have both black and white features in a way that makes us unique."

"Because of a win, Ethiopia got a promotion to the corner office, right next to classism and racism."

"I'm only trying to explain my parents' point of view, their pride, their nationalism."

I took a breath. Tried to remember my history, when I had heard of African Americans having such a victory.

I told her, "To win is to become white."

"Don't misquote my words."

I let that go, went back to my original desire. "Well, I want to see you again."

She inhaled deeply. "I want to see you too."

"Do you?"

"Yes. I don't want this high to end. Would be nice to see you one more time."

"Just let me know when and how much time you think you'll have, even if we have to meet at an intersection. Or in the aisle at a grocery store, and kiss each other as we pass, then go on about our way, I'll do that."

"You'd drive this far for a kiss?"

"Yeah, I would."

She reached, held my hand, squeezed my hand over and over, maybe matching the rapid beat of her heart, pondering as she hummed. "I'll see what I can do. If they don't ground me after tonight."

"Do what you can do, but don't get in trouble with your parents."

"I am always in trouble with them."

"You're breaking free."

"You have no idea. I can't wait until I'm at Harvard. I'll bet the air back east will seem so fresh."

"You're going east to get away from your family."

"Not to get away, but yes to get away. You have to leave home to be respected as an adult."

"You're preaching to the choir."

"When I was born, they put books in my hand. I have studied all my life. All I know is studying. And books. Now I get to live. I get to feel free for once. I get to dance. I get to be an adult. I get to make love. For a season before university. Then it will be back to studying and studying and studying for the next six to eight years without pause."

"And here I was complaining about two more years at UCLA."

"An undergrad degree isn't enough to be competitive. At least get your master's."

"I know. Undergrad is the new high school diploma."

"No. A master's degree is the new high school diploma."

"You have your head on right. Even with a master's, black men don't make as much as white men. And black women with the same degree are getting shortchanged. But you're right. It's better to have the master's."

"Who were your role models?"

"The streets."

"Not your dad?"

"Not my dad."

"You and your dad get along?"

"We don't not get along, but we don't get along."

"Is he a mean man?"

"He didn't come from a nice world. No black man in America has."

"Your mother?"

"Can't say I'm my mother's favorite child."

"Is she a nice woman?"

"The world is harder on black women than anyone."

"But is she nice?"

"She is her own special version of nice."

Jimi Lee took a deep breath, shuddered, looked at the horizon. Vampire too close to sunrise.

She sounded tense. "I have to go now. I have stayed out too, too long."

"You're scared to go home."

"A little."

"You're scared."

"I hope they aren't up. I know they are angry, drinking coffee and waiting."

"Don't challenge them."

"It's been worth it."

"Getting too big for your britches never comes out in your favor."

"I'm an adult."

"Never in your parents' home."

"By law, I am an adult."

"Never under their roof."

She asked, "Were you too big for your britches?"

"Once upon a time, my dad let it be known there was only one king in his house."

"That's why you have your own apartment?"

"In my parents' home, the day you hit eighteen, they bake a cake and leave your suitcases at the door."

"At least in your purgatory, they make you a cake."

"The cake's for them. They celebrate kicking your ass out. Won't even cut you a slice."

"You're joking."

"I wish."

"Wow."

"On that note . . ."

"Wait."

"You have to go."

"I did something adventurous. I did something dangerous. I flew close to the sun and survived."

She kissed me again.

Jimi Lee said, "You were the blues in my left thigh. And you definitely became the funk in my right."

We smiled, the darkness around us not as thick as it had been two minutes before.

She said, "I smell like you. All over, I smell like you."

"Same here."

"I can still taste you too."

I wanted to kiss her again and again, but I broke free, had to be the one to say good-bye first, and with a deep breath I got out of Jimi Lee's parents' car. She crawled over to the driver's side as three cars pulled into the 7-Eleven. Asians. Whites. Pacific Islanders. I was a stranger in a strange land. Jimi Lee was still panicky but didn't see anyone she recognized. She pulled off my Malcom X hoodie, tossed it to me, thanked me for getting her near home, thanked me for being a gentleman, then put the car in gear, zoomed away, tires screeching across fresh blacktop pavement like she'd robbed a bank and was leaving the scene of the crime. She drove fast, like she was trying to speed back in time. I knew I'd never see Jimi Lee again. She didn't ask for my house number. Didn't ask for my beeper number. She'd hit it and quit it. Cool by me. This was Los Angeles. That was as normal as palm trees.

I was around thirty-five miles from home. On a weekday, with traffic going west, that was a two-hour ride. In the evenings, that ride took another two hours. If it was Friday, when everyone was heading toward Vegas, add an hour and a half to that ride. If it was raining, add at least another hour to the time as the freeway became a parking lot.

Jimi Lee was area code 909. I was area code 213. A handful of area codes lived between us. We were just over thirty miles apart, struggling to breathe under the same smog, same sun and moon, but different worlds.

In Southern California, every four or five miles was a different city, had its own area code, and it was rigged to cost a grip to call from area code to area code. Everybody was being robbed by the phone companies. When I used the cellular it cost at least three times as much as using the house phone. That bill looked like a car note last month. Most people didn't use their cellular to call anyone before the rates dropped at seven P.M. That was why most people carried pagers and told folks hit them on the hip, then used a germ-ridden pay phone to call them back.

The Harvard-bound girl from Ethiopia was right. We were geographically undesirable.

I inhaled, smelled her on my fingers, smelled our combined scents on my clothes, tasted her honey on my tongue, then nodded as the sun yawned and struggled to rise. The sun was coming up. It was a new day.

Time to move on.

My beeper went off. It was an LA area code, but I didn't recognize the number. It wasn't San Bernardino or Jake Ellis, and I was about to let it go. I clocked a line of pay phones at 7-Eleven. I wasn't in the mood to see who was hunting for me this damn early in the day, but it could be a hoochie momma from my past feeling lonely at sunrise. I'd drop in a few quarters and call from a pay phone, call from a Diamond Bar number.

"Who paged me this early?"

"Don't answer you phone acting like I didn't raise you right."

"Momma?"

"And good morning to you."

"Good morning."

"Where are you answering your phone sounding like a heathen?"

"Where are you?"

"I'm at home."

"I don't recognize this number."

"We had to get a new number."

"Again?"

"Your daddy and those loose women. They're calling all times of night."

"Where is he?"

"Says he's at the gym training somebody. Some Mexican boy. But you know how he does it."

"I'll try and stop by the house later."

"That's not why I'm calling. Today's his birthday."

"Okay."

"I know you forgot."

"Well."

"You don't remember nobody's birthday but your own, when you bother to remember that."

"My brain doesn't work that way."

"This funny number on my caller ID. Where are you calling me from?"

"Diamond Bar."

"What's going on out there in no-man's-land?"

"Nothing."

"You still working for those people?"

"Not right now."

"Your daddy wants you to work for him."

"I can't do that. Not anymore."

"Well, come see him for his birthday."

"Will see what I can do."

"You live five minutes away."

"Sometimes a five-minute drive can be the hardest drive to make."

"Why?"

"Familiarity breeds contempt."

"You haven't been here in over a year."

"I have to go now. Will stop by if I can, if

I'm not too busy."

"Your big sister came by with her new boyfriend. He was black as a Kodak negative. Told her about bringing those ugly dark men around her. She don't need another dark baby with hair nappy enough to break three combs."

"I gotta go."

"I'm still talking. You not still dating that black Mexican that worked at Robinsons-May, are you?"

"Why? What's it to you if I am?"

"It was rude how she came over and you and her sat around everybody talking in Spanish."

"Momma, it's too early for this."

"I need to tell you what people been doing since the last time you walked out of here angry at everybody."

"Momma, I'm on a pay phone and it's asking for more money and I'm out of change."

"Well, when you get to your little apartment, come up the hill and say happy birthday to your daddy."

"I'll do my best to make it up there today."

"Do better than your best."

"I'm an adult. I can come if I want to. If I don't want to, then I won't come. End of story."

"Don't be that way."

"Only so much of y'all I can take, and you know that."

She hesitated. "Love you."

I hesitated. "Yeah. Love you too."

"Just do your best to come up here and —"

The phone company ended the call. I wished I hadn't called that number back. Once I got to Africa, I wouldn't look back. Not at this shit, not at this family. This time next year, like Jimi Lee, I'd be free. I felt a tightness in my chest, inhaled a stench, the rank of fertilizer, and realized it was all over the place. It was that cow smell coming from Chino. It was unbearable to me. I felt the morning chill on my heated mood, pulled on my hoodie, covered my head, then saw a bus. That was my ticket out of the far end of LA County. I sprinted toward Sunset Crossing, ran like it was Harriet Tubman and this was her last trip toward the North Star. As I hurried, a hard bass line rose and N.W.A. cursed the police. Trunk rattling, bass line cracking, the hard beat from gangsta rap rose at sunrise when a four-door Chrysler with immaculate rims and a cracked windshield slowed down, saw me, scoped me out South Central style, then accelerated, cut across two lanes at me, came like a bull and arrogantly cut off my charge toward emancipation. I didn't have on gang colors, but this was some Crips and Bloods shit. Gangs had originated in LA, but they also had franchises all over Southern Cali. I'd stumbled into the wrong zip code, no gat at my side. Windows down, drive-by style. My heartbeat sped up, and I stopped where I was, hands in fists, body in fight mode, nowhere to run, but ready to duck, drop, and roll. I expected to hear a gunshot and feel the sizzle of hot lead.

"Niggerrrrrrrrrrr!"

Two white boys threw something at me, and I jumped like it was a bomb. What they threw hit the ground and scattered. I thought it could have been acid. But it was fast food and trash. They threw fast food at me. Tires screeched. The Chrysler zoomed away. Just like that, I was ready to fight until I was the last man breathing. I shouted at those motherfuckers, wanted them to come back. Had my eyes on that car until it vanished. I yelled and begged them to come back and call me a nigger to my face. I was from LA by way of Mississippi by way of Oklahoma by way of Charleston by way of Africa. They had incited me and three thousand ancestors. They were fucking with me and every black man killed during the

Black Wall Street massacre. They were fucking with every single body left dead in the Middle Passage during the African Holocaust. And I knew if I beat the fuck out of them, the police would show up, take their side, then take out their nightsticks, raise them high, and do the same to me, then charge me with a crime and sue me to get me to pay for them having to get my blood cleaned out of their uniforms. I didn't care. I was too far from home. I beat ass for a living, and I was good at what I did when I was paper chasing. Diamond Bar might have been cleaner, but it was not better than Los Angeles. Not for a black man.

Being called a nigger at sunrise made me want a pound of flesh.

My Malcolm X hoodie had aroused the racists. Or maybe it was just the hue of my skin.

The life out here was definitely geographically undesirable.

As soon as I got on the bus and dropped my coins, my beeper went off again.

Sun was rising, but this area was already feeling hot, and before the day had started for normal folks, San Bernardino was anxious, trying to get in touch with me. Didn't bring my Nokia. Nothing I could do riding the bus like I was Rosa Parks. I'd find a pay phone and call when I changed buses. Seconds later, my beeper went off again. It was Jake Ellis. He hit me with a code. He never hit me with a phone number. Kept us from being linked or traced. The code told me he'd been summoned too. San Bernardino hit me again, this time with a 911 appended to the code. That meant it was time to do bad to make some more good money. I nodded. I was almost done with this occupation. I'd graduate from UCLA, like I had promised myself. Get that undergrad degree. Then I'd sell my shit; quit the red, white, and blue; leave the smog, skinheads, and racists behind; and go to Africa.

I imagined Jimi Lee was home, arguing with her parents, being subjected to corporal punishment.

I bet there were a thousand women like Jimi Lee in the motherland. Maybe a hundred thousand.

Soon I would be there and find out how many tasted just as sweet.

CHAPTER 7

Long Beach, California

Willie Boy saw me, then turned around, left his ten Mexican employees standing where they were, and bolted toward the back of the nursery. He tried to escape. I chased him past giant palm trees, through Japanese blueberries and Indian laurel columns, and he ducked and dodged by Italian cypress and wax leaf privets.

Underneath the blazing sun at ten in the morning I yelled, "Stop running, Willie Boy."

He yelled back, "Stop chasing me, motherfucker."

"It's hot as hell and you're making me sweat."

"Because you're going to make me bleed."

"Pay your debts and stop dodging phone calls and this won't happen."

"I heard what happened on Sunset last night. Fucking San Bernardino is the devil."

Five foot nine, 140 pounds, a long-distance runner but not a sprinter, he darted through shrubs, roses, past pottery, jumped over bags of fertilizer, knocked over flowering shrubs and hedge plants, trampled decorative grass, until he realized all he was doing was running right toward a grinning Jake Ellis.

Jake Ellis was ten yards in front of Willie Boy and I was twenty yards behind him.

Wearing workman's gloves, steel-toe boots, baggy jeans, and a Lakers jersey, Willie Boy ran to the right, climbed up a forty-foot evergreen tree. Climbed up that tree as high as he could, until the top started swaying.

I yelled, "What are you, part monkey?"

"I ain't coming down."

Jake Ellis said, "You have to come down."

"Says who?"

"Says gravity. Says your bladder. Says your bowels, unless you're making human fertilizer."

"I ain't coming down. I heard what you did on Sunset."

Jake Ellis walked away. Two minutes later he came back with a Mexican carrying a chainsaw.

Willie Boy yelled, "Don't touch this tree. This tree is worth five thousand damn dollars. This is top-of-the-line. Go cut down a *Ficus nitida* or a camphor. Knock over a pineapple palm. Get away from this tree, you morons."

I said, "Five grand for a tree, and we're morons?"

Jake Ellis saw me looking around the nursery and asked, "What are you thinking?"

"My folks need a couple of trees in their backyard."

"You talking to them again?"

"My momma called."

"Who died?"

"Nobody. My old man's birthday is today."

"What that have to do with trees?"

"House needs some yard work."

"You been up there?"

"Passed by once or twice. Didn't stop. Wanted to. Tried. Wasn't in my heart."

Jake Ellis chuckled. "You remembered somebody's birthday?"

"Shut up."

Jake Ellis and the Mexican started shaking the tree. I joined in, made it rock and sway.

Willie Boy yelled down, "Look, man, some assholes in Bel Air screwed me over. They got me to put in seventy grand in trees, gave

114

me five thousand for a down payment, said they would send me the goddamn money in a week, then the motherfuckers filed for bankruptcy. I had cashed the check, so I can't get them for fraud. Law says they get to keep my goddamn trees. They conned me. Sixty-five grand. That put me in a bind. Work with me. How about this? I can sell you three giant trees, three instant evergreens, three palms, ten shrubs, plus I'll throw in a jug of moon juice and a bag of soil conditioner. That's twenty grand worth of trees, but I'll let them go for ten thousand."

"How much you owe San Bernardino?"

"Five thousand this week. Next week I'll owe ten."

"I'll give you five thousand for the trees. And I want three jugs of moon juice and three bags of soil conditioner. And don't use the cheap crap. You have to deliver them and plant everything today."

"You fuckin' serious?"

"Or I can give you what we gave the fool on Sunset last night."

"Damn you."

I stood by Jake Ellis, anxious, throwing jabs, uppercuts, and left hooks at the wind.

He said, "You said a carload of white boys

came at you when you were out in Diamond Bar?"

"Yeah, man. Sun hadn't come up yet."

"First-shift racists."

"They work round the clock, and put in overtime when they can."

"They act real bad in a group."

"Or when they have guns."

"Get the plates on their car?"

"You know I did. Might run it through the DMV and take a ride back out that way."

"Let it go."

"Yeah?"

"Let it go. It's just a word."

"Might be just a word in Africa, but it's black history here in America."

"Let it go."

"They threw trash at me."

"So what?"

"That's a metaphor."

"Last time. Let it go. San Bernardino is hot on us. We have bigger fish to fry."

Willie Boy fell out of the tree. Fell hard, knocked the wind out of his lungs. We watched him struggle to breathe. Tree branches were all over his body. He was scratched up. He was in so much pain, it looked like his eyes crossed over and changed sides. Jake Ellis couldn't help but laugh. I had to laugh too. Shit was pretty funny. I took out a disposable camera, took pictures of Willie Boy on the ground, covered in dirt and fertilizer, bleeding from his nose, looking like he'd had his ass kicked. The disposable camera would be mailed to San Bernardino. Proof of work.

Sweaty, Willie Boy fought to breathe, looked up at us, terrified. "You promised not to hurt me."

Hands in fists, both hands wrapped in boxer's tape, Jake Ellis looked at me. "It's your call."

"I don't feel like hurting a black man today."

"That little drive-by in Diamond Bar got to you."

"I wanted to beat those racists the way Jack Johnson beat James J. Jeffries."

My cellular phone rang. I answered.

"Ken Swift?"

"Who is this?"

"Lila."

"Who?"

"Jimi Lee's friend."

"Little Red Corvette."

"Yeah. The girl in the Corvette."

"I'm busy right now. Whassup?"

"I didn't hear from Jimi Lee like she promised and was scared to call her house before I heard from her."

"She got home right before sunrise."

"Are you serious?"

"As a heart attack."

"Wow. Well. I was concerned. I'll give her a call at home, then."

"Tell her I said hello. And let her know I wish her all the best at Harvard."

I closed the cellular phone, then dropped it inside my front pocket.

Willie Boy got to his feet, then leaned against a tree, still shaky, panting, expecting me or Jake Ellis to attack him. Jake Ellis walked away. I gave Willie Boy my parents' address. Then I wrote him a check for five grand.

I told him, "Cash it and pay San Bernardino before midnight. I want all those trees and bushes put in before the sun goes down. Tell them I sent you. Say it's a birthday present. And I'll be in touch whenever I get in touch."

"You must really love somebody to buy these trees."

"The opposite. Sometimes you buy shit to show people that you're better and you don't need them."

"Well, if you have more people you don't like —"

"Don't push it. Motherfucker, don't push it."

118

■ ■ ■ ■

Not long after we squared away with Willie Boy, we hit the gym on La Brea and Pico, did a boxer's workout. I was jumping rope, working the speed bag, and sparring with a hard-hitting boy from Argentina while Jake Ellis was shadowboxing, hitting the heavy bag, and sparring with a contender from Boyle Heights. We knocked them out, then took on more challengers. We hit the showers. Talked shop while we groomed. We were in separate cars. Jake Ellis went his way, went to meet the dirty cop from last night, was taking her to lunch at Roscoe's Chicken and Waffles.

I dropped the top on my ride, cranked up R and B on KJLH, and headed back toward zip code 90008. A surprise was waiting on me. Trouble was there. When I pulled up and parked two buildings over, a Toyota I didn't recognize was squatting in front of my spot. Windows were up, and they were tinted, so I couldn't see who was inside. The horn blew when I was close to my building. I stopped, considered the .38 I had in my gym bag, always on edge. When you hurt people, when the police aren't your friend, when you are a black man, you stay

119

on edge.

The car door opened and she got out. It was Jimi Lee.

The white skirt was gone and now she rocked baggy jeans, sandals, a loose-fitting T-shirt with Amharic writing across the front. Janet Jackson in *Poetic Justice* with an East African twist. Jimi Lee wore a Harvard baseball cap, her wavy, bushy hair pulled through the opening in the back. The Ethiopian girl who called herself Jimi Lee looked like the perfect girl next door, like a petite, cerebral, sexy nerd. She hurried toward me.

"Ken Swift, is it too soon to say I missed you and I was very worried?"

Dressed in sweats, carrying my gym bag, I reached for her. She hugged me, smiling. She smelled good. Her aroma reignited what I had felt hours ago. We stood on the street and shared tongue like we had last night.

"How did you get free?"

"I made up a few lies, said I had to go to Malibu. I made it into the house without being seen, took a quick shower, made breakfast for my parents, and then parts of my anatomy started to twitch, because of you."

"How long you been here?"

"About an hour."

I smiled. "Spending the night, or just stopping by on your way to see Little Red Corvette?"

"I'd rather spend the night with you. If that is still cool. If not, I can go to Lila's and crash later on."

She handed me a bag. It was different types of coffee.

She said, "Ethiopia Yirgacheffe."

I smelled the bag. It was a good scent, citrus and flower tones.

She hurried back to her car, grabbed her overnight bag and a book.

I asked, "Studying for something?"

"I was hoping you could help me with my lessons."

"What do you have?"

"The Complete Kama Sutra."

"Don't threaten me with a good time."

"Yes?"

"Yes."

"I saw you have a VCR and a very nice television, so I brought a movie too."

"Which one?"

"The Lover. We can watch it together."

"I have a VCR in the living room and bedroom."

"Two VCRs?"

"Two televisions too. The new Sony Trini-

121

tron is in the bedroom. Thirty-two-inch screen."

"That's a big screen. The television in the living room looked smaller."

"It's a Sony too. You can pop a movie in either one when you feel like it. Make it a Blockbuster night."

She moved her bushy, wavy hair, licked her lips, grinned. "It's strange to feel this way."

"What way is that?"

"To crave you. That's all I've been thinking about. I want you inside me again."

"Do you?"

"I'm tingling now, knowing that within a few minutes, that's how we will be."

CHAPTER 8

We were naked on the come-stained bed. Sheets rumpled. Pillows knocked to the floor. Curtains closed enough to make the afternoon look like dusk. Almost an hour had passed. We were spent. I staggered to the bathroom, flushed the condom, then soaped up a hand towel. I went back to Jimi Lee, cleaned her, then used a second towel to dry her.

This was different from last night. Today we were sober. Sober and capitulating to biology.

She spoke in an exhausted tone. "No one has ever done that."

"I'm your first."

"In more ways than one."

"In what other ways?"

"That freaky thing we did yesterday."

"You like that."

"I must have been intoxicated to even consider doing that."

"You liked it."

"I did. It hurt at first; then it felt amazing. Indescribably amazing."

She had found the remote when I was in the bathroom. The big Sony television was on. A special about the OJ Simpson case. Johnnie Cochran. Chris Darden. OJ squeezing on the bloody glove.

" 'If it doesn't fit, you must acquit' is bullshit." Jimi Lee yawned. "That was real bullshit. Do people not know how leather gloves work? Do they not know that when they get wet, they shrink and get tight? Is everyone so dumb?"

"You sound sexy when you cuss."

"Shhh."

I imitated her, *"Bullshit."*

She laughed, rocked against me, watched more, ceiling fan moving in slow motion over our heads.

Jimi Lee asked, "Where were you when the *bullshit* OJ verdict was announced?"

"Few blocks away at Boulevard Café. Same restaurant OJ went to after he was set free."

"I was in a room of white people. It sounded like the end of the world."

"Bet that had to feel uncomfortable."

"How was it where you were?"

"Cheers and high-fives like the day President Lincoln freed the slaves."

"First it was silent where I was. People called out in pain, broke down, literally collapsed."

"They got beat at their own game."

"What game? OJ did it. Do you not understand DNA? There was a plethora of evidence."

"Law didn't prove it."

She inhaled sharply. "Black people danced the Cabbage Patch and cheered for a murderer."

"Do I need to explain this to you?"

"Please do."

"Black life has no value in the white community. Locking the black man up is a sport. OJ killed a white woman. The prize of all prizes. And the message you heard when all the black people applauded and cheered was that since black lives don't have value on that side of the tracks, and since they never have, white lives have no value in our community. And that's not being evil. That's playing by the rules the man created. You're watching the oppressed imitate the values and ways of the oppressor. Hate begets hate."

"That's evil. To even think, let alone say, something like that, Ken Swift, is evil."

"I'm just keeping the shit real. That applause was the sound of anger."

"No one deserved to die like that. At the hands of a madman."

"Consider the concept of slavery. You think slave owners weren't madmen? You don't think the government is being run by madmen? They have maintained a war against my people since we've been black."

"She was a human being."

"I'm just trying to explain to you how I see it, how I interpreted what went down."

"I don't need to be explained to. I am well-read."

"But you're sheltered. Books don't give you the knowledge of the streets. I told you. Three hundred black people were killed in Oklahoma by white people. Not one went to jail. Not one. And show me pictures of a crowd of happy black people standing around a dead white man hanging from a tree with a rope around his neck."

"Being resentful of your history and applauding for the death of an innocent white woman serve no purpose. You can't fight their resentment for you with your disdain for them. You don't fight ignorance with ignorance. You don't fight evil with evil. You live that way and the nonsense goes on and on, generation after generation."

"Well, tell the other side that."

"Cheering when a woman has been murdered is wrong."

"Let me know when you feel black and want to talk about the white man's wrongs. Like I said, I have books with black-and-white pictures, crowds of white families laughing and smiling as lynched black men hang from trees. White women were there, smiling, holding their white man's hand like it was the best date night ever."

"There needs to be a statute of limitations on the things black people won't let go."

"It's called history. Let that go, and it will be repeated."

"Still, you can't spend every day living in atrocities from the past."

"Do Ethiopians let go of the atrocities in their past?"

"You don't hear me going on and on like the Energizer Bunny. Take the batteries out."

"Pretend OJ was Ethiopia and the system was Eritrea. Would you applaud then?"

She laughed and shook her head, then playfully pulled at her hair and did a silent scream. She was idealistic. Too idealistic. She was eighteen. And I was twenty-one, had my own view of the world, not much better.

She said, "Good thing we didn't have that

127

conversation last night."

"Bullshit."

She laughed, walked across the room, stomach flat, breasts high, hair wild. She knew she had a nice body, and had it on display. Her thighs were strong, her arms toned, her ass taut. Music was bumping from all directions.

I said, "You work out."

"Step aerobics, then twenty minutes on the treadmill at level six. Weights on most of the machines. Pretty much go to Family Fitness every day. Not much to do in Diamond Bar but go to the gym and eat."

Jimi Lee's voice trailed off as she looked out the window at my world, tsking, shaking her head.

I asked, "What's wrong?"

"People here enjoy their music so much they want everyone to hear."

"They can get spirited. A few people have a contest. Only lasts about ten minutes."

"It's rude. I can hear five different songs competing for attention."

"Ever lived in an area lined with apartment buildings before?"

"No."

"Around black people?"

"Not like this. We have one or two black families in our area, but not like this."

"Didn't think so."

"I live around people who have great credit scores."

"Don't fool yourself. Credit scores are a way of discriminating against black and brown people."

"Is that how you see it?"

"That's how it is. Same people here who pay their rent and bills on time can't get a place west of Culver City because of credit scores. You can show them you have a job and make a grip, but they keep you out. And the white people who live west of here are filing for bankruptcy day and night but still are allowed to rent those same spots."

"Are you a militant?"

"I'm just keeping it real."

"I see."

"Maybe it's different in Diamond Bar."

"It's better."

"Diamond Bar ain't Beverly Hills."

"Militant."

"Realist."

"Before this gets out of hand, can we call a truce?"

"Sure."

She went to her bag, took out her video. I told her how to operate the VCR and she started the film. It was a number that took place in the 1920s. A young French girl met an important Chinese diplomat on the boat down the Mekong River. I thought it was a political film, about class. When he looked at her, he looked at her the same way I had looked at Jimi Lee in the club. She looked at him the same way Jimi Lee had looked at me. He was attracted to her. She was attracted to him. Soon they were in bed, going at it hard. I pulled Jimi Lee closer, held her as we watched the lovers make love. Jimi Lee was soft, warm, made me want to drink Yohimbe and grow inside her and do to her what they were doing in the movie again and again and again. She made me want to never leave this bed.

I asked, "This is your favorite movie?"

"I've watched it more than twenty times. In this movie, the actress, Jane March, how her character is so restricted and innocent, yet so curious, she reminds me of me. And the harsh family dynamics resonate. It feels like I am looking at a version of myself."

I kissed her neck, touched her breasts, pinched her nipples.

She said, "The way you hold me, you're one of those people who like to cuddle."

"Yeah. I am. I like to kiss. I like to cuddle, skin against skin."

"I've never done that. The cuddle part. Never done that."

130

"Never?"

"I've never spent the night with a boy."

"I'm your first."

"Not only this. You're the first lover I've come with."

"That means when you get to Harvard, you won't forget me."

"Hush and show me how to do this cuddle thing properly."

"Turn on your side. Now back that cute ass up. Jesus, this ass."

"Mmm. The way you hold my bottom. The way you massage my bottom. I have never been touched that way before. You take my body like you own my body. And I surrender. I never give in to any man."

"Let the curve of my body mold into yours until you can't tell where you end and I begin."

"I like this. Mmm. Soul Stealer is throbbing against me."

"Soul Stealer."

"Each time you are inside of me, you take part of my soul."

"Same here."

"You made it jump."

"You wiggled against me and made it jump again."

"Make it do that again." She laughed. "It jumps and grows."

As the lovers in her favorite movie made love again and again, I became aroused, felt her body get warm. I kissed the back of Jimi Lee's neck, moved my hand up and down her curves, did to her what the young French girl let the Chinese businessman do to her with an intensity I'd never seen in a movie that wasn't rated XXX. Like the young girl in the film, Jimi Lee was on fire, aroused, insatiable.

She moaned. "Keep touching me like that. Don't stop."

I moved her hair, sucked her ear. That was her spot.

I told her, "I'm tired, but Soul Stealer wants to steal some more of your soul."

"I am exhausted too, but I want some more of you, too."

"We're going to wear each other out."

"They will find carcasses here, sexed to death."

"With smiling faces."

"Being with you, doing this right now, it feels so urgent."

"Why does it feel urgent?"

"Since I am here today, and this might be the only time I ever see you again, I want to do this as much as I can, just to see what that is like, to have amazing sex until I can't have sex anymore. Want to see how many positions you can teach me. We just did it and I want to do it again. Would that make me a slut to want to do it again so soon?"

"No more of a slut than I am."

"All men are sluts."

"A coconspirator can't call his companion a criminal."

She opened her legs and I two-fingered her and sucked her nipples, did that and she arched back and sang a sweet, spiraling moan. I went down on her, became a lazy cat lapping milk. She purred and wiggled and held my head, became loud, sounded beautiful, her moans riding out the windows into the boulevard. I licked her until my tongue was tired, licked her sweetness until she couldn't take it anymore. And as her legs shook, she summoned me to her, held my face, sucked my tongue while she masturbated me. Soul Stealer hardened in her hand, throbbed while we kissed. I reached for a condom. Jimi Lee mounted me, sucked my lips, sucked my tongue again, kissed me.

Breath ragged, she whispered, "I am so curious. So many things I want to try."

"Show me."

She made me straddle her, put Soul Stealer between her breasts.

"I want to see what this feels like. I want to see if I like the way this feels. It always sounded silly to me to hear girls do this."

"Still seem silly?"

"Not at all. I like this. I can tell you do, and that arouses me."

When it felt too good, I moved away from her.

She reached for the condom I had in my hand, put it on me, got on top, became aggressive, took control. My pager buzzed while Jimi Lee rode me, buzzed while she drove me mad. San Bernardino wanted me to call. The boss wanted my attention. But I couldn't break free. I didn't want to break free. Jimi Lee owned me. Soon I had Jimi Lee on the bench in the workout room, and I owned her.

She moaned, "The way you look into my eyes, that gives me chills. It turns me on so much."

She let me lead and I didn't rush, moved in slow motion. Did Kama Sutra positions. Clasping position. Indrani. The tigress. Splitting of a bamboo. The milk and water embrace. Ate those yams. Had her climbing the walls.

She whispered, "This makes me feel so beautiful. I don't want this sensation to end."

We moved around the apartment, from armless chair to floor, relocated to sofa, changed positions, kissed, laughed, evolved from one Kama Sutra pose to another. The positions had interesting names. Amazon. Arch. Brute. Cowgirl. My San Bernardino pager buzzed again. I knew Jake Ellis's pager was jumping about the same time.

When we took a break, when Jimi Lee had gone to get water, I yawned, dragged myself to the landline, and called Jake Ellis. San Bernardino had more issues to be resolved. We had a job up near the Ashram in Calabasas. Needed to talk to a man about a debt. I told Jake Ellis I was balls deep and he told me he could go and handle it alone.

I went back to Jimi Lee. We turned the page in her book, did that like we were students in a classroom, read the instructions while I was inside her, went back to Kama Sutra lessons, page after page, position after position.

Breathing heavily, I wiped sweat from her face, kissed her, asked, "Having fun?"

Panting, eyes closed, Jimi Lee sucked my tongue. "Fuck. I love this. Love the way you make me feel."

After we showered, I put clean sheets on the floor, then had her get down on the carpet. I broke out the lotions and oils and straddled her back, started at her shoulders, rubbed her down, gave her a head-to-toe

135

massage.

She asked, "Do you treat all of your lovers like this?"

"Only the special ones."

"The Afro-Mexican?"

She said that and I paused, waded through memories. "Yeah. I gave her a few massages."

"If she's not missing this, then I know she's missing your Soul Stealer."

"I'll bet your ex is missing you."

"But I'm not missing him. These things, I'd never do with him. This movie, I'd never watch with him."

"Has he called?"

"Yes. Over and over. He's angry."

"Tell him to come see me."

"He wants to know if you were really my boyfriend."

"And you said?"

"I told him that the way he walked away, obviously I was not his girlfriend."

"Obviously not."

"He didn't even try and defend me. He just walked away like property had been transferred."

"He's an intellectual. His brain told him that was the safest thing to do."

"Whatever."

"Where were we?"

She motioned at the movie. "That. Do that to me. He's so passionate."

"She's on fire."

"I want to feel what she feels. I want to be on fire like that."

Jimi Lee admired the French girl who had gone to bed with a man she didn't know. The girl in the film was with a man from a different culture, a man her culture looked down upon, no matter how much money he had. That was the part of the film I noticed. The eroticism was what Jimi Lee saw. Was all she saw. Like it was to the girl in the film, sex was new to Jimi Lee. Only the girl in the film had been a virgin. Jimi Lee felt tight enough to be the same.

I know my downstairs neighbors heard us. But they didn't bang on the ceiling or come knock on my door.

The provocative movie ended and we were still in motion, now in slow motion, on the other side of orgasm, barely awake, still touching. I rubbed Jimi Lee, massaged her until she fell asleep. Her breathing was deep.

I rested next to her. Worried. She was lying to her parents to be with me. Lying over and over.

I was putting new sex in front of my new money. In the land of capitalism, no matter how fine the woman was, in the long run, that was never a good thing. I was twenty-one. Sex and women were all a man wanted.

I looked over at the dresser. Six condoms looked back at me, wondering who was up at bat next.

CHAPTER 9

After we had a disco nap, I woke up with Jimi Lee grinning and playing with my face. She had nap and sex breath. So did I. She touched my eyelashes and brows, smiled, touched my nose, put soft kisses on my lips.

She whispered, "I'm so hungry right now."

We ran through the shower again, brushed teeth, put on lotion, dressed in baggy jeans and Ts that represented our respective universities, became collegiate, and I drove her ten minutes away to a spot in Inglewood.

Relaxing in the passenger seat, she whispered, "Stop rubbing between my thighs."

"You don't like it?"

"You're. Making. Me. Wet."

"When I rub you right there?"

"Stop pressing your finger in me like that before I go mad."

I took my hand back. She took deep breaths, fanned herself.

She asked, "Where are you taking me?"

"It's a surprise."

I was tired and excited. I wanted to be seen with her. Show her off. We had laughed all the way.

When I pulled into the small parking lot, Jimi Lee tensed up, froze when she saw I had stopped in a strip mall featuring Fresh Ethiopian Restaurant. It was next to Beach Side Ethiopian and Mexican Café and several other East African businesses. Jimi Lee reacted here the same way she had when I had pulled into the lot at the 7-Eleven in Diamond Bar, only more intense. Ethiopians were all over; some went to the van on the passenger side of where I was parked. They saw Jimi Lee's striking features. Her telling features. Jimi Lee shook, pretended she was busy in her purse, didn't acknowledge them. The East Africans paused, said something in Amharic, but Jimi Lee didn't respond. They assumed she was American, then moved on. Ethiopians were going to the many shops, patronizing their own.

When the van was gone, Jimi Lee asked, "Why in the world did you bring me here?"

"You don't like Ethiopian food?"

She snapped in Amharic as she pointed. *"Menna* Mini Market. *Menna.* There is a

140

woman named *Menna."*

"Is there a problem bringing you here?"

"Yes, there is a problem. A big problem. Menna is my mother's name."

"This is your mother?"

"No. They share the same name. This is a sign."

"Sign of what?"

"Since I have lied and told my mother I'm in Malibu at Lila's parents' home, it is not a good sign."

"Why are you freaking out?"

"This is a reminder that I am not supposed to be here and this is a warning."

"We still need to eat." I took a breath. "We can get burgers at the joint next to the restaurant. It's black owned. Place doesn't look like much, but they make the best turkey burgers in Los Angeles."

"What is that place rated by the board of health?"

"The sign in the window said they were given an A."

"I only eat at places with an A rating."

"So, burger or no?"

She sucked her teeth, did that and irritated me. "Mind if I wait in the car?"

"Why can't you get out?"

"These people."

"What people?"

141

"Pants sagging. Gold chains. Girls look like strippers. People out here look like slaves."

"Whoa. Slaves? You just jumped the shark."

"What would you call a person who dresses like they are still in prison?"

"There were never any slaves. No woman or man is born a slave. Our people were enslaved because the devil looked in the mirror and thought he saw an angel. And the Bible he carried told him what he did was the will of God. The will of his god."

"That was then, *Farrakhan*. This is now. Two hundred years later. What's the excuse?"

"Black man wasn't freed two hundred years ago. We walked out of slavery into Negro Codes, Jim Crow, and every evil law they could think of. We're still begging for equality."

"I get the point. No need to become Malcolm X. I understand your history. I know about the nationalism, patriotism, and white supremacy they hide behind false Christianity. I know firsthand how they resent minority groups. I know how it is being seen as black and a woman, then to be seen as African and a woman. And don't think that people aren't racist toward me.

It's worse for Africans. Yes, I said worse. I've been bullied since I was born. By white people, Mexicans, Africans, and by black Americans. Ignorant people don't care what kind of black or brown or what part of Africa I am from. It's all the same to them. We didn't have to be in the boat to be on the boat."

She lectured me on being black, female, and African in America.

I told her, "Let's not talk about this. Let's just have a good time."

"If people had conversations like this up front, then they would never have sex."

"Jesus Christ. Pop a fucking Valium."

"Don't disrespect me. I am a woman, a black woman, an African woman, I get too much disrespect. I speak and either I am not heard or my every word is challenged by some guy."

"I apologize. If I did, it wasn't intentional."

"Pop a fucking Valium? Really? I'm not some South Central hoodrat."

"How many times will I need to apologize?"

She rolled her eyes, away from me. "You're different than you were last night."

"Sun came out."

"You're more fun in the dark."

"You're more fun when you're drunk and rocking a miniskirt that barely covers your ass."

I was about to tell her that last night I thought she was sugar and spice, that I'd had nothing sweeter, but now, the morning after, I'm realizing that even salt looks like sugar.

I said, "Tell me what you want."

"You're angry."

"Just tell me what you want."

"Truce?"

"What?"

"Let's call a truce."

She leaned over and kissed my cheek. Then held my face, gave me a quick taste of tongue, and it hit me like it was a shot of Jack. That burst of anger, then rescinding, seeing my change in mood, then calling a truce to control that, in two seconds she let me know she could be passive-aggressive. She needed to control the moment.

She whispered, "Truce?"

"You can't pull that bratty act and just yell you want a truce."

"Apology blow job? Will that make it better?"

"Will it? Don't know. Never had one."

"I've never done one."

"That's supposed to do what, exactly?"

"Bet you're the kind of nasty boy who would prefer *soixante-neuf,* right?"

"I have no idea what that is."

"That was French. Simultaneous oral sex, like doing the sixty-nine."

"So technical."

"I am a nerd. I am analytical. I like to be precise. And things I don't know how to do, I like to read about so I know what to expect. I have never done sixty-nine. Let's see how that works for us. You can get on top, put that here. I put this there. And we do this in slow motion while Luther Vandross sings in the background. Can you handle that?"

I didn't say anything.

"You're mad."

"Tell me if you want a burger from here, or should I roll over to Simply Wholesome and get healthier food? But let me warn you, some of your cousins will be there too. And at Starbucks. At the grocery store. Everywhere."

She took a second. "What do you do for a living?"

"What do you mean?"

"You have a swank apartment. You drive a nice car. You dress nicely. You own a lot of books. Own a lot of music. You have a computer. Not a lot of people have computers in their homes. You have a DVD player. You have a CD player. Two VCRs. A very big television in both the living room and the bedroom. Your furniture is new and too nice to be in an apartment. Your bed is new. Skateboards, snowboards, skates, and Roll-erblades."

"You took inventory."

"By my calculations, you must have a lot of debt."

"By yours, but not by mine."

"Your money goes toward bad invest-ments."

"You've evaluated me."

When I said that, my beeper went off. It was San Bernardino trying to reach me.

She hesitated. "Are you a drug dealer?"

I verified the number to call, then faced Jimi Lee, laughed. "I'm not a drug dealer."

"What type of work do you do?"

"I work for a small security firm."

"And you go to UCLA? You sure about that, or are you just trying to impress me with a lie?"

"I go to UCLA. I'm off for the summer. I usually take a couple of classes in the sum-mer, but I guess like you, this is my break. I get a gap summer and you get a gap year. And, damn, drug dealer? Really? Drug dealer?"

She hesitated again. "Do you know any drug dealers?"

"Why would I know drug dealers?"

"Look, don't judge me, but I . . . time to time . . . not often . . . I partake of the sticky green."

"You're a pothead?"

"Recreational user. Not often. Told you. You don't know me."

"Ethiopians smoke weed."

"Blame Lila. She got me started. All of my bad habits came from her."

We laughed, but it wasn't a hard, true laugh. It was a revealing laugh.

"I get migraines. Helps the migraine. And now I have a headache. And it is your fault."

"Want an apology pussy licking?"

She laughed. "I won't turn it down."

I said, "I'll see if anyone on the block is holding."

"Holding?"

"Holding means selling drugs."

"One more thing." She hummed. "I want wine. Riesling if you can find a bottle. I love Riesling."

"You're not old enough to drink."

"My age wasn't a problem last night."

"You look all of sixteen today."

"That wasn't a problem two hours ago."

"You're eighteen, pretending to be twenty-one, and you claim you've barely broken the seal on that coochie, but you work that ass like it's a '64 Chevy lowrider with sixteen switches. Up, down, back, forth, round and round."

"You are twenty-one and make love, do freaky things like that is what you really do for a living."

"Is that what you think? I'm a drug-dealing gigolo?"

"I wouldn't be surprised."

"And for your information, I don't sixty-nine. I ninety-six. My shit is advanced."

She laughed. "Get the burgers."

"You sure?"

"A double-meat hamburger, two slices of cheese, extra mayo. Get weed and wine if you can."

"Sure."

"Maybe we can pass by the so-called Black Beverly Hills on the way back. You said it was close by. We can do that, then eat at your well-appointed bachelor pad and fall asleep watching *The Lover*."

"*The Lover* was something else."

"It's a deep movie. Has levels. But the passion. In so many ways, like I told you before, she reminds me of me."

"How so? You're not a poor French teen-age girl in Saigon in the 1920s."

148

"Her family. Her life. Her angst. Her restlessness. I know I feel the way she feels on the inside."

"The lover she chose?"

"I know how she feels for him, for that stranger. That craving, that awakening. It makes me feel normal."

"And I am the Chinese man."

"He has the apartment. And she has a place she can go to and feel as if she is in control of her life."

I leaned toward her.

"You are rubbing between my thighs. You're massaging that thing that men want."

"Like it when I touch you like this?"

"You're. Making. Me. Wet. Again."

"Good."

"If I had a dress on."

"Wish you did."

"You're really good with that hand, those fingers, and you're good in bed."

"Trying to be like you."

"I am a freshman when it comes to sex. You're a grad student."

"Like it when I rub you right there?"

"Stop before I go mad."

I took my hand back. She took deep breaths, fanned herself.

With that, I eased out of the car. Jimi Lee let her seat back so she couldn't be seen.

■ ■ ■ ■

I hit Phat and Juicy, put in our order, then wiped down the nasty receiver, dropped in some coins, and used the pay phone to call San Bernardino. Jimi Lee watched me. She also watched the Ethiopian workers and customers coming and going from the restaurants and the other businesses. Jimi Lee was comfortable with me in bed, but not in public. Most men were looking for a woman like that, something that had an expiration date and would never be more than a booty call. I hadn't known Jimi Lee twenty-four hours. I knew it was the last day I'd see her. This wasn't going to be a summer thing. I had access to women in LA, women who were geographically desirable, and didn't need to drive an hour to get a hookup. I was sure boys and men in Diamond Bar were hot on her. I told myself to feed the East African, slap that humble ass one more time, and send her home to her strict momma and heavy-handed poppa.

She lived with her parents. She had to have permission to leave home, had to lie about her whereabouts. I was a grown man. She got an allowance and I had worked since I was barely a teenager.

150

I didn't have a curfew.

I could have taken her to Beverly Hills to eat, but I hated spending my greenbacks in places that didn't care about my black skin, places where they might spit in my food or do something twice as disgusting to get their rocks off. I had come here to patronize people who looked like me. People who looked like her. My money went to Africa and a black business. Anger rose. Jimi Lee was right. I did want the Ethiopians to see me with her. I wanted to show her off. I wanted to be seen as part of the tribe, as part of the global struggle. Like them or not, understand their tongue or not, we were all from the same baobab tree. But Jimi Lee showed me that looking like me didn't mean thinking like me. I wished I had ended it in Diamond Bar at sunrise. Then she would have remained perfect in my mind. While I talked to San Bernardino, I looked back out toward my car, saw Jimi Lee hiding from the world.

Made me feel like I was a black man who had taken a white woman to a meeting at Nation of Islam.

I was done with Jimi Lee.

I'd feed her, be a gentleman, hit it again, make her say my name, then be done with her.

CHAPTER 10

But after we had eaten the burgers, Jimi Lee came to me, and the apology blow job she threw down changed my motherfuckin' mind. Had me whimpering and saying her name over and over. She used me like she was in summer session at an Ivy League school taking a class dealing with sensual and erotic matters.

Jimi Lee whispered, "I read a lot."

"That's obvious."

"I read that the penis has about four thousand nerve endings."

She took control of me. Owned me. Comfortable now, exponentially better than yesterday.

She whispered, "I love that you moan. You're never quiet. That turns me on."

She left me in the fetal position, shivering like a child.

She whispered, "That time I did it right. And I didn't expectorate."

"I see."

"I like you."

"Do you?"

"I feel like I can be free sexually with you. I'm physically attracted to you. I need to be like this with someone who can't hurt me, someone who doesn't want too much, someone I can see this way and be free, go wild, do things beyond the normal things that people do. I want to be with someone and not have to hide this part of me."

"I'm your guy."

"Just for the summer. Just until I leave for Ethiopia."

"That works for me."

"This is what we are about. Just fun. Just this."

We fell into more touching, ear nibbling, tongue sucking that became habanero kisses, fingering that made her murmur, stroking that made me whisper to God and his son, panting that echoed wall to wall, husky exhales that made me sound like an unleashed animal, curt inhales that made me think she was drowning, and with all of that, as the intensity grew, the desire to devour each other was so damn strong. When I was so hard I was about to explode, her legs opened and I felt her fire, a heat that needed to be resolved. And to ease her ache, to soothe her pain, there was the offering of her flower, the willingness to give me her body for more penetration. There was slow penetration that quickly turned intense, turned into a passion she didn't want to end. Right away we exploded, came at the same time, came hard, came panting, moaning, screaming, rocking the bed, shaking the room. Jimi Lee took all of me that time. Took all of Soul Stealer. And when that was done, panting, we fell into tender kisses.

She whispered, *"Soixante-neuf."*

"That what you want?"

"I want to try that next. I want to see what that is like."

We napped again, woke up separated, reached for each other, kissed, touched, cuddled, the thirty-two-inch Sony Trinitron glowing, sound muted.

"Ken, question?"

"Shoot."

"Do you know where the Hustler store is in Hollywood?"

"Yeah."

"Is it far?"

"Thirty minutes." I turned to her, kissed her. "You want to take a ride and go there?"

"I might buy my first vibrator."

"That's the spot to get a portable penis. There or the Pleasure Chest."

"When I leave for Ethiopia, I want to take a discreet toy with me. Something I can hide and my mother won't find when she snoops and looks in my things. I don't want to shop for one in Diamond Bar. You can be anonymous in LA. Diamond Bar is like a small town. People talk. I look young and if I go to one, they will ask for my identification; then they will know I am African and know my address. If I am carded in Los Angeles, it will not matter so much."

"Know what you want?"

"A vibrator. I want to see what Ben Wa balls look like. And plugs."

"Been to an adult store before?"

"Never been old enough to go in one, only heard my mother tell someone those places are Sodom and Gomorrah. I'm curious. I want to know what goes on in there. I want to know the secrets."

"And you want a souvenir."

She laughed. "Wouldn't want anyone to see me buying a toy or a butt plug in Addis Ababa."

"How do you know about all this stuff?"

"Guess."

"Lila."

"No. I went to school with rich girls. Rich

girls get bored and are very experimental."

"What are rich girls into?"

"White girls at my old school? Everything. They lived for LSD and debauchery."

"LSD?"

"LSD. Three students passed out in class. And they carried vodka in their water bottles. They had been coming to school high for months. They were high or getting intoxicated right in front of the teachers. Nobody noticed. All were top students. An ambulance came. That was the talk, until the science teacher was taken away."

"Why?"

"He did something with a student."

"Sex?"

"He was old. Forty. And the girl was twelve."

"You get caught doing way more stuff out there in cow town, and y'all chastise folks in LA?"

She laughed a soft laugh, kissed me again, changed the subject, controlled the conversation. "I was a virgin ten months ago. I was scared to think about having sex. My father would kill me if he found out. If I had done drugs or was found with alcohol at school and brought shame on my family, I would have run away from home because he would have beat me within an inch of my life. If I embarrassed my family, I'd die of shame; then he would kill me."

"He thinks you're a nonsmoking, non-drinking, non-sex-having virgin."

"Until the day I marry, that is what he and my mother must believe. Anything less is not acceptable."

Two days later, Jimi Lee broke free again and came back, showed up by eleven in the morning. I took her to eat breakfast at Simply Wholesome, then hopped in traffic and battled my way to 6540 Hollywood Boulevard. When we pulled up at the Hustler store, Jimi Lee was as excited as a kid at Disneyland. We walked through a sea of strap-ons, vibrators, couples' toys, cock rings, anal toys, dildos, masturbators, prostate toys, whips and paddles, bondage kits, nipple suckers, gags, ticklers, and nipple clamps. I bought her a few things; then we went to Universal City, took in a tour of the back lot, ate seafood, caught a movie. After the movie, we hit World on Wheels. She could skate, but not like I could. She had learned to skate down in Cerritos. I had learned to bounce and rock on my skates in LA, grew up hanging with some of the same people who skated on Venice Beach every weekend. I reminded myself this would end soon. I was her boy of summer. After skating, we went to the Comedy Store, watched comics, had drinks. Then we went back to Leimert Park, hung out at 5th Street Dick's coffee shop, listened to jazz for about an hour, then headed back to my place, showered, kissed, and tried out her new toy. We had a quickie on the sofa. I took her from behind, our pants pulled down to our knees. I made her come before she had to hurry back home. There was no time to shower or cuddle. Again, she had to be back in her parents' house before sunrise. I drove her while she slept. Jimi Lee sped away and I had Jake Ellis meet me at the 7-Eleven on Diamond Bar Boulevard. He showed up thirty minutes later. I had downed an energy drink and had a honey bun. We had to drive four hours to Vegas and take care of a problem for San Bernardino. This time the issue was a woman and her husband.

I asked Jake Ellis, "How San Bernardino want this one handled?"

"No mercy."

"Wake me up and I'll take the wheel at the McDonald's in Barstow."

"Ethiopia wearing your ass out."

"Shut the fuck up."

■ ■ ■ ■

Seventy-two hours later, Jimi Lee was back. Again, she had lied, said she was going to be in Malibu with Lila. Jimi Lee had arranged it so she could spend two nights with me. I dropped the top on the Benz and drove her to Morro Bay one day. Lila and some dreadlock-wearing white guy she was dating followed us up the 101, his convertible BMW challenging me and racing me all the way. Lila and her white boy walked around with us. Two couples strolling, holding hands. Jimi Lee called her parents from a pay phone with Gelila at her side, all of them talking in Amharic. Once she had used Lila to make sure her lie worked, we all went our separate ways. Lila and her friend had booked a hotel room. Little Red Corvette was using Jimi Lee as her alibi, her way to get away from her Malibu parents. I had my own spot. I didn't need to rent space to knock boots, but I booked us a room anyway. Got us some room service, made love with the windows open to the Pacific Ocean, made her feel so good she cried.

Soixante-neuf. She whispered she wanted more *soixante-neuf.*

I did my best to give her everything she wanted, how she wanted it.

The next afternoon, I made a stop on the way back into Los Angeles and took Jimi Lee hiking at the Griffith Observatory. We stood up on the hills, disposable cameras in hand, and took maybe fifty pictures with the Hollywood sign behind us. I kept a stock of disposable Kodak cameras with me. I took pictures everywhere we went, grabbed memories of all we did. She was my girl of summer and I didn't want to forget her, wanted to be able to look in my photo album and remember the time I had with the girl who was going away to become an Ivy League queen.

After dinner in Santa Monica, we held hands and walked the promenade. Just the two of us.

Again, I took more pictures. Took roll after roll. Loved photographing her.

Jimi Lee said, "This is getting too serious."

"What's got you upset?"

"We should take a break."

"I thought this was the break from the other parts of our lives."

"From each other."

"I do something wrong?"

"My father almost found out I have been lying to him."

"How?"

"He's been checking the mileage on my car."

"Get the fuck outta here."

"He found the receipt from the Hustler store."

"What did he say?"

"I told him it was Lila's receipt."

"Lila is your fall guy?"

"I had no choice. I put it on Little Red Corvette."

"Did he investigate?"

"I don't know."

"You're scared."

She didn't answer, but said, "I feel so much with you."

"Is that bad?"

"I must get this under control."

CHAPTER 11

San Bernardino sent Jake Ellis and me to San Diego. We arrived at nine in the morning, hurt a man at eleven, hurt another at two, then were back in Los Angeles eating chicken at El Pollo Loco by sundown.

When Jake Ellis dropped me off at my spot, Jimi Lee was parked out front, waiting.

I saw her and she saw me, and we smiled, and I got all the feelings in the world.

She said, "I tried to stay away from you. I can't. What have you done to me?"

"Same thing you've done to me. Exact same thing."

"I didn't see you for a day and I went mad. I couldn't sleep and couldn't eat."

Within five minutes of my arrival, we were in the shower. Shower sex was as spontaneous as it was hot, never gave us a chance to put on a condom. We were too busy capturing corners of each other's souls. After the shower, it was the bed, and from the bed, we slid to the floor, continued on the carpet, bucking like broncos.

Then we were frantic, feral, out of control until we climaxed, first her, then me, and when I slowed, when I softened, we rolled away from each other, panting, skin covered in sweat.

She whispered, "Without a condom, Jesus, it feels twice as good."

"Ten times as good."

"Too damn good."

They say it takes about sixty days to create a new addiction.

This compulsion took half that time. Being inside Jimi Lee was more potent than cocaine and twice as habit-forming as crack. And the way she drove thirty miles one way in LA traffic, traffic that could make a one-way thirty-mile drive take as long as two hours, longer in the rain, told me she felt the same, had the same infatuation.

She hated waiting for me to get back home, didn't feel safe being alone on the streets in Leimert Park, didn't think it was ladylike for a woman to be sitting in a car waiting for a man to come home, so I gave her a key to the front door, a key to the back door, and the password to my computer so she could dial up AOL and go online if she needed to. I'd come home and she'd be there, in shorts, no shoes, comfortable, doing her version of surfing the Internet, bouncing from chat room to chat room, talking to strangers on blackvoices.com and playing music. I came home from another job in San Diego and she was in the kitchen cooking. She was dressed in lingerie and heels.

With a big smile, she hugged me, kissed me, said, "I am preparing *tibsi, dorho, kwanta fitfit.*"

"You went shopping, or did you bring all of this from Diamond Bar?"

"I went shopping. Menna Mini Market in Inglewood. I went there to get the things I need."

"She sells all the breads like injera and spices like berbere. I say those right?"

"What do you know about berbere?"

"It's a dope spice."

"It has chili peppers, garlic, ginger, basil, *korarima,* rue, *ajwain* or *radhuni,* nigella, and fenugreek."

"I bought that and *mitmita* before."

"You know spices? I thought black Americans just used Lawry's seasoning salt and called it a day."

I laughed. "I don't eat out much because

164

I love to do my own cooking. I buy different spices. African and East Indian spices are the best. Would've cooked for you, but I haven't been food shopping in a long time."

"You eat all of that Mississippi food."

"Did when I was growing up."

"Shud I mek ya a big ole bucket of chitterlings and some hot waddah kawwwn bread?"

"It's pronounced *chitlins*. And I don't miss eating out of a hog's ass."

"You seem obsessed with my culture. You've dated an Ethiopian before me, haven't you?"

"Had a few Ethiopian friends growing up."

"Northern Ethiopia or southern?"

"Never asked. What's the difference?"

"Were they darker-skinned, like the south, or more like mulatto in the north? We have a range of complexions and features in Ethiopia. From thin noses to broad. Dark skin and light. All noses. All complexions."

"Brown skin. Asymmetrical features, like you. Nice people."

"Yeah, you're obsessed."

"Aware, not obsessed."

"But not intimate like we have been with an Ethiopian before me?"

"You're the only girlfriend who invited me inside the walls of East Africa."

"I'm not your girlfriend."

"I stand corrected."

"Now come eat. Eat and make love to me so I can hurry back home."

Sometimes I wouldn't hear from her all day, and I'd be in bed and the door would open. She would call my name, then run to the bedroom and drop her overnight bag. Once she had on a trench coat and nothing else. She would dance, do her tease, do her belly dance, arouse me as she undressed to her skin, and jump under the covers with me. She would go to Malibu, to Lila's place, call her parents from there, say good night, then drive to my bed.

And as we calmed down, we rested, touched, held fingers, cooled in beautiful silence.

She glowed. "Never felt this way."

"You have to get home before the parents wake up?"

"My parents think I am staying in Malibu with Lila. She's covering for me again."

"Lila has it covered?"

"They never call her parents' home, so her parents have no idea. It's all sorted out."

"Good to know you're an expert at logistics."

"But I have to leave early in the morning. We have relatives coming from Addis Ababa.

It's my parents' twenty-fifth wedding anniversary, so we will have people coming from Ethiopia, Brooklyn, Minneapolis, Tampa, Boston, and Washington, DC. Everyone is staying at Ayres Suites. I will be overwhelmed. I won't be able to see you for two days, so I want all the kisses I can get so I can survive."

"Need a date?"

She made an "I'm sorry" face. "I have a date."

"Really?"

"I have to go with an Ethiopian boy. For appearances."

"Are you sleeping with him?"

She made a "yuck" face. "No."

"You like him?"

"He's gay. It's illegal to be gay in Ethiopia. I keep his secret and he keeps mine."

"Bet you're going to be dressed nice."

"I'll take pictures and get them developed at One-Hour Photo or Costco."

The conversation was broken by the sound of sirens and ghetto birds. I eased up and looked out the window, made sure the doors were locked, took off the used condom, went back.

I asked, "So, you said that the Ethiopian calendar has thirteen months?"

"Twelve months of thirty days and then a

thirteenth month. We celebrate our New Year with a lot of dance and song, and we have an Ethiopian coffee ceremony, a cultural fashion show, and storytelling from our leaders, the elders."

"How long is that thirteenth month?"

"Five or six days, depending on whether it's a leap year."

Condoms were on the nightstand, but Jimi Lee took a toke, then mounted me without asking me to roll on another jimmy hat. She put me inside, made a sound that told me she was ascending to heaven, made me do the same, let me feel her again without the latex, controlled me, weakened my heart for her, moaned, moved slowly as she smoked her joint. She clouded my life, perfumed my space with what was illegal, with what had led to the incarceration of many black men, and while she made cumulus clouds over our heads, while she rode and hummed and exhaled and inhaled, she licked her lips and taught me the basics of her native tongue. She closed her eyes, took short breaths, fought the feeling, and told me basic phrases, schooled me. She had taught me enough to be respectful, but not enough to remove my ignorance.

I caught my breath. "I was reading . . . about Abyssinia. Ogaden. Eritrea. The modern . . . Ethiopian Empire."

"I am impressed . . . by your effort. I love . . . the way you . . . are interested . . . in me."

"C'mon, Jimi Lee. Teach me more Amharic words and phrases."

"So you can be prepared when you meet another Ethiopian girl."

"Teach me while you move your body like that."

"I can't focus with Soul Stealer inside me pulsating and growing like this."

"You can. Focus."

She moaned. "I will say the months."

I panted. "Have fun. Belly dance."

"Then you repeat the months."

"Let's have class while we make love."

"Let me see if you are focused."

I struggled, did my best to pronounce each correctly, managed to whisper, "Meskerem, Tikemet, Hidar, Tahesas, Tir, Yekatit, Megabit, Miyaza, Ginbot, Sene, Hamlé, Nehasé, Pagumé."

We made love without reaching orgasm. We were trying some tantric shit. Mindblowing. We treaded in the feeling, treaded in the heat, lived in the heart of the need to come until we were so hot and sweaty we slid away from each other. She fell away from me, aching. Again the room was humid enough to swim through the air. I turned on the floor and ceiling fans, opened the window and let in the city sounds, the night in the desert chilly and dry.

She whispered, "I adore you."

"You adore me. Adore. What does 'adore' mean?"

"Get back on top of me."

"What does 'adore' mean?"

"Adore is like love. It is like infatuation, admiration, respect, and with you it is also desire."

"You adore me."

"I adore you too much."

"What's too much?"

She shivered, closed her eyes, reached for me. "Bring Soul Stealer back to me. I need to come, baby."

"Do I bore you?"

"I love the way you bore me."

"Do you?"

"Bore me now. Bore me good."

When Jimi Lee calmed down, she crawled to me, put her head on my belly.

I played in her hair, pulled her curls. She hummed, sang; then we had more silence.

She whispered, "I'm going to miss this."

"Yeah?"

"Best summer ever."

"Yeah. Best summer ever."

"You have made me a junkie. I will have to go through withdrawal."

"Twelve steps for me too."

She hesitated, had an internal debate, then whispered, "I think I could love you."

"Think you could?"

"I could. But I can't."

"Why can't you?"

"With love comes responsibility. Love is a choice, and we must choose carefully. And love requires both time and presence. I can't start something I know I can't continue."

"Sometimes we choose, and sometimes we are chosen. Cupid and that arrow."

"It's a choice. There are different kinds of love. Affectionate love. Familiar love. Playful love. Obsessive love. Enduring love. And there are different levels of each love, in my opinion."

"What kind of love do you have for a man like me?"

She hummed, bounced her leg. "I think it's a playful, erotic love."

"You like sleeping with me."

"I have a strong sexual desire for you. I can tell you enjoy my warmth too."

"Enjoy your warmth?"

"I don't want to be crass."

I hummed. "You're going to Ethiopia soon."

"Then to university so I can start the next phase of my life. You are my interlude."

"What will you become?"

"A doctor. Not sure what I will specialize in, but I will become a doctor."

"You won't be back."

"I won't be back."

"You'll meet someone else."

"I'll meet someone else."

"You will meet an Ethiopian."

"More than likely."

"I can see you with a white guy."

"Can you?"

"That offend you?"

"My parents see the world this way: Ethiopians are on top."

"You told me that before."

"If I married an Italian or a white, they wouldn't complain, not so much."

"So in your parents' eyes, I'm not good enough. Will never be good enough."

"Don't be offended. That's the way my parents see things. They carry their cultural and political values and it's based on years of struggle back home, on their philosophy and how they want to be viewed and treated here."

"I should've stuck to chasing the light-skinned Ladera Heights girls."

"Do they have dark-skinned girls there?"

"Maybe in old Ladera. Have to pass the paper bag test to get up the hill."

"And I should've bypassed this gap year and gone straight to Harvard."

"Or stayed with the Ethiopian you ran away from the night we met at Club Fetish."

"I really think my parents would prefer me to be with a well-educated white man."

"Why?"

"I think my parents would respect me more."

"Why would that get you more props?"

"My brother was engaged to a beautiful girl named Bewunetwa, but they broke up. Now he's married to a white girl, Kristen. She's Welsh. Born and raised in Swansea. She went to Brown. And my parents are happy to have her as a new daughter. It shocked me. Kristen is an ophthalmologist. Has her own practice in Chino Hills. Bewunetwa went to UCLA, owns a restaurant on Fairfax. They have embraced Kristen more than they did Bewunetwa."

"Because their minds have been colonized."

"It would be like I escaped orbit. They would praise me. A white Ivy League graduate? A son-in-law from Brown, Columbia,

Cornell, Dartmouth, Harvard, the University of Pennsylvania, Princeton University, or Yale?"

"Could you marry a white man?"

"I could."

"Really?"

"Yes. But if I married a white man, I would not love him. Not like an Ethiopian man."

"Then why marry the pink stick and have beige children stuck in between?"

"When you don't love someone, they can't control you. If they cheat, you are not destroyed. If they choose to go away, you don't lose sleep at night. You don't go crazy. You won't be weak for them. And I wouldn't be bound by my parents' traditions. I could still get away and be me, the version of me I love to be. It's hard to explain. I feel like a modern African woman fighting against her own culture. My parents say that I am living like the white Americans while trying to be like the black Americans."

"Am I just an escape?"

"What am I to you? You are so fascinated about my culture."

"I've met girls from Gambia and Malawi. Knew girls from Botswana and Nigeria."

"Funny how some blacks want to date Africans to feel closer to Africa, as if seducing or fetishizing an African is part of a spiritual journey, and Africans will date Americans to have an international experience, the same way blacks date whites just to see what it's like on the other side of the racial barrier, to have experiences beyond that which they know, to achieve a certain type of growth. But this is more of a cultural thing, I suppose, and when the fun is over, most of the curious always go back home to family, to the familiar, go back to their tribe in the end."

"If that were true, there would be no bicultural or biracial babies."

"Maybe not in Ladera Heights."

"Stop stealing my jokes."

She said, "There are accidents every day. Most living creatures are accidents."

"As long as there is alcohol and weed, there will be accidents."

"The strong become weak and have accidents."

"Is that what you did?"

"Don't ask me that."

"Are you weak for me?"

"I went home with you the night I met you."

"Soon as I crowned you my girlfriend."

"Like I was a slut."

"Don't say that. You were no more slut

than I was."

"I had known you for maybe two hours."

"Three."

"That's not much better."

"You work fast. Got me to give up the boxers."

"You came to me."

"You looked at me. Gave me all the right cues."

"Your eyebrows and lashes."

"That white dress."

"It was a skirt."

"Whatever it was, the way it hugged your ass."

"Your dancing aroused me."

"So did yours."

"The way you held me close and looked into my eyes."

"You did the same."

"I didn't intimidate you. That aroused me."

"You still arouse me. Like never before."

"I have sex with you as much as I can, even if I am bleeding and we have to do it in the shower."

"I can't stop wanting you."

"I drive to LA two or three times a week, over thirty miles one way, and in traffic that could take two or three hours. I am out of control. Over sixty miles from my door to yours and back home."

"You don't have your own place. If you did, I would drive to you. Or come there and get a room."

"I lie to my parents every day."

"Most kids do."

"What I do is against my parents' wishes. I have gotten comfortable with you and now I only want to have sex with you without a condom. I am smarter than that. Much smarter than that. But I have allowed emotion to defeat logic. You are the second man I've been with, and the first always used protection. I have trusted you but betrayed myself. My heart has made me do things my mind told me weren't good for me. I don't know how to stop. I can't stop."

"I'm a good boyfriend."

"You're not my boyfriend."

"I'm your fuck buddy."

"We're not buddies."

"I'm your booty call."

"You're my lover."

"Temporary lover."

"For now."

"For now."

"We will move on and have other lovers."

I paused. "Are you dumping me?"

"I'm not sure if I can dump you if we're not in a relationship."

"You're dumping me."

"I'm not dumping you. Only saying what is inevitable. This will end."

"Yeah. What doesn't have a name, a title, or a label will end."

"Each time I'm with you, it gets harder and harder."

I asked, "When will this end? Have you circled a date?"

"I don't want it to end. But I'm leaving. You've known that from the start."

"I'm not Ethiopian and I can't pass for white. You've put me in my place."

She sighed. "I shouldn't have told you that. You're taking it the wrong way."

"Only one way to take it, Jimi Lee."

"You're angry."

"Not angry. Enlightened. That nonsense is what I'd expect from white people in Mississippi. You're African. How can you put Europeans ahead of all other Africans? Where you are from probably makes Mississippi look like Rodeo Drive, and you're looking down your nose."

"Those are my parents' values. I don't see you that way. I adore you. You know I do."

I chuckled. "You said you'd rather marry a white guy to get a better parking space."

"You like sex with me?"

"I do, but it's more than sex."

"I like sex with you too. I have a good time with you. It's exciting. Let that be enough for us."

I nodded. "Sure."

"You can go back to your girls from Gambia, Malawi, Botswana, and Nigeria."

I said, "Maybe we should end this now."

"Wow. Okay."

"I'm just a place holder for some white guy who wants to conquer the Horn of Africa."

She tsked. "Someone's feelings got hurt."

"Yeah. Maybe we should stop seeing each other."

"That's not what I want, but if that's what you want, then I'll have no choice."

"You're leaving, so there is no choice."

"But it doesn't have to end now. It doesn't have to end like this."

"Maybe we should just rip the Band-Aid off and let this open wound start healing."

"You've fallen in love with me."

"No, I haven't. I'll never fall in love with an African from Bourgeoisie Town in Ethiopia."

"I didn't want you to fall in love."

"I don't love you."

"This was about fun and you had to go and fall in love."

It started suddenly. It had to end the same

way. Tears and a good-bye kiss.

I asked, "Have we exhausted all possibilities?"

"This has never been a romance."

"Then it ends like *The Lover*."

"It ends because it has to end."

CHAPTER 12

Jimi Lee called me and told me we needed to talk face-to-face.

I met her at Mimi's restaurant off the 60, a few exits shy of her moneyed and gated community.

I hadn't seen her in three weeks. That had felt like forever.

We stood in the crowded parking lot on a Sunday afternoon, under dark skies and clouds that promised rain, multicultural people lined up, waiting at least an hour to have brunch. Jimi Lee wiped her eyes, eyes that cried their own rain, and told me that she had missed her period. She had taken a pregnancy test. It was the only test she'd ever wished to God she had failed.

I asked, "It's mine?"

"Are you serious?"

"I have to ask. Momma's baby, Poppa's maybe. That old saying."

"Are you insane? Of course it's yours,

Kenneth Swift."

I had never seen a woman look so angry, terrified, and remorseful.

She looked like she wished we'd never met.

She said, "My parents don't know. No one knows."

"We're keeping it?"

"You want me to?"

"Of course."

"Why?"

"Certain things I don't believe in. But you have the final say."

"This is a lesson. A hard lesson. I have succumbed to the nature of the flesh. I did not stay focused. My analytical mind was offline. I was guided by the flesh. By drink. Smoke. Fornication. I have been taken over by a sickness. I was challenged and I failed. I lost to the enemy. This is the penalty for being disobedient, for being an arrogant daughter. Now part of you lives inside of me as punishment. I had a hard head and a soft ass. I can pray for forgiveness, but there are things you can't get forgiveness for. The payments will last most, if not all, of your life."

I bounced my leg, took deep breaths, and let the terrified girl rant.

She said, "I'm afraid to tell my father."

"Is he violent?"

"He is from another time. If you knew him, you would be afraid of him too."

"I'll be a man, will come to your home and be there when you tell your parents."

"This will devastate my mother. My siblings will lose respect. People will talk."

I contemplated what to do. "Let me be a man and face your parents."

"No. You don't know what type of father I have. My father is a hard man. He has come from a very hard life, and he has achieved, and this is not the life he wants for his family."

"He's strict. I get it. He's going to be pissed off. His daughter got knocked up by a random guy. Your mother is strict. They expect more of you. But we are where we are. We talk to them."

"They will throw me out on my face. I will be disowned and cut off financially. If I bring shame to my family, I might as well commit suicide. I might as well go kill myself."

"Move in with me."

She laughed like that offer was north of ridiculous. "Have you gone mad?"

"I'm serious."

"I'm not going to shack up with you."

"We're adults. If you're carrying my baby,

that means we're family. They might not like it, but the child in your belly links your family to mine. It's where separate family trees converge."

We stood still for a moment. Silence burned like hot iron poured on flesh. It disturbed me. When you loved a woman, she had too much power. When Jimi Lee was silent, either she was overthinking, depressed, mad as hell, falling apart, crying inside, or breath-by-breath dying inside.

At that moment, how she looked so aged, I knew she was doing all of those things.

She took a breath. "Happy birthday."

"Yeah. Happy birthday to you too."

Her tears fell, and they fell hard.

She shook her head and dabbed her eyes. "I can't do this."

"Because of your father?"

She stressed. "I can't, I can't, I can't, I can't, I can't, I can't."

"What do you want to do?"

She swallowed, could barely talk. "I have the three hundred dollars."

I asked, "What are we doing? I have the money."

"It will cost three hundred. I took it from my bank account already."

"I'm not letting you use your money."

"You have no choice. No arguments over

this. I am stressed enough."

"You picked a place?"

She nodded. "Just come with me."

I understood. It took me a second to nod. "I can pay for it."

"Would you hate me after?"

"I won't hate you."

"You hate me now."

"I do not. I'll pay for it. I'll make sure you're okay after."

"You've done this before?"

"No, but I know people who have. I'm sure you know people too."

"This is my fault. My carelessness. I just need you to drive me."

"When?"

"In the morning. First thing in the morning."

I realized she had already booked it. She'd wanted me to say I didn't want the child, to tell her to get an abortion, but I didn't. Her plan had failed. Now I knew she wanted freedom.

She said, "They won't let me have the procedure unless I check in with someone who will drive me away from the scene of the crime after."

She laughed; then she cried like she was dying. Cried the tears of a murderer yet to be.

She said, "I didn't want to ruin our birthdays."

We ate at Mimi's Café, ate in silence while she drank mimosas; then she followed me home.

It was odd, but she was tipsy and wanted to have sex, wanted to feel me inside her. Like she needed my cock to open her pussy and massage her, give salve to the pathway to our sin. Or maybe she had gone numb and needed to feel something, and I was the old, familiar drug she went back to. I took her from behind, and she stood on her tiptoes, moved up and down, her back to me, slightly bent, pushed against me, went hard, pumped like she was trying to make me fuck her into a sudden miscarriage. It was different. It was desperate. There was no lust. It was awkward sex. And at the same time, it was necessary. Bond-breaking sex. It was the prelude to good-bye sex, if not our good-bye sex itself. Maybe it was sex to calm me, so I wouldn't see the fast-approaching end of the road.

She moved up and down on her calves, worked me hard, massaged me while I massaged her.

Then we stood in the shower until the hot water turned cold, damp, panting, silent.

I asked, "You okay?"

She wiped her eyes with both her palms, got out of the shower.

She went to sleep, then woke up hungry again. Pregnancy had her starving day and night. I took her to Culver City to a restaurant that served authentic food from Oaxaca, Mexico. Tamales. Moles and margaritas. She drank like a woman who had no intention of keeping the second heart, the embryo growing in her womb.

I imagined a son. I imagined us fixing cars, camping, hiking, at Dodgers and Lakers games. I imagined us traveling, finally making it to Africa, Jimi Lee and at least two more siblings at our side.

She asked, "You okay?"

"Happy birthday."

"Happy birthday to you too."

Tomorrow, when she got the abortion, this affair, this summer fling, would be a wrap.

There would be no son. No other siblings. No more Jimi Lee.

She wouldn't want to see me after the crime was done.

Looking at me would only serve to remind her of the things she wanted to forget.

I wished I could do this for her, but this time the cause couldn't be the solution.

She'd opened her legs for me many times. Now she would open them for another reason.

She'd have to get on that table alone, feel the pain alone, and I'd just remind her of her shame. And there would be a fear. She would be afraid that she could get knocked up again. She would jettison me and deal with the psychological damage alone. It would be a secret between us, one lived, endured, but never discussed.

CHAPTER 13

Jimi Lee wore one of my UCLA sweatshirts, light blue, and loose gray kick-it sweat pants. She also wore a hijab. I had never seen her in a hijab. But she took it off, then put on a baseball cap and her glasses. Cold outside at five A.M. California cold. Los Angeles cold. I doubt if either of us slept through the night, but we got up acting like it was just another day. By five thirty, we sat at the dining room table sipping Ethiopian coffee, the early morning news on, talking about AIDS and Crips and Bloods and all the things that made LA yawn and struggle to pay attention.

Jimi Lee smiled. "Guess I'll be saving you a lot of money."

"Don't be cynical."

"A bill, a never-ending obligation. This insufferable moment is why men run."

"Weak men."

"That's just for the basics. What a baby

needs every day, things beyond Pampers and food, I can't even imagine. Being a responsible adult is a full-time job. If you have a baby, it's a 24/7/365 lifetime job."

She looked at the time. Tears fell. She wiped her eyes. Her difficult expression said she had sold her soul to the devil and for three hundred dollars she could buy part of it back. I went to her. She waved me away, didn't want to be hugged.

She stepped around me, grabbed her identification.

She reached into her purse and took out three hundred dollars, then handed it to me. Wanted it to look like I was paying when the time came. All about appearances.

I said, "I can pay."

"You don't want me to do this, so why should you pay? Add insult to injury."

"I work; you don't."

"Just because I don't have a job doesn't mean I don't have any money."

"I will pay."

She shook her head. As if paying was a way of punishing herself for our crime.

She adjusted her baseball cap. "I don't want to be late."

"Okay."

"Which is ironic, because being late is the goddamn problem."

■ ■ ■ ■

In two blinks, we were on the other side of town, in the heart of urban LA, the part of town the news never had anything good to say about. Signs were in two languages. WELCOME. BIENVENIDOS. First sign for foreigners, second for the indigenous people treated like foreigners.

This was the Mexican and Central American version of Lagos, their Addis Ababa.

We were the first ones there. No protestors outside in the dark off I-10 on Kingston Avenue at Marengo Street. Planned Parenthood–Bixby Health Center. Blue, one-level building, hardly noticeable, with a light blue metal door and intercom. Looked vacant. But cars were parked outside. As soon as we went to the door, someone spoke to us over an intercom, asked our names, and Jimi Lee said her birth name, her true Ethiopian name, and a buzzer sounded. We opened the heavy metal door. As soon as we did, car doors around us opened. People followed us. No one spoke. No one was here to make friends. Cold tile floor, some shade of gray, maroon chairs with gray arms. Bland decorations. Again the buzzer rang. They buzzed us from behind a desk. A heavyset Hispanic woman in dark blue scrubs rushed in, a plastic bag that held her lunch rustling at her side. She had a tense morning face, the kind that needed a carafe of coffee from Starbucks to flip a frown. She rushed through a yellowish door. Buzzer sounds. Black woman, brown skin, tall, black hair in a ponytail, hurried in, did the same as the Hispanic woman.

I said, "Workers are rolling in."

"I'm early. Very early. Two hours. I should have waited in the car longer."

"Why so early?"

"Wanted to see if someone didn't show up; then I could be seen sooner."

"Looks like it's gonna be a full house. You will be lucky if you're seen at your scheduled time."

"We will be here for hours."

"Here or home, we will be waiting and nervous."

"What do you have to be nervous about?"

"What's in you is mine as much as it is yours."

Jimi Lee filled out paperwork. Her gynecological history. Her family history.

Lila was her emergency contact.

She scribbled things about her I didn't know, all written fast in black and white.

She said, "I'll use your phone number and

address as my own."

I told her my address on Stocker, then nodded. "You okay?"

"I want this over with."

"Take a breath."

"I want to be on the other side of this."

Buzzer. Buzzer. Buzzer.

A thirteen-inch TV was anchored in a corner. There were billboards for EC — Emergency Contraception pills, another route to termination. Buzzer sounded. Girl in gray sweats came in a cappella.

The nervous girl said, "I have an appointment at seven."

Buzzer sounded. Hispanic girl in Old Navy sweats. Boyfriend with her wore a leather coat, gray skullcap. Buzzer. Two white girls. Buzzer. Buzzer. Buzzer. Everyone found their own part of the room. No eye contact. No conversation. No music. Silence. The kind that forces you to think.

I asked Jimi Lee, "Will talking help you calm down?"

"Sure. Let's talk about the Balfour Declaration, which proclaimed British support for the establishment in Palestine of a national refuge for Jews."

"Okay, I'll shut up."

"Thank you."

Buzzer. Buzzer. Buzzer. Buzzer.

Birkenstocks. Timberlands. Uggs. Converse.

"Lorena to the window. Lorena."

A brunette got up and rushed through the yellow door, which was decorated with happy colors and a dull and faded image of a Santa Claus mask on display in the summertime.

Jimi Lee said, "So that's where it will happen."

I squeezed her hand. It was 7:35. This was taking forever.

I asked, "What do I do?"

"I go back behind that yellow door."

"I don't go with you?"

"No. You wait."

"Okay."

"They will come for you when they are done, and you will pull the car up to a door outside. Then we leave here. We leave here."

"You're familiar with this."

"Told you. Went to school with rich girls who have been doing this since they were thirteen, if that old. They sit around and talk about it. Never imagined I would join that club. But here I am, no better than they are."

"Renita to the door. Renita."

Jimi Lee said, "If anything goes wrong . . ."

"It won't."

"If it does, if this goes wrong and I have to go to a hospital, call Gelila."

"Little Red Corvette knows what's up, then."

"She knows. I had to talk to someone about this."

"Does she know all of our business?"

"She knows my business. She would have come with me if you hadn't."

Buzzer. Jimi Lee almost jumped out of her skin.

Buzzer. Buzzer. It was like she was being shocked each time.

I looked around. Black Barbie in gray sweat pants, gray and red top, permed hair, brown with highlights, she got up and hurried through the door with the Santa Claus mask. Renita came back with her paperwork. She was frazzled. Jimi Lee glanced at the girl, then quickly turned away.

"Don't stare at people, Ken Swift."

I shifted. "Okay. Just surprised how many women come and do this alone."

"Girls."

"Yeah. Girls."

"Without the guy."

"They look so afraid."

"And embarrassed."

"And defensive."

"Or just sad."

"Hallmark doesn't make cards for days like today."

"I guess nobody would want to open an envelope and read that card."

"Not even if you put a ten-dollar bill and a grape lollipop inside."

"What rhymes with abortion?"

"Extortion."

"Proportion."

"Absorption."

"If only the egg didn't absorb the sperm."

"One sperm."

"One was one too many."

We laughed a soft, misplaced, nervous laugh. Then seriousness blanketed us again. Jimi Lee sighed. "To be honest, I'm surprised you came."

"I came. That's the reason we're here. I came and I came hard."

"So not funny."

More people arrived. I imagined their occupations. Equipment operator. Dishwasher. Lawn care worker. Clerical. Gutter installer. Assembler. Forklift operator. Landscaper. FedEx employee. Hairstylist. College student.

It was a room of people who had been drunk on sex and were now sober. Each face wished they could take back one night, that love hangover gone, but the headache was left behind. One of the parties involved could cut bait and run like Carl Lewis, but this couldn't be run from. The up and down was all fun and games until the egg was cracked. Beverly Hills, Bel Air, and Rodeo Drive, they had their own places to handle their problems. Special offices that had no protestors, and patients all had private waiting rooms. Yet a few of the Beverly Hills girls were here.

Jimi Lee said, "I'm better than this. I'm better than this."

"I know."

"I tried to have fun like Lila. Fake ID. Party on Sunset. Everything she does looks so easy, as if there will be no penalty for misbehaving. Grass looked greener where she stood. But now I realize it was only a field of weeds."

"She's your closest friend."

"I know. Still, she is narcissistic and sees beauty as a shortcut to success."

"She's smart too."

"Not Yale or Harvard smart. I tutored her most of her life. She is stuck on beauty."

"You're painfully beautiful too."

"She drives one hundred on the freeway and gets no tickets. If I do one mile over the speed limit, the highway patrol are on my bumper anxious to pull me over, ticket me, and send me to traffic school."

"Everybody can't be Lila."

"No, everybody can't be Lila."

A white girl in jeans and a black top got up and sniffled her way to the receptionist window. The window was thick, bulletproof, protected the employees. I took in all the security doors that were impossible to open without being buzzed, realized the room had just as much bulletproof glass as they had at Bank of America or at Yee's Chinese Food on Slauson and Angeles Vista Boulevard. Not for the safety of the customers. The bulletproof glass was in a spot that would do us no good. It protected the employees. Buzzer. Jimi Lee jumped. Buzzer. She jumped again. Buzzer. Again. Jimi Lee took it all in, brim of her cap down, hiding as much of her face as possible. Eleven people were waiting, including an Asian couple. A Hispanic couple with a little boy, barely walking, maybe a year old, was in the small room too. Jimi Lee glanced at them, saw the dichotomy. One got to live. One wouldn't have a say in the matter.

Wendy was called.

Jimi Lee's leg bounced without pause, like a drummer playing a hard-core rock number.

One by one, tense, jittery, unhappy, sad,

stressed, overthinking women vanished through the door with Santa Claus's face, the door where two heartbeats went in and one heartbeat came out. It was that mysterious place where pregnancy ended.

Jimi Lee held my hand tighter, almost broke my fingers.

It felt like if she let me go, she would fall through the floor, straight to hell.

The little Hispanic boy in the Champs top, black and red, practiced walking around the room, went from spot to spot, advertising life, saying, this is the miracle that happens if you let me live. I can become this, I can become more than this. He had no idea that his sibling wouldn't be able to do the same. He'd been lucky to be the first mistake. I cleared my throat. Jimi Lee handed me a tissue. I dabbed my eyes.

She said, "Didn't expect this to be that hard on you."

"What did you expect?"

"I thought you would be relieved."

Buzzer. Buzzer. Buzzer.

Jimi Lee rocked, fidgeted, mumbled to herself in Amharic.

I asked, "What's the problem?"

"Place feels like a mortuary."

"Well. It is."

"What do they do with the . . . after it is done?"

"Garbage."

"Just like that."

"Maybe use for research."

"Garbage."

Buzzer. Buzzer. Buzzer. Buzzer.

Sign on the wall assured all stressed-out customers that the emergency contraceptive pills could prevent pregnancy if taken within seventy-two hours of unprotected sex. Jimi Lee read that sign, sighed, shook her head, tsked like she wished she had known that shit.

Then it was 9:15.

Sixteen people were in what felt like a holding cell, most of the conversations in Spanish. Outside, still overcast. Weather to honor the dead and dying. Was supposed to rain tomorrow.

Some laughter was in the room. Felt like chuckles at a funeral.

A black girl in an Eddie Bauer sweatshirt sat, back slumped, face in hands, eyes down, frowning. She had a look like she'd never fuck the Bruce Banner–lookalike boyfriend at her side again in her life.

Jimi Lee had the same look. Waiting for two to again become one.

By ten in the morning, the room looked

like a *sala de espera* in the heart of Tijuana. There was so much Spanish chatter that the signs in English seemed out of place.

Blacks. Three flavors of whites. Asians. East Indian. And an African.

"Irma Flores to the window. Irma."

Hispanic. Mid-thirties. Wide hips. Dark blue sweat shirt, jeans, flip-flops on her feet.

Jimi Lee squeezed my hand, leaned in close to me.

She whispered, "I can't."

I nodded. "Then we won't."

"I have no money. I have some savings, but not a lot."

"I will make sure you are taken care of."

"I am carrying a baby."

"The baby will never want for anything. And neither will you."

"I have nothing. I own nothing. I have never had a job."

"We can do this."

The tears flowed. "I'll have to tell my parents. That. I am. Pregnant."

"I have to tell mine too."

"They will hate me. Say I trapped their son. And I ruined his days at UCLA."

"Your scholarship?"

"Scholarship aside, they will be angry. I've taken classes, have enough units already from attending summer school since I was in middle school, and I would enter with enough credits to be a sophomore. I did the dual-enrollment program, went to high school and college at the same time and earned my gap year. I earned it. Gave up summers. And for what? For what?"

"You're entering an Ivy League institution as a sophomore?"

"Yes. I've taken eight classes. Two each summer. Statistics. Sociology. Physiology. Geology. Calculus. Physics. Economics. Spanish. Twenty-four units. Easy, boring stuff."

"You never said that you were already a college student, more or less."

"Wasn't important, not so far as this thing between us, not until now."

"Wasn't my business because I'm not your boyfriend."

"You might have to get a temporary promotion. Boyfriend. For the day."

"Think about this. I mean, if you take the scholarship, can we work this out?"

"With you at UCLA and doing whatever you do to earn so much money?"

"I'll follow you east."

"I am sure I could still . . . but to be pregnant . . . African . . . and in college. I know that many universities haven't set up an environment and procedures to handle their pregnant students, because they don't want pregnant students. They don't want a campus of pregnant women walking around as if to say it's okay. They don't want that and I will bet that the health centers haven't prepared very well for it, and never will prepare for that. All they have at universities is condoms, some other birth control, and information on STDs. I've never seen a college pamphlet mention anything regarding pregnancy. I've never seen a movie with a pregnant college student. This will change everything. I can't do that and I can't do this. I can't do this."

"They don't want you pregnant in the dorms?"

"The shame."

"So, basically, you read that they abandon pregnant girls."

"Yeah. That's how I interpret the literature."

"Boys who knock those girls up?"

"No penalty. No shame. A boy can have ten girls pregnant, and he continues his life. But one pregnant girl. Some force pregnant women to live off campus after their second trimester."

"Why?"

"For liability reasons. You have to pay for your own housing and your own transportation. And on top of that, you're pregnant. You're carrying a full load in more ways than one, and you're alone, and the university pretty much wants nothing to do with you, from what I have read. Not all universities are like Georgetown. They have made town homes available. And most girls who enter pregnant don't finish their degrees. When the baby comes, it becomes impossible."

"So abortion becomes an option."

"Lots of rich girls have flushed one in the name of higher education and opportunity."

"Your trip to Ethiopia?"

"I can't think that far ahead right now. I need to get through today. Through this moment."

"Don't hyperventilate."

"But to go there, to show up in Addis Ababa pregnant, would bring insurmountable shame."

"When you face your parents, I will go with you."

"No, that can never happen."

"I told you. You didn't do this alone."

"No. In their eyes, I did do this alone. I was irresponsible."

"And me?"

"You were only being a man."

She squeezed my hand. The room was

filled with people disgusted by the conse-
quences of sex. People who had fucked like
rabbits and now regretted that orgasm.

I asked Jimi Lee, "Still with me? We're
leaving? Your legs are shaking."

"I can't stand up."

"You're a mess."

"We're staying." She dabbed her eyes.
"They can do this. Some have done this
more than once. I overheard the white girl.
Her third time. I can do this. I can be done
with this soon."

"Okay."

"Then I'll rest at your apartment a while.
Maybe Lila will come sit with me, if that is
okay."

"Pain meds and antibiotics."

"Then I'll drive home tonight."

"You'll be on meds. I can drive you home
again."

"You'll be stranded."

"I can get a room out that way tonight.
You can call me in the morning. If you need
to get to see a doctor, drive to me and I'll
get you there. If not, I'll MTA it back to
Leimert Park."

"Okay. Up to you."

She squeezed my hand, grinned at me like
I was a nice guy.

She whispered, "Thanks."

Children played, laughed, watched cartoons, as their mothers waited their turns to ensure that the embryos within, that the new heartbeats, that the children's siblings, those new souls, would never be a burden, would never open their eyes or live long enough to play.

Then, for the final time, Jimi Lee said, "I can't do this. I can't use a crime to hide a sin."

Just as we stood to leave, the door opened. Little Red Corvette rushed in, dressed in baggy cotton sweats and K-Swiss trainers. Lila had broken away from whatever obligation she had and come, literally at the last moment. Jimi Lee went to her and they hugged, both of them crying. I followed them outside wiping tears from my eyes.

CHAPTER 14

Jimi Lee went to break the news alone.

It caused complete chaos.

She said she was knocked up by a black American, and it created an earthquake felt from Diamond Bar to Addis Ababa. Jimi Lee told them the father was a boy she had met a few weeks ago. Her mother broke into tears and ran out of the room crying. Jimi Lee sat in a chair, sat where her father had screamed and told her to sit, and she sat shivering, hands on her knees, head down, crying as her father yelled out his disappointment. Her siblings were asked to leave the room. She had to face her father's wrath alone. Jimi Lee said she came from a hard family. Her cousin had dated a man who wasn't of their religion, and her uncle had beaten the girl half to death as punishment. He didn't approve of whom she dated and would have killed her if he hadn't been stopped.

She was pregnant.

Her father didn't touch her, didn't strike her, but she was so terrified, she almost pissed herself. Her father had beaten her all of her life. He had been beaten in school, had received cruel and inhumane punishment, and had passed that way of life, that slave-beating level of discipline, on to his children. Jimi Lee's father didn't want her to keep the baby. Right away, he wanted to drive her to Planned Parenthood in Mo Valley on Frederick Street, pay cash, and force Jimi Lee to send his bicultural bastard grandchild down the toilet. The shame. And the scholarships. They didn't want Jimi Lee to lose them. She was destined to become a doctor.

There was no place for a bastard baby in her future.

Her father told her that she would have the abortion.

And he had the final word.

Or she would be put out into the streets.

Jimi Lee refused to get an abortion.

Her father disowned her. Told her to get out, to leave and not take one thing he had paid for. He wanted her to leave with nothing but the clothes on her back. Said she was an adult, and adults took care of themselves. Her mother agreed but argued she should be allowed to take her clothing and her car. Jimi Lee's mother wanted her to lose the baby and dump me, the black American, and do both before she ruined her life more than she already had. Even her mother wanted her to send our child down the toilet. That would have been their way of pushing reset. If she did that and stopped seeing me, if she had an abortion and denounced me, they would take her back into the fold. If it was too late for the scholarships, they would help pay for college. Offered to buy her a new car. All she had to do was come back home. And not be pregnant with the child of a black American they knew nothing about. And it would be a secret kept in the family. But Jimi Lee chose me. She chose our child. She met me downtown against her parents' wishes. Early in the morning, we went to the diamond district and bought wedding bands. Then we waited to get married. Jimi Lee held flowers, looked at other ecstatic women doing the same.

I asked, "What are you thinking?"

"I wonder how many of these women are pregnant."

"This isn't a shotgun wedding, Jimi Lee."

"Not everyone looks happy. I see a lot of

false smiles."

"It's the biggest decision most of us will ever make."

"We're up next. I'm about to become your wife. Surreal. I've had my license to drive less than a year, and now I'm in line to get a marriage license, like this is my graduation ceremony."

"You will be my wife. For the rest of your life."

"Because I had the blues in my left thigh, and it became the funk in my right."

"Smile. They are trying to take our photo. Smile like you know why we're here."

"We're here because I couldn't stand the additional friction from a condom."

"Cheer up. Ease up on the self-deprecating humor. And smile."

"Hard to smile when you feel like your life has become a cautionary tale."

CHAPTER 15

As husband and wife, we sat at a table in Pho Palace, a restaurant in Chinatown. We were in a hole-in-the-wall filled with Mexicans, whites, and interracial couples, all getting Vietnamese food. A city of working-class Asians moved up and down the burning sidewalks and did business around us, this being their preferred zip code, their restaurants, their swap meets, the ornamental structures and images of dragons etched in the sidewalk showing they had staked a claim on this part of the land. We sat at a second-rate table, staring at each other, occasionally looking up at the dirty ceiling fan as it spun and circulated heat. We took in the noise from the kitchen, the sounds of pots and pans, the noise from five other conversations, but between us, silence. Uncomfortable silence had visited us more and more. Followed us everywhere we went.

She said, "I don't feel like I just got married."

"How do you feel?"

"Like I was just adopted. Or sent to a foster home."

"We are husband and wife."

"Feels like I was on the auction block and you purchased me for twenty-five bucks and a kiss."

"We're married."

"You say that like you own me."

"You're my forty acres and a mule."

"Romance is over. Let the business of marriage begin."

I smiled but stopped trying to make her feel like it was all to the good.

Love without conversation was impossible. Mortimer Adler said that. He was right.

I said, "You look like you're getting sick."

"Suddenly I smell everything in the world. This city reeks like an unwashed intergluteal cleft."

"What's that?"

"Butt crack."

"Why can't you just say butt crack and not use a twenty-dollar word?"

"Fine. This overcrowded city stinks like an unwashed butt crack. I'm inhaling stale booty and it's disgusting. Happy? Were all of my words on your level? Do they meet with your approval?"

I took a breath. "Well, pregnancy heightens the senses of smell and taste."

"Duh. I know that. I don't need a guy to explain to me how a woman's body works."

"I apologize."

"You do that all the time, you know?"

"This guy will refrain from explaining anything outside of galactic astronomy from here on out."

"And my nose stays stuffed up now. Never been this miserable in my life."

She reached for the napkins on the table and accidentally knocked over a glass of water.

"To top it off, I'm suddenly very clumsy. An alien has taken over my body."

Mature waitresses ran to clean up the mess. Jimi Lee went to the bathroom to blow her nose. I checked out one of the interracial couples. A tall black woman, as dark as midnight, and the man she was with was as pale as twelve noon. They had a baby with them. Beige skin, curly red hair. Two tables over were a brown-skinned black man and a white woman who had her hair in braids. They sat on the same side of the table, holding hands, laughing. When Jimi Lee came back and sat across from me, I reached for her hand. I was the black man many generations removed from an un-known part of West Africa reaching for an East African woman's hand. My wife of one hour and a few minutes shifted and pre-tended she was still reading the menu. We'd ordered three minutes ago. Jimi Lee hadn't mumbled ten words since she'd paused before saying, "I do." She had paused. Paused. Then looked around the court at the others waiting to get married, had looked at people who didn't practice any particular religion, had stared at couples who were blending religious backgrounds, at the interracial couples, at the intercultural couples, and had chewed her bottom lip and rocked long enough to make the justice of the peace uncomfortable. For twenty-five dollars, we now had a legally registered mar-riage, one that provided medical and tax rights, legal protection, and other financial benefits that you don't get from shacking up. Divorce is never so cheap. Never.

She put the menu down, then looked at her wedding ring. It had cost fifty Benja-mins.

Taking it all in, taking a deep breath and exhaling, I asked, "You okay?"

She tendered an unsmiling glare. "What have I done?"

"We did it together."

"I'm married."

"We're married."

I reached for her left hand, but she gave me her fingers. "What's wrong?"

"My hands tingle, Ken. My feet feel like boats and my hands are uncomfortable."

I said, "Well, your skin looks healthy. You have a glow. You're beautiful."

"What have I done to my life? I should be on the way to Ethiopia for six months."

After she pulled her fingers away, I told her, "One day at a time, and we can do this."

"I was to end my gap year in Addis Ababa, then return and go directly to university."

"We have to be a team. We have to look forward. We have to plan this out."

"This is going too fast. I'm going to have a baby. I'm married. None of this was supposed to happen for another ten years, if it happened for me at all. I'm married and I am having a baby."

I reached for her hand again. "We're going to have a baby."

She gave me the tips of her fingers again. "Why aren't you scared?"

"I am terrified. But I can't let fear own me. You do. What are you afraid of?"

"You'll abandon me. I'll be a single mother with a high school diploma. I'll look like a fool."

"I'll be there every step of the way, Lamaze classes to birth and beyond."

"Did you want me pregnant?"

"What do you mean?"

"Did you do this on purpose?"

"You were the one who jumped on me and rode me bareback."

"You know how I get into it. And you didn't tell me you were about to come."

She bounced her legs, drummed her fingers, the blame resting at my feet.

I said, "Guess we won't need condoms for a while."

"Wrong. A woman can get pregnant while she is pregnant."

"That's some bull."

"It's called superfetation. Rare, but it happens. With my luck, it will happen to me."

"Those ten-dollar words."

"That is my normal vocabulary. I simplify things when I talk with you or other Americans."

"Other Americans? Other black Americans?"

"With anyone who is comfortable with not knowing anything other than the lyrics to a Tupac song."

We both sighed.

"Who are you, Ken Swift?"

"I'm your husband. Been that guy for the

last hour and a half."

"This is surreal."

"Your parents said harsh things to you."

"To them I am not an adult. Not even now that I am married will I be an adult to them."

"By law, you are an adult."

"In my home, I was not treated like an adult."

"You're old enough to join the military. Or do jury duty. If they call you for jury duty, you can't tell the court your parents said you can't go do your civic duty."

"To them, I am still a child. An irresponsible, uneducated, careless child, it seems."

"In America, a black child is seen as an adult from the age of five."

"Good thing I'm not a black American."

"Your brown skin is darker or just as dark as any black person in Watts, Harlem, or Oakland. You think you're not black like me, but the government won't treat you any differently."

"They will treat me like you, until they detect an accent; then I am treated worse."

"I want to ask you something. Something that bothers me."

"Okay. Ask."

"You never want me around other Ethiopians, not when you're around. We were at

217

Magic's Starbucks in Ladera two days ago, and that Starbucks is Ethiopia Central. I went to the bathroom and came back and you were off to the side talking to three guys. Ethiopians. I was there with you and you didn't introduce me to the East African men you were chatting with. You were uncomfortable. You chatted in Amharic and your body language was so distant."

"Didn't I introduce you?"

"You know you didn't. That's why I walked away; went to have a seat. It was fucked."

"What's the issue?"

"When you get around Ethiopians, or if we pass a group of Ethiopians, you move away from me. I feel like a white man and like you're afraid to take me to the black community. But if we are around my people, or the Hispanic crowd, you are all over me, like I'm your man. You hold my hand when no Ethiopians are around."

"They say things, usually in Amharic, and with a smile. Some of them will say things."

"Like what? What do they smile and say in your language?"

"Men from Awassa confronted me."

"What did they say to upset you?"

"Like, oh, 'One of your own is no longer good for you? Are you American now? Have you packed your bags and moved away from your culture? Men like your father are not good enough?' So if I move away from you, it is out of fear, because I loathe conflict; it is because I do not want to have to explain myself to people I do not know."

"It's because of shame."

"They say things. They say things that disturb me. They say things that upset me."

"Now that you are pregnant, they will joke that your ovaries were colonized."

"I'm serious. This is a serious issue for me. Basically, they say I have sold out."

"Why don't you point these people out?"

"You think I can't handle it?"

"Can you? I don't see them stepping to me with that bullshit."

"It's nothing personal against you. They just love Ethiopia and want to protect me."

"Well, I love you and I want to protect you. You're my Ethiopia. You're my wife."

She bounced her leg, tapped the table with her nails.

She moaned, "I never should have wanted a gap year."

"Stop beating yourself up."

"I never should have argued with my father and then compromised to spend at least half of that gap year in Ethiopia. But I wanted at least six months of freedom. Six months of fun. I wanted to be like Lila. I should have backpacked across Europe with friends, and from there gone to Ethiopia, and then I could have gone straight to uni."

"You hate that you met me. Don't you?"

"Don't ask me that."

"You regret meeting me, don't you?"

"What did I just say?"

"You're looking at me like you hate me the way America hated the Soviets. Am I disgusting to you now?"

"Relationships aren't singular. Delusional or real, I contributed to this."

"But it feels like you're pinning the whole thing on me. Am I delusional or real?"

"*Don't ask me that.* Not now. Not when I'm feeling this way. Not when I'm pregnant. I don't want to say things because I know my emotions will be speaking and my mind has nothing but unkind thoughts and I know once a rock is thrown, it cannot be *unthrown.* So please, let me sit and keep my words and thoughts to myself."

"Shutting down is not effective communication."

"But it is safe communication. You can't fault me for things I don't say."

I paused. "Are you ashamed?"

She snapped. "Yes. I am insane. My breasts are sore. I have morning sickness. I have to depend on you for my every meal. My life depends on you. I hate that. And I am going insane."

"I said ashamed, not insane."

"You have eyes. Look at my face and you tell me how you think I feel."

"Well, I'm sorry."

She dabbed tears from her eyes. "You should be ashamed too. Have you no shame?"

"What's done is done. We have to move forward. Crying over it will solve nothing."

"You were unmarried and got a girl pregnant. Your parents? Were they disappointed?"

"I'm a grown-ass man paying my own bills."

"Why didn't your family come to the courthouse?"

"I told them. They knew. I guess they were busy."

"So much for family and community."

"Don't do that shit. Not now."

She looked into my eyes. "What do you do? Where does the money come from?"

"Let me worry about that."

"You're my husband. Now I have the right to ask. What do you do?"

"I do collections. I do maintenance work."

"Like in the movies when people get hurt

and beat up and stuff?"

"Yeah."

"You are paid to beat up people like in the movies?"

"Like in the movies. It's a professional service."

"It's a criminal service."

"So was J. Edgar Hoover and the FBI. So was William H. Parker. And so is Daryl Gates. If you define crimes by what white men do and not the laws they make, I do nothing wrong."

"You're smart. Articulate. Intelligent. You go to UCLA. How did you get into such a thing?"

"Family business. Was kind of handed down from generation to generation."

"Family, as in the *Godfather* family, or Kentucky Fried Chicken family?"

"My grandfather fought in Vietnam. When he came back, after he had put his life on the line for the country, he was spat on, called a baby killer, couldn't wear his uniform, couldn't put Vietnam on his résumé, and as a black man, he couldn't find a job. When people get hungry enough, it becomes about fixing the missed-meal cramps."

"What did he do?"

"He started to do what he had to do to

pay the bills."

"That's no excuse."

"He hooked up with some other white boys who had been in Vietnam, joined their clique, and strong-armed people, became a collector. My father did the same."

"What is your father like?"

"My father is a bit of a gangster."

"A gangbanger?"

"Like James Cagney, suit and tie. He was a black man with an office in Beverly Hills for a while. My grandfather wanted to be more like the Joe Kennedy clan, people who did illegal shit and made a lot of poor people money, only he's never made a lot of money."

"And your father and grandfather now have you doing the same."

"I don't work for them."

"But you do the same thing."

"No different than the Kennedys and Rockefellers did in their day."

"Both you and Jake Ellis. I can understand Jake Ellis doing that. He has Nigerian blood and Nigerians are criminals. They run cons. They hustle. You can't trust them. But not you."

"That's harsh. I mean, fuck. What if Nigerians were spitting out Ethiopian insults?"

223

"Nigerians always insult us. They do starving Ethiopian jokes day and night. How many Ethiopians can you fit into a phone booth? All of 'em. How do you tell if an Ethiopian woman is pregnant? Hold her up to the light. How do you start a riot in Ethiopia? Roll a biscuit down the street. What's the best part about marrying an Ethiopian woman? She'll swallow every time. What's the worst part about marrying an Ethiopian woman? She's a nigger."

"Okay, okay. Maybe they see it as a farce. An unfunny farce."

"Being called a nigger is as much a farce as a woman being called a bitch."

"And as long as there are black people or women, neither will ever end."

"I am called a nigger because of my skin and called a bitch when I stand up for myself, then called a cunt before they walk away and the next arrives. Lather, rinse, and repeat."

"I'm sure more than a few Mark Fuhrmans are in Diamond Bar and Phillips Ranch."

"American blacks call me the same names racists use to rile me. Everyone jokes about my country's plight and it hurts. My country is your punch line. It's an insult. It's demeaning. It's meant to degrade a culture."

"Okay, okay, okay. But I've never heard Jake Ellis do one insult. Not one. Have you?"

"Stay on point. There is a bigger issue. What happens to us if you end up incarcerated?"

"Look, for me this side gig is short-term. Only been in this three years."

"Three years is not short-term. Three years is a career. Your side gig is your main gig."

"It was part of the four-year plan, so for me, it's short-term. There is no scholarship for me."

"How did you do in school?"

"My GPA was just below a 3.0 and we're not going to talk about my SAT score."

"But you were admitted to UCLA."

I nodded. "I'm an average guy trying hard to be above average. I read about the world; I study everything; I know a lot, but I'm not close to being a Mensa. I am . . . was . . . paying for my own college. I don't . . . didn't want to get out of UCLA and have a huge student loan left to pay. It's easy money; at least it is for me."

"That's why you have so much cash in a shoe box in the back of your closet."

"Yeah. I claim some of it, tell the IRS I'm a bodyguard."

"Why do all that?"

"That way I can have credit, and a black man needs to have credit."

"Why the fancy car?"

"I bought the Benz, not because I wanted to floss, but to have a big-ticket item on my credit report. The only thing worse than a man with bad credit is a man with no credit. That's why I use credit cards and just pay the minimum. If I pay the bill off each month, it will be like I have never had credit at all. So, I'm just playing the game."

"And you own a gun. I saw it."

"It's legal. Registered in my name."

"Have you ever used it?"

"No bodies are on it. Nothing to worry about."

"Why do you have a gun?"

"Have it to protect myself."

"From?"

"People like me."

"Be serious. You have a questionable, complex occupation. You're a criminal."

"No more criminal than any bank that gives a black family a bad loan."

"Banks don't go to jail. Banks don't get shot by LAPD."

That silenced me.

Her expression said that this was too much. "Are you going back to UCLA next semester?"

"I have to take care of you and get ready for a baby. Not going back next semester."

"What about your undergraduate degree? What about your fantasy of touring Africa?"

"You're pregnant."

"But you're not."

"A baby isn't cheap. Neither is a wife. I'll need to make a lot more money."

She twisted her lips, lowered her voice. "I've become a burden."

"I've changed your life."

"I have become the opposite of independent."

"We're a team."

"I am not ready to take on the role of motherhood."

"I'm scared too."

"I'm supposed to have a career before I have a family, and now I have destroyed the rest of my life."

"Don't say that."

She sighed. "I live with you now. I live in Los Angeles, in an old apartment building."

"Historic apartment building."

"I've never had a job. And now I'll have to stay home and raise a child."

I took a breath. "We have to buy things. A lot of things. We need a list."

"Stroller. A crib. Changing table. Diaper

pail. Car seat. It's going to cost a lot."

"I'll take care of it all."

"Your toys will have to go to storage. Or be sold."

"I know. The second bedroom will have to get sorted."

"And I need Ethiopian Yirgacheffe coffee."

"Your wish is my command."

"I want Sidamo, Jimma, Limu, and Ghimbi coffees too."

"I will buy enough Ethiopian coffee to fill an Olympic pool."

"I'll need maternity clothing."

"Okay, my queen."

"And you have to get rid of all the weights."

"Anything else?"

"Since I live with you, we need some changes. The place is too masculine. I want to lose some of the ugly colors, and the furniture with hard edges. I want to change things so I can feel more comfortable."

"I have two new charge cards you can use to get whatever you need."

She looked at me, shook her head. "You're excited about this. Unbelievable."

"I have a smart, beautiful wife."

"I'm not smart. If I were smart, we would not be here."

"I'm happy about you."

"I know you are."

"I just need you to be happy too."

"This is a lot for me. I just need time. This is an adjustment."

"I would love for you to be happy about me, but we can start with you being happy about you."

"And when the baby comes, I ask one thing."

"What?"

"There will be no spanking."

"Are you serious?"

"Beating a child does no one any good. It does not address any real issues."

Jimi Lee had said that children who weren't spanked had higher IQs, and spanking children confused them about love and punishment and turned them into lawbreakers. At the same time, I knew Jimi Lee's dad had had a heavy hand. He didn't spare the rod. So I agreed. Our child would never be spanked.

Jimi Lee hummed. "You've surprised me."

"In what way?"

"You didn't run. I have given you every opportunity to go in the other direction."

"Is that what you wanted?"

"I thought you would vanish when I said I was pregnant. You did the opposite."

"Well, Soul Stealer turned out to be an egg breaker and a baby maker."

"Not funny."

"It is funny. You want to laugh."

She smiled a difficult smile. I smiled an unsure one, again glancing at the interracial couples. Heard bits of their flirty conversations, as they laughed and touched.

I said, "Let's drive up to Santa Barbara for a couple of days."

"For what?"

"We can have a honeymoon."

Her lips turned down; she looked out toward the streets, toward a flock of tourists.

I asked, "What's that expression?"

"Overwhelmed."

"Talk to me."

"My life has changed. I hate myself. I have become one of those girls."

"One of what girls?"

"The ones I've always chastised. The ones who I saw as unfocused, undisciplined, and turned my nose up at. I've become a hoochie momma wearing Gap clothing."

"You're married. Anything after this is honorable."

"I married after I was pregnant. Because I am pregnant. I was forced to marry."

"Be optimistic. What you give the universe

is what the universe will give you."

"You're not pregnant. You can still walk away at any moment."

"We're married."

"So what? Husbands go out for cigarettes and don't come back all the time."

"Be positive."

"Trying. But this tunnel is long and there is nothing but darkness before my eyes."

A moment of silence passed; then I said, "You will have to plan a baby shower."

"No, I won't be having one."

"Won't Lila throw you one?"

"What we have done does not deserve a celebration."

I pulled my lips in. "I'm here for you, no matter what."

"Are you?"

"I'll never let you down. I'll get you back to your dreams. You'll get your degree. You will get your master's, and you will get your PhD. My mission is to make that right. Our child will have everything he or she needs."

Jimi Lee put her hand on her belly, rocked. "We're having a girl."

"How do you know? You have to get an ultrasound."

"I'm certain it's a girl. I saw her in a dream."

"You and those dreams."

"I have picked her name. I prayed and her name also came to me in a dream."

"Well, I want to name her Margaux."

"Tsigereda will be her first name."

"Can we be patriarchal for a moment? Can you give the Simone de Beauvoir act a rest?"

"No, I cannot. Don't silence me. If you like, then her second name can be Margaux."

"If you're wrong and it's a boy?"

"You can name him. And raise him. I don't do boys."

"Oh, yes you do."

She put the tips of her fingers in her water, flicked it in my face.

We laughed. It felt good. Laughter felt like hope.

"I know we just met, but I love you, Adanech Abeylegesse Zenebework-Swift."

"I want to keep my maiden name."

"No."

"At least for a while."

"No."

"Until I adjust to this change."

"I want you to take my name."

"No."

"We're black people. People don't look at us the way they do white people. You're not a liberated white woman. You're African and

232

I'm African American. They see us as **niggers**. I don't want us in the hospital having a baby and we have different names and getting those negative looks."

"No."

"You have our baby in your belly and we're a family now. If we walk around with different last names, we look like a black stereotype. People should see our names and know we're married, not shacking up."

"Then take my name. Take my Ethiopian name and that will fix your issues."

"I'm sure that would make your daddy happy if I took your family name."

"Quite the opposite."

"I was being facetious."

"Now who is using ten-dollar words?"

"That's a five-dollar word."

I gazed at Jimi Lee and she turned her head, gave me her profile.

I said, "I'll change my name to Kayode Euruchalu."

She laughed. "But that would be West African."

"No one will call it a slave name."

"You would be Nigerian."

"So what?"

"I would not marry a Nigerian."

"Fine. Pick an Ethiopian name for me and I will change my name today."

Not amused, she said, "Our chicken and seafood pho is here. Let's eat and leave."

I said, "Honeymoon or not?"

She replied, "I'm not in the mood."

"Things have changed."

"I don't feel sexy. Or like having sex. Feet swollen. Breasts tender. Skin breaking out. So, no."

Again I looked at the happy interracial couples, touching, laughing, loving. Then a black woman and her Asian husband came in. He had no issue being with her in front of other Asians. I smiled at them, smiled with envy.

I said, "Jimi Lee?"

"What?"

"Get that stick out of your ass."

"Excuse me?"

"We're going to Santa Barbara for three days."

"Did you not hear me say I'm not in the mood?"

"We're having a honeymoon."

"I'd imagined that if I married, my honeymoon would be more, that my husband and I would travel through Europe. We'd wake up with a view of the Eiffel Tower, dress and go downstairs, walk Paris in search of coffee and a croissant, then hold hands as we walked along the Champs-Élysées. We'd be there a week, maybe two, then leave, move on to the Amalfi Coast, and we'd hire a boat and sail to the waterfalls of Marmorata and the Emerald Grotto."

"We're doing Santa Barbara. I booked us at the Four Seasons."

"Okay. You sound so 'me Tarzan, you Jane' all of a sudden."

"And we're going to go Rollerblading on the beach; we're going to go shop for maternity clothing, and we're going to have dinner and fuck like rabbits. We will copulate like bonobos. Fornicate like the brown Antechinus. We will knock boots and when the cops come knocking, we will not stop coming. We're going to humpty hump like all those horny bastards. And no matter where I put it, I'm not wearing a condom."

She grinned. Then she broke down and laughed. "Okay. You are one lecherous man."

"Guilty. I'm horny for my beautiful, sexy, pregnant wife. Sue me. I want to get my freak on with the woman I married. That's not a crime in any man's Bible or illegal in any state or country in the universe."

"Are you that attracted to me? Even now, since you know I'm pregnant? I feel so disgusting. And you want to have sex with me. My hair is dry. I need to shave my legs.

You are attracted to me like this?"

"Mind, body, and soul. But right now I want some of that pregnant booty."

"Gross. The idea of having sex with a pregnant woman turns you on?"

"Will that be like a three-way? Will I be poking Margaux in the top of her head?"

She laughed. "Tsigereda."

"Margaux."

Jimi Lee put her fingers in her water, flicked them at me. "That is just . . . gross."

"You're turning me down on my wedding day? You don't want none of this?"

"I always want you. Was horny for you at first sight."

"What's the problem, then?"

"I have to process a lot. My life has changed. But that desire has not changed. That desire scares me now. My vagina is horny for you even when I'm angry. Already I'm starting to feel very randy all the time."

"Then act like it. Stop poking out your lip and let's go to Santa Barbara and get down and do the nasty, freaky, funky, stinky, junky, and bump uglies in the nighttime down on the beach."

"Now I stay awakened. My breasts feel alive. My body feels like it belongs to someone else and I am inside of this woman, just visiting. Pregnancy will exacerbate the arousal issue."

"They have this new stuff called Viagra. I can score some if I can't keep up."

"If I let loose and become feral, if I give in to my urges, you won't be able to handle this."

"I'll handle it like a package at FedEx. Absolutely, positively overnight."

"Oh God. Your ego."

"And I'm still not wearing a condom."

"That baby-making, soul-stealing come hydrant barely fits inside a condom anyway."

"Come hydrant?"

"It's like watching a fire hydrant. With come. You come like you're trying to put out a fire."

"Soul Stealer fits inside you, oh so well. You know you want some Soul Stealer."

"Maybe."

"I want some pregnant pussy."

She laughed, put her hand on her belly. "I'm married and I'm going to have a baby."

"We're having a baby."

"Yeah. We."

I said, "A real African American baby."

She corrected me, "*African* African American."

I corrected her, "*African American* African."

"Whatever."

We were afraid, unsure, unhappy, but we laughed.

She said, "You love me."

"Yes."

"You really love me."

"Yes."

"I will learn to love you."

"I can't ask for more than that."

I leaned in, kissed her. She kissed me back.

CHAPTER 16

Being married excited me. Making love to a pregnant woman aroused me. Sex with my pregnant wife turned me on. After a round of *soixante-neuf,* a session that had both of us over-aroused, I took her ankles in my hands, eased inside her. She pulled at her hair and made breathy sounds, totally lost in rapture. In the softest voice, she said things in Amharic, her tone hot and provocative. I couldn't take it. Felt too good. I stopped moving. She sped up, moved her ass and made me hold on. She worked me from the bottom and when she couldn't get it the way she wanted, she made me turn over. She got on top and she was wicked. She worked me. Impressed me. She was passionate, not wild, but intense and focused. Lots of kissing, licking palms, sucking fingers, lots of nibbling, lots of massaging. Jimi Lee was loud. She set free a telling moan, one that sounded like she was at the precipice, one that told me orgasm had its hooks in her. I was almost in the same place. I put my hand around her neck, held her like that. Her mouth opened wide, her face elongated, and her breathing stopped for a few seconds. She was silent. Then she exploded, started moving her ass at a hundred miles an hour, bounced on me, sounded like it hurt so good, and her breathing was hard, her chest rising and falling, her breasts dancing, erect nipples giving me the thumbs-up. My East African wife stopped again and strained, held on to me. The shakes started; then the shakes moved up and down her spine. Her toes curled. Her nails dug into my skin. I gave up my own pain as she came again. She was overpowered, same as she had been the first time, and her orgasm amazed me. Then she moved her ass, worked me and looked at me, determined to make me finish, resolute to make me come again. She achieved her goal.

That was our first time as husband and wife.

She rested on her back and I had my head in her lap, my hand on her belly.

I whispered, "Daddy wants to tell you about Mississippi and Oklahoma."

"Stop it."

"Fine. Then I will tell you about the important African empires that came after Egypt. Let me get comfortable and tell you about the Empire of Ghana. The Hausa States. The Kongo Kingdom. Songhay. Empire of Mali."

"Ken?"

"Yeah, babe?"

"Stop talking to my belly."

"Okay."

"Rub my feet."

I rubbed her feet awhile, rubbed them and massaged her legs until my wife pulled me back to her and we kissed a good-night kiss. Then she put her back to me and we cuddled skin to skin. In the darkness, I felt her smiling.

Jimi Lee had no friends except Lila, and it felt like she was shutting her best friend out of her life. Jimi Lee was with me, but I hadn't seen her loneliness. Someone could be with someone else, feed them, make love to them, engage them in conversations about sub-Saharan African empires, talk about Egypt, Carthage, about the Songhay Empire, about the Kingdom of Aksum, keep them intellectually stimulated, take them to the beach, or take them to Santa Monica and ride all the rides on the pier, and they would smile, chat, laugh, and still be bored. Maybe she was lonely the night she met me and had sought out what she felt now was the wrong kind of friendship. If she were in bed sixteen hours a day, wrapped in covers like it was a cocoon, like she was back in her mother's womb protected from all negativity, I wrote that off to her pregnancy. I would get in bed with her, put my arm around her. Sometimes fear was silent. Same for her constantly eating. She was sad most days and I had failed to see her depression. Had been so busy smiling and trying to make us happy that I had ignored what this life change had done to her. She was supposed to go to Harvard. I hadn't seen that she felt as if she had lost everything and gained nothing by being with me. If I had a chance at Harvard, then had gotten a DUI or some shit, or if some cop with LAPD had stopped me, then made up some charges and caused me to lose it all, then had my scholarship revoked and had to settle for a community college lifestyle, if I were forced to go to a place that I knew I'd already exceeded, yeah, I'd be in a serious funk, have an attitude, be angry at the world, look down on everyone.

I would guess that to her, my life was a rung below being in community college.

Sometimes she looked at me like I was that cop who had caused her to lose it all.

And no matter how she felt, bills had to be paid, money had to be saved, and I had to hustle.

I had to go hurt people to keep our lights on.

CHAPTER 17

Atlanta, Georgia

I rang the doorbell at least thirty times. Rap music thumped in the mansion, an erratic pulse.

Finally, a soft silhouette crept down the curved staircase, book in hand, puffing on a joint as she came to the main door at a snail's pace. She put her face to the door, saw me standing under the lights from the motion sensor, scratched her butt, danced to music that should outrage halfway intelligent women.

She asked, "Dafuq you?"

I adjusted my round-lensed, John Lennon–style glasses. "Postman."

"Postman this time of night?"

"Got a package."

She opened the left side of the French doors. Made of thick wood and thicker glass. Solid. Locks that went from the top to an inch down into the concrete. Had to cost at least twenty thousand. She wore a sheer baby doll number and a G-string, all of it purple. I saw what she was made of, but she was so high she couldn't care less. She was a shorty with a bushy red Afro. Slim, but her full face said she'd get fatter later on in life. But for now, she had a nice body. Had an ass that looked like she tortured her buns with two thousand squats every four hours.

"The mailman ringing the damn doorbell like he lost his mind at three in the god-damn morning."

"Ran behind on my route."

She looked at my designer jeans, jacket with patches on the elbows over a shirt that sported cuff links. Again, she looked at my glasses, stared at the circular, silver-frame John Lennon glasses the longest. She stared at them as if she were trying to see my eyes, but she only managed to see the reflection of her own.

"The mailman dress like that in the Cascades?"

"Uniform dirty."

She nodded as if, while in her purple haze, that made sense to her.

I showed her a box. "It's certified and I need a signature from Jason Starr."

"Who?"

"Jason Starr the Third."

Another girl click-clacked down the wooden stairs, took the stairs slow and easy — heard her before I saw her — and then she appeared behind the black girl. Number two was a gum-chewing white girl, urban attitude. Colorful tats ran from her neck to her ankles. Pink Mohawk. Sweet little ass and breasts about the size of a newborn's. She rocked a sheer lace chemise, padded cups, adjustable straps. Yellow G-string, six-inch red heels.

White girl said, "Black Keisha, that's Fourth Street Steve's real name."

"Get out. You mean Fourth Street Steve, his name Jason Starr the Third? There are three of them?"

The white girl said, "I'll sign."

I interrupted them. "Only Jason Starr can sign for this package."

The black girl looked at me. "Shit. Fuck. You ain't with the IRS, are you?"

"Post office."

"The place the IRS uses."

"But not the IRS."

"Cause his paranoid ass told me not to let the IRS in if they came to the door."

"Post office. Not IRS."

"Well, is that a certified bill from the IRS?"

I looked at the box. "Not from the IRS."

The white girl took a deep breath. "Follow me. I'll take you to 'im. He in his special room chillin' and smokin'."

The black girl said, "I'm going back to bed, White Keisha."

"Nobody gives a fuck, Black Keisha."

"Don't make me snatch that wig off your head."

"Be the last thing you snatch."

Black Keisha danced to the rap music, made her booty shake as she headed up the extravagant staircase. She looked back and saw my eyes following her retreat.

She slapped her ass and moved on. "Get your last look, then move the hell on."

"Yes, ma'am."

"Pervert."

"Nice bottom."

"Baby, I am nice top to bottom, and especially in between."

"I heard that."

"Flirty mailman."

"Postman."

"Whatever. You better not be from the IRS."

Black Keisha disappeared and I followed the white girl's rotund bouncing bottom.

I said, "This is some place. I bet it costs a lot to maintain."

White Keisha nodded.

"Who else is here?"

"Place is usually packed with freeloaders, but nobody here but Black Keisha and Fourth Street Steve. He got mad and kicked everybody out. Begging relatives, bloodsucking friends, smiling haters, and three baby mommas were here eating up the food and smoking all of his weed. Baby mommas always come without the babies."

"Sounds like he has temper tantrums."

"You're looking at my booty?"

"No."

"And why not?"

"You're built like a black woman, if that's okay to say."

"And Black Keisha is built like a white woman. She hates that."

"She's slimmer but has Africa all over her body."

She laughed. "I walk into a room of black men, wake the haters, and shut it down."

"A black woman can walk into a room of white men and do the same."

"Yeah, but nobody in America won't look for her if she goes missing."

"You have a black woman's body and have the advantages of being white."

"Free, white, and twenty-one."

"Won't argue with that."

She slapped her backside. "Winning."

"Yeah, to be honest, and no offense meant, but I don't see the point of a man wanting a white woman who looks like a black woman, when there are already black women. I prefer the original, not the imitation. A Pinto isn't an Aston Martin and a Celica isn't a Bentley. Black women are Astons and Bentleys."

"I'm still the white girl black men leave black women for."

"Well, congratulations on picking up the traitors and the trash."

"Traitors? You're watching my ass like you want to change teams."

"Stop making it jiggle."

She slapped her booty again.

She led me past fireplaces and two dining rooms into a sunken den. No library. Not one book from what I could see, unless he kept his literature in the refrigerator. House was devoid of knowledge, draped in materialism. Wooden floors throughout the house. Four-inch recessed lights. Contemporary furniture framed by tacky art. In the den, the room was lit up by seven televisions, all tuned to what seemed like random shit.

Rap music played like it was the gospel that ruled this household.

Jason Starr the Third was on a bright red leather sofa, bare feet on an ottoman. Six bottles of Smirnoff were on the table. No glasses. No one else was in the room. He was a big man dressed in gray sweats and a black hoodie. He rocked the type of unique designer sweats sold in downtown LA boutiques for about two grand.

"White Keisha, who dis nigga walkin' up in my personal space like he know me?"

"He say he got a package for Jason Starr, but Jason Starr have to sign to get it."

He exploded, "Don't ever say my government name out loud."

"Sorry."

"Too late now. It from the IRS?"

"Naw. At least I don't think it is."

"Did you fuckin' check?"

"Naw. He said it's for Jason Starr and only for Jason Starr."

"White Keisha, don't say my government name."

"He said it first."

"What good are you? Bet you were a test-tube baby."

"Mad at me like I named you a name that sounds gay as fuck."

"What was that?"

"Your momma shoulda swallowed or left that nut on her forehead."

"What you say about my momma?"

"I'm going upstairs and kick it with Black

250

Keisha."

"Does it look like I give a fuck where you go?"

She walked away. "Right in the middle of her fuckin' forehead. Splat. Done."

He looked me up and down. "Who the fuck you, nigga?"

"Post office."

"Nigga, I know my fuckin' postman, and she a cross-eyed yellow girl with a fat ass."

I grinned. "I need to see your government-issued ID before I give you the box."

"Fuck you do."

"Jason Bartholomew Starr the Third, from Buckhead, graduate of Wadsworth Magnet School for High Achievers, went to Ivan Allen College of Liberal Arts for a minute, then went to GSU and dropped out. After that you hit rock bottom. You are a long way from San Quentin. Thirty-one counts of pharmacy robbing under your belt. You should've been in jail for the next thirty-eight years, but money had bought a good lawyer, and more money had found its way into a corrupt judge's personal coffer."

"Fuck you know all that?"

"Classified."

"Fuckin' government. You probably done tapped my cell."

"And the phone in your basement."

He threw me his ID card. Flicked it at me, and it hit me on the forehead.

I read the name, gave it back to him. I handed him the box. He rushed and opened it.

Nothing was inside.

He looked up at me. "What the fuck this?"

"That's the promise you made."

"Box is empty."

"Again, like the promise you made."

"What the fuck is this shit?"

I said, "San Bernardino sent me."

"San Bernardino sent you."

"Did I stutter, motherfucker?"

"You came all the way from California to bring me a box?"

"You were a hard man to find. But you were found."

"Why the box?"

"To put the money in. That twenty-four thousand you owe."

He slapped the box away. "You're a long way from home. Over two thousand miles from San Bernardino."

"The Confederate flags and the indecipherable accents told me that."

"You know who the fuck I am?"

"Ask me if I care."

"Nigga, I'm the Pope of the Cascades."

"San Bernardino wants you to take a call

and talk about your debt."

"San Bernardino."

"Take a call."

He stood up like he was ready to paint the walls with my blood.

I asked, "Do you know who I am?"

"You in my goddamn house talking like a dead man walking."

I adjusted my John Lennon glasses. Thought. Then I took them off, eased them into a case that was in my suit coat pocket. Next I took off my jacket, rolled up my sleeves. I eased off my tie, wrapped it around my right fist.

He asked, "What you getting ready to do?"

"My job."

Before he could reach under his seat and pull out his gun, I was across the room, on top of him. I was twenty-two, fast, moved like a cat, a panther, and my speed surprised him. My first blow hit his chin and he went down. Before he hit the ground, I had hit him five more times. I tenderized him but didn't want to overdo it.

He said, "I'm hurt. Nigga, I think you broke my fuckin' arm."

I stomped his left ankle. He screamed.

I looked behind me, saw two Keishas in the doorway, mouths wide open. I was surprised they had heard the noise over the rap music. Black Keisha saw Jason Starr on the ground, fucked-up, and she laughed.

White Keisha asked, "What kind of postman are you?"

"Kind that delivers, rain, sleet, or snow."

Jason Starr screamed, "What you bitches looking at? One of y'all better be dialing nine-one-one."

Black Keisha shook her bottom to the beat and said, "Mailman done beat the mess outta you. All that shit you talking about how you beat up people in jail and shit, and a motherfucker walk in your house and beat you like —"

He exploded. "Get the fuck out of here."

Both Keishas turned around, shared a joint as they headed back toward the stairs.

"I want both of you bitches out of my goddamn house."

Black Keisha said, "Boy, this ain't your house. You know you're in foreclosure."

"I knew they after him for child support, but didn't know he was in foreclosure too."

"I'mma call me a taxi and go back to my momma's apartment at Collie Park."

"Let me pack up my stuff too."

Jason Starr pulled himself back to his chair, face bloodied, eye swollen, and he looked left, looked right, considered his options, then cursed and kicked the empty box. He took out his phone.

I rubbed my aching hands, spat again, then nodded and said, "Call. Now."

"What if I don't want to call? What if I don't?"

Someone walked in behind us. "He's giving you a problem?"

That was Jake Ellis. Dressed in black sweats and an ATL baseball cap he'd picked up.

I said, "Another stubborn one."

"Let me take over."

"I can handle it."

"Your clothes too nice, bruv."

As Jake Ellis drove us away, I called home and there was no answer, so I called my wife's cell, worried, hoping the baby wasn't coming early. Jimi Lee answered, told me she was at Lila's place in Malibu. She said she had driven up and they had gone to dinner and caught a movie, some chick flick starring Julia Roberts.

She asked, "When are you back home?"

"Tomorrow."

"I didn't want to stay in the apartment alone."

"How are you feeling?"

"She's in my belly playing soccer."

I smiled. "Yeah?"

"Your daughter won't give my bladder a break."

"Put the phone to your belly so I can sing to her."

"Not now. Let me rest."

"Love you."

"Bye."

It was a girl. Jimi Lee's dream had been right.

Jake Ellis said, "You're going to be a daddy soon."

"And you're going to be a godfather, bro."

"Real soon."

"Yeah. Soon."

Something wasn't right. Jimi Lee had dreams, and I had a gut feeling.

I called my wife back on her cellular phone.

She didn't answer. Her phone was turned off.

I called the house phone. She didn't answer.

Jake Ellis asked, "You okay?"

"I'm cool."

"You look worried."

"Just want to make sure Jimi Lee is okay."

I called the number I had for Lila in Malibu. She answered. Said she was home, reading. She told me that she hadn't seen Jimi Lee in over a week. I told her my wife was fine and I was just calling to say hi, then let her go.

As we pulled up at our hotel, Jake Ellis asked me, "What's wrong?"

I answered, "Nothing."

Wherever she was, whoever she was with, she had sounded happy.

I tossed my John Lennon glasses, grabbed my backpack, got ready to go back to my room at Howard Johnson's in the area known as College Park, but for some reason pronounced as Collie Park.

Jake Ellis asked, "Bruv, want to have a couple of drinks?"

"Nah. Long day. I'mma shut it down."

"Atlanta is the place to party. Magic City. Strokers. Strip clubs all over the place."

"Not tonight. Not this time."

"You good?"

I nodded. "Make sure you're ready in the morning."

"What time we have to be at the airport?"

"Noon. So be ready to bounce by ten."

"Eleven. Airport is five minutes away."

"Bro."

"Bruv, you don't want to hang?"

"I'm good."

"All right, bruv."

Jake Ellis went to his room, talking, laughing, followed by ebony and ivory, two girls

named Keisha.
I called my wife again and again and again.

CHAPTER 18

Margaux was born at Cedars-Sinai.

I was there, panting along with Jimi Lee during labor, holding her hand as she pushed. It was just us. Her parents and siblings knew she was in labor, that they were about to become grandparents, uncles, and aunts, but no one came. My parents knew I was about to become a father, but no one came.

The first month, I doubt if Jimi Lee held Margaux six times.

She wouldn't give her the nipple but would use a pump, put the milk in the refrigerator. If I was at home and it was feeding time, Jimi Lee would tell me to feed Margaux, and I would give our child the bottle. Jimi Lee stayed in bed, was low energy, and her face began breaking out. She had bad acne for a while but couldn't take anything because she was breastfeeding. One minute she was constipated, the next minute, the opposite problem.

Our days of sleeping in were over. Margaux became our alarm clock, our queen, the one who called out when she needed me to wipe the yellow shit from her ass. Within three weeks, I'd never felt so exhausted in my life. Jimi Lee's skin changed. She looked worn, like she needed Calgon to come and take her away. But we had done it. We were parents. We had Margaux. I was in the room when Margaux was born, saw her come into the world, touched her before her mother did. I was twenty-two. Jimi Lee was nineteen. We looked like children with a child.

Our lives changed. No sleep. No sex. The apartment stayed disorganized. That drove me mad, so I cleaned up behind them all day long. And we could no longer just get up and walk out the door to go somewhere. Jimi Lee had to feed Margaux first, change her, gather diapers and anything Margaux might need, load her into the car seat while I loaded the stroller into the car.

It took an extra hour to get out the door. It became easier to just stay home. We watched the same movies over and over. When I lived alone in a two-bedroom apartment, the place felt spacious. Now it was like someone had cut the size by a third and

260

closed in the walls.

Margaux wouldn't stop crying. Sensory overload. A high-speed chase came through the area, and that brought helicopters and a parade of sirens. It was hot and dry and the air wasn't moving, not even with the ceiling fans on high. Someone blasted N.W.A.'s "Fuck tha Police" like it was their national anthem. Sounds of Blackness was thumping too. God's Property tried to stomp out the noise and failed.

Margaux cried and cried.

Jimi Lee pulled at her hair.

Neighbors tried to drown one another out by cranking up TLC, Mariah Carey, and Donell Jones. The Japanese joined in. All competed for the crown against the West Indians. Buju Banton, Beenie Man, and Machel Montano were overpowered by Ricky Martin, Enrique Iglesias, Marc Anthony, and Santana.

Jimi Lee screamed, "How can you expect us to live like this?"

"They'll stop. It's the call-and-response game they play once every blue moon."

"I have a child. My child is crying. They are so fucking uncouth. I'm calling the police."

"No, don't call the cops. Just let the candle burn out."

She yelled out the window, "They could at least play the same motherfucking song."

I'd never heard her curse that way. It didn't sound right coming from her mouth.

Jimi Lee put my boom box in the window, cranked the volume up, and shook Stocker Boulevard with Ethiopian music by Mulatu Astatke and Tewelde Reda. Forever went by with Margaux shrieking and Ethiopian funk shaking the apartment so hard the downstairs neighbor banged on the ceiling. I turned the boom box off.

I massaged my temples, counted backward from ten, took a deep inhale, a slow exhale, searched for the right words, but simply said, "You're traumatizing Margaux, Jimi Lee."

"This neighborhood is traumatizing me. It is traumatizing your daughter."

The rest of the community didn't follow suit. We sat in dry heat and madness, rocked a crying baby, then changed her diapers as walls and windows vibrated. I grabbed the sports stroller, told Jimi Lee to get dressed. She rebelled against me, didn't change, had been walking around tired and wearing wrinkled Old Navy sweat pants, a pair that swallowed her like a whale. She rocked a messy ponytail, no makeup, and she left the house just like that, in worn-out-mommy mode. Margaux laughed. I put on fresh baggy jeans, Tims, and a Superman T. I had my arms out, was black-man sexy. We left the apartment, strolled down Degnan into the heart of Leimert Park. We sat down at 5th Street Dick's Coffeehouse, ordered brewed coffee, listened to jazz. John Coltrane, Monk, and Miles Davis put Margaux in a better mood, and Jimi Lee too.

She sipped her exotic coffee, now calm, and said, "It's all about Margaux now."

I held the handle on the stroller, moved it back and forth. "It's about you too, Jimi Lee."

"No, not anymore. A baby is a black hole, sucks all the money out of your pocket."

"How do you feel?"

"Afraid. All mothers are afraid."

"Fathers too."

"I understand my mother now."

"How so?"

"I feel how she wanted to protect me. From the world. She wanted me to be educated and independent, break the chains. But here I am. And I feel ugly and fat. Nothing fits. I am inside someone else's body."

"Margaux took over everything, even owns the breasts I'm crazy about."

"Don't be shallow."

"I loved sucking your breasts."

"I was telling you my fears, and you say something stupid like that."

"She should share the milk. I'm the daddy. I have needs. At least let one titty be designated for me. Bet that titty milk goes good with some hot-water cornbread. Stop frowning. You could feed us at the same time."

"Don't be gross."

"When are we going to start having sex again?"

She huffed. "Never."

"Are you serious right now?"

"How can you even think about having sex again?"

"We're married now."

"You saw her come out of me and you want to go back in there again?"

"What are you afraid of?"

"The pain told me to never have sex again."

"You're scared you'll get pregnant again?"

"Yes. I will make sure that doesn't happen."

"Never? So, we're done in the bedroom?"

"Not until we move. I might give you some then."

"Maybe?"

"We need to move."

"Move? What are you talking about?"

"I don't want to live in this area anymore. There have to be at least three million apartments near here. Apartment dwellers are nasty and loud. People stop at the corner blasting music, then open their doors and throw all of their Popeyes and El Pollo Loco garbage on the streets. People walk and eat and throw trash on the ground without blinking. Blame the white man for many things, but you can't blame him for black people being disgusting."

"And Diamond Bar is cleaner."

"From the 57 to the 60, hell yeah."

"Until you get to where it touches Pomona."

"I don't live up there with those people. Not the kind that throw trash everywhere."

I sipped my coffee, thought of a dozen counters, but said, "Okay. We'll talk."

Soon a lot of cats and kittens our ages showed up, women who were on the Erykah Badu and Lauryn Hill vibe and brothers who were smooth as D'Angelo and Maxwell. Pelle Pelle. Starter jackets. Lugz. Wu Wear. Kani. Ecko. They all went to a spot on the other side of the Vision Theater, a spot on the corner. Neo-soul drifted our way. We went down there, watched about sixty people getting their party on. Baggy jeans, Kente cloth, pro-black T-shirts, X caps, and hoodies. It was Saturday night. Sisters were getting their sexy on. Hot music, DJ slamming, sexy dancing, ganja in the air. Brothers were selling TUPAC, BIGGIE, OJ, RODNEY KING, and I SURVIVED THE LA RIOTS APRIL 30TH, 1992 T-shirts. I doubt if anyone in the crowd was over thirty. The spot was eighteen and older. Jimi Lee wanted to go inside. A lot of people were outside playing the let out, trying to get their mack on. Her energy changed. Jimi Lee wanted to be with those strangers. There was nothing like that in Diamond Bar. People drove from fifty miles away to come here. Men looked at Jimi Lee, saw her with me, saw we wore wedding rings, saw we had a baby. Jimi Lee looked at Margaux.

Music played, the rhythm fire, and I danced up behind my wife. I rolled my hips against her and she looked back at me. I kissed her on her neck. Tried to get her to move with me.

Jimi Lee looked down at Margaux, like she was embarrassed for our child to see her mommy and daddy being lovey-dovey, then proffered a sad smile. "Let's go home, Ken Swift."

"We never get out."

"I'm not dressed properly."

"Let's chill out outside the joint, dance,

266

and enjoy the music."

"Margaux is getting restless. She's hungry. Let's go before she starts screaming."

"Dance with me."

There were girls from Saint Kitts and Nevis, Saint Vincent, Guadeloupe, Belize, Tortola, Anguilla, Turks and Caicos. It looked like the sign-up for a Baby Got Back contest. They were shaking their bottoms, moving like Janet Jackson in that song featuring Q-Tip and Joni Mitchell. I saw a few Mother Sally– and Rachel Pringle Pol-green–sized bottoms and fell into a trance, looked at those well-blessed sisters the way Jimi Lee grinned at the brothers who were tall, bronze, and handsome. Jimi Lee walked away first, pulling at her hair, head down, no eye contact. I pushed the stroller, caught up. We went a different way back, inhaled the scents from Phillips barbecue, then walked up side streets that had single-family homes. The side streets that had homes were neat from end to end, and the streets weren't covered in trash. Older people waved at us, smiled. The young black couple. The black man pushing the stroller. The dad. I wanted to stay out forever. But we had a child to tend to. By the time we left the residential areas and were on apartment row, it was a different world. Custom cars and lowriders had taken over the streets. The cruisers and car clubs had appropriated Crenshaw Boulevard. Traffic was backed up for miles. Cars with switches dancing, bouncing up and down. Men fighting in the streets. Women doing the same. Alcohol. Weed. LAPD. Any car that passed the same point twice in thirty minutes would get a ticket. More sirens. Another swarm of LAPD and news helicopters. Loud music. Margaux cried again. I was losing it too. It felt like I had two children to please.

Jimi Lee said, "I can't take this. I'm your wife. For your child, I beg of you. Do something."

The next day we looked at rentals in Culver City.

But I didn't have Culver City money, not with a baby and a wife. Culver City rented at white folks' rates.

Jimi Lee wanted to move to the Valley.

The Valley was hot and dry, bland, and devoid of black culture. It was where Mexicans and blacks sounded like the ditzy Valley girl Whoopi portrayed in her one-woman show. Jimi Lee was used to that Diamond Bar desert heat. I had to be where it cooled off at night, where it was twenty degrees cooler in the summer.

I needed to be around soul food, not tofu. Being in a black area made her feel like a failure. I wasn't one of those people who measured success by how white I became on my journey. Traffic was better on this side of town.

Dressed in an Ethiopian coffee dress, a casual number she wore only while we were inside the house, her hair in two ponytails, Jimi Lee sat on the living room floor and fumed, "So we're not moving to a better area."

"This is a middle-class area. They only act up every now and then, not every day."

"You promised to take care of us. Keep your promise."

"The money's not there. San Bernardino has hit a dry spell. We have to make sure we have money for Margaux. And you ain't cheap. I might have to get a nine-to-five just to pay for all the toilet paper you use."

"Did you hear about the Jamaican girl on Garthwaite whose apartment was broken into by drug dealers? Two black men in masks jumped the fence, kicked down her back door in the middle of the night, went in with guns and machetes. They kicked her back door off the hinges."

I paused. "What happened?"

"The idiots realized they were in the wrong apartment and ran back out. That was two minutes away. What if that happens here, or someone comes because of the things you do?"

"If I stop doing what I do, then we will all be living on skid row. And before you say get a regular job, there is no regular job I can get with half of an engineering degree that will take care of you and Margaux like this. I walk away from San Bernardino, then we're pushing shopping carts and collecting bottles and cans to get by. You're too cute to live in a cardboard box."

"Well, this ain't much better. People blasting music, car thefts, everything."

"You miss being the queen living behind the big gate in Diamond Bar."

"I miss being able to hear myself think. I don't need my neighbors to hear everything I do. Margaux cries, they hear. If we have sex, they hear. If I fart, they complain about the smell."

"You fart?"

"Shut up."

The men who had kicked down the wrong door had been me and Jake Ellis. Well, it was the right door. But the guy who owed San Bernardino ten grand had fled to Suriname a month before and the landlord had rented out the space without changing the names on the mailbox. The stress she felt wrestled with the anxiety I felt.

I needed brown liquor and a Valium.

In the middle of the night, Jimi Lee reached between my legs, made me rise, crawled on top of me, rode me hard and fast, no kisses, came and eased the tension in her body, then rolled away from me, scooted to the far side of the bed. I was surprised. She had been sneaking into the bathroom with her vibrator, pleasing herself in the shower while I kept Margaux. She didn't know I knew, but she had left the vibrator humming on the counter.

I asked, "What was that?"

"I'm tired. I can't sleep. That was therapy. I did that so I can sleep."

"I'm awake now."

"Don't touch me."

Margaux started crying.

Jimi Lee kicked me. "Go check on your daughter. She wants you. Not me. Go."

"We're going to finish curing my blue balls when she goes back to sleep."

"Just make her stop crying. She hates me. She hates to let me rest one second."

"And one fuck can't hold me."

"One time."

"Twice."

"Once. And don't be trying to go on and on. Get to the point. I need sleep."

"African bad gyal, I need you like you needed me and we're going twice."

"Once. And you can jack off the second time."

"If I jack off, I'm waking you so you can swallow."

"Wake me and I'll bite your dick off to your nuts."

"Then you go get Margaux."

"Go get her. She's calling for you. She doesn't even like me."

"Get your ass up and go tend to your daughter."

"Fine. Two times. Whatever you want. Just get her to stop crying. I can't take this."

Neighbors banged on the ceiling, angry at Margaux's misery.

I put my daughter in the car, drove the streets of LA, cruised into Hollywood and back, and that calmed her down. Aggravated, I drove her around until five in the morning. Then we went to Starbucks, watched the sun rise. Exhausted, afraid of failing at this shit, I looked at my child's beautiful brown skin, her bright eyes, felt hope, and I smiled, then went home to my sleeping wife. I changed my daughter's diaper, undressed and put her in the king bed next Jimi Lee, then eased in our bed, left Margaux stirring between us. When I closed my eyes and started to doze off, Jimi Lee reached across Margaux, found my fingers, tugged, and we moved closer to each other.

She held my hand, our arms over Margaux, and we all drifted off to sleep.

CHAPTER 19

Miami was a special kind of hot. It had a hellacious heat from a part of south hell that was yet to be discovered. Air was thick as a bean pie. It was so humid my sweat had sweat on its sweat. Had to be over ninety degrees in the shade with humidity at damn near one hundred percent. When we had landed at Miami International and were outside catching a cab, it was like breathing through a damp paper towel wrapped in a soggy blanket.

Jimi Lee and Margaux had traveled with me. First-class. We'd landed six hours ago. Checked into a suite on South Beach, our hotel across the highway from the Atlantic Ocean. Had amazing room service. Laughed. Played in the hotel's pool a while. Jimi Lee and Margaux were excited but tired, so they went to take a nap.

While they did, I pulled on jeans and a T, checked in with San Bernardino, then left to run a few errands. Jake Ellis had checked into a separate hotel on South Beach. He had come on a separate flight and stalked the target, made sure everything was in place and we could get into his mansion unseen and unheard. We met to take care of San Bernardino business. We cruised the primary streets in Miami Beach. Ocean Ave. Collins. Washington. Everything was on and popping. Amazing clubs and bars. Women dressed in anything that left them damn near naked. Lots of black women with African bodies and a European mind-set. But after a few drinks, nobody cared about mind-sets, only where they could get that ass to sit. It was an erotic show, a cousin to the one on Sunset in LA, only here the heat forced women to strip down to the bare minimum. The section below Twenty-Third Street was a paradise lost. Lots of people walking. Legs everywhere.

Taking it all in, I said, "Must be nice to live like this all day, every day."

"These Cubans and Puerto Ricans make me want to relocate."

"You could. I saw some dark-skinned Cubans and Puerto Rican sisters that would make you pack up and move here and never think twice about LA. You could trade Disneyland for Disney World."

Jake Ellis shrugged. "I like Hollywood."

"They have a Hollywood down here too."

"This heat. If I wanted to sweat this much, I would have stayed in Africa."

"If I wasn't married, I'd tear up my return ticket and start all over, live in South Beach."

"If I find a pretty woman who loves to talk Sartre, Baldwin, Camus, and Fanon, I might do the same. Might cook her a big Ghanaian meal while she does the salsa and has a deep conversation."

"You're becoming pretentious."

"I'm on my journey of enlightenment. I'm here absorbing knowledge about your American icons. Woolf, Hemingway, and also people like Mayakovski. Mayakovski's futurist poetry is off the hook, bruv."

"Throw W.E.B. Du Bois and Langston Hughes in that pot of knowledge before it gets stirred."

"And you throw some Kwame Nkrumah, John Akomfrah, and Joe Coleman de Graft in yours."

The sights were amazing. But we had to pass by and move on. We were on the clock.

I had a wife and child waiting for me to get back to the room.

As Jake Ellis drove the van along the beach, I asked, "What's this guy's name?"

"Balthazar Walkowiak."

"San Bernardino?"

"Already here. Up by Pembroke Pines. Waiting for us to deliver the package."

"If San Bernardino has traveled across the country, this must be serious."

"Flew on a private jet to get here."

"We have another job this time next week."

"Something about a winery back out in California?"

I said, "Some guy is supposed to be some kingpin supplier of wines. He's hawking the rarest of the rare. Sells to deep-pocketed winolas. Wine he's slanging cost seventy grand per case."

"Must be nice, bruv. Must be nice."

"All had been consigned from his supposed magic cellar. San Bernardino invested in that guy's so-called business. Then our boss found out it was all bogus. This motherfucker was selling Domaine Ponsot vintages that didn't exist. He was selling faux Ponsots."

"I don't know wines like that."

"Well, imagine you bought a Maserati, paid top dollar, then opened the hood and found you're running a Pinto engine. He made a pretty bottle with a pretty label, but the shit inside was a Pinto."

Jake Ellis chuckled. "San Bernardino got conned out of close to a quarter million."

I laughed a little. "I guess going to court over this is out of the question."

"You know how San Bernardino rolls."

"Well, let's focus on this job today. We'll worry about that one in a few days."

I looked behind me, saw Jake Ellis had picked up ropes, blindfolds, and tools from Home Depot.

Hand wraps were on the dash. I picked up one, looked at the gauze and tape worn under boxing gloves. Jake Ellis cranked up the music while I wrapped my hands to support the wrists and knuckles.

He asked, "How's Jimi Lee?"

"She's happy."

"About time."

"I mean, not all the way."

"No one is."

"I know."

"People know how to maximize when it comes to some choices and satisfice on others."

I nodded. "She's happy today. Ask me about tomorrow when tomorrow gets here."

A book was on the dashboard too.

I said, "You're down here with all these women reading Dostoyevsky?"

"*Crime and Punishment.* Started it on the plane."

"I was pretty impressed with it. Liked *House of the Dead* more, though."

"You have to read *Brothers Karamazov.*"

"I'll pick it up and start it on the plane back home. If Margaux sleeps."

"How you feel about Tolstoy?"

"*War and Peace* is one of my all-time favorites. Read that in high school."

"I lived it in what you would call high school."

CHAPTER 20

Soon we were inside the target's well-appointed crib, the home of a man who had wealth and glory. Sun was going down, but the oppressive heat stayed high. Each inhale reminded me this wasn't California air. Cali air was arid. California air didn't make you sweat like a river. I could row a boat or swim across Florida in this air. Despite the discomfort, the land was beautiful. It was nice to see skies not polluted with smog. Coral Gables and Miami Beach were crowded with spectacular mansions, the kind larger than the average hotel, private homes on steroids. In this part of the world, a small crib had nine bedrooms and thirteen bathrooms.

A money launderer named Balthazar Walkowiak was six figures in debt with San Bernardino. Six figures in debt and two months behind in paying Caesar what Caesar was due. San Bernardino had to send a message. Each message was about maintaining and solidifying a dangerous reputation.

San Bernardino said Balthazar Walkowiak was a cunning man, a rough man in this business.

But San Bernardino was ruthless. San Bernardino was more cunning than anyone I'd ever met.

Our boss was becoming more powerful and the jobs were becoming more intense.

I needed to get out of this business, needed to exit before it all fell apart.

But now I had a wife and child. Every dime was spent before it was earned. I would never have enough dimes. Being in Florida, seeing how people were living, I knew I'd never have enough money to have that kind of life for myself and my family. But I was still happy with that. I loved my wife. I loved my daughter. I just had to keep making dirty money good and figure out how to get us to the next level.

Still, being in South Beach, seeing the single people, I saw a life I'd missed out on.

Miami, Florida, was beautiful in a way Los Angeles never would be. Maybe it was the Cubans and the Haitians and the Dominicans. The humidity was a beast, but the women in bikinis were beauties.

I was twenty-seven hundred miles and some change from home. I stood in the window of the estate, looked at the docks, at the palm trees, at the boats headed toward the tempting blue waters of the Atlantic Ocean.

Jake Ellis did African finger snaps. "Seven miles of beaches, three golf courses, twenty parks."

"I admire his taste. Art in every corner. Not my kind of art, but it's classy."

"Restaurants and that South Beach nightlife every day of the week."

"The women."

Dressed in shorts, sandals, a South Beach tank top, his hands wrapped up in boxing tape, just like mine, Jake Ellis came and stood next to me. I had on jeans, Nikes, and a tank top. I started unwrapping the boxing tape from my hands. Jake Ellis did the same. The tapes on both of our hands were bloodied.

A cough and a groan came from behind us. Then came a series of farts.

We turned around at the same time. Dressed in thousand-dollar jeans and a shirt that cost just as much, Balthazar Walkowiak was a bloodied mess. In too much pain to get on his hands and knees, he did an army crawl across the marble floor. His place was

amazing, should have been in a movie like
Scarface.

I asked, "Where you think you going?"

"Bathroom. I need to use the bathroom."

We took a few steps across the massive room and stood over Balthazar Walkowiak.

He moaned, "Please, no more. No more."

Jake Ellis said, "San Bernardino demands a face-to-face."

I added, "San Bernardino has flown across the country to make that meeting happen."

Jake Ellis stuffed his bloodied wraps in his pockets. "So, get ready to make a drive."

Balthazar Walkowiak moaned. "I'm going to shit my pants."

I said, "If San Bernardino had flown across the country to see me, I would too."

"Before we go . . . please . . . allow me to use the bathroom first. You hit me so hard, I have to shit."

Jake Ellis told him, "Hold it."

"I beg you. Let me use the bathroom. Please, please, please. I am in pain," Balthazar Walkowiak cried out. "Plus, this is so, so, so embarrassing to say. I have hemorrhoids. You hit me and now I am all messed up."

Jake Ellis shrugged. "I guess we beat the shit out of him."

"The man has a bad case of the piles. And

we kicked his ass." I laughed. "Let the man take a dump. I don't want him losing control of his bowels and stinking up the van. We have an hour ride to get him to San Bernardino. We'll tie him up, lay him down in the back."

"Bruv, go in there with him. Keep an eye on him."

"Bro, I ain't going to watch no grown man do the number two."

I reached for Balthazar Walkowiak's trembling hand. Pulled him to his feet. Six feet tall. Not big, but toned. He reminded me of the actor who played the bad guy in the movie *Die Hard.*

I told Balthazar Walkowiak, "Leave the bathroom door wide-open."

"I will."

"Don't try and jump out of a window."

"I just need to use the bathroom before I embarrass myself."

"Are your speed bumps inside or outside your fart hole?"

"Both. With this pain, I will have to have surgery again."

Jake Ellis said, "And turn the fan on while you're in there."

As I moved toward his bar, I asked, "Mind if I make me a drink?"

Balthazar Walkowiak said something ugly

in French. Jake Ellis snapped back at him in the same language.

Balthazar Walkowiak limped and groaned toward the guest bathroom on the main floor. With each wobbly step, the sartorialist in thousand-dollar pants wiped blood away from his mouth. He touched his wounds, made a sound like his insides were about to explode. He walked funny. We laughed. The Frenchman moved like he'd be eligible for handicap parking until he died. It was going to take him forever to get across the room to the nearest bathroom. I grabbed an exotic beer, something that had been imported from Paris, opened it, took a sip, then tried to get to the bottom of the bottle in one gulp. Jake Ellis followed Balthazar Walkowiak, then stopped, saw the image of a sexy woman, of many sexy women from all over the world, then stood outside the bathroom looking at erotic pictures on the walls. The place was filled with larger-than-life professional photos of women in various stages of undress. The same for men. He had more seminude and erotic images of men than he did of women. Some of the men were in wet tank tops, naked from the waist down. Booty or coochie, that was his business. Balthazar Walkowiak finally staggered into the bathroom. Right away the toilet flushed. An alarm sounded in my brain. He flushed the toilet as soon as he went into the bathroom. That meant the water was draining out of the reservoir. I turned around and Balthazar Walkowiak was stumbling back out of the bathroom, right hand raised. He had a goddamn gun. He pulled it out of a wet Ziploc bag. A piece had been stashed in the bathroom. The man who had looked so defeated now had the eyes of a deranged killer. I yelled at Jake Ellis. Everything was in slow motion, even my scream. The gun fired and hot lead took flight. Jake Ellis was damn near pointblank range.

Balthazar Walkowiak was wounded, could barely aim, yelling at us in French.

The Ghanaian was hit. Jake Ellis went down and Balthazar Walkowiak stumbled and aimed at me. I was running toward him, and it was too late to change my course. Fight or flight had sent me sprinting in the wrong goddamn direction. Room was wide-open. I saw my own death. I saw my wife being a widow. I saw my daughter growing up without me. I saw me and Jake Ellis in body bags.

Balthazar Walkowiak aimed at my head, cursed me to hell, and pulled the trigger.

The gun jammed. A casing didn't eject. His eyes widened. So did mine.

Screaming as Jake Ellis yelled out in pain, before Balthazar Walkowiak could figure out what went wrong with his gun, I rushed him, hit him hard, took him down on the marble floor. He didn't give up. Motherfucker was desperate, knew he had fucked up, and now he had to fight. He used the gun and tried to pistol-whip me. I caught a blow in my left eye, then hit him with a barrage of blows, hard blows, threw a dozen knockout punches. He dropped the gun, but no matter how hard I hit Balthazar Walkowiak, he wouldn't surrender. I held him down on the floor, flopped around. It was like trying to hold a snake. He tried to bite a chunk of meat out of my arm. We wrestled and traded blows until I flipped him and caught him in an LAPD chokehold, put the bone in the forearm hard across his windpipe. I called out to Jake Ellis. He was still alive. He stood up, holding his arm. He'd been shot in the arm, not the head. He came over, scowling, pissed the fuck off. I did my best to strangle Balthazar Walkowiak. Jake Ellis stomped on Balthazar Walkowiak's legs like he was trying to break them off the man's body, then started throwing furious blows with his uninjured arm. He hit Balthazar Walkowiak in his face hard enough to break his jaw. Jake Ellis had hands made of East African concrete, but that didn't stop Balthazar Walkowiak from trying to get free. I had a hard time controlling that snake. Jake Ellis had been shot, but his adrenaline was high and he used the uninjured arm to throw more knockout blows. Nothing made Balthazar ease up. He got to his feet while I had him in a headlock. He threw blows at my ribs. Hit me over and over while I strangled him. We tussled from living room to dining room to the kitchen. Next thing I knew, Jake Ellis had run to the counter and come back with a butcher knife. He gritted his teeth and stabbed Balthazar Walkowiak. Stabbed him over and over, that sound of a knife cutting into human flesh strong in my ears, louder than the screams, yells, curses, and grunts. Jake Ellis lost the plot, was angry because the man had tried to kill him. When a man saw his own blood, he felt his mortality, and survival kicked in. Balthazar Walkowiak bled all over me. With the knife stuck in his chest, Balthazar Walkowiak pushed me across the room, fell down on one knee, rose again, tried to shake me off of him. Blood drizzled like a warm summer rain. He was slippery, but I never let him go. I felt his fear, inhaled his desperation. He was terrified of our boss, of having to stand face-to-face with

San Bernardino. The Frenchman didn't want to die and showed me how much he wanted to live and did what he thought he had to in order to escape. The Frenchman caught his breath, then dragged me, tried to shake me, pulled me across the room, knocked over anything not attached to the wall or floor. Lamps toppled. Chairs turned over. Jake Ellis kept hitting him. Balthazar Walkowiak threw his head back into my face and smacked my nose. With that pain, I loosened my grip for a second, and that gave him air to breathe. Eyes watering, nose feeling like it could be broken, I doubled up on the choking, got my breath, growled, summoned all of my energy, growled again, and twisted his goddamn neck like they did in the movies. I didn't hear Snap or Crackle, but there was a pop.

Balthazar Walkowiak stopped fighting, exhaled once, and went limp. The Frenchman dropped. I held on to him a good twenty seconds, kept choking him, was enraged and couldn't shut it down. He'd tried to shoot me. He'd outsmarted me. He'd head butted me. When I was sure he was gone, I collapsed on the floor next to him, drenched in sweat. Jake Ellis did the same, scowling, biting his lip in pain, bleeding from his gunshot wound. Blood covered me like warm piss. I got to my feet, almost slipped and fell just as Jake Ellis was trying to get his tank top off. He ripped it away and tied it around his arm to slow the bleeding. Rivers of DNA were all over the place. Then I used the bottom of my T to wipe the blood and sweat away from my face. Nose was bloodied, ached, but it wasn't broken. I looked at the gun that Balthazar Walkowiak had stashed in the bathroom. I picked it up. It had been in that plastic bag a while. Too long. The gun had gunk built up near the firing pin. That was why it didn't move forward properly. Trigger mechanism was probably fucked too, or the gat had a weak firing-pin spring. A worn ejector wouldn't provide enough energy to cycle the gun. That first shot had jammed it all up. Jake Ellis's brains were still inside his head because the Frenchman was terrified, was in a lot of pain, and had poor shooting technique. He wasn't a marksman, but if Balthazar Walkowiak had cleaned his gun last week, even with the bad shooting technique, the injuries, and the fear of San Bernardino in his heart, Jake Ellis and I would be dead.

Jake Ellis held on to his wounded arm. "Goddamn gun-in-the-toilet trick."

I looked at Balthazar Walkowiak. Filled

with stab wounds. Neck broken. Face slack, eyes half-open, not breathing. He was gone. I'd killed a man. When I popped his neck, that shut him down.

I kicked that motherfuckin' lying-ass bastard. Kicked him as hard as I could.

"Why couldn't you just take a shit and call it a day?"

Jake Ellis said, "He was on something. Some PCP. Something."

"The way you stabbed him and he kept going like he felt nothing, he had to be."

"Call this in to San Bernardino. I'm going to look around for a first aid kit."

Bleeding, sweating, panting, I made that call.

It wasn't an easy call to make.

"Boss. Ken Swift. Good evening. We have a little problem over here."

San Bernardino was angry as hell at this monetary loss, but told us what we had to do.

CHAPTER 21

In the thick of the night, we wrapped Balthazar Walkowiak up in painter's plastic and an Oriental rug that cost more than a luxury car. We went out to the Everglades. There were more than two hundred thousand alligators in the Everglades. I'd heard that they didn't really eat humans, but we didn't care. All I know is that when we dropped his body, it sounded like gators rushed to feed on his corpse. We had to do as told and make Balthazar Walkowiak disappear.

It was dark and I was on edge, expected Swamp Thing to leap out of the water and take us both. Whirligig beetles, maybe a hundred species of butterflies, yellow garden orb-weaver and all kinds of spiders, lubber grasshoppers. Centipedes. Millipedes. Dragonflies. Mites, ticks, and whip scorpions. A million female mosquitoes were hungry for blood, were out hunting for mammals like me and Jake Ellis to eat alive. The air felt twice as thick, the air three times as hot, and smelled putrid as fuck, worse than rotting vegetation, worse than clothes left in the washer a week too long. Each inhale reeked like we were riding up a dead skunk's ass. Maybe all of that horrific stench didn't come from the Everglades. It might've been the dead man's pong. Death had loosened his bowels.

Jake Ellis was in pain, the bullet wound alive and kicking. "Our blood was all over the main level."

As we sped out of the Everglades I spat into the waters. "Our fucking DNA was like soup."

"Haitians showed up. San Bernardino getting that spot cleaned."

"Balthazar Walkowiak is big shit down here. People will be looking for him before noon."

"We need to get out of Florida. I didn't leave anything at my hotel room I'll miss."

"I did. I left my wife and my child."

"I have to get my arm looked at first. Can't risk getting an infection."

"Handle that. Then get out of Dodge."

"What about you?"

"I have to go and get my family."

"You should leave first. Tell Jimi Lee to leave tomorrow. By herself with Margaux."

"Can't do that."

Jake Ellis winced. "He shot me and I bled all over the place."

"He busted my nose."

"Fuck." Jake Ellis screamed into the night. "Fuck."

Jake Ellis had the same concern I did. We didn't know how good the cleaners were. We were in the age of DNA. It took one speck of blood to identify a man, and that speck was better than fingerprints.

We set the van on fire, then got into a different car. When that was done I dropped Jake Ellis off at a doctor, a mature Dominican woman who worked off the books for San Bernardino. The bullet was removed.

Soon Jake Ellis went left, and I went right.

CHAPTER 22

I'd vanished, been MIA for hours. I couldn't call Jimi Lee and tell her I'd be late getting home from the office, not after what had gone down. I had killed a Frenchman, then carried his dead body out into the Everglades as an offering to prehistoric reptiles. I had to sneak back into my five-star hotel. I was worried about my wife and child. It was three in the morning when I made it inside. I looked like shit and smelled twice as bad. I hadn't changed T-shirts.

Jimi Lee sat up, turned on the lights.

She had been waiting for me to come back.

I knew she was angry because she had waited all day.

She had been here with Margaux all day.

She saw me before I could get from the door of the suite to the bathroom.

I stood still, like a burglar caught in the act.

"Oh my God. Is that blood?"

"It's not ketchup from In-N-Out."

"You're covered in blood."

"Some."

"You were in an accident?"

Margaux was in the bed, sleeping. She didn't wake up. I was glad she didn't.

I said, "I'm okay. Most of it's not my blood."

"Most of it isn't yours? Whose blood? Were you in a fight? Where have you been all day?"

Hands were shaking. Could hardly breathe. Legs wouldn't move. I was traumatized. I had killed a man with my bare hands. I had to force myself to snap out of it, to keep moving to keep from falling apart.

I said, "There is nothing to worry about."

"I'm your wife. You will tell me what has happened. And you will tell me now."

Jimi Lee followed me to the bathroom, angry still, but now mixed with worry and fear. She was a smart woman. Any lie I told her wouldn't make it to her ears before being slapped down.

I said, "There was this guy . . . Balthazar Walkowiak . . ."

"Who is Balthazar Walkowiak?"

"Either you talk or I talk."

"What happened?"

"Had a problem."

"What type of problem did you have with Balthazar Walkowiak?"

"Shit." I wished I hadn't said the man's name. Excited utterance had me. "We had a problem."

She panted. "Answer me. What kind of problem?"

"He shot Jake Ellis. Then tried to shoot me."

"Jake Ellis is dead?"

"He was shot."

"What does that mean? Is he dead?"

"Lower your voice."

"Answer me."

"He was injured, but he's going to be okay."

"Who is Balthazar Walkowiak?"

"He tried to kill Jake Ellis, shot him, then tried to shoot me in the head."

"Why would he do that?"

"I went to talk to him and it got out of control."

"Talk to Balthazar Walkowiak about what?"

"Money."

"What money?"

"San Bernardino business."

"What happened to Balthazar Walkowiak?"

"He left me no choice. I had to take him out."

"You . . . you . . . you killed a man?"

"He tried to kill me."

"Did you kill that man?"

"He had a gun. Was determined to kill Jake Ellis. And me. I did what I had to do."

Jimi Lee shook her head, processing this. "Wait . . . you said we were here on vacation —"

"We are on vacation."

"This trip is a charade. You bring me here, use me, to hide San Bernardino business?"

"I told you to relax, get a massage, get a manicure and pedicure, while I ran an errand."

"An errand? I run errands all day. No one shoots at me. No one ends up dead."

Jimi Lee ran to the bed, woke up Margaux, and right away my daughter started crying.

"What are you doing?"

"I have a daughter. I can't be here, not with my daughter. This is beyond irresponsible. Beyond unacceptable. I can't believe you lied . . . used us . . . brought me and your child to Miami and you —"

"You're scaring her."

"You're scaring me. I've been scared since I met you. I'm tired of being scared."

"Scared of what?"

"A moment like this. Look at the blood on your shirt and answer your own question. I can't do this. If you had ended up dead, at least my daughter wouldn't be old enough to remember . . . to remember . . ."

"Jimi Lee."

"If you go to jail, know this. I don't visit jails. My daughter will never visit a jail."

Jimi Lee was built for Harvard. She wasn't built for this. I wasn't built for this either.

I hurt many, but I wasn't made to kill other men.

My wife started packing, started getting Margaux together.

I took a step toward my crying daughter, did that out of parental instinct.

Jimi Lee snapped, "Don't you dare kill a man and touch her. Don't put that energy on her body."

"I need you to lower your voice, Jimi Lee."

"Keep away from us. Look at your face. Look at your nose. You have scratches all over your arms. Your eyes are black. You look like a homeless man and smell like day-old sewage. That blood that came from someone else, the blood on you could have AIDS in it. And you bring that back to this room?"

"You're leaving?"

"On the first flight back to Los Angeles.

I'll sit and wait at the airport as long as I have to."

"At least let Margaux rest and leave when the sun comes up."

"What if the police come for you? What if they kick down that door and arrest me too?"

"Don't leave now."

"They will take my daughter from me and I will hate you like I've never hated anyone."

"No police are coming."

"How do you know?"

"No one knows what happened. No one knows who I am, or where I am."

"The room is on your name."

"Jimi Lee."

"Keep away from me. Keep away or I will scream that I am with a murderer."

"I need you to believe that everything is under control and I have to be able to trust you."

"Am I supposed to trust you? You've lied and involved me in your San Bernardino bullshit."

"I didn't lie. I ran an errand. Did you want me to lie and say I was out with some woman?"

"I wish you had been. Anything but this madness. You come in . . . looking like that . . . smelling like that . . . blood all over you . . . your nose . . . your face . . . your eyes . . . and tell me you killed a man, and what do you expect from me? What would a sane person do? I'm trapped in Miami in a room with a murderer."

"The man tried to kill me. And right now, dealing with you, I wish he had."

She shouted at herself, "This, Adanech? This instead of Harvard. This. This. This."

"Lower your voice before someone sends up security."

She went off on me in Amharic as she pulled off her pajamas and searched for clothes to wear.

I was exhausted, traumatized, and I wasn't going to stop Jimi Lee from leaving. I had to change, had to tend to my wounds, check out my nose, and scrub Balthazar Walkowiak's blood off my skin. I had touched the doorknob. Had touched the wall. Now his DNA was probably all over my hotel room.

Jimi Lee's anger and Margaux's cries followed me into the bathroom as I shut the door. I took the plastic liner out of the trash can, shoved all I had on into that bag, and stepped into the shower.

I would've rather Balthazar Walkowiak shot me in my head than to have to face Jimi Lee.

I hit the shower wall with my fist, banged

it hard. I had told Jimi Lee that Frenchman's name.

She had looked at me in a way that made it possible for only the truth to exit my lungs.

I was a big man, but in my life, she was a giant.

She was my wife. I didn't want to lie to my wife. I'd killed a man. The night had left me shaken. I needed her now more than anything. I saw she was scared, but I had to act like I was wearing the skin of a man like Leroy Brown.

My daughter cried for me to hold her, but I wasn't sure I was a good father.

Blood rinsed from my skin, turned pink as it circled the drain.

I closed my eyes. Heard the sound of a body being dropped in the Everglades. Saw the eyes of oversize reptiles glowing in the night. Heard them easing into the water in search of breakfast.

The hotel door opened and closed, made me blink that memory away. My heartbeat sped up. Jimi Lee was gone out the door, walking down the hallway, hurrying away from me. Margaux's cries faded as she went down the hallway. I beat the wall again, felt disgusting, then tried to get the water hotter. I soaped and scrubbed and soaped and scrubbed for the better part of an hour. Jimi Lee had walked out on me. She might betray me. San Bernardino would drag me to the swamps if Jimi Lee caused trouble, and her body would be chained to mine.

Jimi Lee and I were married.

If the police did come, she was my wife. They couldn't force her to testify against me. Unless she was pissed, wanted to become a turncoat, tell them I'd been missing all day, tell them I'd crept into the room in the middle of the night, bloodied and battered, smelling like the Everglades. Not unless she wanted to tell them I'd mentioned Balthazar Walkowiak. I'd had Jimi Lee's back since day one, but she wasn't ride or die. I was Clyde without a Bonnie. With a mother, the child always came first, as it should be. I should've stayed out all night, not come back to the hotel room until I had on new clothes, came back smelling like a brand-new cologne, let her think I was dancing salsa with the cokeheads on South Beach, or swimming in some bodacious Cuban pussy until the sun came up.

No man ever went to jail for infidelity.

Never would, not as long as men were the judges.

But a good husband wasn't supposed to stay out all night, not the way my father used to do to my mother.

I wasn't my old man, but I wasn't a good husband.

CHAPTER 23

By the time I stepped out of the shower and wrapped myself in a hotel towel, the door flew open, opened fast and hard. Paranoia told me the slave catchers had arrived and were here to drag me away. My heartbeat accelerated. I imagined my wife turning me in, in order to save Margaux from me. Jimi Lee stormed back in the room, our child in her left arm. Jimi Lee also carried a bag of hotel goods in her left hand. She had gone shopping at the all-night gift shop. My wife was on her cell phone, had it up to her right ear, was talking in Amharic, talking fast, animated, upset, raging, every other word my name. Across the room, her bags and Margaux's toys and dolls were packed.

I asked, "Who are you talking to?"

She rolled her eyes at me and moved across the room, violently threw the bag on the bed. Then she marched around me, went in the bathroom, and gathered her toiletries and things that belonged to Margaux.

Swimming in paranoia, patience lost, I asked, "Jimi Lee, who are you talking to?"

She ignored me and that set me off. I knew her relationship with other men had never stopped. I knew I'd never be good enough in her eyes. I reached for her hand, took the phone from her.

I demanded, "Who is this?"

"This is Menna. I demand to know what is going on. Why is my daughter so upset?"

"Menna? Jimi Lee's mother?"

"My daughter's name is Adanech Abeylegesse Zenebework."

"Adanech Abeylegesse Zenebework-Swift."

"You have taken her name, changed it, and changed my granddaughter's name as well?"

"My daughter's name is Margaux."

"Her name is Tsigereda."

"Well, I call my daughter Margaux."

"What have you done to upset Adanech so?"

Before I could utter another word, Jimi Lee yanked her personal phone out of my hand, gave me hard eyes as she vented to her mother, again in Amharic. She vented to a mother who had allowed her to be put

306

out into the streets when she found out she was pregnant. Her enemy was no longer her enemy. Now I was the odd man out. Jimi Lee was her daughter, but her daughter was my wife. I wanted to know what the fuck they were saying. My Amharic was decent at that point, but Jimi Lee was talking at one hundred words per second, each word hot like molten lava. Her native tongue sounded like a string of gibberish laced with fear and animosity, each word as sharp as the blade Jake Ellis had stabbed the Frenchman with.

Killing Balthazar Walkowiak had been easier.

Jimi Lee ended her call, gave me hard silence. She handed me Margaux, did that gently, then stormed back into the bathroom. My daughter cried until she was in my arms. She looked at me and fear left her eyes.

Jimi Lee yelled, "She hates me."

"She felt your energy and anger and that scared her."

"Don't talk to me. Don't fucking talk to me."

I stood in the door, rocking Margaux back to sleep while I stared at my enraged wife.

"You and your mother are talking again?"

"I called her."

"Why did you call your mother?"

"Because I don't have Oprah Winfrey's phone number."

"What did you tell her?"

"Is it safe here?"

"It's safe here."

"I don't feel safe."

"Your mother."

"I called her."

"Why?"

"She's my mother."

"Why call her now?"

"Because I was scared and upset."

"But why call her?"

"Because I felt like . . . a scared child."

"You're not a child."

"Because you are like my father."

"What does that mean?"

"She told me that I have Stockholm syndrome. She said this life is my punishment."

"You're not a prisoner. You haven't been kidnapped."

She wiped tears from her eyes.

I took a breath. "Are you leaving?"

"We're leaving."

There was a tap on the door. I jumped when I heard the rapping. Jimi Lee heard the noise, wiped away tears, and hurried out of the bathroom, ill at ease, eyes red, not blinking, too scared to get comfortable.

She asked, "Who is that?"

"No idea."

She took Margaux from me, hurried across the room.

I asked, "Who is it?"

From the other side of the door someone said, "Nobody. It's Nobody."

"Give me a second."

Jimi Lee asked me, "What's going on? What is this all about?"

I pulled on fresh jeans, a T-shirt, then opened the door. It was a well-dressed Cuban woman. Sexy, sophisticated, and sweet. A curvaceous size-ten body with 34E breasts, looking like the ultimate girlfriend experience. Nobody looked like a succulent angel, like she could be a man's perfect companion, the kind he'd want for the rest of his life, or at least until the next sunrise touched his eyes. Nobody smelled like heaven and smiled like she was as savage as she was comprehensive between the sheets. Her outfit was top-shelf, a white dress that hugged her frame, and her taste spoke volumes. Said she was expensive, said she knew where the best restaurants were. But her curves said she knew her way around the kitchen. She could make a married man regret being married.

"Ken Swift."

"Nobody."

"Long time."

"Been a minute."

"Looks like you had a rough night."

"Looks like."

She looked beyond me and saw my wife standing there holding our child.

I said, "My wife."

"Heard you married."

"Found the one."

"And a kid?"

"A daughter."

"Congratulations."

"Thanks."

She reached into her oversize designer purse and handed me a bulky golden envelope.

I took it from her hand and she said, "All the best."

"Likewise."

Then she left, her rich and sweet scent lingering as I closed the door.

In a tone as stiff as it was harsh, Jimi Lee asked, "Who was she?"

"Nobody."

"Nobody."

"Like the Keith Sweat song. Nobody."

"Did Nobody think me and my daughter

had already left? Is that what that was?"

"She's a lesbian."

"She's exotic."

"So are you."

"You like exotic women."

"But I love you."

"How old is she?"

"Between your age and mine."

"Have you fucked her?"

"Strictly business."

"Would you fuck her?"

"I'd fuck you while she went down on you."

"That's disgusting."

"You said Lila tried that."

"This has nothing to do with Lila. And don't repeat things I tell you in confidence."

"Jimi Lee, you need to keep what happens in this family between us. Even from Lila."

"Why was that hoochie momma here at this hour?"

"She did a delivery for San Bernardino."

"At this hour?"

"Money never sleeps. And for the people who are partying on South Beach, it's not late. Sun's not up."

"San Bernardino hires pretty women who walk around half-naked in the middle of the night."

"Every woman in Miami is half-naked in

the middle of the night, if not buck naked."

"She's pretty. I look like this . . . like a mother . . . and she comes to the door looking like that."

"You should see San Bernardino's girl from Aleppo, Syria. She's so beautiful her name is Beautiful."

"I bet you've slept with them."

"You're jealous."

"She knocks on the door at this hour? Looking like that? I bet she was hoping you were here alone."

"Did you not hear me say she was a lesbian?"

"I'm not stupid. You don't dress that way to drop something off. She planned on staying."

I walked away from Jimi Lee. Tossed the bulky envelope on the desk. Jimi Lee followed and picked it up, opened it, turned it upside down. Ten thousand dollars in cash rained to the table. We stood looking at what some said was the root of all evil. Others said the lack of money was the root of all evil. I tended to side with the people who believed the latter, but I worked for San Bernardino, and my boss was making me a strong believer in the former.

My wife whispered, "Did you really kill a man?"

312

"Yes."

She gulped. "While I was in this room with your daughter."

"Yes."

She blinked nervously. "A man who was trying to kill you."

"Yes."

"Balthazar Walkowiak."

I put a finger to my lips, my way of telling her to not say that name anymore.

Jimi Lee touched the money and shuddered. Ran her fingers over what I had earned, scowled like she wanted to burn it all. Then she stepped back shaking her head like she was in the middle of a nightmare.

Her fear remained. "Get me and my daughter another room."

"Okay."

"In another hotel."

"Can you just change rooms here?"

"It's not safe to be with you."

"I'll get you a room, and in the morning. I will get you a room at a different hotel."

"I want a room in a different hotel and I want it now."

"It's late. You know rooms aren't available until noon."

"There is always an available room."

"Margaux is finally going back to sleep."

"And I want us a very nice hotel. I want

the presidential suite. You can afford it."

"Okay."

"Under another name."

"What name?"

"Daffy Duck. Superman. I don't care."

"So, you're not leaving for Los Angeles in the morning?"

"Just get us another room."

"Okay."

"Get me and my daughter away from you and your San Bernardino business."

"I need to know this, and know this now." I took a breath. "What did you tell your mother?"

"Nothing."

"Don't play with me, Jimi Lee. What did you tell her?"

"That you were like my father."

"What does that mean?"

"Get me a room. Please."

I called downstairs, arranged for her to have another suite, on a different floor.

That done, I motioned. "What's in the gift-shop bag? What did you run out and buy?"

She wiped away tears of anger, then snapped, motioned at a chair. "Sit."

Compared to me, she was vertically challenged, should have been terrified of me, but she talked to me like she was twice my size. If I were a bear, then she was a wolverine. Bears were larger than wolverines. People with common sense were terrified of bears, but bears never fucked with wolverines.

My wife opened the bag. She'd bought things to tend to my wounds. She took wet towels, cleaned me up, put peroxide on my scratches, cleaned blood from inside my nose. It hurt for her to touch my face.

I asked, "How bad is it?"

"If it were broken, I think it would be more crooked or bent-looking."

"Okay."

"Can you breathe?"

"It hurts around the nose and the breathing is blocked."

"From one or both nostrils?"

"Left side."

"Some bleeding. Do you hear a crackling or crunching sound when you move your nose around?"

"No. Just hurts."

She said, "It's not broken. Just bruised. You will be ugly a few days."

"Good. Always wanted to be ugly and see the world from that perspective."

"You're going to have two black eyes. People will stare at you."

"I'll say I'm an abused husband."

"And this is funny to you?"

"I will tell everyone you beat me."

"And I will tell everyone I kicked your ass and will not hesitate to kick your ass again."

"And that is funny to you."

"Hush."

She finished cleaning my face, gave me two Tylenol, made me rest with ice on my face. She stood, arms folded, rocking from foot to foot, frowning at the pile of money. Frowned at it a long time.

I asked, "What's wrong?"

While Margaux slept, Jimi Lee spread the money around on the carpet, stared at the poor man's fortune, then reached for me, and we eased down on top of my payday. She held my head, pushed it south, wanted me to eat her. That evolved into us doing ninety-six on a pile of cash. She mounted me, fucked me, rode me good, hard, and strong. Seeing that money did something to my wife. Money was an aphrodisiac. Capitalism made it hard for a woman to love a broke man. It was hard to love a man when you were broke and suffering from missed-meal cramps.

Money made it easy for a woman to love a bad man.

CHAPTER 24

We didn't change rooms. But after room service brought breakfast, we left without a formal checkout, caught a cab out front, changed hotels. We stopped being Mr. and Mrs. Swift and became Mr. and Mrs. Daffy Duck. We checked into another five-star spot that charged five hundred dollars a night. We chilled out by the giant swimming pool in the heat. Jimi Lee played with Margaux in the shallow end. I got in the deep end, swam a few laps.

Margaux was soon dehydrated, exhausted from the heat and the playing.

Balthazar Walkowiak was on my mind. The blood that we had left behind, blood that had to be cleaned. I worried that one drop had been overlooked. I closed my eyes and felt the heat from the Everglades. Heard flies and mosquitoes buzzing. A few of the latter had stung me.

Jimi Lee sat next to me. "I was thinking."

"About?"

"Last night."

"What part?"

She bit the corner of her lip. "Let's go back upstairs."

"Margaux is awake."

"I'll put her to sleep."

Margaux crawled into my arms.

I smiled. "Okay."

"I came to Florida to have a good time, Ken."

"We're having a good time."

"We could have a better time. Try not to kill anyone else while we're here."

Back in the new room, a suite made for a king and queen, while our daughter slept, again, we fucked hard, fucked hard on a bed of money, left come stains on the faces of Presidents Hamilton, Jackson, and Grant. She fucked me like she was trying to get me to put another baby in her belly. She sucked me good; then she offered me her bottom. She came, legs shaking, thighs quivering. I was slow stroking. We fucked as quietly as we could, like teenagers when adults were in the next room. Quiet, but intensely, we fucked all over the luxurious suite while our child slept. It was like we had been at the start, the night we had met at Club Fetish. It was the kind of fuck a woman gave when she loved a man. It was also the kind of fuck a woman gave when she was leaving a man.

The beautiful Afro-Mexican I had fallen for had loved me hard before she cut me loose.

It had been a fuck of closure. It felt like Jimi Lee was loving me hard before she said good-bye.

We showered together; then we crawled in the bed, tried to get in a nap before Margaux woke up again.

Jimi Lee's cellular rang and woke us up. She said it was her mother calling again. This time Jimi Lee was soft smiles and polite laughs. My wife said it was her mother, but the voice on the other end carried. It was a male's voice, and he was talking in Amharic. Could've been her father. Jimi took the phone and went inside the bathroom.

Margaux stirred but didn't wake up. She snored like she was in her twelfth dream.

When Jimi Lee finished her call, she hung up and came back to me, put her head on my shoulder.

I asked, "What's wrong?"

"My mother wants to meet her granddaughter."

I asked, "You're going to take Margaux to Diamond Bar when we get back?"

"In a few weeks. It must be discussed, planned. She wants to meet you as well."

"Your voice is shaking."

"I guess I will have to see my father again."

"Do you want to see him?"

"No. But he is my father. I am his daughter. He is our child's grandfather."

She was scared. I felt her tremble from head to toe. My wife was terrified.

I said, "Margaux and you haven't met my parents either."

"You say we live five minutes from your parents."

"We do."

"They are on the hill, in the big houses in the so-called Black Beverly Hills."

"In that area. They have lived up there since the seventies."

"You sent them trees. I heard you and Jake Ellis talking about that."

"I sent them the best trees I could find. Spent a lot of money. It was impulsive."

"Why?"

"To show them I was doing okay without them."

"But you won't call them or go drive five minutes from Leimert Park to see them."

"I haven't in a long time. I invited them to the wedding."

"Were they too busy?"

"They chose not to come."

"They are our daughter's paternal grand-parents."

"I know."

"Our family trees have merged."

"I know."

"Starting with Margaux, your family and mine will forever be part of the same tree."

"Ethiopia and Mississippi are connected."

"And you have siblings."

"Not all have the same mothers."

"I wanted to ask about that, about your family, but I didn't."

"My father sent my other siblings to private schools. I went to public schools."

"Why?"

"He said I didn't deserve it. Refused to help pay for any of my college."

"That's why you went to work for San Bernardino?"

"Part of the reason."

"Why would your dad not want you edu-cated?"

"I don't want to talk about it. My life is fine. It is what it is, and it's fine."

"It would be better. Safer. That would have made all the difference in the world."

I took a breath. "You want me to arrange a lunch or dinner with my parents and siblings as well?"

"Yes, I think it's time. We live like no one else exists in the world but the three of us."

"Will see what I can do."

"It's claustrophobic. We're living in a bubble. All bubbles burst. Sooner or later, all bubbles burst." She pulled her bushy hair away from her face, saw Margaux was still asleep, then put her arms around me. "Ken?"

"Yeah?"

"I'm your wife."

"Yes."

"I have a question. A serious question. I have to know. I really have to know the truth."

"Yeah?"

She was afraid to ask. "Because you are my husband, and I am your wife, I need to know."

"Okay."

"How many people have you killed?"

"One. Only one."

"Was there any other option?"

"He shot Jake Ellis. Tried to shoot me in the head. There was no other option."

"You killed a man. Like my father has done before, in a war, you killed a man."

"I killed a man who tried to make you a widow and leave my child fatherless."

"If you go to jail, what will the difference be?"

"I'm not going to jail."

"If you go to jail, you will be dead to me. *Dead.* I will be a widow and my child will be fatherless."

"I don't want you stressed."

"You have to turn your life around. We have to turn our lives around. For Margaux."

I fell asleep. Tossed and turned. Relived the Frenchman being stabbed. Heard his neck pop.

When I woke, Margaux was next to me, still asleep. Jimi Lee was at the desk, had a little notebook open, was writing. She saw I was awake and put her notebook away. I headed for the bathroom, took another shower.

When Jimi Lee slept I looked at her phone. Three calls had been to Gelila. Damn phone bill would be sky-high. I saw the call to her mother. Her last call had been an incoming call from someone named Yohanes. The number was in the 909 area code, maybe the same sector as Diamond Bar. He'd called her yesterday, while I was gone with Jake Ellis. They had talked for more than three hours. She had just talked to him again, in my face. I found her notebook. She had written more than a hundred pages in Amharic, in a language I couldn't read. That pissed me off.

When Jimi Lee woke up, Margaux and I were on the carpet, playing with her toys.

Jimi Lee smiled at us, said things in Amharic to Margaux, and our daughter laughed.

My wife gazed at me. "Ken?"

"You ready to lose at Scrabble?"

"Give me a second. I'll run downstairs and buy the game in the gift shop."

She bit her bottom lip, wagged her butt side to side. "Truce first, then Scrabble?"

"Margaux is wide-awake and bouncing around like she's been drinking coffee and taking NoDoz."

"She will be fine for five minutes."

"Why do you come between me and her when we're having a good time?"

"Because she always comes between me and you when I want to have a good time."

"What if she starts crying?"

"Let her cry. Stop spoiling her and let her cry."

"Wait until she falls asleep."

"I don't want to wait. Put one of the *VeggieTales* tapes we brought in the hotel's VCR. Prop her up in front of the television. She won't miss us. She gets mesmerized by the talking vegetables. Then we won't have to rush."

"Jimi Lee."

"I need to meet with Soul Stealer."

"Jimi Lee."

"Two times. Second time can be when she's asleep."

Jimi Lee was away from Leimert Park, living in luxury, and that left her aroused.

She whispered, "I brought sexy lingerie. I know I won't get a chance to put it on until later, if at all."

"Put it on now. I'll meet you in the bathroom."

Jimi Lee grabbed things from her suitcase, winked at me, kissed Margaux, then went into the bathroom. I popped in a movie. While our daughter played in front of the VCR, my wife rocked her lingerie. She sat on the toilet, had me stand in front of her, and she took me in her mouth. When I was hard, Jimi Lee held the counter.

She moaned. "Wish we were on the bed."

"Yeah?"

"Soixante-neuf."

"When she's sleeping."

I took my wife from behind, loved her, felt good, told myself that Yohanes didn't matter, that her secret notebook didn't matter.

She knew I had sent a man to Valhalla. She stayed with me. This was all that mattered.

Margaux became restless and we took her out of the room. I carried her and we walked her around the glorious hotel and we all ended up in the rambunctious lobby. The city came to life after dark. Was like we had stumbled into a new world, one that overwhelmed Margaux. While some people our age got dressed to go party out by the pool until the break of dawn, while others went out into the land of cocaine and one-night stands, we moved around the gift shop with geriatric Coppertone-tanned couples old enough to be our grandparents. Margaux was scared, reached for her mother's arms. When she did, as Jimi Lee bounced and cooed her, an older black woman asked my wife if she was babysitting her little sister. Something shifted in Jimi Lee. My wife told the woman she was holding her daughter. The old lady told Jimi Lee she was too young to have a child. Jimi Lee showed the woman her wedding ring, did that to ward off shame. The old lady told Jimi Lee she looked too young to be married, said my wife looked like she should still be in school getting her education. Jimi Lee gave a stiff smile and walked away, seething. We bought Scrabble from the gift shop, then went back to our suite, not one word spoken along the way.

Both of us were good at Scrabble.

Jimi Lee wanted to show me the Harvard in her brain, show me how much smarter her private-school brain was than the brain of a guy who had gone to Audubon Middle School, Crenshaw High, and UCLA for a hot minute. She challenged me and wanted to flex that African superiority. We played for hours. Game after game, as we sipped sodas and ate chips, as Margaux went from Jimi Lee's arms to mine, we filled the Scrabble board with ten-dollar words like *oxazepam, quetzals, quixotry, gherkins, quartz, muzjiks, syzygy, zincate, capeskin,* and *barfi.* We also hit the small words like *pya,* and the two-letter words like *jo, ka, ki, qi, ex, xi, xu,* and *za.* Jimi Lee had lines in her forehead, was serious. It took the Everglades off my mind. We played with strategy, blocked each other, went for double- and triple-word scores. The way we played, they should have called the game Chess with Words.

Jimi Lee said, "I had no idea you were this good."

"Surprised?"

"Very. You're brilliant at this."

"Grew up playing cards, dominoes, and board games."

"We're tied. One more game. I will kick your butt; then we can have a truce."

On the last game, the tiebreaker, I was cursed with the letters *BKNSST* and a blank tile. Jimi Lee played *OP.* With my tiles, *OP* became *stopbanks.* One in a trillion chance of that happening, and it happened. I won.

I laughed and she was about ready to flip the board. My wife showed me she was a sore loser.

Then as our child slept, I went down on my wife, calmed her, licked the animosity out of her soul.

Jimi Lee moaned. "The way you eat me. I love your tongue and the way you eat me."

I wished she had moaned she loved me. That was all I needed to hear. Soon we slept. While people partied and danced to a salsa band outside, ten stories below, we tried to sleep. Margaux was in the bed between us.

Jimi Lee shifted, bounced her feet, sighed, then pouted. I asked her what was wrong.

In a delicate tone she said, "We leave tomorrow afternoon. I don't want to go back home."

I asked, "What's wrong?"

Forever passed before she replied, "I wish I had never contacted my mother."

I didn't question why, just told her, "We have to go home."

"I know. It feels nice to be away from everything."

Nightmares dragged me back to the Everglades. I jerked awake, sweating, panting, and Jimi Lee wasn't in the bed. She was on the other side of the room, hair wrapped, wearing colorful pajamas, her silhouette in the window, gazing down on the party people, watching them enjoy life, sighing like she wished she was down there, not up here. She wanted Harvard. That notebook with her secret writings was clutched in one hand. Her phone was in the other.

CHAPTER 25

Jimi Lee was as tense as a june bug in a henhouse. Within thirty minutes, I'd be as nervous as a long-tailed cat in a room full of rocking chairs. Storm was coming. A few drops of rain fell as I drove my family east toward Diamond Bar. I navigated five lanes of maniacal traffic and Jimi Lee was in the back seat with Margaux, our six-month-old restless in her rear-facing child seat. Jimi Lee sat in the back so our baby could see her mommy. Jimi Lee had on a conservative business suit, her hair pulled back in a bun, eyeglasses on, like we were off to a Fortune 500 meeting. I had on a suit and tie, hair cut in a Caesar to meet her approval. Had a long day with Jake Ellis yesterday, long day at the gym, a five-mile run, and then two jobs for San Bernardino down in San Ysidro, just this side of the Tijuana border. I got home and Jimi Lee handed me Margaux, then went to sleep while I took care of my child, while we bonded. I'd only gotten two hours' sleep.

I asked, "None of your relatives have ever married an American?"

"Slow down."

"I'm doing the speed limit, which is already a crime. Speed limit is speed limit plus twenty on the freeway."

"It's raining."

"Sprinkling."

"Slow down. Turn your windshield wipers and lights on."

I did what she said as I moved to the slow lane, did five miles under the speed limit and pissed off the world.

Jimi Lee played with Margaux as she answered me, "No, but friends of friends have married Americans."

"How did that work out?"

"They didn't last long."

"Why not?"

"Culture clash."

"They married black or white?"

"I have met people who have done both. Same result."

"They all failed?"

"There are no absolutes."

"Well, they might see us as Romeo and Juliet, but Margaux will bring the families together."

"Your optimism astounds me."

"Well, we'll meet my family too. We should've done it all the same time. Two birds, one stone."

"That would be too much for me."

"How do you feel?"

"Fat."

"You look good to me. Your shape has filled out. And that booty."

"Nothing fits."

"Don't fret."

"Slow down."

"If I go any slower, we'll need to take the surface streets."

"I should have done this alone. This time. Then had you come the next time."

I knew it wasn't my driving, wasn't my speed. She wasn't in a hurry to get to her family. They didn't invite me to their home but said they would meet us at Mimi's Café, would break bread with us and have French and American staples in a rustic-inspired setting. In public. Jimi Lee hadn't seen them since she was put out of her home, since she came to me broken down, since she married me. And now the girl who had left Diamond Bar was wife and mother. She was an adult.

"This rain."

"It won't last forever."

"Doesn't feel that way."

"Jimi Lee."

"You can't call me Jimi Lee with them."

"Everyone else calls you Jimi Lee. Lila calls you Jimi Lee."

"Not in front of my family. Not in front of my mother and father. They have never seen me with a boy, not like this. I am their daughter. You have to use my real name. They will think I now want to be American."

"How about I just call you my wife?"

"Use my name. Please? They will take it as a sign of respect."

"Queen of Sheba, your wish, my command."

"And don't be touchy. And don't touch me below the waist. No grabbing my ass."

"So don't act like a newlywed."

"Act civilized. Don't objectify me."

"That's how we ended up where we are."

She toyed with her wedding ring, anxious. I was nervous too.

My mobile phone rang. It was in the back seat.

I told her, "San Bernardino is sending someone to meet me at Mimi's. It's probably them."

"Meeting you why?"

"To drop off money. That thing I had to

take care of up in wine country a few days ago."

"How much?"

"About four thousand."

"What did you and Jake Ellis do? Please tell me it wasn't like Florida."

"Just take the call and say I'll be at Mimi's in the parking lot in twenty minutes."

Margaux sang for attention while Jimi Lee flipped open the phone and answered.

She said, "Ken Swift is driving. I am his wife. My name? Mrs. Swift. And yours? Ethiopian. And you?"

I asked, "Who is that?"

Jimi Lee handed me the phone. I thought it was San Bernardino calling. It was my ex. I hadn't heard from her in more than a year. My Afro-Mexican was back in California and had been trying to get in contact with me.

I said, "I'm married now."

"Married."

"With a beautiful daughter."

Jimi Lee said, "You're on the phone and driving in the rain with your beautiful daughter in the car."

My ex said, "Wow."

I said, "I'm on the way to break bread with my in-laws."

"Wow. In shock. Well, I'm happy for you."

Jimi Lee said, "Please make the call short. For our safety."

I asked my ex, "What are you doing back here on the West Coast?"

"My mother died."

"What happened?"

"She had a heart attack while she was at work."

"Sorry to hear that."

"The funeral is day after tomorrow."

Drivers flipped me off, and I returned the middle finger. People cursed me for my slow driving, honked horns, tried to cut in front of me and make me wreck, and I was tempted to follow one or two and show them who they were fucking with. I sped up. It was hard to ignore people you wanted to gun down to salve road rage.

My wife said, "Ken. The rain is coming down harder. First rain makes the roads slippery."

Then I slowed down, focused, and told my ex, "Let me know where the funeral will be."

"Was hoping to connect with you."

"Well."

"Needed to see you."

"Well."

"A day late and a dollar short."

I paused. "Sorry for your loss. I will try

and send flowers."

"Angelus Funeral Home on Crenshaw. Come to the wake if you can."

"Good hearing from you. Sorry about the circumstances."

My wife said, "Ken."

My ex heard her and said, "I understand. I didn't mean to disrespect your wife."

I exhaled. "She understands."

"Take care."

"You too."

I ended the call and to keep the peace I told Jimi Lee what had happened.

She asked, "Did you love her?"

"We dated."

"How long?"

"Not long."

"A physical relationship."

"We dated. Had fun. Then she left for Johns Hopkins."

"No secret baby?"

"No secret baby."

"Why did she call you?"

"You heard the conversation."

"The connection was severed."

"Guess there was some friendship. I met her mother three or four times."

Jimi Lee nodded. "You were close to her mother?"

"She didn't dislike me."

"Sex the first night?"

"We had a half-dozen dates before it evolved into that."

"Where did you take her?"

"Comedy Act Theater. Eso Won bookstore. World Stage for poetry. Roscoe's Chicken and Waffles."

"Same places you took me."

"I took her wherever I went."

"How many times you sleep with her?"

"Not as much as I have slept with you."

"Afro-Mexican."

"They exist."

"You make her sound like a unicorn."

"Those don't exist."

"Is she pretty?"

"I thought she was. Not many men see the beauty in dark berries and crave a sweeter juice."

"I asked you a yes-or-no question."

"Not as pretty as you."

"You never said that you and she were that close."

"We didn't get married and have a child."

"Slow down. Before we have an accident."

Jimi Lee sucked her teeth, mumbled in Amharic, then went back to tending to Margaux.

Assholes cut me off, cursed, blew horns, and I think I saw one or two brandish guns.

In the back seat Margaux and her mother laughed while I waved at drivers like I was an idiot. In my rearview a car came up fast, switched lanes, zigzagged, and passed in a blur. Little Red Corvette passed us by, doing over a hundred. From the Crenshaw Boulevard on-ramp and at least thirty miles east, CHP had people pulled over at least every mile.

Gelila and her little red Corvette had sped by them all as if the world belonged to her. She was dangerous. Exhilarating. Still had that single-woman, no-kids body and disposition. She reminded me of what life was like when I lived in the fast lane. Too bad Jake Ellis hadn't gone after that. If I were him, I would have fucked the Africa out of her.

CHAPTER 26

Then came the disaster.

God cried hard by the time we squeezed off a sudden traffic backup due to an accident. We hit the crowded parking lot at Mimi's. We were thirty minutes late. The rain and traffic had a few of the other attendees running late, but almost everyone was waiting. The only parking spots were in the back forty, so I had to get Margaux sorted, then let Jimi Lee out at the door. I pulled out the car seat, then handed her and Margaux off to Little Red Corvette.

"Hey, Lila."

"Hey, Ken."

She kissed me on both cheeks, same as she would do when she greeted Jimi Lee. In their culture, cheek kissing was a common greeting between relatives and friends. It didn't mean anything sexual. It was a handshake. Still, it was weird when a woman was close to me like that. My culture never taught me to process that as friendship.

I asked, "How many are here?"

"Quite a few. More people are coming. More than expected."

"Why?"

"The woman you married is very special to them."

Umbrella in hand, Lila had parked and was in the doorway waiting by the time I pulled up. She was dressed in a colorful Ethiopian dress, one that was white and gold and the right hue of red to match her ride, and a colorful shawl. The dress stopped below her knees, and she rocked expensive and beautiful low heels. Her long hair was down, cascading over her shoulders. She looked like a woman who would never use fake ID and sneak into clubs on Sunset, or go off to Santa Barbara to get her freak on with a trust-fund baby. She always had to be the best-dressed and prettiest woman in the building. Not my thinking, but what Jimi Lee had told me about my child's godmother. With a big smile, Lila carried Margaux. More brown-skinned people entered from the rain, older men and their wives, kings and queens, talking in Amharic. They spoke to Jimi Lee and Gelila — she was Gelila now, only Gelila, and not Lila — but once they realized I didn't speak fluent

340

Amharic, saw I wasn't East African, they ignored me.

Lila and Jimi Lee kissed cheeks, did the same with the new people, then joined a few more well-dressed Ethiopians as they walked in. Everyone spoke to one another in Amharic, cut me out of the conversation.

Feeling intimidated and pissed off, I walked away, went to handle my business.

They went inside and by the time I found an empty space, one of San Bernardino's workers was in the parking lot. She pulled up in an '88 Toyota Celica. Her name was Alma. She was three years older than me. A short woman with silver-capped teeth and long hair. She had on a worn Selena T-shirt and baggy jeans. She had crossed three deserts from Central America to work in this America. Her four-year-old daughter, Esmerelda, was in the car with her. Esmerelda had made that three-desert trip with her mother and was born en route.

With a kind, nervous, preoccupied smile, Alma spoke as she handed me an envelope stuffed with cash.

"I have a question, Ken."

"Yeah. Whassup?"

"Should my daughter learn only English, or should I teach her Spanish as well?"

"Why would you only teach her English?"

341

"Maybe she will be treated better."

"Don't rob her of your culture. She should know the language of her people. And California is a very bilingual state, and the way your people are moving up this way and reclaiming your land, the rest of America will eventually be bilingual as well. Being bilingual will get her more career opportunities than only speaking English."

"I asked because a woman I know told me to not teach my daughter Spanish and then she will not have an accent, and then people in her school and everywhere we go will treat her better."

"White people."

"Others too. The Latinos born here treat the ones from Central America and Mexico bad."

"I never knew that."

"Many of them pretend to be white and are ashamed of their parents. That scares me. They refuse to learn Spanish at home, then fail Spanish when they have to take it in school. How is that even possible?"

"I thought all of you were from the same place and worked as one."

"I wish that were true. *Gracias,* Ken."

"*No hay de que,* Alma."

"San Bernardino needs you and Jake Ellis to go to Sacramento next week."

"Can San Bernardino send someone else?"

"I can only tell you what I was told to tell you."

"Hard to leave so much with this new baby in the house."

"Welcome to my life."

I nodded. "How's her dad?"

"He's met a Latina born here, one who sells houses and speaks better English."

"Sorry to hear that."

"She's pregnant and he moved in with her and now he wants to marry her."

"So sorry to hear that."

"We will be fine. We have to be fine."

She drove away, her windshield wipers moving fast while I jogged to get inside Mimi's.

As I trotted, I saw a car I'd seen before. It was the same car I had seen that morning when I was leaving the 7-Eleven on Diamond Bar Boulevard. That Chrysler that held some tough boys who had called me a nigger. I knew it was the same car. I had memorized the plates when they sped away. Was going to ask San Bernardino to get their info, or walk into a DMV and say we'd had a fender bender and get the info myself.

A year had gone by. I was a father now. A year ago, I would've found them in the restaurant and given them some manners. I spat on the car six times as I passed by. If I hadn't been going inside Mimi's I would have left a footprint in its door, then waited for the driver to come out and ask him to repeat what he and his friends had shouted. Every man had to reap what he sowed. A year ago, I would've kicked his ass. Before I was a dad.

Had to focus.

I was here to meet the maternal side of my child's family.

I was here as a father, representing my side of Margaux's family.

I was here to make my first steps toward befriending the Horn of Africa.

Rain dripped from my suit. I made my way through the crowded eatery. This area was mostly white people, Hispanics, and Pacific Islanders, and usually had few people with brown skin at any one spot at one time. Today that had changed. For a moment, I thought I was on Pico and had accidentally walked into an upscale version of Roscoe's Chicken and Waffles, only it was located in the heart of the motherland. All shades of black. I smiled because this was the world I wanted to live in. Well dressed, beautiful, African, cultured. Murmurs in Amharic filled the room. Jimi Lee had reached out to her mother. I knew that Jimi Lee's strict parents were coming, and maybe her siblings would come to see the baby, but there were at least fifty people there. Men were in suits. Women were in formal Ethiopian dresses, beautiful dresses. They had pretty much booked half the eatery.

With each step I felt like I was moving closer to acceptance, to resolution, to a new beginning, but instead I walked into a wall of coldness, was stopped by a collection of attitudes colder than Siberia.

Women who were near Jimi Lee and my child saw me coming and then moved away, went back to their seats, sat next to dates and husbands. I saw people who had to be Jimi Lee's siblings, saw cousins, saw people I had only seen in photos she had brought with her when her parents had thrown her out of the kingdom.

Jimi Lee's father and mother sat at one end of a long table, across from my wife, across from the spot where I was to sit. I spoke to people, in English, as I moved to my seat. No one said anything. Then I spoke in Amharic, said a basic good afternoon. People here on behalf of Jimi Lee looked at me, and very few replied. A few were offended by my tongue speaking their language. I inhaled this family's politics and philosophies. I wasn't from their tribe. Jimi Lee's father scowled at me once, then turned away. So did his wife. I spoke to them but guessed I had become invisible. Jimi Lee said something to her mother in Amharic; then her mother deferred to the patriarch.

I asked Jimi Lee, "What's going on?"

She commanded, "Change Tsigereda's diaper."

Put off by her tone, I paused, then asked, "Why can't you do it?"

Without looking at me, she responded, "Because I told you to."

African-born or -nurtured men looked at me to see what kind of man I was.

"Why don't you change Margaux's diaper?"

She emphasized, *"Tsigereda."*

"Sorry about that, *Adanech.*"

"Change Tsigereda's diaper, please."

My wife ordered me to change my daughter's diaper in front of the men in order to show her dominance over me. I was about to say something and embarrass us all. But the room was filled with beautiful people, beautiful women. The women looked smart, enlightened, intelligent but at the same time were very unlike African American women,

346

women who looked just as fine as the women from Africa who had their eyes on me. These women were strong, but the men had position, said that no matter how hard their woman worked, when the man came home from his job, he would enter a home where food was prepared, where his clothes would be ironed on weekends.

I regarded her father, a slim man at least thirty years older and six inches shorter than I was, and with a Mississippi smile I said, "How are you doing, sir? We haven't been properly introduced. Mr. Zenebework, my name is Ken Swift. I'm married to your daughter and I am the father of your beautiful granddaughter, Tsigereda. We really wish you could have come to the wedding. I wish we had met before now. Despite the circumstances, which I apologize for, it's a pleasure and honor to finally have a chance to meet you and the rest of your beautiful family."

I extended my hand, the only olive branch I had to offer, and he still didn't look my way.

He whispered something to his wife, to Jimi Lee's mother, to the woman I knew was named Menna, to a woman who refused to acknowledge my existence, and she shifted, body language closed, and said something to Jimi Lee, spoke to Jimi Lee, and my wife was nervous, a little girl in their presence. I'd never seen Jimi Lee in that subservient mode. I stopped standing like a statue and took my hand back. Lila was seated next to Jimi Lee, and she saw the awkwardness, understood something I didn't, and she stood up, offered to change her goddaughter's diaper, but Jimi Lee didn't hand her over.

Her father looked at me, then turned away and mumbled, "You are not worthy to breathe the same air."

I said, "Excuse me?"

Brows furrowed, he frowned. "This, Adanech?"

"Father."

"This, instead of being almost a junior at Harvard. Your friends are attending Brown University, Columbia University, Cornell University, Dartmouth College, Harvard University, the University of Pennsylvania, Princeton University, and Yale University. Your friends are making their parents proud. Your friends have taken the road that will give them amazing futures. Yale and Harvard wanted you. And this, this is what you have chosen."

Those words, in English, were directed at Jimi Lee, but I knew they were meant for my ears.

Jimi Lee opened her mouth to speak again, but no words came.

Tears fell, but there were no words.

Her mother didn't reach for her, didn't try to console her, and no one else did either.

Margaux cried.

Jimi Lee's father adjusted his necktie and frowned, took in the restless grandchild who cried and made this moment real, shook his head and said, "Of all the lives, this is the life you have chosen."

I stood tall, dark, handsome, and fearless. Barely an adult, but still a man.

A husband. Not a child.

Again, I addressed the patriarch, said, "Adanech is your daughter, but she is also my wife. Man to man, no matter your age, there is some bull I won't tolerate. Not even from you. Please, address my wife with respect."

My words made Jimi Lee shudder and shake her head, but I remained invisible to him.

I said, "I came here to make friends, make new family, not become enemies."

A twenty-something guy seated on the other side of the table facing Jimi Lee spoke up, said something in Amharic, sounded as if he defended Jimi Lee, and Jimi Lee countered, made him stop talking. Her father owned the room. He said what he wanted to say, said what he wanted me to hear in English, then turned away and talked in Amharic to the men seated near him. I took my daughter and headed to the bathroom to change her, and Lila walked with me, did her best to keep up with my aggravated pace. Her heels clicked as she carried the diaper bag.

Lila said, "Let me take Tsigereda into the proper girls' bathroom and change her expeditiously."

"Her name is Margaux."

"Let me do my duty as godmother."

"And her last name is Swift."

Not many changing tables were in men's toilets. In public, it was still a woman's job.

But that didn't bother me. I had no problem wiping the excrement from my child's ass.

I asked Lila, "Who is the guy seated directly across from my wife?"

"His name is Yohanes."

"A sibling?"

"Family friend."

"Where is he from?"

"We all grew up together."

"What does he do?"

"Rocket scientist."

"He's very interested in my wife."

"Well."

"Why am I getting the cold shoulder from my father-in-law?"

"He's the leader. They will do what he says. Unless Menna disapproves."

"So, he's the slave master and this is his plantation unless Miss Ann disagrees."

"He's an elder. Everyone here is under his influence."

"He's rude as fuck."

"Strict and can be violent. The Ethiopian National Defense Force is still in his blood."

"Ruder than white people when King tried to cross a bridge in Selma, Alabama."

"Of all of his children, Jimi Lee was his special pride and joy."

"What did he say in Amharic?"

"You . . . basically he says you ruined her."

"She was ruined when I met her."

"That her life will be the life of a *black American* now."

"He said that?"

"Yes. Well, he didn't call you a *black American.*"

"What did he call me?"

"Well."

"What the fuck did he call me?"

"He pretty much called you N.W.A. without the W.A."

"Half of your people are darker than burnt toast, and he called me —"

"Don't let him upset you. He has his ways."

"And I have mine."

"Well, from a father's perspective, you ruined his perfect daughter."

"Jimi Lee ruined me."

"Well, her need for coffee and jazz met your need to jazz, and here you are."

"She wasn't the only one who had plans."

"Just ride this out. Just have dinner and ride this out. It won't last more than two hours."

"My wife tried to emasculate me."

"She's stressed."

"She talked down to me like she was better than me."

"Jimi Lee wanted . . . needed you to leave the room so she could talk to her mother and father."

"They brought a nation."

"Jimi Lee is . . . was very important to them. She was their intellectual Doris Day. Their Shirley Temple in brown skin. She was the last one anyone imagined having a child. Everyone is shocked to see her like this. They want their daughters to see her, to see what happens when a girl fails to do as she has been instructed."

"She's afraid of him. He used to beat her."

"He is from Ethiopia. Not here. He is from where children still experience corporal punishment at schools and severe punishments at home. Corporal punishment is lawful in the home. It is required for proper upbringing. You won't understand that. Here in America, a parent spanks a child, the child calls nine-one-one, and the parent is arrested."

"You think it's any different for children in Mississippi? My people don't spare the rod or spoil the child."

"Tsigereda is crying, Ken."

"Here, *Gelila*. *Margaux* is reaching for you."

"Because you're scaring her."

"Nobody wants shit to do with me now."

"Don't say that. That's how Jimi Lee's father wants you to feel."

Lila took Margaux, grabbed the diaper bag, and hurried into the ladies' room.

A brown-haired white boy passed by, bumped me, didn't apologize. Of all the people to body check me and keep going, it was that motherfucker. Baggy jeans. Lakers jersey. Kareem's number. Lots of people stopped wearing Magic's number after they found out he was HIV-positive. He went into the men's room. Amazing how a white

353

boy could call a black man a nigger, dress like Tupac, and listen to Cube while he rocked Air Jordans and Kareem's number. While my daughter was being changed, while my wife was being treated like a child, as my temper flared, I followed that brown-haired boy. Wanted to see if he remembered me. Needed him to know I remembered him from a year ago. Needed to hit somebody, pretend they were Jimi Lee's dad, and make them feel my unwarranted pain.

CHAPTER 27

The next week I took Jimi Lee and Margaux to meet my parents and my siblings. My parents lived less than two miles away from my spot in Leimert Park, up in the hills. I hadn't seen them in two years. No love was lost between us. After that two-hour visit, Jimi Lee didn't want to meet my southern-born and raised parents again. I felt the same about hers, and it didn't matter that they were from the Horn of Africa. Her parents and my parents would never break bread. Mississippi would never invite Ethiopia to the Black Beverly Hills for a backyard barbecue.

I wished I had never bought my old man those trees.

I was so pissed off I wanted to rip them all from the ground.

Jimi Lee said, "I hate your mother. I will hate her beyond my grave."

"Calm down."

"After what she has done, the way she treated me, don't tell me to calm down."

"I'm sorry."

"She's a goat."

"Don't call my mother a goat."

"Donkeys have better manners. Your father and siblings are no better."

In Amharic I told my wife, *"Ayzoh."*

She snapped, "No, it will not be okay."

"Enen."

"I don't need your damn apology. She insulted me and my child. She should apologize, not you."

"Jimi Lee."

"I repeat, your mother is a goat. A donkey. No better than a cow. And you defended her."

"She is no worse than your father. No worse than your mother. They were no better than hogs."

"Fuck you. Motherfucker, fuck you."

My jaw tightened and I gave her silence. It was for her own good. For my own good.

Then, brows furrowed, ignoring our crying child, over and over she said, "This, Adanech?"

I reached for Margaux, but my daughter rejected me. She wanted her mother. Her mother wanted nothing to do with us. So we had a triangle of anger, rejection, and misery. I picked up Margaux anyway, held her in my arms.

Jimi Lee said, "You talked me into this. You bamboozled me into this world of yours."

Jimi Lee wanted that other life. The one where her parents were proud of her.

The life in which my daughter and I never existed.

CHAPTER 28

Back at home, days later, tension high, we sat at the dining room table.

I looked at Jimi Lee, saw she had the blues, then asked, "What's the new issue?"

"I talked to a couple of friends. They are at Yale and Harvard studying, going to frat parties, being courted by sororities. I feel like I'm living in an alternate universe and I keep waiting to wake up in my bed at Diamond Bar."

"You're singing that woe-is-me song every goddamn hour of every goddamn day."

"Don't curse me. Don't ever talk to me in such a way again."

"Go. If you are that miserable, leave Margaux with me. We'll be fine."

"I'm not abandoning her."

"I'm her father. You won't be abandoning her. This isn't the front door of a fire station."

"Mothers can never abandon their children and be considered worthy of living."

"What do we do then? How do we take care of Margaux and get you happy again?"

"I'm married to you. No longer eligible for my scholarships."

"Your father has gotten in your head."

"And we're living in this small apartment. I can't breathe. My parents had a large home, and I had my own room, I had peace and tranquility, but here, nothing but chaos, and this cave feels like a dungeon. I hear rap music; I hear street sounds; I hear adults cursing; I hear children cursing; and I hear it all day long."

"Well, I've missed my escape from here, just like you."

"I was Ivy League. Ivy League."

"And when you made it to Harvard, they'd still call you a nigger."

"Do you know how hard I had to work from the beginning, how careful I had to be, how hard I had to study, how much I had to sacrifice in order to be smarter than every white boy and girl in every class in Diamond Bar? And even then, they wanted to create two valedictorians, let one be white, when my GPA was much higher."

"I didn't know that. And at the same time, I'm not surprised."

"You know nothing about me."

"Your first time living in an apartment and you act like this is a concentration camp."

"You think I've had no struggle. My mother counseled me all of my life, and I have let her down. She told me not to go into the arts, to select a field that pays, a field that is new and go into it through the front door. I was to pick one subject and focus, pick a field and become the expert, because that is what an African woman has to do. She wanted me to be powerful and self-sufficient, not dependent on any man."

"I'm sorry."

"Stop saying you're sorry about everything."

"Well, it's starting to feel that way."

"And make Margaux stop that damn crying. Tsigereda, please be quiet. Shut up."

Jimi Lee showered, dressed, stormed by me as I held Margaux, the colicky child still crying in my arms. Jimi Lee left the apartment, hurried down the thirteen concrete stairs out front, went to the curb, hit the remote, got into our convertible Benz, let the drop top down, sped away, left us to sort it out, and didn't come back until two in the morning. She staggered in, smelled like Riesling and sticky green. That meant Margaux's food source was tainted. I was pissed as fuck. We argued until the sun came up; then I tended to Margaux all day, and as soon as she took a nap, I was in Jimi Lee's face, and we argued until the sun went back down.

While we stood in the kitchen, as Margaux slept, I asked, "How do we fix this?"

Jimi Lee slammed a glass onto the floor, made it shatter into a thousand pieces.

I yelled, "Have you lost your goddamned mind? Why did you do that?"

She looked at me, tears in her eyes, and asked, "How do you fix that broken glass? How do you put that back together? Everything can't be fixed, so stop asking me how to fix it."

I grabbed a broom. "Margaux could crawl and get glass in her knee. Or get it in her hand. Or pick up a piece and eat it. What the fuck were you thinking? You stupid . . . stupid . . ."

"Say it."

"I'm getting tired of your shit."

She sat down at the kitchen table and cried, gave up her pain, sorrow, hate, grief.

I said, "Let's take parenting classes. Let's be better parents, for Margaux, if nothing else."

She marched away, opened and closed drawers, made them bang with her ire. Two minutes later, she was out the door. She left

361

without a good-bye. She wasn't back home at sunrise. I didn't look for her. After lunch, I took Margaux to the park in Ladera, put her in a swing for a while. While she laughed and went up to the smog-tinted clouds, while I hoped she didn't get allergies or asthma breathing this shit, I cried. I was glad Jimi Lee was gone, and I was crying because I knew she would come back. I wanted her to go the fuck away, vanish from my life.

When we made it back home, Jimi Lee was in the kitchen, cooking.

I handed her Margaux; then I walked out the door. Margaux cried, broke into tears, didn't want her mother to hold her, called for her daddy, but I kept going until I couldn't hear her cries.

I used Margaux's cries to punish Jimi Lee.

Jake Ellis was in front of my building, waiting on me to come down.

He asked, "You good with this local job, or should San Bernardino send in someone else?"

"Let's do this shit. Let's bust some heads and pay some bills."

Horns blew over and over. A U-Haul truck was out front, across the street. Four Mexicans were blocking the one lane of traffic on that side of Stocker. They unloaded enough furniture to fill a one-bedroom apartment. A taller-than-average girl was on that side, a light-skinned black woman in her early twenties. She yelled and pointed at what to take where. She had a small waist, wore itty-bitty pink shorts and a yellow top, a UK-branded hoodie around her waist.

Jake Ellis said, "She's from London."

"You know the yellow gal."

"Bernice Nesbitt. She's here to go to LMU."

"Loyola Marymount University. The Christian university on the hill."

She waved at us, smiled. We kept going, not in the mood to move furniture.

Unsettled, unhappy, I looked back up at my window. I saw Jimi Lee and heard Margaux's cries.

I told Jake Ellis, "Let's go."

He waved up at my window, said hello to my wife, then followed me and caught up.

Jake Ellis said, "So her folks actually did that shit?"

"Yeah. The tab for that dinner at Mimi's ended up in my lap."

"You paid?"

"Maxed out my Discover card."

"They played you."

"Motherfuckers didn't even leave a tip."

"Well, you tried."

"I had on new socks and drawers and was treated like I was a crackhead."

"That's why your momma wasn't nice when she met Jimi Lee."

"That meeting with my people was worse than the one with Jimi Lee's people."

"Jimi Lee doesn't want anything to do with your family up in the Black Beverly Hills."

"As much as I want to do with her folks out in white-ass Diamond Bar."

CHAPTER 29

Jake Ellis and I walked out of Leimert Park, went two miles away to an area called the Jungle. The area was built in the forties and was one of the first developments of high-density apartment living in Los Angeles. It used to be a prestigious white area. Banana plants, palm trees, begonias. Now it was a Mexican and black neighborhood; signs said Section 8 was accepted. There was a con man there who owed San Bernardino some money.

I knocked on that man's door, and when his guard answered, I rushed in, knocked him to the floor, and beat him half to death. My mind was still at Mimi's Café. Jake Ellis had sprinted by me, beat the Mexican con man to his gun, then knocked that man into the floor. Jake Ellis was done with the job and I was still taking my frustrations out on that delinquent Mexican's bodyguard. Then I went after the Mexican. After a half-dozen knockout blows, Jake Ellis reined me in, pulled me away. I was still back at Mimi's, imagining I was beating Jimi Lee's dad into the pavement.

Jake Ellis said, "Fuck, man. We just supposed to scare 'em and give 'em black eyes."

"They're scared."

"As fuck."

The bodyguard moaned, *"Señor."*

At the same time Jake and I snapped, "Shut up."

Jake Ellis went to the refrigerator, took out two beers, tossed me one. I opened mine and poured it on the men at my feet. Then I motioned for Jake Ellis to toss me another one. I popped the top and took a swig.

Jake Ellis said, "Jimi Lee got you twisted and acting like a fool."

"Señor."

At the same time we barked, "Shut up."

I sipped my beer again, sat in a worn-out chair, vented, told Jake Ellis all of my problems.

He asked, "What you gonna do?"

"I'm married with a kid."

"Trapped."

"Only takes one good nut to put a man in a bad predicament."

"A bad nut can have the same result. But

I don't think there is such a thing as a bad nut. It doesn't matter if the nut is good or bad; it can put a woman with a good egg in the same position."

"Señor."

"Shut up."

I nodded. "If Jimi Lee left, Margaux and I'd be fine."

"You'd keep the baby?"

"Margaux is mine. That's my daughter. She's my blood."

"What about her momma?"

"Jimi Lee is just some crazy chick I met in a club. A Diamond Bar chick looking for LA dick and I fell for a cute little butt and a smile in a white miniskirt and slipped and dipped and tripped myself into the trap of all traps."

"Whatever you just said, you don't mean that."

"Bro, sometimes you have to show a motherfucker that fat meat's greasy."

"Bruv, I have no idea what that means either."

We dragged both of the men downstairs, stuffed them in the trunk of the wounded man's car. We drove them to San Bernardino, made that three-hour drive, and dropped them off with the person they feared most.

We were paid, offered three more jobs, one in Memphis, one in Florida, and another in Utah.

We had another beer; then we caught a taxi back to Leimert Park.

Jake Ellis said, "Worried about you, bruv."

"What's wrong?"

"You're drinking too much."

"Alcohol was made to numb the effects of marriage."

"I guess your wife needs an AA program."

"Fuck you."

I stopped by Jake Ellis's apartment. His spot was like mine, filled with modern furniture nice enough to be in a middle-class house. Enough books for a library. He had two West Indian girls come by. One was from Trinidad and the other was from Antigua. Two hot women with million-dollar shapes. Jake Ellis put on soca and the girls started drinking Jamaican beer and whining, set free fluid, sensual, and rhythmic dances. Jake Ellis took out the pots and pans, broke out the special spices, the recipes from Ghana, and cooked *chichinga*, red red, *banku*, and fried rice with chicken. Homie made Jollof rice better than anyone from Nigeria, Senegal, Gambia, Sierra Leone, Liberia, Ivory Coast, Togo, or Cameroon.

While Jake Ellis threw down in the kitchen, Ghanaian music by Akyeame, Daddy Lumba, and Kojo Antwi played. Some soca by Red Plastic Bag, Mighty Gabby, and Edwin Yearwood was in the mix too. Jake Ellis was living the life I had given up. The island girls danced the island dances, drank, smiled, flirted, would have kicked it with me, but I walked away, left both with Jake Ellis. I was angry, but I was still a married man.

When I made it back home, Margaux was no longer crying. She was on the floor in a sea of toys. The television was on, a Christian kiddie video. *VeggieTales.* Jimi Lee looked at my bloodied knuckles, then took our child and hurried into the bedroom. She locked the door behind them. The house was a mess. Jimi Lee never cleaned up. She was always too tired. I didn't make a big deal of it. I did what needed to be done. I washed dishes. Swept. Mopped. Vacuumed. Cleaned the toilet. Wiped away dust. Cleaned the stove and the top of the refrigerator. Emptied the diaper pail. Cleaned inside the microwave and countertops; did the same for the cabinet doors. Put toys away. Opened windows. Sprayed the house to make it smell as fresh as I could. I heard Margaux crying; then the weeping stopped. I assume her mother gave her the titty, tainted or not. I tended to my knuckles, took the two baskets of laundry we had, and drove to a late-night Laundromat in Hollywood on Western Avenue. Washed clothes. Dried clothes. Folded clothes. When I returned, Jimi Lee came out, dressed to the nines, nice pants, sexy top, high heels, face done, perfume popping. Without saying a word, she handed me Margaux and walked out the door.

It wasn't easy taking care of three people. A lot of women assumed that there was no stress in a man being a provider. It was hard. But I did it. People never talked about the stress a man felt when he was trying to keep the ship from sinking, when he felt like he was on the *Titanic* throwing water out with a teacup, and no one was helping him keep what he had afloat. It felt like for every cup of water I threw away, someone threw in two gallons of piss.

Jimi Lee couldn't stand being with Margaux all day long.

If I didn't have anywhere to go, Jimi Lee would leave first thing in the morning and not come back until it was time to put Margaux down for the night. If I had to go off to work, she would bail the minute I got in from doing a job, would be at the door waiting for me to pull up in my car, and would be out the door before I made it to the porch. I felt for Margaux. No child should have to go through that, but that was where we were. Jimi Lee would snap at me and scream that being with the baby all day was driving her mad, said she had to go out and drink some dark liquor to calm her nerves, needed to dance away stress. She was nineteen, a mother, using a fake ID to hit all the clubs.

She said, "I should be back east, halfway to my bachelor's, planning to work on my master's. I'm living in the ghetto. I flew too close to the sun and this is where I crashed."

"This isn't the ghetto. I'm fucking tired of you calling my zip code the ghetto. I can take you to Mississippi and show you trailer parks where white people live and wish they had it this good."

"Please don't."

"It's not Bel Air, but nobody is walking the streets barefoot. This is a working-class neighborhood. This isn't an African American version of poverty-stricken Coronation Park in Johannesburg. This isn't as dangerous as Cape Town. This isn't the suburbs. This is LA. You're around real people."

"A store called the Liquor Bank is on the

corner."

"So what?"

"Liquor Bank? How many hot wings places are there in a square mile? How many barbershops and beauty shops do they need? Crenshaw Boulevard is atrocious from the 10 freeway all the way down to the 105, and it's been that way since the lootings and arsons from the LA riots. There are no pleasing aesthetics."

"And Ethiopia has streets of gold and families have a camel in every pot."

"Go to hell. You know nothing about where I am from."

"Tell Sally Struthers those commercials don't exactly make Ethiopia look like Rodeo Drive."

"*Nothing.* Reading a textbook, reading a few paragraphs about Africa, learning a fact or two, does not mean you know Africa. You have to travel and experience a place, know the five senses of a place, meet the people."

Sober, not having sex, having to share a bathroom, a kitchen, having to become parents, our focus changed and we'd become as compatible as oil and water. We had arguments over everything and nothing, became as explosive as Coke and Mentos. She would get angry and yell at me only in Amharic, and she knew that pissed me off because I couldn't understand. We were as dangerous as drinking and driving. Every quarrel left my mouth tasting like toothpaste and orange juice. It was complicated. But that didn't make me want Jimi Lee any less. I loved her.

Every time San Bernardino paged me, I went to make that money. I went to work out my rage. I hurt men, beat men like it was personal, made money, and gave Jimi Lee most of the dead presidents I made.

CHAPTER 30

Margaux took her first steps.

I was twenty-three. Jimi Lee was twenty, still rocking illegal identification, her hair long, pressed. She looked amazing with her hair straight. Like a model. And she knew she did. We were kids trying to be adults and failing with every breath we took. I had enough to deal with trying to keep Jimi Lee in line. It felt like I'd taken her father's place, had become strict, had to lay down rules, and she refused to follow any of them. She continued to rebel.

Somewhere between sucking tongues and being fondled by a stranger, she'd forgotten she had a husband and a daughter waiting on her at home. Once she woke up at the motel at the top of Overhill, two miles from our apartment. She had woken up alone, with a hangover, and called me crying, begged me to come get her because she was in a fix. Whoever she had been with had stolen her clothes and taken her purse. She was too naïve for my zip code. Once I ended up banging on some six-foot-tall guy's front door, Margaux in my arms, telling the half-naked guy to send me my child's mother so I could take her home because I had to get my ass to work. Her boy toy challenged me. A minute later, he was upside down in a corner, begging for mercy, my knuckles bloody red from trying to bust him every way I could.

While my daughter cried and my wife yelled at me like I was the one in the wrong, I stepped away. My unfaithful wife went to him, was apologizing to him, told him this verified she had married the wrong man.

I grabbed Jimi Lee by her hair and dragged her with me. She was screaming in English and Amharic and my child was in my other arm, crying in what sounded like English.

When I looked in a mirror, I no longer recognized myself.

I didn't know who the fuck I was.

It took a couple of months, but Jimi Lee was back in our bed, sometimes sleeping naked under a T-shirt. Sometimes I woke up and she had her head resting on my chest, or she had her body wrapped around mine, spooning. Sometimes I woke up to her playing Ethiopian reggae music and dancing in the glow of happiness. She had become passive-aggressive, oscillated between love and hate, between liking me and not being able to tolerate my existence. My heart and mind couldn't take her bullshit, and that made every day a struggle to cope.

I asked, "What's going on?"

In the softest voice, she whispered, "You're a good man."

"I could be better."

"You're a good father."

"But am I a good husband?"

"You are a better husband than I am a wife."

"When you want to be a good wife, you're damn good."

"I'll do better. I promise. I'll do better."

"We have to be a team."

"Margaux is sleeping."

"She's knocked out."

"Truce?"

"Truce."

"Shower and I'll give you an apology blow job."

She became her child's mother again and became as busy as a hen with one chick, had time for no one except her child. We went to Disneyland. To parks. To beaches.

Margaux loved Build-A-Bear. We did it all as a family. Soon I couldn't get Jimi Lee to put Margaux down for longer than two seconds. Both smiled, played, and laughed. They had finally bonded. We had a few good weeks. Then Jimi Lee's mood changed again.

Recidivism. She went back to her old ways.

One night, around midnight, there was a knock at the door and a college boy was out there asking for Adanech Zenebework. Jimi Lee had given him her Ethiopian name. He had to be a junior, no more than twenty, said my wife was his girlfriend. Said he had been seeing her for almost two months. I smiled, opened the door, shirtless, a pistol-grip pump at my side, asked him if he was sleeping with my wife, and the butter-and-egg man took off running.

He had already been to my apartment. Had been naked in my bed. Had shit in my toilet.

Weeks later, it was some professor she had met at the grocery store.

Then a CSULB grad student she had met at the mall.

After that, a New Yorker she had exchanged info with at the public library in

Culver City.

The next one was some light-skinned brother she had met when she was pushing Margaux in a stroller, exercising on the track field at Dorsey High.

She was young, needed to have fun, had to dance and de-stress. I had no problems with that because I liked having a good time too, but she wanted to get sexy and party without me. She wanted to get away from me like she'd wanted to get away from her strict parents. She lied to me the same way she had lied to her father.

She told me she was going to have drinks with Lila at a bar near Malibu. Lila. The one she'd used as an excuse with her parents for her sins and indiscretions. People show you who they are when you meet them. But I'd been too busy looking at her ass to listen to her words.

Jimi Lee would get drunk and too friendly, cause trouble, just like she did the night I met her.

When an unhappy woman was that damn fine, there was no shortage of erections volunteering to get her through the night. She was beautiful. Men would fight over her like she was the last woman on the planet.

I was twenty-five. My unhappy wife was

twenty-two.

The innocent one in all of this, Margaux, was three.

I grew tired of fighting motherfuckers. I got tired of hitting motherfuckers when I wasn't being paid.

A lovesick fool would knock on the door, and I'd tell Jimi Lee to go see what her newest butter-and-egg man wanted before I put both of them in the ground, and to make sure that motherfucker never passed by my door again.

I turned twenty-seven. Jimi Lee turned twenty-four.

Margaux was five. She was taking a nap.

Jimi Lee and I were at the kitchen table, at the end of our millionth argument.

I sipped Ethiopian Yirgacheffe coffee and said, "I can't do this another year."

Without hesitation, she responded, "I feel the same way."

My skin was breaking out. My sanity was loosening. Murder stayed on my mind.

Love made men murderers and made many women become the same.

One of us would kill the other.

I told her, "We can't stay together. I can move out, if that will make it better."

"No, stay. I want to move back to Diamond Bar. I need you to get me a place out there. I found a rental on Golden Springs Drive and it will cost two thousand a month, plus utilities."

"So, you've already found a place?"

"An agent showed me a two-bedroom condo."

"An agent?"

"I need first, last, and security deposit."

"Sure. If that's what you want. Move out. Send a postcard or visit us when you can."

"Margaux goes with me."

I was about to challenge her, but she was the mother. "I won't argue."

"And I've already worked out how much support I'll need."

"Already worked out the money?"

"We both know this is coming to an end."

"Do we separate?"

"Let's not drag this out."

"Divorce?"

"Yes. I have the papers."

"You have this mapped out, all the way to seeing Judge Mablean Ephriam."

"We have been married long enough for a quick divorce to seem respectable."

"Respectable?"

"Yes."

"A five-year marriage isn't a state record."

"But it's respectable. For both of us.

You're a man who stayed married for five years."

"You're unhappy."

"I feel like I have no options. Like I'm imprisoned at times."

"We had a baby, Jimi Lee. All we did was make a beautiful baby."

"I never wanted this life."

"Then I won't belabor the point and act like wanting a divorce from me is unexpected."

"Don't be dramatic. Let's not make this any harder than it needs to be."

I took a breath, then told her, "Happy birthday."

"Yeah. Happy birthday to you, too."

"I guess we're not going to Harold and Belle's for dinner."

She said, "Would be better if we talked about child support."

"Okay."

"And alimony."

"I'll pay alimony. For one year."

"Four years."

"One year of reparations."

"Four years."

"Your college years."

"Even if I marry again, I deserve alimony for four years."

"You're entitled to four years of reparations."

"Don't call it that."

"What would you call it?"

"Reimbursement for tuition lost."

"You want me to repay you for your scholarship?"

"I deferred my entry into university by a year, had a gap year, met you, got pregnant, had your child, lost scholarships, and I have lost a career where I would make much, much more. I should be in grad school. No, I should be working on my PhD. I should be ahead of Lila. I see her growth. When I go for drinks with her, I meet her friends, her new friends, say I am married with a child, and the look they give me cuts deep, like I've wasted my life."

"Classism."

"I see the types of friends she has. Intellectuals. They have conversations about meaningful things, conversations with a worldview, conversations not as myopic and repetitive as yours. So, yes, four years of alimony. Four years of tuition. I am not asking for any more than I already had before I met you. I want what I have lost. That is the least you can do. I need help getting on my feet. I'm still depending on you."

"I'm not a bank. And if you remarry, you

become someone else's bill."

"In that case, I will never marry. You'll pay. And I'm depending on you to pay child support and to pay for her education, for day care, for her private schools, until she's twenty-one."

"Law says eighteen, and private schools aren't required, not when public schools are around. You can't ask me to pay for what the government has made available to the public."

"My daughter will not go to a public school. The schools are filled with gang-bangers. They have metal detectors at the front doors and they look like prisons. The children curse out the teachers. I've talked to other mothers when I've gone walking. Every child in Baldwin Hills, View Park, Windsor Hills, and Ladera goes to a private school. They refuse to send their kids to Crenshaw and Inglewood High, and those schools are no more than five minutes away. They'd rather drive an hour in traffic one-way and pay to get their kids educated in the Palisades."

"With the snowy faces."

"At the better schools, so they will have a better chance to achieve in this country."

"How'd that work out for you?"

"Fuck you."

"Child maintenance and four years of reparations. Any other demands?"

"Don't forget. I know about Florida."

"Is that a threat?"

"A gentle reminder. I remember that man's name. Balthazar Walkowiak. It came up in the Florida newspapers that he went missing. He was never found. He had a memorial service. Police had all kinds of theories. The news in Miami did a big special on Balthazar Walkowiak. I followed the story in case it came to my front door."

"Now you're saying you'll bring it to my front door, if you have to."

"I can't get the name Balthazar Walkowiak out of my head."

"Neither can I."

"Nor the time and date you came back to the hotel room covered in blood."

"Neither can I."

She handed me a worn sheet of paper.

Months ago, she'd worked out how much she wanted. It was an outrageous amount of money. Forty grand a year, health insurance, clothing, and a dozen other things. Middle-class families didn't make that much in a year. I read the demand and laughed, then tossed it in the trash. Wanted to punch a hole in the wall.

A man was born free but was not content

until he had made himself someone's slave.
Jake Ellis knew that. His life would always
be better, because he was emotionally
smarter.

I said, "We'll come up with a fair amount
and it's done."

"We're depending on you. Your daughter
is depending on you to be upstanding."

"I can't pay that kind of money if I don't
have that kind of money."

"Then you'd better tell the thugs in San
Bernardino to keep you busy."

The way she said that told me she wanted
a fight. I didn't give her fuel.

I just nodded and said, "I will do just
that."

"When do you leave again?"

"In three days."

"For how long?"

"Will be gone two days."

"We'll be gone when you get back."

"You don't want me here?"

"It will be easier that way."

"What are you taking?"

"Her stuff. My stuff. Things we need."

"Furniture?"

"We need some furniture. What can I
take?"

"Take it all if you want."

"The Compaq laptop?"

"You use it more than I do. Take it."

"Are you sure?"

"I'll get another one. Take all the floppy discs, but leave the ones with the photos and videos."

"I don't want to take everything."

"What I own belongs to Margaux. Take it for her. She needs familiar things."

She nodded. "Then we have an agreement."

"Who is going to help you move?"

"Lila will help me."

"Then you won't take much."

"We will take what we can carry and fit into our cars."

Two days later, I held my laughing daughter as I packed my bags, took what I needed to be gone across the country for a couple of days. I packed, head hurting, heart aching, mood foul, knowing Jimi Lee was leaving. I would have bet my last dime her mother and father were celebrating our breakup. I should have celebrated too.

While we were in the car, Jake Ellis asked, "Jimi Lee's moving out?"

I told him, "She said she is."

"She packed anything?"

"Nothing I could see."

"She's bluffing. When you get back, she'll

have a big Ethiopian dinner and apology ready."

"Lila is helping."

"That's the one you should have been with."

"You didn't tap that?"

"Lila? Nah, bruv. I'm the wrong kind of African and not the right kind of white man for her."

"I could say the same thing about Jimi Lee."

CHAPTER 31

I returned to an empty apartment.

All the furniture was gone. Except for the Italian bed and the Sony television. The Sony television was state-of-the-art and weighed more than a hundred pounds, took two or three people to carry. The television in the living room was gone. It would've been easier to carry. I opened her closet and saw nothing but hangers and poles. This was real. She had taken the car too. The car was five years old now, had depreciated, like we had. I was surprised she didn't demand a new ride. Divorce papers were on the counter. Her section had already been signed, and signed hastily, like she couldn't sign those papers fast enough. I signed them. Brought this failed marriage to an end.

Jake Ellis stood in my empty living room. "Damn, bro."

"Yeah."

"Well, you free now. You can come back to Africa with me."

"I should do that. I should just vanish. I have enough money to last a while."

He took me to grab a bite to eat at Roscoe's Chicken and Waffles in Hollywood, where the stars and pretty women went to be seen sucking on greasy chicken bones. After we ate, he drove me to buy groceries. Jake Ellis dropped me off at my new life, then headed back to his apartment up the way, on the other side of Leimert Park.

I sat on the tossed bed.

I had silence once again.

I had peace.

It wasn't freedom. But it was peaceful.

I went to the closet, looked in the shoe box that doubled as my bank.

All the money was gone.

I was penniless except for the money I'd just made. Escaping to Africa was out of the question.

But I was free. Freedom ain't never been free. Now, like Haiti had been forced to do to France once they had been liberated from slavery, I'd have to make payments. She had had the first word, the last word, and most of the words in between. But I was free. I'd never have to look at Jimi Lee again.

That felt good and bad at the same time.

But what felt horrible was that Margaux was gone, and I had left her crying and my heart breaking.

That was her last image of me.

In the bathroom, taped to the mirror, Jimi Lee had left me one picture of her holding my child. My wife was smiling, my daughter laughing. It was like she was telling me they would be happier without me.

I saw that photo and cried.

Their happiness didn't include me.

Once again I felt .38 hot and needed to calm the hell down.

I picked up the phone and called Jake Ellis.

Jake said, "Wash your ass and put some clothes on. We're going to hang out at the spot."

By eleven P.M., we were on Rosecrans Avenue in a skanky strip club in the mostly Japanese American city called Gardena. I was getting a lap dance from a shorty with a big ass, a brown-skinned black girl with perm-straight hair. She could dance so good she could make men come in their pants, and she did that with a flashlight glowing in her vagina. I'd never seen a woman with that much energy, one who could move like that. Had never seen a glowing coochie. Two shots of rum and a beer later, I said two tears in a bucket, wanted the glowing coochie.

I asked, "What a bro gotta do for you to help him get off after you get off?"

"Boo, I'm a lesbian."

"You tricked me."

"I trick all men because all men are tricks. I take their money and laugh all the way home."

"How does lesbian sex work?"

"Both women come, no one gets AIDS, then they go shopping."

"The way you work that ass."

"I'd hook you up for a fee."

"Thought you were lesbian."

"I can be straight for pay. But not tonight. My girlfriend is here watching me."

"Who else is working on tuition or paying off student loans?"

She motioned. A pretty girl was on stage, complexion by Europe, butt by Africa, hair in a big reddish Afro, naked from the top up, all of five feet tall, dancing like sin, in clear heels tall enough to give somebody a nosebleed.

She said, "I bet you'd like her."

"I like dark-skinned women."

"Close your eyes and we're all dark-skinned."

■ ■ ■ ■

A little after three in the morning, I was half-drunk and had a Rhode Island woman in my bed, on her knees, and I was giving her back shots like I was trying to bang thoughts of Jimi Lee out of my head. Jake Ellis was in the empty front room on the floor with another dancer, giving it to her Ghana style.

About thirty minutes later, the college girl from Rhode Island went to Jake Ellis. His girl came to me, smiling. She was from Philadelphia. Student at Santa Monica College.

I asked, "What's up?"

"You want next?"

"Switch?"

"Yeah. Side out, rotate."

She looked like Toni Braxton, but with more curves and less money. College girl took the back shots well. Almost broke the bed. No matter what I did, she didn't complain. Based on the sounds from the other room, Jake Ellis was having twice as much fun.

When the sex was done, as two college girls slept off alcohol and gave a sexual fragrance to my apartment, in the middle of the night I staggered to the phone. I called Jimi Lee.

My words slurred. "I want to see Margaux. Call me back. I want to see my daughter."

Jimi Lee didn't return the call. She didn't return the twenty-seven calls that followed.

The next week, I had the lesbian stripper who was straight for pay. She showed me how to make a woman feel good. She took me to school and I graduated with flying colors, at the top of my class. Two nights after that, the redbone came to see me again, and she brought a girl from Lakeland, Florida, a sister who looked like Mary J. Blige. Found out both were bisexual. A week later, it was a dancer from a club in Long Beach, a CSULB student who reminded me of Aaliyah. Then there was the white girl I met on Hollywood Boulevard, a girl fresh to California from the Midwest, an aspiring actress who looked like Lisa Stansfield. She attended Point Loma Nazarene University and drove up from San Diego to work where no one knew her. Then there was the Swedish girl, a student at Cal State Northridge. I met her at a coffee shop in Encino. She came on to me. She loved brothers. Next there was a girl from Clarita who looked like the Swedish singer Robyn. I didn't bring them to Leimert Park, same as Jimi Lee would never take me to Ethiopia. But the best I met during that season of wildness was a Coke-bottle, full-figured Jill Scott number. She was the best lover I'd ever bedded. She had Suriname and Guyana in her blood, was dark-skinned, East Indian, not of African descent. I met her one night when I went with Jake Ellis to a club in Hollywood and danced to calypso, soca, steel-pan, and *parang* music. She was from Tobago, could drink and party like no one I'd ever met, and the girl won the limbo contest at the club. She was curvy, flexible, had a Jessica Rabbit build. Two weeks later, Jake Ellis picked up two girls, one vacationing from Martinique and Guadeloupe, and the other a dance-hall queen from Jamaica. He dropped one off at my apartment, then took the other one home. Jake Ellis was a man and knew that for us the poison was the cure. It would take a new woman to make me forget an old woman. But there was no cure for Jimi Lee. Never would be. I was lost. A brokenhearted man lost at sea, in a rowboat, no paddles, adrift.

I called again, said, "Jimi Lee. What's going on? Why haven't you called me back?"

Someone answered. An angry man, his accent thick, definitely from Ethiopia.

I asked, "Who is this?"

"This is Adanech's father."

"Where is my wife?"

"Do not keep calling this number. Do not disturb my family."

"Adanech Abeylegesse Zenebework is my wife. That makes her my family."

"She is no longer your wife. She is here, back with her family, starting a new life."

"By law, she is still my wife. I need her to arrange for me to see my daughter."

"You have brainwashed her. You brainwashed a child. I will correct that."

"Brainwashed? Do you know your child? All she wanted to do was get away from you."

"I see the damage you have done. I was wrong to turn my back on her for the devil."

"Fuck you, old man."

"Do not call over and over."

"Fuck you."

"Do not bother her again."

"And damn you for the way you treat your daughter."

"You have been warned."

He hung up.

CHAPTER 32

Jimi Lee had been gone eight months before she called.

She had waited for the uncontested divorce to be final. She'd left with twenty-five thousand in cash, so I guess it had taken her most of a year to run out of money. I hadn't seen Margaux since her mother took her back to the nothing in Diamond Bar. It was the longest I'd gone without having Margaux in my arms. Jimi Lee called at three in the morning. It sounded like she had her windows open, or was outside standing on a deck under the stars.

I said, "I want to see Margaux. I'm getting tired of repeating myself."

"She asks for you every day."

"Does she?"

"All day, every day."

"How is she doing?"

"She's different. She misses you."

"Do you miss me?"

"We are still adjusting."

"We're divorced."

"Yeah. Now I have to check that box on every application for the rest of my life."

"That will please your father."

"Let's not talk about him. Or the disrespectful way you spoke to him on the phone."

"He hasn't earned my respect."

"Elders are always to be given respect, even when you disagree."

I took a breath. "I want you back. I hate that you left. I miss you every day."

"Don't do this."

"I could move out there. Rent a condo in Phillips Ranch or up in San Dimas. To be closer to both of you. To help with Margaux. I could take her to school or pick her up. I want to let her friends see she has a father."

"I don't want you with me and Margaux. I don't want any more confusion for her."

"Then bring her to me. Bring her or have someone else bring her."

"Wednesday."

"The weekend would be better. Less traffic. We can go to the park, or out to the pier at Santa Monica."

"Wednesday. Take it or leave it."

"What time?"

"After morning traffic dies down."

"So around ten or eleven?"

"I have to be back on the freeway by one."

"I only get two hours with Margaux? That's not good enough."

"It's the best I can do."

"Well, can you at least stay until evening traffic dies down around seven or eight?"

"No. I have an afternoon appointment in Chino Hills. This is my only offer."

"You can leave her with me."

"No, no, no, no, no."

"Well, I can cook breakfast for her."

"I might ask Lila to meet me."

"To cover for you. In case someone calls, you're with her. Same old game."

"Would that be a problem?"

"That's fine."

I rubbed the bridge of my nose. "Can I say hello to Margaux now?"

"Ken, it's three in the morning."

"Okay. Sorry. Tell her I said I love her."

"Wednesday. Don't have me and Lila drive there in traffic for nothing. And Lila is busy working on her advanced degree, so time is precious to her. She has to beat traffic and so do I."

"Can I call you back at the number that's on my caller ID?"

"I'm at a pay phone at the 7-Eleven on

Diamond Bar Boulevard."

"You had to sneak away and call me at three in the morning."

"Just be glad I called."

"I almost didn't answer."

"I wish you hadn't."

It took her three Wednesdays to finally show up at my door. Each week she had a new excuse. She had to get a root canal. Lila wasn't available. Margaux was sick. On that third Wednesday, when I had no idea she was coming, Jimi Lee came back to the apartment by herself, wearing tight jeans, flattering top, new perfume. Lila wasn't with her. And she showed up at my door without Margaux. Said we needed to talk about financial arrangements, away from Margaux. She wasn't working, and the bills were more than anticipated.

I was twenty-eight. She was twenty-five.

Margaux was six years old, in the first grade.

There were boxes by the front door.

Jimi Lee asked, "What are those?"

"Presents for Margaux."

"I'll try and bring her next time."

"Can you take them to her?"

"Those should be things she keeps here."

Jimi Lee's hair was shoulder length, colored three shades of red, like a rock star.

She had lost all the weight she had gained; was back to the size she was when I had met her. She was back in the gym in Chino five days a week, back on a diet. She had a glow. She smelled good. She wore Chucks, ripped jeans, tight blouse, jean jacket. She looked sixteen again.

I tried to hold the words in, but they came out on their own. "You look nice."

"Thanks."

If we had just met on that day, it would have been perfect. She would have been on the other side of grad school, and I could've had my PhD. We would have been different people.

She said, "I need more cash, Swift. Never realized how expensive it is to be alive."

"I don't have more cash. Ain't nothing left to give, until I work again."

"I need more. Or I'll tell the LAPD and the feds what I know about what you did in Florida."

"Men I know hear you say that, even as a joke, they will bury you after they bury me."

She took a moment, gave me a vulnerable look. "You haven't seen me in a while."

"You're the one who left. You wanted the divorce. I've always given you what you want."

She hesitated. "Truce? Can we have a truce?"

"I can't do that anymore."

"Don't you miss me at night?"

"I miss you all day. And at night."

"Truce?"

"No."

"Truce."

"Stay on point. I want to take Margaux to Disneyland."

"No."

"I just need you to drop her off. I'll have her back to you in three days at the most."

"No."

"It doesn't work that way. You don't get to steal my child from me."

"You're raising your voice. You're upset. Am I getting under your skin?"

"I don't want any of that worn-out roast beef. Mud flaps on an eighteen-wheeler are cleaner."

The sophomoric insult hit her hard, was too personal. She cursed me like she'd never done before. I didn't have time to play childish games, but she pulled me down to her immature level every goddamn time.

If I had wings, I would've flown toward the sun, never come back to Earth.

I told her, "We can lawyer up and go to court. I'll get Johnnie Cochran. See what a judge says."

"Miami. Oh yeah, I'll bring that up as soon as anyone subpoenas me. If I ever get one letter, one note, one phone call from anyone saying you're trying to take my child, then Miami. Johnnie Cochran might have gotten OJ free for killing Nicole, but you'll be the one doing time. You killed a man in Florida. Both you and Jake Ellis will get extradited. Johnnie Cochran can't do a thing for you in Florida. No Dream Team would get you out of that nightmare."

I went to her and grabbed her shoulders, screamed in her face, then backed away.

She shivered, rattled, adjusted her top. "That was some reaction."

"Get out."

"If I get out, I will make a few phone calls to the feds and to the IRS, and I will be honest and I will mention the money you gave me. Money I doubt you've ever claimed on your income taxes."

"You'll get laughed out of court into the streets."

"You'd get dragged to jail."

"You're not fit to be a parent."

"She's my daughter. Mine. Ken Swift, she'll be looking at you through Plexiglas if you think about taking her from me. You're not on the list, so don't even try and go to her school and talk about picking her up. They'll call the police so fast, your head will still be spinning. Don't threaten me. Don't you ever threaten me. You understand?"

"This is a new you."

"I'm a grown-ass woman now. I'm not the little girl you married."

"You went to Diamond Bar and you've changed."

"I'm no longer under your roof. I am no longer a little girl."

"Your father and mother have put bullshit in your head."

"They've counseled me. They have accepted me back into the family."

"Under what conditions?"

"That is not your concern."

"You divorced me and now you're keeping Margaux away. Nothing an attorney can't fix."

"Don't make this a legal thing. You know you're not fit to be her father. Stop pretending you're someone you will never be. Make this a legal thing, take me to court over my daughter, embarrass me, and I will do what I have to do to win. I know things. You'll end up in jail with every other black man and black woman President Clinton and President Bush has locked up. Your government doesn't give a damn about you. And since you're not OJ, neither will a jury in Florida, and it won't matter if Johnnie Boy is representing you and throwing race cards like darts. Dealing from the bottom of the deck doesn't always work. Keep this shit real. You're a black man, Ken Swift. Do we have an understanding?"

Her rage was strong, her intent powerful.

"I keep paying."

"She's your child."

"Not for Margaux. For you. You're seeing other men and I have to pay alimony."

"I can date whomever I want."

"You're dating?"

"Mind your own business. I'm sure you have your Gambian, Malawi, and girls from Botswana and Nigeria on rotation. I will try and not stay so long as to disrupt your lifestyle."

Seconds passed, and I had no defense, so I told her, "Jimi Lee. You win."

"Ken Swift."

"Yeah?"

"Ken Swift."

"What?"

"I've missed you."

She kicked off her Chucks, eased off her ripped jeans. Soon she stood in her Victoria's Secret, that body designed by the devil himself. She unsnapped her bra, let it fall.

I asked, "What are you doing?"

"Truce."

"No."

"You want me."

Soul Stealer strained against my pants, became my Judas, tried to lead me to the cross for another crucifixion. Jimi Lee shook her head, eased off her bottoms, and did a slow sashay toward my bed. My heartbeat accelerated. My palms were damp. My mouth watered for her. I struggled with myself and I lost. I followed her. She undid my pants, tugged my pants to my knees, then straddled me, moved Soul Stealer against Soul Sucker, and moaned like she was dying. I thought that was as far as she would go, thought she was about to rub me against her until she came to her senses, but she moved me against the mouth of her vagina, across the lips, teased the head in and out, teased it as if she couldn't make up her mind if she was going to put me inside.

She shivered, moaned. "I didn't think I'd miss this, but I do. I have."

She put the tip, the head, at the mouth of her vagina, then panted and mounted me.

The mother of my child, my ex-wife, she

405

moved up and down, and it was a subtle motion, just a little up and down, enough to make me want to erupt, to make me need to erupt, and weakened me more. She shook me, and she shook me good. Shook me and I felt an earthquake and hurricane dancing in my body. Each time I moaned, she did the same. Then I turned her over. It was too much. It was heaven and hell. I wanted to come fast, not allow her to have any pleasure, but she came with me. We had orgasms at the same time. Lust felt like love, and we clung to each other, skin slapping, primal grunts and moans. I exhausted myself inside of her as she called out, then began to whimper, and then my grunts and her cries turned to pants. She tried to kiss me, and I didn't let her. I rolled away.

When that was done, she rested with her head on my chest, her hand tracing my skin as I played in her hair.

She showered.

I closed my eyes.

She left without saying good-bye.

Black pussy supreme.

Because I loved her.

CHAPTER 33

After that, Jimi Lee would show up at my door, always looking good, always smelling good, always with an unsure smile, and I would weaken, want her, and let her in. Straight to the bedroom. No conversation. No arguing. I was tired of arguing. No fighting. Was tired of fighting a battle I didn't know how to win. I treated her like she was a girlfriend. No, actually, it was like she was less than a girlfriend. She was a one-night stand happening over and over again. Groundhog Day. That went on for several weeks. I bored my angst into her and made her have a tongue-speaking conference with Jesus and his daddy. She had made me her fool and I made her my whore. She was bad for me, wrong for me, but part of me couldn't break away from her magic.

She had spent a thousand dollars and bought a camcorder at The Good Guys, the kind that had recorded Rodney King being clubbed like a savage animal. Jimi Lee lugged the camcorder with her twice, brought it and I hooked it up to my Sony television from Circuit City. We sat side by side and looked at videos of Margaux. Jimi Lee wouldn't let me keep the VHS tapes. But she promised to bring me a new video every two weeks. Like a prisoner, I accepted that which the jailer offered. I saw my daughter in two-week intervals, but she saw nothing from me.

I asked, "Can you record me and let me send Margaux a recorded message?"

She rubbed that space between her brow and exhaled.

She said, "I'll record you. I have to get a new tape. A separate tape."

"Will you show it to her?"

"We'll see."

I didn't hear from Jimi Lee for more than a month. Then she showed up without the video camera. She had on workout clothes and was wearing a new wedding ring.

As she lay next to me naked, in a whisper I asked, "Who is the lucky man?"

"Yohanes."

"What does he do?"

"Rocket scientist at JPL in Pasadena."

"Oh. He's literally a rocket scientist."

"Yes. And his parents own a set of businesses."

"You love him?"

"He adores me. Has adored me since I was ten or eleven. He was fifteen."

"So you've known him most of your life."

"Our parents are friends. Political allies. They have done business together for years."

"Why would you marry Yohanes if he is just another man you didn't care about?"

"I missed my family. I wanted my daughter to know my parents. It killed me every day she didn't see my parents. They are getting older. Yohanes is smart. Has a PhD. So I married, had a traditional wedding they could come to, tried to bring all of us back together as a family. We dressed like royalty; had our wedding in Ethiopia; had a three-layer cake that was decorated to look like Kente; and we danced, prayed, celebrated, tried to restore our family's good name."

"Do they accept Margaux?"

"They only call her Tsigereda."

"Her name is Margaux."

She snapped. "Her name is Tsigereda. Not Margaux. That was for you."

"Adanech Abeylegesse Zenebework, do they accept Margaux?"

"Did your mother accept me, Kenneth Purnell Swift? What did your sweet mother,

Edith Lucille Swift, say when she met me? 'Oh, you're from Africa. You don't look like one of them people from the Tarzan movies.' Oh, and the killer. 'You ain't dark enough to be from Africa.' "

"It was a joke. My people play the dozens."

"A joke? It was ignorance. 'You ain't got hair like Africans. You look like you got Indian in your blood. Don't y'all live in huts over there? When you married her, how many goats did her African father give you?' Have I ever seen a gorilla? Or a giraffe? The nerve of that woman. The ignorance. Then she said at least I wasn't too dark-skinned. She said I was darker than a paper bag, so that would take the family in the wrong direction."

"It was a joke."

"But I was smart, so that might offset the deficit."

"Black Americans, colonialism brought us enslavement, rape, disease, and colorism. When the slave masters and Euro-rapists working on their behalf created mulattos, then gave preferential treatment to them the way rappers still do in videos, they created colorism."

"And *dinik'urina.*"

"What?"

"And ignorance. Ignorance is no excuse. People choose to stay ignorant. Insulting. Your mother, with her cheap wigs, wide nose, monkey lips, and rotund butt that looks like pigs fighting in a soggy blanket, she made a stank face and called my daughter — her granddaughter — a half-breed. And your stupid father and ugly siblings laughed like it was the best joke in the world. They insulted me and my daughter. I wanted to die. That broke my heart."

"Remember it in context, or not at all."

"Again, defending her. You read all those books on Africa, and remain ignorant."

"You told them that the color of the skin does not tell the race. And you . . . educated them, told them that some Ethiopians are Caucasoid. You went on and on about your connection to Caucasia. You said that some of you are as much forty percent Caucasoid. That's close to half."

"Your mother said that explains my hair. What the hell was that? She attacked my hair. Am I supposed to have hair like a Nigerian? I am not Nigerian. I am Ethiopian."

"To my people, saying you're Caucasoid, talking about the Italian, Danish, English, and Greek in your blood, and smiling about it, to them that means you think you're white."

"I intimidated your mother. She was color struck and threatened by my skin. She was threatened by my hair. Before I said a word. It's not a weave. My kitchen is not kinky. It grows this way; no need to add any poisonous product sold in Chinese beauty shops. Your family thinks they are less than white people, yet imitate white people, and that is not my problem. But your family is delusional if they think that since my family is African we are less than the dirt between their toes. I'd challenge your family to an IQ test any day of the week, and win, hands down."

"Okay. I don't even know what to say about that flaming diatribe."

"I looked at them, your family, and felt nothing but sadness for them, because in each one of your parents and siblings I saw the lingering impact of this country's slavery."

"I defended you. I defended my child. I told my own mother to close her mouth."

"You said no such thing. You defended them. You told me to stop talking."

"They are my family. Bad African jokes aside, they are not bad people."

"Isn't that what white people say about

412

other white people in the KKK?"

"You have jumped the shark and now you're going for the blue whale."

"They are racist toward me. Toward my people."

"They don't have the power to be racists."

"Then they are a league of bigots. I will not have Tsigereda around them."

"Her name is Margaux, and my mother would love to see her grandchild again."

"No. I will not subject Tsigereda to such foolishness and ignorance. The things your mother says will be bad for my child's self-esteem. I will not have that shit, not on my watch."

"Margaux is her only granddaughter."

"She called my daughter a half-breed. Half-breed? Ha. My child will never know them."

"Adanech Abeylegesse Zenebework."

She screamed, "I hate the way you butcher my name. Have always hated that."

"Were your parents any better to me than mine were to you?"

"Your mother is the tackiest woman on the planet. Whatever evil lives in her soul, she touched my child and some of that evil went inside her. I felt the energy in her change."

"No matter what you say, your parents

413

were no better. They went cold real fast."

"My parents are polite. Even when angered, they are polite."

"Your father wouldn't even hold his own grandchild."

"They don't see my child as true Ethiopian."

"She was born in America. She's American."

"She is Ethiopian American."

"She is African American."

"Margaux doesn't speak Amharic well, can't communicate with most of the elders. She won't wear a *kemis*. Doesn't like Ethiopian food, and won't sit and share food, unless she can use a knife and fork. She wants her own plate and refuses to tear off a piece of injera and use it to grab beef or other foods and put it directly into her mouth. She looks at our intimate way of eating and sharing as something primitive and savage. She knows nothing of the struggles in Ethiopia, doesn't care how we are mistreated in Israel. She knows nothing about Ethiopian jazz and won't listen to Mulatu Astatke. She only speaks one language, and she thinks that is enough to get her through life. She's lazy, too American. She has been taught to reject Africa. To reject her heritage. That is my fault."

"What's the real issue?"

"Kids at school tease her for being part African. She comes home crying."

"You live in an area devoid of black people and wanted her in private schools."

"What is your issue with nicer areas and people going to the better schools? The public schools where you live have barbed wire, graffiti, and metal detectors and all look like prisons."

"When you send a black kid, a half-African child, to an expensive private school with a conservative curriculum, what do you expect? The Mexicans and Pacific Islanders out there are confused and think they are white because they have the skin. And they have the same type of hair. Mexicans don't want their kids to speak Spanish because they want to be seen as white, or close to white, or not ethnic, by the white man. Black kids being educated by people who don't understand their history and resent them from hairstyle to toenails; this is the result. The weak ones buy into the madness, sip the Kool-Aid, and learn to hate themselves and their reflections."

"Lay off the Farrakhan juice and stop reading Malcolm X's anti-Semitic rants."

"You're no better than the white people out there. You're ashamed to be African."

"No, I'm ashamed I haven't been more *African.* Your *African* wife wasn't *African* enough."

"You know what I meant."

"I lost my Ethiopian culture along the way, didn't pass Addis Ababa on to Tsigereda."

"Margaux."

"I was here drowning in your toxic culture."

"Well, for me, yours hasn't exactly been chicken soup for the soul."

"You entered me, took parts of my soul, and I'll never be the same."

"I've taken nothing from you that you haven't taken from me."

"I let you lead. I had no choice."

"You've always had a choice. Don't fault me if you don't like the outcomes of the choices you made."

"I felt powerless."

"Bullshit."

"Trapped between you and my father."

"Bullshit."

"You're the man, the leader of this household. My parents blame you. I said I was done with you. I put my hand on a Bible and swore to my mother, father, and God that I was done with you."

"Is that why you won't bring Margaux? Is

that why you tell me lie after lie?"

"I'm sorry. I told them you were no longer in Margaux's life."

"Tell them the moon is made of cheese, I don't care. But bring me my daughter."

"I can't bring my child here, then instruct her to lie to her grandparents."

"I get it. Margaux will talk, be questioned when you're not present, and ruin your secret."

"It will slip that she sees you."

"You're worried about all the lies you've told."

"Then all hell will break loose in Diamond Bar."

"It will slip that you lie to them, like it has come out you have lied to me."

"Tsigereda will talk, will tell them I come to visit you."

"Her name is Margaux."

"If Tsigereda was here, she'd get used to that, come to expect being around you, and I can't start what can't be finished."

"She would get used to being around her father. What a shame."

"Don't."

"But you will keep visiting me."

"I'll bring you videos to see. I will bring you pictures to look at. You deserve that much."

"You will bring me images, and keep sleeping with me, if I play your game."

"This isn't a game."

"It's been years of Chinese water torture."

"Knowing you has done me no true favors, except Margaux. You gave me a beautiful daughter and I am trying to be a worthy mother to her. I am trying to fix what is broken."

"The broken glass will always be broken. Everything can't be fixed. You taught me that."

"She doesn't have to know it's broken."

"I want to protect her too."

She pulled at her hair. "You are part of the problem, not the solution."

"I'm the problem? Because I want to see Margaux, I'm a problem?"

"You bring conflict. You bring confusion. Your bloodline brings ignorance."

"Then leave. Don't come back. Don't keep hurting me and Margaux over and over."

"I have never hurt *Tsigereda*. Don't lie on me. I have never harmed her."

"You keep her away from her father. What the fuck you think that is?"

"I protect her like a mother should."

"Protect her by not letting her spend time with her father?"

"You are a criminal."

"And you haven't hesitated to spend every dime that came in that door."

"I've never hurt anyone. You killed a man in Florida. Jake Ellis was with you."

I made fists and barked, "We don't talk about that. We don't ever talk about Florida."

"Sending you to jail would solve all of my problems, so don't threaten me."

"Get the fuck out of my life. Go the fuck back to Ethiopia and ride a damn camel."

"I should. I really should. Sign the papers that give me permission to take her out of the country and I will do that. I will sell all I own and get on the first flight back to Addis Ababa."

"And I'll never hear from you again."

"Or Tsigereda. I will tell her you are dead. I need you to become dead to me. That would fix everything. If one of those times you went to work, if someone just killed you . . . I wish they would. I'm not your wife anymore and I would not have to bury you. I would be free of you."

She cried. I didn't hold her. I just let her shake, cry, and blow her cute little nose. Her shoulders began to heave; then she let it go, began wailing, a wounded-animal sound.

I watched her. Wiped tears from my own eyes and watched her deal with her angst.

I cleared my throat, wiped my eyes with the back of my hands. "Stop crying."

She said evil things in Amharic, then shouted, "Don't tell me to stop crying."

"You tell me you wish I was dead, then cry. Fuck you and your bullshit."

She threw one of her shoes at me, popped me right above my eye. Then she threw the other shoe and hit my arm. I picked it up, acted like I was going to throw it back, then threw it up against the wall, knocked down a framed picture of Martin Luther King Jr. The noise from the violence dissipated, left us once again in silence.

She faced me, whispered, "Truce?"

I was sleeping with a married woman. My child called another man her father. My unfaithful ex-wife was now his unfaithful wife. I scowled at her. I remembered how she had looked the night I met her. That smile was gone. I wiped tears from her eyes. She held me like she adored me, like she always would, but hated herself for doing so.

I held her the same way.

I whispered, "Truce."

Jimi Lee came like there was thunder in the

420

sky. I came pulling her hair, growling, lost in lights that had every color in the rainbow. My orgasm ended, and all of my strength was gone. She went to the kitchen and cooked. She made us a meal that consisted of injera, the large sourdough bread. She made vegetables and spicy meat dishes. Ethiopian cuisine. We sat on the living room floor, the food on a large dish between us, and ate with our hands, no utensils, ate only with our right hands, ate as if we were in an Ethiopian restaurant on Fairfax.

She asked, "Where is Jake Ellis?"

"Africa."

"He went home. Did immigration kick him out of the country?"

"Not at all. Wants me to come visit. He's going to university there."

"What's his major?"

"No idea. He'll be back in America after he graduates. He's pretty busy over there. Training boxers. Training cooks. In university."

"Where?"

"Igbinedion University."

"That's in Okada. It's new. They say it's the best university in Nigeria."

"And he's building a house in Accra."

"All of his dreams are coming true. Good for him."

"Why you ask about him?"

"Lila asked about him."

"Really?"

"Surprised me too."

"What's Lila up to?"

"School. Stressed out. Working on her PhD."

"You would've been her mentor."

Jimi Lee's nostrils flared as she pulled her lips in. She measured herself against Lila, measured who and what she was now against the life her best friend had, then softly asked, "You said you had some money for me?"

In the end, everything was about money. Money, not love. I handed her an envelope.

She asked, "How much?"

"Five grand."

She said, "Thanks."

"Margaux?"

She took out her purse and sat next to me. She pulled out pictures she had had developed at One-Hour Photo, took out others she had had developed at Costco, showed me month-old pictures of my child.

I said, "Can I have these?"

"No."

"Can you make copies for me?"

"I can't."

"Why can't you?"

"Because. I can't."

"Let me have one."

"No."

"Give me the negatives and I can go to Walgreens and make my own."

"No, no, no, no, no."

Our dance was getting old, yet I knew it would never end.

I wiped tears from my eyes. "I want to show them to my parents."

"They don't deserve to see one photo of my child."

"Just one fucking picture."

She wiped tears from hers. "Sorry. Don't make this any harder than it already is."

"I hate you."

She held my hand a moment. I held hers. Soon I let her hand go, got up and went to the kitchen, needed to get away from her. I heard her gather her things. She left without saying good-bye. When I went back into the living room, I saw she had left me one photo. Margaux on a swing. Laughing. The photo was stained with Jimi Lee's tears.

CHAPTER 34

Jimi Lee showed up every two weeks. She always came on Wednesday mornings. I found out that was because she got her hair done on Wednesday afternoons. And hump day was the day her cuckolded husband worked long hours. It was the day she could be free. We could mess up her hair and she would have it done in a new do before she went back to her happy home. On Wednesdays she kissed, sucked, swallowed, made love, fucked me like she was still my wife. As we always did, we assaulted each other like we were furious, drowning in love and hate.

She moaned. *"Ewedishalehu. Ewedishalehu."*

She moaned until we were going at it hard enough to bring down the building.

As she was coming, someone banged on my door.

They kicked my door and stopped my

down stoke midstride.

A man yelled her Ethiopian name, called for her in Amharic.

She shoved me away from her and leapt to her feet, terrified.

I asked, "Who the fuck is that?"

"Yohanes."

I opened a drawer, took out a .38, sat it on my lap.

She freaked out, shuddered, waved her hands, said, "Please, no."

"I'm about to learn him some manners."

Jimi Lee said, "Balthazar Walkowiak."

"What that have to do with this mother-fucker?"

"Touch him and I swear, I will tell the police about Balthazar Walkowiak."

She was scared that I was about to kill her husband. I probably was.

I barked, "You'd better get that mother-fucker away from my zip code."

"I will; I will."

"How did he find you?"

"I don't know."

I sat on the bed while she gathered her things, while she hurried away from my bed.

She left, and when she stepped out, he was there, waiting, in front of my building. Yohanes was in the grass under my window, a large rock in his hand. I thought he was about to hit her in the head.

He screamed, "I heard you; I heard you; I heard you; I heard you."

Heels in hand, head down, Jimi Lee hurried by her husband, moved too fast for him to grab her by the arm. She was rattled, terrified, could barely walk without tripping. She struggled with her keys, adjusted her dress, ashamed, humiliated, and she hurried into her car and drove away. Yohanes stayed behind, challenged me, then threw the rock into my bedroom window. It bounced away. And that pissed him off. He picked up another rock.

He roared up at my window, screamed like a wounded animal, hot tears raining from his eyes. He lost the plot the way I had, shouted at me the way I had shouted at men when I had been cast in the role of the brokenhearted husband. Neighbors came out into the streets. Cars slowed. He had an audience. People knew me. I had lived here for years. They had seen me married. They had seen my wife pack a U-Haul truck and leave. They saw her come back on Wednesdays. A thousand windows faced mine. A thousand eyes. He let the world know my offense, that I had seduced his wife, that I was a monster he wanted to kill, but I didn't go out. This could go a couple of ways. Jail or the grave for one or both of us. Only the men would lose. Jimi Lee would be free of both of us. He wiped his tears, saw the crowd, saw how they were more amused than sympathetic. If Jimi Lee was out there in tears, if she had our child on her hip and was screaming I'd been unfaithful, every black woman from between here and Harlem would be outside my window with torches. Some with nooses. No one cared for a crying man. A sad man wasn't seen as a man. He spat in my direction, then left, hopped in a car, a four-door Nissan that had a car seat in the back. Rage fueled his self-righteous indignation. This was the man she had married. The man my child saw as her father.

I was still feeling .38 hot when I went back to my bed.

The room smelled like my ex-wife.

Jimi Lee's purple panties were on the floor.

Her matching bra was on the nightstand.

Her come stains made a Rorschach on my fresh sheets.

I studied them until they made sense.

It showed me the image of a man separated from his child.

I screamed and threw a glass on the floor. It shattered into a million pieces.

I got down on my haunches, studied it, saw no way to put it back together.

CHAPTER 35

Two evenings later, I was going to put in a ten-mile run. Ran the hills in View Park; ran the streets in Windsor Hills; ran Stocker and Valley Ridge. Then the rain came. It was sudden, strong, and cold enough to turn me around. I was sprinting back down two-mile-long apartment row when I saw a lot of brown people congregated in front of my building. I slowed. There were at least thirty men. Half of them had on suits; half of them held umbrellas over their heads. It looked like a funeral procession. Slacks, nice jeans, Dickies, Dockers. More men with umbrellas appeared as I walked up, soaking wet, rain dripping from my head into my eyes. Might have been closer to forty in that group. When I was closer, I could tell they were East Africans. Didn't matter where they were from. This was my country. My zip code. I walked to them and a thin man with a receding hairline stepped up to me.

It was Jimi Lee's father. Mr. Zenebework had dressed to come see me. Brown oxfords. Gray suit. A professional man. The other men were sons, uncles, brothers, and other men from his community. I saw Yohanes, as angry now as he had been two days ago when he heard me fucking his wife. Jimi Lee's bitter and broken husband had brought them to my door.

A man next to Jimi Lee's father held an umbrella over the older man's head, kept him from getting wet from the waist up. The patriarch of my pain. I told him good evening in Aramaic, said, *"Inidemini āmeshehi."*

"Speak to me in American English."

"You were not invited to my home."

"Neither was the rain. Yet here it is."

"Is there a problem?"

"I have come to put things in order. You will not see my daughter again."

"What about my daughter? My ex-wife and I have a child."

"Will you be honorable, sign the papers, and allow her stepfather to adopt her? They will move away from all of this, return to Addis Ababa, and start their marriage over, away from America. Allow my daughter and my son-in-law to have a marriage, uninterrupted by chaos."

"They would go to Ethiopia. Relocate. Never return. With my daughter?"

"Allow Yohanes to adopt Tsigereda so she can be raised properly."

"Are you crazy?"

"My daughter agrees that will be the best. It will free her from this situation."

"I'm not giving my daughter away to make your daughter's life easier."

"How much do you want to sign the papers? What is your price?"

"You can't bribe me."

"Then this will not be as easy to resolve."

"My daughter has been kept from me for years and you want me to give her away?"

"For her own good. And keeping her away, those are my instructions. She is young. Time has passed. Now she has no real memory of you. She does not cry for you. You are but a fading dream. She can be free of you."

His words felt like a blade made of fire. I barked, "When do I see my daughter?"

"You will not see your daughter, nor will you see my daughter."

"I don't give a fuck about your daughter. I have fucked her every way but loose and Yohanes can have the sloppy seconds. I have fucked her in every orifice and left my mark all over your daughter. So, fuck all of you

African motherfuckers. Now. For the last fucking time, when will I see my goddamn daughter, motherfucker?"

Winds blew, and cold rain saturated my skin as six of the East Africans grabbed me. I fought them. The first five took hard blows, and four of those five went down for the count. But the sixth, seventh, and eighth ones attacked me at the same time, from three directions. They rushed me like it was planned, threw blows until they could manhandle me, then wrestled with my strength until I grew tired, and a half-dozen men held me by my arms. They yelled at Jimi Lee's husband, urged Yohanes in Amharic, told the cuckold to have his revenge. I spat over and over but I didn't fight them anymore. I could've, but I chose not to. Jimi Lee had caused this. If I died, I hoped she was haunted with guilt the rest of her life. I wanted her to feel all the pain I felt. They held me, and Jimi Lee's husband looked me in my eyes. He had come to fight me over Jimi Lee the way Ethiopia and Somalia had clashed over the region called Ogaden in the seventies. For him, this was about territory, about ownership, about his ego. Jake Ellis, the Ghanaian warrior who could have been my one-man Soviet army, was in Africa. Yohanes caught his breath and hit

432

me again. Showed his family he was a man.

Mouth bloodied, violence framed by palm trees, I said, "*Yetewabe.* Are you mad that your wife comes here to pretend she's Monica Lewinsky? She told you my *biliti* is bigger than yours?"

He lost it, went mad, hit me over and over. I struggled and the others pummeled me until I capitulated to the agony. Then he resumed his revenge. His heart was broken, and he needed to release his pain. Jimi Lee had given me the same pain, but I had been able to control it.

"You pig. You dumb Negro."

"Dumb Negro? Have you been watching black exploitation movies?"

"Asinine porch monkey, do you not know who I am?"

"You think I give a fuck, you stupid fucking fuck?"

Surrounded by men holding umbrellas, they held me like hunters trapping a raging bull. Yohanes hit me until his bloodied hands hurt too much to strike me anymore. Then Jimi Lee's father took his place. Next her brothers attacked me. Then her uncle the attorney. Followed by another uncle, a podiatrist. They were smart men who had grown up having rivalries and skirmishes with Bantus, Somalians, and Eritreans.

When the whipping was done, when they had beat up my face, ribs, and stomach, when they were exhausted, when their hands hurt, they let me fall on the ground, dropped me on the wet concrete, on the nasty pavement. Then it felt like all forty of them began kicking me at the same time. It felt like they marched over me in one direction then turned and marched back in the other. Rain made me feel like I was drowning. I made it up to one knee, scowled up at them.

Jimi Lee's sweaty father rubbed his knuckles. "Pray to your god we do not return."

I spat blood, wheezed, coughed, found enough air to say, "I want to see Margaux."

"There is only Tsigereda. She is not yours. And you are not worthy of her. Or my daughter. This has gone on long enough. This has gone on for too many years. It is done."

"We're not done. You'd better kill me, because my next stop will be Diamond Bar."

"Then before you come in my direction, dig a hole as deep as your body is tall, as wide as you are from shoulder to shoulder, and shop for a tombstone, unless you want your grave unmarked. You come in my direction, that will be the last trip you ever make in this lifetime."

I lived in a moment of irony. They did unto me as I had done unto others.

My debt to them was the shame I had brought upon their family.

Someone else moved through the crowd, a small body, no more than five feet tall. Light brown and comely. A beautiful woman. Rain fell, but never touched her skin. God knew better. I saw the power in her eyes. I saw elegance and astuteness as well. She was angrier than the men. I had offended the husband and the father, but I had offended the matriarch the most.

It was Menna. It was Jimi Lee's mother, dressed in beautiful, colorful, flowing materials.

She said, "Heed our words, bad man."

She nodded twice, then walked away.

She walked away and with the motion of her right hand signaled they were done.

This was her army. A king was nothing without a queen. And I no longer had a queen.

Menna was Cassiopeia, Sheba, Amanirenas, Amanishakhete, Nawidemak, Amanitore, Shanakdakh, and Malegereabar amalgamated. Menna showed me she was the queen's queen.

She took Jimi Lee's failures personally. As any parent with half a soul would do.

The army of beautiful people marched away like they were returning to the Kingdom of Aksum. If all fifty-four African nations had been that organized, there would never have been any colonization. Slavers would have been killed on the shores of Africa, and as a result, India would have never been robbed and raped, and on this side of the pond, Native Americans would still own prime real estate. The African men kicked my ass and left, umbrellas high, everyone talking in their Semitic language, raining insults and spitting on me as they passed. I coughed. Two dozen car doors opened and closed. I struggled to breathe. I heard faint music. God's Property chanted "Stomp." It came from a neighbor's open window. I heard several songs at once. Engines started. Ice Cube rapped about "No Vaseline." I collapsed and heard Prince singing about the year 1999. Two dozen modest cars pulled away and took to the streets that led to the 10 East, back toward the Inland Empire. They left me bleeding in the rain. I was on the ground for at least five minutes after they were gone.

People came over, stood by me. Neighbors watched from windows. Cars slowed down, then kept going.

A curvy, light-skinned woman wearing

loose jeans, Birkenstocks, and a Loyola Marymount hoodie and carrying a large blue umbrella hurried across Stocker and asked, "Are you all right?"

She had a strong British accent. She looked like she was barely twenty but sounded more mature. I'd seen her around, but we'd never shared words. She always had a man on her arm. A mixed-race woman with a British accent was common across the pond, but a rarity in this zip code. She was seen as exotic in Leimert Park.

She asked, "Should I dial nine-nine-nine for you, Ken Swift?"

"Nine-nine-nine?"

"I mean nine-one-one. It's nine-nine-nine back home."

She talked to me like she knew me.

I asked, "Sister, what's your name?"

"Bernice Nesbitt. I live across the street from you. If you need a witness, I saw the whole thing."

When she spoke, her British accent made her sound like a movie star.

I said, "Bernice Nesbitt. I don't need a witness. Just an issue between a man and some men."

"You're bleeding."

"I'm fine."

"You have someone to make sure you're okay?"

"Neighbor, I'll be fine."

Pain as I inhaled, suffering when I exhaled, anger when I blinked.

I crawled to my ride, drove to urgent care. Said I had been mugged but didn't see who had done it. I wasn't a snitch. This was a family matter. Still, that didn't stop me from wanting to go rabbit hunting in Diamond Bar.

When I returned from urgent care I loaded my .38. Took a box of bullets.

I was ready to go Rambo on the Horn of Africa.

I sped east out I-10 and the 60 like a demon, made my car move like a jet plane until I was coming up on Rowland Heights, changed lanes like a maniac until I was a few seconds shy of zip code 91765.

I made it that far before I came to my senses.

I put the weapons under my seat and turned my wrath back around, pulled over, and stopped at Mimi's Café until my urge to kill a nation of distant cousins had dissipated. Margaux was in my heart. I didn't want my daughter to have to make prison visits to be able to look me in my eyes.

My father, mother, grandmother, siblings, none would visit me in jail.

Jimi Lee would be free of me, married and growing old with Yohanes.

Back at home, I took pain pills, kept my .38 at my side. Bernice came and knocked on my door. She smiled, said she wanted to make sure I was okay. I invited her in, and she stood in the kitchen while I cooked spaghetti with turkey meat and garlic bread. She stayed long enough to sit down and have dinner with me. I noticed her. She had a small waist and killer curves, breasts like pillows, and the kind of thighs a man wanted to crawl between from sunset to sunrise, then lounge in until the sun set again. She smiled like trouble was built like a money trap.

She asked, "You're married?"

"Not anymore."

"The girl who comes over on Wednesdays?"

"You see her?"

"From my window. I get a better breeze from the front window."

"My ex-wife."

"I thought that was the same girl you lived with."

I nodded. "Same girl."

"I saw her the day she moved out."

"What did you see?"

"She was crying."

"Who was over here?"

"She had four or five men over moving all the furniture out."

"African men moved her out?"

"Yeah."

"A woman about her age helped?"

"I didn't see a woman."

"Okay."

"I thought you had moved out too; then I saw you a few days later."

I told her about the child custody issue. "So, her family didn't care for me."

"They came after you like they were the Black Guerrilla Family. I dated an Ethiopian in London and it was a marvelous experience. We did museums, gallery exhibitions, lots of walking, photography, dining out, theaters, as well as day and weekend trips out of London. We did the best day trip to Rochester to a Dickens festival, wore costumes, were in the parades, enjoyed street entertainment, had a blast at the readings and lots of free activities."

I refilled her wineglass with Riesling. "You're divorced too?"

"Never married, not yet."

"You're single."

"I'm not single. Met someone last week."

"Good for you."

"A fireman. He thinks I'm hot and wants to put the fire out."

"Good for you."

"Glad you're okay after that incident. You're handsome. Want you to stay that way."

"You're a pretty woman. If that's okay to say without offending."

"Always thought you were cute."

"Never knew you noticed me."

"You were married with a baby."

"I was."

"And I was single. Until last week."

"I guess you were."

"And now you're single and I'm seeing someone."

I nodded. "Well."

"We could've been kicking it."

She kissed me on both cheeks, then took a step away. She grinned and said she'd had a lovely dinner.

She said, "We're going to rent an Eddie Murphy movie and make it a Blockbuster night."

"Take care, neighbor."

"You too, neighbor."

Later that night, I sat in my window, six-pack of beer at my feet, lights off, in the dark.

I sipped my brew, fired up a joint Jimi Lee had left behind, and looked across the way, saw Bernice Nesbitt entertaining her fireman. I'd never looked at her window before. But I guess she had looked at mine.

CHAPTER 36

Jimi Lee lived rent-free in my head every second.

And every second of every moment, I was aware of my own infuriated heartbeat. I called Jimi Lee's cellular again. Her number had been changed. Rule of the streets said I was to go to Diamond Bar and not leave until I was the last man standing. Then do my time like a man, get three hots and a cot at the free hotel until I died in a cold, claustrophobic cell. They had me ready to walk the green mile and break bread with John Coffey.

I looked in the mirrors, scowled and cursed my wealth of scars. I took my .38, removed the bullets, dropped it in a drawer. As soon as I did that, there was a knock on my door. I was surprised to see African trouble standing on my porch. She wore loose jeans. A hoodie from Pepperdine. It was Lila. Jimi Lee's coconspirator.

I said, "Little Red Corvette."

"Ken. Oh my God. Your face."

"Much better than it was."

"Who did that?"

"What are you doing at my door?"

"Was in the area. Stopped by to check on you."

"Jimi Lee sent you?"

"She didn't."

"What did she tell you?"

"Yohanes was here. He found out about her coming to see you."

Little Red Corvette had come to find out what had happened between me and Jimi Lee.

I didn't realize how badly I had been injured. I could barely stand. Off and on I had a series of spasms that lasted a good minute. I almost collapsed right there. Lila helped me to my bed. I sat on the edge. She made me recline. I pulled up my T. She looked at my healing wounds. She put ice packs on my skin.

She asked, "What happened?"

"I think you know."

"Tell me. Jimi Lee didn't say much. She was distraught. I only know Yohanes is infuriated."

"Jimi Lee's husband came here with Jimi Lee's dad and half of Africa."

"He found out she was creeping."

"She told you enough. You're her girl. You know more than I do. You know the truth."

"I was her alibi. Yohanes called me and she wasn't with me. He caught me in a lie."

I took a breath, didn't want to ask, but I needed to know. "Is she okay?"

"She's not answering her phone. And she's blocked me on AOL."

My ex-wife's conspirator massaged my shoulders. It felt too good, so I sat up, made her stop.

She shivered. "I'll call her from here. On her cellular. Will that be cool with you?"

"Don't call her from my house."

"To see if she is okay. If she sees your number on her caller ID, then maybe she'll an—"

"Don't call that bitch."

That widened her eyes, stunned her more. "Don't say that."

Tears fell from my eyes as anger rose from my heart.

She said, "She might not talk to me anyway. She's mad at a joke I made. She was talking about our culture, your culture, and I told her you were a failed social experiment."

"You were right. We were a failed social experiment."

"It. Was. A. Joke. We were drinking. People say stupid shit while drinking."

"I wish, I wish I was twenty-one again. I would've seen Jimi Lee the first time, nodded, and kept on walking, left that drama in the arms of a weaker man, and saved us all from this hell."

"Would you have turned and walked away? Would you give up the passion you shared?"

"Or I would have just tapped that ass once and moved on. She could've had her fantasy, I could've had mine, and she could've gone to her Ivy League school, been a doctor, and forgotten about me. I could have finished at UCLA, maybe gotten my master's from Pepperdine. I had a five-year plan. I could've moved to Africa years ago."

"I am going to need you to relax. You're saying things I know you don't mean."

"She used you, Lila. She lied and told her people she was with you a lot."

"Oh I know. And they hate me. I am persona non grata with her family."

"And you knew she was messing around on me. You helped her do me wrong."

"I have no control over anything she did. No one can control Jimi Lee."

"I never tried to control her."

"I know."

"I loved her."

"I know."

"She didn't love me back."

"She did her best." Lila became emotional, wiped her eyes. "She did her best."

"Her family. How do they treat her?"

"Jimi Lee has fallen from sainthood, forever desacralizing her place in her family's legacy."

"Her family is a family of thugs."

"They are passionate people. They are political. They are very proud and military-minded."

"Same shit redneck racists say in the South as they hang a black man from a tree."

A few seconds passed. Sirens were in the distance. Someone passed driving fast, music bumping.

That was when I noticed she was tipsy. "You've been drinking."

"I had one beer."

"One?"

"School has me so stressed out. Broke up with the guy I was seeing, so there is that."

"Sorry to hear that."

"Then Jimi Lee has me stressed. So stressed I can't function."

"She's got you drinking, same as she has me drinking."

"Had one drink. Could use another."

I asked, "Another beer?"

"Another anything."

"Asti Spumante?"

"Even better."

"I'll open a bottle."

"You'll have to drink with me."

"Don't worry. I need a drink too."

"I only want half a drink."

"I'll finish the bottle."

"You shouldn't drink like that, not when you're alone."

Lila wiped her eyes again. I did the same. Jimi Lee had us both. I wanted to take a walk before I had a drink and asked Lila to come with me. Sitting too long exacerbated my injuries. And once I had a drink, I knew I'd drink until I was in my twelfth dream. We walked down Stocker toward Creed, took Ninth to MLK, then took Degnan back to Stocker. She was quiet, looked at the triplexes and quads, took in the apartments and single-family homes.

She said, "This is a really nice area."

"I know. News only shows a certain type of black people, and they're not from this zip code."

"It's about to rain."

"We're almost back."

"Gets cold over this way."

"Let's get back and get that drink."

"I'll have one, to be sociable; then I'm gone."

When we made it back inside my apartment, I asked, "Who'd you break up with?"

"He's a professor."

"Naughty girl."

She laughed. "I think I'm over that phase. I already started seeing someone else a while ago."

"I can't keep up with you."

"Hell, I can't keep up with myself."

"You should have given Jake Ellis a go."

"That would have been another failed social experiment too."

She followed me to the barren kitchen. Only paper plates and paper cups had been left behind.

"You still haven't bought any new furniture."

"All I need for now is a bed."

"Don't you ever have company?"

"Just Jimi Lee. And all we needed was a bed. Most of the time we didn't need that."

"I'm worried about you."

"Don't."

I pulled out two cups, poured Spumante like they were two wineglasses, handed her one.

She said, "I didn't want that much."

"My bad. Let me pour it back in the bottle."

"Too late."

"Keeps me from drinking alone."

She stood in the doorway, sipped, made faces like she loved the taste.

She said, "You were really good to Jimi Lee."

"Did my best."

"Never saw a man love a woman like that before."

"A fool is born every minute."

"You still love her."

I shifted. "This love has no exit wound."

"Wow. So, love is a slug and it's still in your body."

"I inhale and feel the shrapnel in my heart."

"God."

"What?"

"Wish I could get a man who loved me like that."

"Be careful what you wish for."

"You have a twin?"

"Nope."

"Cousin or brother? Doppelganger?"

"None that would do you any good."

She took a breath. "You sound as poetic as Jimi Lee's writings."

"What writings?"

"Her journals. She never showed you or read anything to you?"

"What did she write about?"

"Well, she wrote her deepest feelings, and she definitely wrote about sex with you."

"She never shared any of that with me."

"She wrote in Amharic. That was how she practiced and stayed in touch with the language."

"Oh. She wrote it in a way I'd never be able to read what she was saying."

"I only saw a few pages. She was private. I have to be honest. At times, I was jealous."

"Jealous?"

"Just a little bit. At times."

"Jimi Lee was more than a little bit jealous of you."

"Well, most women want to find a man who loves them the unselfish way you loved Jimi Lee."

"I did my best."

"You were too good for her."

"Her folks would beg to differ."

"You were. You were too good for her."

"No one has ever told me I was too good for anything."

I stood by the fridge, tried not to look at her, then looked at her, sipped.

She asked, "Anything to smoke?"

"Really?"

"Yeah. Really."

"Jimi Lee told me you were the one who put her on the puff-puff-pass train."

"And she quickly became the engineer."

We laughed.

She repeated, "Anything to smoke?"

"Depends."

"On?"

"You have photos of my daughter?"

"Blackmail."

"Fair trade."

She nodded. "Some are on my phone. Have better ones of my goddaughter at home. I have saved some videos on a floppy disk too. I kept her a couple of weekends and we made home movies."

"You kept her a couple of weekends?"

"You were out of town working."

She said that like she knew what I did, like the name Balthazar Walkowiak was on the tip of her tongue, but was too afraid to say.

I said, "I never knew you kept Margaux."

"Sorry."

"When I was away, Jimi Lee sent her to you so she could be free and run the streets."

"She needed a break."

I cleared my throat. "How was the time spent?"

"We had tea parties. Played dress-up. Went to Magic Mountain. Played with dolls."

"Had no idea."

"I can make you copies, if you want."

I walked away, found a small stash of weed Jimi Lee had left behind in the dresser, then went back. Lila was sipping, then stopped and rolled a joint. We stood in the empty kitchen and made cumulus clouds touch the ceiling.

I asked, "Shotgun?"

"Of course."

I put the fire end of the joint in my mouth and she came closer. She smelled like cherries, orange blossoms, and peaches. I'd never been that close to her before, not like this. I blew her a shotgun, the smoke flowing out and moving up her nostrils as she gently exhaled. Our lips touched. She blew me a shotgun. Our lips touched again.

She swallowed. Shifted foot to foot. Went back to inhaling the doobie. Small smile on her lips. Sweet woman, but a naughty girl. Soon I refilled our glasses, and she was high. I was tipsy, high on something.

She whispered, "You have soft lips."

"So do you."

"Two pair."

"Really?"

"I shouldn't have said that. I'm rewinding

this conversation."

"Good idea."

We leaned against the walls, then sat down on the floor, the Spumante between us. Windows open. Night breeze. Moon high as we were getting. Soon we were laughing, talking, letting the weed and alcohol take us away.

She asked, "You want to know about my first boyfriend?"

"Yeah. Who was your first?"

"His name was Abdisa. Fine-ass Abdisa."

"Ethiopian?"

"Of course. But he could pass for a white man."

"I'll bet you didn't meet him on Sunset."

"We met during Irreecha."

"What's that?"

"It's the Thanksgiving holiday of the Oromo people in Ethiopia."

"Look at that smile."

"I loved him. He loved me to death."

"What happened?"

"He met a girl he loved more."

"And you haven't been the same."

"Makes it hard for me to connect with a man on that level."

"Once bitten, twice shy."

She tsked. "Some things we will never recover from."

"Heartache is at the top of that list."

"Yes, heartache is at the top of that list."

"You okay?"

"With heartbreak, there is no Ganna, there is no end of rainy season."

"That's how it feels for me. Like this will never end."

"He said I was not political enough for him. He participated in violent protests in Ethiopia, protested political and economic marginalization, but I didn't return home that summer to join him. That was the summer you met Jimi Lee. I didn't want to go there and be surrounded by violence. People died, were trampled in stampedes."

"You'd rather be here, where it's safe."

"I was not the one he wanted to build a strong family with."

"He's missing out."

She told me about her homeland, about Ethiopian culture, her pride. Was different hearing it from her.

I asked, "Ever see a hyena?"

"Yup."

"Get out."

"We were near the ancient city of Harar in Ethiopia."

"Where was it?"

"A man had one as a pet. He was outside with it, like it was a common dog."

"Wow."

"Enough about me and boring Ethiopia."

I told her about my family's journey. The Black Wall Street.

"What was burned down?"

"Six hundred businesses. Twenty-one churches. Twenty-one restaurants. Thirty grocery stores. Two movie theaters. Six private planes. A hospital. A bank. A post office. Schools. Libraries. Law offices. A bus system."

"Wow."

"Evil does what evil does."

"White men in America never cease to amaze me."

I said, "The relationship between America and blacks has always been one rooted in abuse."

"I see. And it scares me."

"Well, you have the same skin color, so you'll have the same problem."

"Or worse, once they realize I am from Africa."

We sat closer, talked politics. Talked, sipped, blew shotguns, made lips touch over and over. Pain pills, alcohol, weed. I was higher than a motherfucker. Lila's eyes were good-high red.

Soon she stood up. Struggled to stand up. Laughed. I did the same.

She blinked a few times. "I need to sit back down and chill a bit before I drive, if that's cool."

"Buzzed?"

"Jimi Lee smokes some potent dope."

"I know, right?"

"I'm walking through clouds. Hell, I've become a cloud."

"You'll be high for hours."

She laughed, played with her hair. "That's not good. I'm forty minutes from home. And suddenly high as fuck."

"LAPD are out there. The local slave catchers might have checkpoints."

"You do have a lot of police in this area."

"On the outskirts. On the main drag."

The skies opened up and rain came down. It came down hard.

She said, "I should have left a while ago."

"Stay the night. Sleep it off."

"Oh? And where will I sleep?"

"You get the bed."

"And you? Will you be in the bed with me?"

She went to the window. Stared at the rain like she was seeing if it would pass. The winds picked up. Rain came down harder. That was her answer. She took a deep breath, exhaled.

I sipped. "You're welcome to spend the night."

"Might have to stay a while. Maybe another hour."

"You're more than welcome."

She came back, sat on the floor, smoked, bounced her leg. Contemplated. "Any more Spumante?"

"Four bottles left."

"Anything to eat?"

"Mostly breakfast food. Haven't been food shopping in a minute."

She smoked more. "I'm tipsy."

I opened another bottle. Refreshed our cups. "Me too."

"You're staring at me."

"What's on your mind, Lila?"

She sang, "I'm high, looking at you, rain puts me in a mood, and now I'm thinking things I should not be thinking."

I grinned. "Too bad I met Jimi Lee before I met you."

She grinned. "You don't want none."

"The way you walk, I bet that shit is fur lined and gold plated."

She chuckled, smoked, sipped. "Somebody's flirting."

I asked, "You said you're with a new dude?"

"I'm seeing someone."

"Often? Being intimate?"

"Well, this past weekend was the most I have seen of him."

"Meaning?"

"We spent the weekend together, so that was the most I have seen him in a row."

"Have a good time? Spend the night?"

"I had a wonderful time, met the family."

"You're beautiful and smart. Be happy."

"He's divorced with three kids. I don't think the kids are ready for him to have a full-time girlfriend. Even though I know they like me and have spent time with me, they think I'm their daddy's friend."

"Three kids. That's a day-care center."

"It's a lot and I'm thinking this might be a little too much for me. You understand what I am saying?"

"Yep. Well, don't give up. Single dads need love too."

"He's only been divorced for two years and wants to be married again, but do I really want to deal, or just cut him loose and wait for someone with fewer issues?"

"You should get with someone who has your profile. Single. Educated. Ambitious. Wants kids."

"That's so fucking hard to find. That's like finding a unicorn. Doesn't exist."

"This guy doesn't want more crumb

snatchers?"

"He wants two more kids."

"Three plus two more?"

"That will be five for him."

"I could barely afford one."

"So, I'd have to deal with five."

"He loves kids."

"I think that's what made me decide to go out with him. When we talked he said he wanted more kids."

"That's good, then. You like him?"

"You're drunk."

I smiled. "Am I being too nosy?"

She smiled. "I'd never ask those questions you ask me."

"Don't sweat it. Just chatting."

"We've never really had a chance to chat before. Not like this."

"Thanks to you the dope is in my lungs and the wine is in my head."

She took a smoke, another sip. "I was intimate with him last month."

"You happy with it?"

"I'm happy with the decision I made to wait. Made him wait over six months."

"Good."

She hummed. "I think sometimes we tend to judge sex partners too harshly."

"That's possible."

"How was being married?"

"What do you mean?"

"I assumed you and Jimi Lee were doing it all the time."

"I am here to tell you it wasn't like that."

"Liar. Jimi Lee loved that part of it."

"We weren't on the same page with a lot of things, so, hell, we didn't talk half the time, let alone have sex."

"My bad."

"It's different when you are married and got drama."

She blinked a few times. "Enough about that, what's with you? Seeing anyone?"

"Nope. Was seeing Jimi Lee when the mood hit her."

"Nobody else?"

"Didn't want to taint no one with my drama."

Lila hummed. "Does that relationship with Jimi Lee even count at this point?"

"Had an affair with my ex-wife. But that's done."

"I guess cheating was more exciting for her."

"I guess it was. Maybe it was for both of us."

"You cheated on her?"

"Not once."

She smiled a naughty smile, then laughed, made that impish expression go away. "You

take care of Jimi Lee and Margaux. You're
the kind of guy a lot of girls dream of having. So. Anyway. I know how Jimi Lee's family is. I think I was worried, making up a
reason to call. I wanted to hear your voice.
And other things."

"What other things?"

"Oh, the alcohol and weed have me bab-
bling now."

"What other things?"

As the rain drummed against the building, she whispered, "I had sexual thoughts
about you."

I grinned. "Maybe we should stop now."

"Can't stop rain once it starts to fall."

"I guess the horse has left the barn."

"That too."

I nodded. "Tell me about your thoughts."

She bit her bottom lip. "Seriously?"

"Tell me."

She hummed a while, then chuckled. "I
had a wet dream."

"I can't imagine you in that way."

"I had a sex dream starring you."

"How was I?"

"I imagined you. It felt so real."

"Did you? Did it?"

"Oh yeah."

I grinned, sipped, inhaled, blew smoke.
"Me and you."

"Soixante-neuf."

"She told you."

She shook her empty cup at me. "Bartender."

Rain exacerbated the mood. I looked at her. Refilled her cup. Gave her a new spliff, fired it up.

She said, "Rain is coming down harder now. I'll bet the streets are flooding."

I nodded. "What do you want to do?"

Her nostrils flared as she licked her lips. "What are my options?"

I took a breath. "You have to stay. Until you are sober enough to drive."

"So I'm spending the night."

"I guess you are."

Lila sipped. "May I take a quick shower and borrow a T-shirt to sleep in?"

I went to her, pulled her close, held her ass. It was soft. She hummed, purred like a cat being stroked.

We stood like that, staring into each other's eyes. High as fuck. Tipsy as hell. Body and heart in pain. I put my lips on hers, nibbled her lips, sucked that erogenous zone and imagined other acts of intimacy. She trembled, lost her breath, and I kissed her. She kissed me like she had wanted to kiss me a long time ago. She kissed me like her secret desire had been exposed, and she surrendered to the moment. I gave in to her too. I tried to kiss the darkness off her skin. We eased down to the floor, to the linoleum. I moved between her thighs. And I looked at her. Tears were in my eyes. Tears were in her eyes too. She felt my pain and offered me her body as comfort.

I whispered, "We should stop."

She held my face and kissed me, inhaled me; then she undid her hair, let it loose, let her mane fall across her shoulders, down her back. I moved her bushy hair, kissed her neck, held her breasts in my hands.

She said, "You can't tell Jimi Lee. She's my best friend. I love her."

I nibbled on her ear. "I won't. I love her too."

Her breathing became staccato. "You are making my labia ache. Like never before. Feels so good."

I put my mouth on her breast. "You're making me ache too. You're making me wanna do some thangs."

She moaned. "Just like in my dream. This is just like it was in my dreams. I felt on fire, like this."

Lila moved against me as she undressed, kicked off her trainers, slid off her colorful socks, pulled away her loose jeans. She smelled fresh, fruity. She was all legs. Sexy, chocolate legs. She took off her Pepperdine hoodie, took off her teal and pink bra and panties. I undressed. She watched. We smiled at each other, smoked and drank naked, my crib our nudist colony. The next shotgun turned into an intense kiss as her skin warmed mine.

She whispered, "Put on some music."

I put on some R and B to go with the sounds of rain against my windows.

On my bed, we kissed, touched, masturbated each other.

She sang, "Damn, baby. Damn."

We became grunts and groans, feral cries in a crude language. I was hard enough to etch names in diamonds. She pulled me between her legs, and I moved against her without going inside, panting, damp, ready, but still felt nervous, tentative, unsure about what came next.

"Soul Stealer."

"She told you that too."

"She told me that too."

Lila reached down, held me in her hand.

She put a little more than the hat inside her.

I moaned in her ear. I broke the skin and she cooed. I put my hand around the base of her neck, stroked her, kissed her, put her in a trance.

CHAPTER 37

Luther Vandross ended one song as Janet Jackson crooned another, hers a tune for the lovesick. By the time Earth, Wind, and Fire started singing "Devotion," Lila was on top. She sucked my neck hard enough to leave a dozen passion marks. Soon she was facedown, ass up, hands clasping sheets as she took the scenic route through Back Shot City.

"Good Lord, Ken. Good Lord."

"What?"

"You can go a long time."

"Want me to stop?"

"Don't stop, don't stop."

"Like this?"

"I'm so damn wet. You're going to make me touch myself."

"Do it. Show me how you do it. Show me."

"You get me high and make me do things that will keep me from getting in heaven."

Winds roared and the streets drowned as I slapped her rear harder, her words now in Amharic.

"Who told you to stop touching yourself?"

"Sorry, Daddy. Sorry."

"You're a little whore."

"You made me your whore."

"Just like I'm your fucking whore."

She laughed a little. "Hand me a spliff."

"I'm busy right now."

She pushed me off her. "I want to smoke while you stroke."

I gave her the last of Jimi Lee's weed. She fired it up, giggled, got back in the position, bottom raised, taking tokes as she made her butt move side to side in a happy dance. I turned her over. Gave her my tongue while she smoked. Did to her what I used to do to Jimi Lee. Addicts did this thing called the double master blaster. Would get head while they smoked the crack. I gave her head. She made smoke and I made her orgasm. I moved away from her, looked at how beautiful and sexy she was. She puffed and touched herself. She handed me the spliff. I stroked and inhaled. Clouds rose above us and danced with liberated moans. Soon my body felt like something else, like something I was fighting to control. I gave her the joint, put her ankles around my neck, eased inside her.

"Yeah. Like that." She puffed. "Oh God. You feel so good."

"Smoke and touch yourself while I stroke you."

The rain made the world outside opaque, made palm trees bend. We were in our own world while more people lined up to sing to us. Bobby Womack, Stevie Wonder, Lionel Richie, and Diana Ross.

I held Lila's waist while she puffed. She made me get on my back, made me inhale while she rode me, while she went up and down.

"I can tell you love being on top."

"Come better this way."

She put the weed away, pushed her hands down on my chest and made her ass rise and fall, made it go around and around with that up and down, then made her body move in erotic waves. I held her hands, our fingers interlocked, clasped, and she rode. She rose and brought it back down, left me moaning and mesmerized.

After she had come again, she used her hands and mouth. When she finished, while I was dizzy and lightheaded, she reached for her clothes, was about to get dressed.

I stopped her. I saw how she had been with other men. Make love, then leave, maybe ashamed.

She bit her bottom lip, looked embarrassed, then asked, "You want me to stay?"

"Stay."

"Ken."

"Stay."

"Ken."

"I don't want to be alone."

"She hurt you."

"This has nothing to do with her."

She panted, took sharp inhales, crawled to
me. Put her head on my chest. I played in
her woolly hair.

I said, "Christ had woolly hair, like yours."

She shuddered. "What are you saying?"

"Your hair is like God's hair."

"I thought your Christ had blond hair."

"The modern image of Jesus is modeled
on Cesare Borgia, a gangster's son. It's a
big hoax."

"I was being facetious. I'd never pray to a
white God. That's false. Mary hid her baby
in Egypt, not London. Only a black baby
would be able to hide in Egypt. Same for
your Moses. I could go on and on."

"God has hair like this. Beautiful. Soft.
Woolly."

"Does God's hair smell like weed and
coconut oil?"

I laughed. "And patchouli."

She hummed as I gently massaged her scalp, purred. "You're taking my energy by playing in my hair. Touching my hair like that makes me weak. I feel like a female Sampson, losing all my strength."

"You took mine."

She whispered, "Ken Swift?"

"That's my name."

"I remember the moment I first saw you. When I pulled up at Club Fetish and Jimi Lee took me to meet you. She was so drunk. Excited. Said you were fine as hell. And there you were, fashionable, tall, dark, handsome."

"And not African."

"My eyes saw you, but my soul felt you. I thought she picked the guy who would've been my type."

"Really?"

"If only for one night."

"Wow."

"It was loud and there were police and an ambulance, and in all that pandemonium, my soul felt you."

"You looked at me like you didn't care for me."

"I was jealous."

"And she was showing me off. Showing she could be free-spirited like you. You tried to shut it down."

"I had to protect my girl."

"You should have done a better job."

Again, the rain picked up, fell hard. Sounded like thunder in the distance. That was a rare sound in LA.

Lila listened to Mother Nature's roar, then whispered, "I had sex with my best friend's ex-husband."

"How do you feel?"

"Dizzy."

"Besides that."

"She's still my friend. We have been best friends since we were born. We were inseparable."

"I'm still her ex-husband."

"Wish I had met you before she did."

"If you had been there on time that night, I might've ended up with you."

"I might've been your girlfriend."

"Your parents?"

"Are not like hers. My parents are very liberal in some ways."

"We could have traveled together."

"You have been inside me." She sighed. "Now you have me feeling you."

"Likewise."

"There is so much I want to tell you about Jimi Lee."

"Tell me."

"You know I can't."

"Did she talk to you about the others? The men she cheated on me with, did she talk to you about them?"

Lila hesitated, then in just more than a whisper she finally answered, "Yes. She did."

"You knew."

"Ken."

"It's okay."

A few seconds passed.

I said, "She never apologized."

"In that way, she's like her father."

"I did my best. I gave up just as much."

"You were at UCLA."

I repeated, "She did me wrong and never apologized."

"You cheat, your fault. We cheat, your fault."

"Maybe we aren't entitled to simple thank-yous and apologies."

"Ken. I was joking."

"She told a lot of lies."

"She acted in her best interest."

"She wasn't a good wife."

"But she's not a bad person. She doesn't handle conflict or her own anger well. People can be very intelligent in one way, but in other ways have no clue what to do. Everything about her changed."

"Was it depression?"

"I guess. I wanted her to talk to someone,

but she had too much pride. But you have to look at things from her perspective. Imagine you were on the fast track to Harvard. When she was done, she would make over six figures a year. She would have had total independence from her family. From men. Her own autonomy. Imagine if you had that, or had an option to go to Yale, and you lost it all, that and shamed your family. I know people, kids, who have killed themselves for less. You have big dreams, then feel like you've lost it all, that and the love of your family."

"She cheated."

"People do things to escape what they feel. She was unhappy with someone when she met you, then was unhappy again. Unhappy people look for temporary happiness. Very smart people, some will always be restless."

"She's bigger than me."

"What do you mean?"

"She had a greater destiny than the one set out for me."

"Well, let her tell it, she's bigger than me, too."

"Until she met me."

"And in my opinion, you were the best man in her life."

"What else did she tell you?"

"You've done bad things."

"That bother you?"

"We've all done bad things."

"Do you know the bad things I've done? What did Jimi Lee tell you?"

"I'm not going to repeat it."

"What did she say happened?"

"She called me crying. Upset. Traumatized by something that happened in Florida."

"What did she say?"

"You were covered in blood."

"What else did she say?"

"She saw how you were living, was scared you might be killed any day, so she stashed money. Said you had money, that you didn't keep track of all your money, and she opened a secret account. She embezzled."

My jaw tightened. "What did she tell you about Florida?"

Lila patted my hand as if to say she didn't want to take it there.

I told her, "I told Jimi Lee that I'd take her to court, said I'd get Johnnie Cochran. See what a judge says."

"I don't want to be in the middle of it, Ken."

"I'm fucked."

"She is a mother. She sees herself as protecting her daughter."

"She's following her father's orders."

"And maybe her new husband's orders."

474

"All I can do is pay child support and alimony."

"You're not the only man paying and can't see their child."

I thought about Miami, and I was pulled back into the zone of the dead. I remembered that motherfucker Balthazar Walkowiak. I thought about that debacle. The blood. I had killed a man, and Jimi Lee knew I'd killed a man.

She wasn't ride or die. She was about self-preservation. Maybe that was what had changed everything.

For her, our marriage had been an act of self-preservation.

Lila whispered, "Ken? You cool?"

Spell broken, I touched my injuries. "You said you had pictures of your goddaughter?"

She nodded. "I like you. Out of bed, I like you. I would have been a better wife."

"You don't seem the type. You rock a little red Corvette and make people think of Darling Nikki."

"A façade. I like being home. If you were my man, I'd find time to be with you."

"If I were your man, I'd make you happy."

"I wish she could see us now."

"She pissed you off?"

"All this drama. She ruined my character."

"She did a JFK on mine, too."

"Anyway. Let's not start talking bad about my girl. We both love her, Ken."

"I love my daughter."

Lila took out her phone, still high, reluctantly showed me pictures from Jimi Lee's wedding. My daughter had been a flower girl. It was a big affair. Jimi Lee looked like a queen. And she looked happy in every image.

She said, "For the record, your lovemaking is all Jimi Lee said it was."

Feeling emotional, I put her phone down. "She talked a lot about our sex?"

"In the beginning. The night you met. When I called her the next morning, she told me all about Soul Stealer. Described how good you made her feel. All she wanted to do was get back to you. She wanted to make love and feel good again. Told me you were very comprehensive. But she didn't tell me about the rest."

"The rest?"

"You make love like a man, not like a boy."

"How so?"

"The way you kiss and how passionate you are. You are here with me. You look me in my eyes. You make a woman feel a connection she's never felt before. Makes me feel like I've been with weak men, or inexperienced boys who didn't know what they were doing. I see why Jimi Lee kept lying and coming back to be with you."

"Do you?"

"Well, on one level. There is more to a relationship than sex. But without sex, most times there is no relationship. You make me feel good. You make love to a woman and she feels love. You are an intense lover. My God. You are intense. And you're not selfish. You care about how I feel. You want to make me feel good and come."

"I want you to come. I want you to feel what I feel."

"It's better than sex."

"Then why did she leave?"

"Make a woman feel this good, and it's terrifying. A woman loses focus and becomes afraid."

"Bullshit. If I were Yohanes, she'd still be here."

"Sex is like alcohol. It gets you high, but then you get sober. People get a sex high, have a love hangover, but they sober up and have a change of heart. Some people might not feel sober for years, some the next day."

She did her inebriated walk down the hallway. Small waist. Real nice bottom. Wrapped in intelligence.

I asked, "You okay?"

"You made me sweat."

"Same here. Sheets are damp."

"My God, Ken."

"What?"

"You loved me long time."

"Weed makes me go on and on."

"Blame it on the rain."

"That too."

She winked. "I needed this."

"You're the one who kept on going like the bunny in that battery commercial."

"Weed gets me in a mood too. You can keep up with me. I'm impressed. Got me hot like a sauna."

"The rain is flooding the city and we made the room humid."

She rose on her tiptoes, stretched, then opened the door. "Need to freshen up."

"That's the closet you're about to go in."

She laughed. "My bad."

"No problem."

She saw what was inside. "What are all of these packages?"

"Gifts."

"For who?"

"Margaux. I buy her birthday presents. Christmas presents."

"Why are they here?"

"Jimi Lee won't give them to her."

"All these toys. She'd love these toys. That's sad."

"Can you take them and get them to her?"

"I can't be involved, not like that."

"I know."

"Jimi Lee know?"

"She knows."

"You were a good dad."

"Did my best."

She closed the closet, then went inside the bathroom. She closed the bathroom door, made sure the lock was on, did her business, then took a shower. Took her more than twenty minutes. While she was gone, I changed the sheets on the bed. When she was done, she came back. Her fragrance arrived before she did and startled me. I guess some of my ex-wife's soap had been left inside the shower. Now Lila smelled like Jimi Lee.

They looked similar in a tribal way. Lila's body was untouched by motherhood.

I asked, "Feel better?"

She sighed and tendered her big smile. "You put it on me, Ken."

"I like you, Lila."

"I'm feeling you too."

"I remember the moment we met, how you looked at me. Never imagined you feeling anything for me."

"I've always felt some kinda way about you."

"Really? Since when?"

"Maybe since you met her parents. I really felt for you that day."

"Well, I'm not married anymore."

"Jimi Lee has moved on and married Yohanes."

I licked my lips. "We could do something."

"Don't play."

"Serious."

"That would be complicated."

"But it could be done."

"Could be a bridge too far."

"Or just a new bridge others will have to learn to cross."

"Wouldn't that bother you?"

"What if we were the love story that was supposed to happen?"

"Yeah. And Jimi Lee was the one who got in our way."

"What if this moment . . . us finally being together . . . our chemistry . . . what if this is what all this has been about?"

She hummed. "If we let enough time go by, it wouldn't look so bad. I'd have to ask Jimi Lee if I could date you, ask her permission, but when I asked, she'd know that I've already seen you in some way."

"Or don't ask. Jimi Lee has moved on and married and never checked to see if I had any feelings. She besmirched your name."

"I'd have to ask."

"Okay. You could ask."

Lila nodded. "She was still coming here to sleep with you. She never really left you."

"That's over."

"You slept with her a few days ago."

"It's over."

"You had an affair with your ex-wife for months."

"I did. Not because I chose to."

"Why did you sleep with her?"

"Kept hoping she would bring Margaux."

"I don't believe that's why."

"All I do is about Margaux."

"I should go get her, tell Jimi Lee I want her for the weekend, let you come to my house and see her."

"You'd only be able to do that once. Margaux would tell."

"Yeah. She tells everything."

"Why did Jimi Lee leave me, then come back to be in my bed?"

"I think she fell in love with you after she left you. I think she was in love with you all the time, but the family she has, she never knew how to stand up to them. Her father is a mean man. She and her siblings are afraid of him."

"I've hurt men for less than what he's done."

"Jimi Lee told me you were capable of doing some . . . dark things. But you were always gentle with her."

"Let's talk about me and you."

"Is there a me and you?"

"There is now."

"Since when?"

"Since I went in you raw and skeeted."

She laughed. "Oh my God."

"You asked."

"This was unexpected."

"Just like the rain."

"Feels surreal."

"The liquor?"

"The weed."

"I'm serious. This have traction?"

She paused. "How would that work out for my goddaughter? Seeing me with her dad like this."

"She'd adjust. Just like I have had to adjust and change my life year after year."

"It's different for kids."

"Kids adjust."

"My father cheated on my mother."

"This isn't cheating."

"But it's wrong."

Those soft words paused me. "Your father messing around impacted you?"

"Yeah. I walked in on my dad while he

482

was having sex with a woman in our Jacuzzi."

"At your home?"

"Yeah. Came home from school. I was skipping school, and he had skipped work."

"How did that work out?"

"The next day he bought me a brand-new, fully loaded red Corvette."

"Wow. That was when you were in high school."

"I sold out for a shiny red Corvette."

"You didn't tell your mother."

"It would destroy her. She loves my father. I couldn't open my mouth and break up our family. I would've been the bad one. My father put me in a bad position. Same as Jimi Lee put me in a bad position with you."

"Hopefully I put you in a good position."

"Oh, yes you did. A few good positions. You put me in a couple I had never tried before."

"You're flexible."

"Had me climbing the walls like Spider-Man."

I paused. "I thought life in Malibu was a lot better, especially for a girl as rich and pretty as you."

She wiped her eyes. "I might have money, might look a certain way, but my life has been complicated."

"You're beautiful."

"Eye of the beholder. White people still find something wrong with every aspect of my physical being."

"You're always confident, always strong, and always smiling."

"The people who smile the most are the least happy. The ones who smile the most have the darkest secrets. Confidence is an insecure person's shield. And you have to be strong or the world will mess you over. People like me, we keep liquor and weed nearby. We medicate with drugs and sex. We find a way to escape. Some keep a razor blade near, in case they want to put small cuts on their thighs, or just go all the way and slit their wrists."

"You cut yourself?"

"Don't ask me that."

I nodded. "What did Jimi Lee say about your father's affair and the Corvette as hush money?"

"She doesn't know. No one knows but you. I've never talked about it."

"Why?"

"Still traumatized. I don't want her to not like my father or behave differently in front of my mother."

"You're not going to snitch?"

"I'm serious. I don't want people to dislike my father or think less of my mother. They'll think she's not a good wife, that she has done something to cause my father to be the whore that he is. I have to protect my mother."

"Family first."

"Everything is about family because family is everything."

"You okay?"

"Get your shower. I'll be finished crying by the time you're done."

"Okay."

"Pour me another tall glass of Spumante before you go."

CHAPTER 38

I flossed, brushed my teeth, showered in cold water because she'd used up all the hot, and came out naked. She was on the bed, inebriated, waiting. She finished her Spumante and pulled the covers back. She turned her back to me and scooted up against me. We cuddled. No words. We listened to the rain. We listened to the winds as they sang. I held her until we went to sleep. In the middle of the night, I jerked awake. The rain had stopped. A ghetto bird was flying over the Crenshaw District. It woke Lila too. She turned and faced me. She eased her hand down between my legs, moved her hand until that part of me stood halfway at attention.

She whispered, "Ken?"

I moaned. "Yeah?"

Her breathing was thick, curt like mine, passion making her pant like she was in need. She gave me her tongue, kissed me hard, and I held on to her breast like it was a gift from God to man.

She bit the corner of her lip, whispered, "*Soixante-neuf.* Show me how you did Jimi Lee."

I gave her what she wanted, gave it to her until tongue wasn't enough to please her, until her mouth was more than I could handle; then she mounted me. She knew how to shake the bed.

"Oh Ken oh Ken oh Ken."

Her orgasm was beautiful, progressive, came in the key of E major. Eight minutes later, the fever was broken, the bed was almost broken, and she fell away from me panting. I rubbed her back for a moment, rubbed her until her breathing normalized. I hadn't come, was still hard enough to not be able to sleep. I eased on top of her, pushed her legs open, and put my hands in the nexus of the place she opened to receive pleasure.

She reached down, held my erection, stroked me as she whispered, "I'm dying to know."

"What?"

"So, who is better in bed?"

"Really?"

"Me or Jimi Lee?"

"Is it a competition?"

"We've been competing all our lives."

"All girls compete."

"All women compete. Boyfriends. Weddings. Marriage. Children. It's all one big competition."

I whispered, "You're better."

"Yeah?"

"Yeah."

"I love the way you use your tongue."

"Yeah?"

"You make me feel like I'm canvas and you're creating art, or writing love letters with your tongue."

With the sounds of LAPD's ghetto birds and the slave catcher's sirens riding into my world, we fell into fevered kisses. We consumed each other again. Lila wasn't a pillow queen. She liked her sex dirty. Once she started, the fire was hard to put out and it was like she was under a spell. I wanted to be inside of her forever. I could love her. With each stroke, it felt like I did love her in some way. I tried to make her come a dozen times. I tried to make her fall in love with me. And if I couldn't do that, I wanted to empty myself of what I felt for Jimi Lee. I wanted to orgasm the love I had for Jimi Lee out of my system.

CHAPTER 39

When I woke up the next morning, Lila was wrapped around me, cuddling, her warmth mixing with mine. I rested like that, felt the alcohol and weed fading from my system, then woke Lila with kisses. I'd never seen her this way. Blemishes. Pimples. All the makeup gone. Away from the little red Corvette. I saw her imperfections.

With the biggest smile I'd ever seen, her morning voice coarse, she said, "I didn't wrap my hair."

I ran my fingers through her mane. "Hungry?"

"Famished. You said you had breakfast food?"

"Eggs. Bacon. Bread."

"Give me five minutes and I'll cook you something."

"I'll grab us some breakfast from Simply Wholesome."

"What's that?"

"They only serve healthy food. Black-owned. Only five minutes away."

"Can you get me an egg-white omelet? Make it vegetarian."

"To drink?"

"Orange juice."

Her big smile was contagious. I leaned to her, kissed her breasts, sucked her nipples.

I asked, "What do you have to do today?"

"Nothing. I'm free today."

"Rain is gone."

"Sun is coming out."

"Let's hang out."

She hummed and kissed my lips. "I have some more clothes in my car."

"Single women always ready."

"Yeah. We are." She laughed. "I can wrap my hair in a scarf."

"Leave it down."

"It's out of control. I look like who did it and what for."

"You look like a queen. Leave it open. Let's ride to Beverly Hills and get a hotel room."

"For real?"

"Yeah. I can get us a room. Pamper you. We can take a bath together."

"Sounds like fun. Maybe we can eat at an Ethiopian restaurant on Fairfax."

"I'd like that."

"I know several. All have good food."

"You can choose."

"Go get food."

"Or I can just eat you and feed you again."

"Get me a different kind of protein." She hummed, the big smile bigger. "I let you put your penis inside me."

"Over and over."

"You are a good lover."

"So are you."

"We have amazing chemistry in bed."

"We made love all night long."

"And I still want more."

Lila kissed me like she was my wife. I wished I had met her, not Jimi Lee. I moved to get out of bed, and she pulled me back, opened her legs for me again, took me inside her, put me inside her, put all of me inside her, made me rise like never before and moan like a man who had lost his goddamned mind, and while her passion wrestled with mine, I made the headboard rock and roll. I looked in her eyes as she came, stroked her as she shuddered and begged me come with her.

Then we were in the shower, cleaning each other, laughing, talking.

All the while I wished the door would open and Jimi Lee would walk in on us.

CHAPTER 40

When I came back with breakfast, music was on, but Lila was gone.

I knew she had left before I came upstairs. The little red Corvette was gone from its spot downstairs. She had been gone long enough for someone to fill her parking space.

Janet Jackson sang to me. Told me about the principle of pleasure.

I stood in the kitchen, ate my pancakes, nibbled her omelet, drank my apple juice, sipped her orange juice.

I understood. We had crossed a line.

Inebriated, she felt desire. Sober, the shame was greater.

She got to see what she had missed out on when we met that night at Club Fetish. I got to imagine I had made a different choice.

One day Lila would have to look Jimi Lee in her brown eyes. She'd have to play with her goddaughter.

What we had done could take that all away.

I'd pretend that night didn't happen.

I'd been with my daughter's godmother. I had bedded my ex-wife's best friend, had put Soul Stealer balls deep inside the woman who had helped my disgruntled wife lie and cheat and destroy my family.

Some revenge had many levels.

If Lila had come back, I would have made love to her again.

It wouldn't have been my intent, but she had a conscience, and I would have destroyed her.

There was a time to plant. A time to reap. A time to build. A time to tear down.

There was a time to dance. A time to sing. A time to laugh. A time to cry.

And there was a time to walk away.

My beeper danced. San Bernardino called me.

An hour later Jake Ellis was at my front door, just off the plane from Africa.

He said, "Bruv, I have a Senegalese girl in Ghana waiting on you to come over."

"Yeah? What she look like?"

"The kind you like. And I showed her your photo, so you're the kind she likes."

"She smart?"

"She's attending university now. She speaks English, Spanish, German, Italian, a mix of Wolof and French. Bruv, you hear her tell you, *Bonjour,* one time and you'll be buying another wedding ring."

"I might get on the next plane with you."

"You should have been on the last plane with me."

"If I was a single man with no responsibilities, I would've been sitting in first class next to you."

"Bruv, you won't come back to this side of the Atlantic Ocean, not to do more than visit."

"Bonjour."

"Bonjour."

"Senegalese."

"Straight out of Dakar."

We did what men do and talked about women.

I told him about Jimi Lee, about her Wednesdays, our affair, about Yohanes coming to my door.

Jake Ellis said, "If you ever want to go to Diamond Bar and settle the score . . ."

I shook my head, thought about Lila, said, "Nah. Far as I'm concerned the score is settled."

Jake Ellis told me about the women he'd entertained in Ghana and Nigeria.

I almost told him about Lila. Almost.

But I kept that to myself, between me and her.

He showed me photos of the home he had built in Ghana. And he'd gotten his bachelor's degree.

After a few laughs, I packed a few things and asked, "Where we off to?"

"Vancouver. San Bernardino doesn't like being robbed."

"Three-day drive."

"We can do it in two. But we'll do it in three."

"Safeguards in place?"

"Yeah, bruv. We can't have another Florida."

"Word."

"I don't plan on getting shot again."

"You didn't plan on getting shot that time."

"I don't want to have to feed another alligator."

"Or crocodile or whatever was out there."

It was time for me to work. I had child support to pay. I had to make sure my daughter had food on her table. I kept my word. I took cash and went to the Bank of America, wired three thousand dollars to Jimi Lee's account. I was angry with Jimi Lee, dreamed about killing her father and siblings both day and night, but I made sure Margaux had food, clothing, shelter, and wipes for her tender ass. Each day I hoped Jimi Lee would call. That never happened. I had to go on with my life.

People lived with shrapnel in their bodies all the time.

I had to learn to do the same.

I asked Jake Ellis, "Know any girls up that way?"

"Oh yeah. I know a model from Lodwar, Kenya, and an actress from Durban, South Africa."

"Call 'em up."

"Already did, bruv. Already did."

I didn't call Lila.

I'd take the blame for what happened between us.

I was drowning and had tried to cling to her like she was a life preserver.

We had crossed a line. It couldn't be undone.

I doubted if she would ever call me again.

But she had my address and mailed me about two hundred photos of Margaux. That had meant more than the world to me.

She had felt something.

And that something would keep her away.

I was going to send a thank-you.

I didn't.

That might have been too much.

It might have started something.

Those photos of Margaux were all that mattered to me.

I bought four photo albums from Costco, added those pictures to the ones I had.

I was a man obsessed with his own child.

A man with a war in his mind.

Then I stood in my window, looked out at Leimert Park like I was its pope.

I watched Leimert Park refuse to change.

I watched it hold on to its past.

And it watched me refuse to change.

It watched me hold on to my past.

But we changed.

Bit by bit, in ways we never noticed.

Like it or not, want to or not, we changed.

I was no longer the man I had been at twenty-one.

Jimi Lee was no longer the girl she had been at eighteen.

But whoever she was, whoever I was now, I still loved her.

CHAPTER 41

A year went by.

Then two.

Then three.

Pain lessened with time.

But time never erased all pain.

For that to happen, time would have to be able to give a man amnesia.

Jimi Lee never went away from my thoughts, but she was reduced to a low hum.

We had a child, so I was sure that a low hum existed for Jimi Lee as well.

That hum wouldn't ever go away.

That hum reminded me of my obligations. That hum told me whom I had loved once upon a time.

Each year I bought Margaux a birthday present and a card, added whatever I picked up to the other birthday cards and Christmas presents, let them accumulate. Like a heartbroken fool. Like some sort of a hoarder. I had no idea where Jimi Lee and my daughter were, what they were doing, didn't know if they were dead or alive.

I was at the same spot on Stocker, same apartment, with new furniture, and the same old cellular number I had had since I bought my first mobile phone. Maybe I was waiting for them to come back.

At times, I felt like a man with his feet stuck in concrete, and that concrete had dried many years before.

I wondered who I might have been, if not for one night, if not for going to do one job.

I'd had my eyes on Africa, but I had stepped into Club Fetish, become distracted, and taken my eyes off the prize. America had never felt like home, and I had been homesick for the motherland all of my life. The distance between me and Africa felt the same as the distance between me and the moon. Most days the moon felt closer.

I had had a five-year plan.

Jimi Lee had had her eyes on Harvard.

She had had a ten-year plan.

She was going to be a doctor and heal the world.

I was going home to Africa.

A black man planned, and God laughed.

I guess when a black woman planned, God laughed harder.

CHAPTER 42

I was twenty-one when I met Jimi Lee.

The nineties had come and gone; rap had evolved into trap.

Now I was forty-three, a few years younger than Barak Obama was when he was elected president of the United States of America. Not young, but not old. Not a word from the former in-laws in Diamond Bar since that night they came and jumped me like I was from a rival gang. Not a word from that faction that hailed from the Horn of Africa. Not a word from my ex-wife. Hadn't seen my daughter's face or heard her voice since she left as a child. That closet had collected at least two presents a year. It looked like a broken man's obsession. A father's obsession.

I no longer pined for Jimi Lee, but I had wished to see Margaux every day. A man had to be careful what he wished for. My wish came true today. My phone rang this morning, before the rising of the sun. It wasn't San Bernardino calling with another job. Jake Ellis and I had finished a job yesterday out in Palm Springs, had put a good hurting on some bad folks. I knew we had a job later in Pasadena, had to visit an Ivy League man named Garrett. It wasn't my girlfriend, Rachel Redman, calling and I didn't recognize the number. It was one of Los Angeles's area codes. Had to be a telemarketer with a lot of nerve. I was in bed alone. I was about to send the call to voice mail, had meant to hit the red button, but I accidentally pushed the green button and answered.

In an early morning dehydrated voice I managed to say, "Hello."

A woman with a strong, articulate, bill collector's voice asked, "May I speak to Ken Swift?"

"Yeah." I cleared my throat. "What can I do for you this early in the goddamn morning?"

"It's Margaux."

"Margaux who?"

"My mother was married to you a long time ago. They tell me that I'm your daughter."

"Margaux Swift?"

"Yes."

"Tsigereda? Don't play with me. Is this you for real?"

"Just call me Margaux."

I heard edges of Africa in her voice. Not much. It was in the background, but it was there.

I sat up. Big smile on my face. Tears trying to form in my eyes. I hadn't heard from Jimi Lee in years. I had resigned myself to thinking I'd never hear from them again. I walked and stood in the window facing Stocker, looked out on apartment row. I saw Bernice Nesbitt in her window. The woman from London was still living there. A lot of people had come and gone from Leimert Park, but we were still here. Down below, early risers were up. It was summertime. One of the hottest days on record. Wildfires were on the other side of Burbank. White people were walking dogs, jogging, pushing baby carriages as arrogant traffic moved up and down the tree-lined avenue. Signs protesting gentrification were on telephone poles. None of that mattered to me. I had been pulled back in time.

She said, "I need to meet with you today."

"Tomorrow would be better."

"Well, Ken Swift, this is urgent and I need you to make yourself available today."

"Excuse me?"

"You heard me."

Two decades of anger were alive in her voice.

The sudden attitude and palpable hate shocked me.

I told her, "I have to work, but we can meet at Zula's."

"Zula's? What is that?"

"Zula Ethiopian and Eritrean Restaurant."

"No. Not there."

"It's a nice spot. Won't be crowded."

"Meet me at TGI Fridays in Ladera, not far from where you live."

"You do know you're talking to your father, right?"

"Ken Swift."

"And this is my daughter?"

"The daughter you abandoned."

I hesitated. "And you're calling me for what exactly?"

"To meet."

"For what?"

"Fifty thousand dollars."

"What?"

"Ken Swift, I need you to give me fifty thousand dollars."

Again I hesitated. "For what?"

"Not over the phone. Face-to-face."

"What's this all about, Margaux?"

"Be at TGIF." She told me the time.

"Don't be late."

"Will your mother be there?"

"Worry about the money, not my mother."

"Is this a joke?"

"This is serious." Her voice strained. "Ken Swift, this is serious."

"Margaux Swift." I nodded. "Okay. I'll meet you at TGI Fridays."

She hung up.

Hers was a voice I didn't recognize. Last time I'd talked to her she was a child, had a child's voice and temperament. She'd loved *VeggieTales* and American Girl dolls. That image of her in my mind was outdated. Margaux was a grown woman with a disposition to match. I'd paid, had sent money to Jimi Lee for Margaux until half a year past her eighteenth birthday. Not one phone call had ever come this way. Not one thanks for doing what I'd promised I'd do. But I guess a man wasn't supposed to get thanked for doing what he was supposed to do.

I didn't know Margaux anymore.

Soon Margaux would let me know she was the same kind of fool now that Jimi Lee had been back in the nineties. She wanted fifty thousand dollars from me, the dad she had been taught to despise.

Soon I'd realize my child knew things, knew about Florida, and had called me so she could blackmail me.

But for now, the call ended as abruptly as it had started.

I didn't know if I should be excited or scared.

But I was both.

I saw my battery was low, so I put my phone on a charger, then went to my hall closet and took out my old photo albums. Heart thumping, I looked at pictures of my daughter, images of her from birth until she was five.

Her bushy, wavy hair. Her brown eyes.

Her beautiful brown skin.

My beautiful brown baby was a beautiful black woman now.

She was an angry woman, an angry half-African woman.

She came at me like I was the epicenter of her pain.

My daughter had called.

That hum. Now it was louder. Loud enough to make me cringe and rub my temples. For a moment, that hum was unbearable.

The proverbial saying said that curses were like chickens; they always came home to roost.

Many moons had come and gone, and now my daughter was a beautiful brown bird returning to its old nest. In anger. Demanding money. Extorting her old man.

This morning, all I'd had to worry about was another job for San Bernardino with Jake Ellis. But now I had to meet Margaux first.

I pulled a pair of straight-leg jeans from my closet, tossed them on the bed, did the same with a Muhammad Ali T-shirt and a trendy gray suit coat.

I was more scared than excited. The past was never done with us.

In a few hours, I'd know my estranged daughter knew about Balthazar Walkowiak. I'd realize that my only child was my enemy and our family tree had become a wild rat snake and was about to try to cannibalize itself.

I didn't know what Jimi Lee had to do with this, but it was my time to reap.

ACKNOWLEDGMENTS

Hello, O ye faithful reader! You are the best of the best!

Once again, thanks for checking out my latest offering.

While creating *Bad Men and Wicked Women,* I started working on a short scene to show Ken and Jimi Lee's backstory, but it was more than could be contained in a few paragraphs. I was interested in their entire relationship, before they were wicked, well, as wicked, the details, not the surface stuff. So, I packed my bags, hopped in my secondhand time machine (bought it used on Craigslist, formerly owned by some guy named H. G. Wells) and went to the 1990s. ☺

For *Before We Were Wicked,* I wanted to cover Ken Swift's life from the moment he met Jimi Lee in the '90s until Margaux returned, in the present day, so this novel actually flows right into the first page of *Bad*

Men and Wicked Women seamlessly. I know, they dropped in reverse order, but that's because they were written that way. So it goes. I hope you enjoyed the ride back to the '90s as much as I did. I'll park my time machine in the cluttered garage. Or put it back on Craigslist.

Usually I say a lot, but that's all I got. Been a long day.

Stephanie J. Kelly, my amazing editor, thank you so much for believing in this. Thanks for all the hard work back there in NYC.

Emily Canders and everyone in publicity, thanks so much!

To everyone at Penguin Random House, thanks for the love.

To my agent, Sara Camilli, we're getting closer to book 100. Hmmm. We're about a third of the way there. LOL! Thanks for everything.

Drum roll!

And you, special person, invaluable one, friend of all friends, as always, I'm not going to forget ya! Always saving the best for last.

I want to thank _____ for their assistance, love, turkey bacon, and conversation while I was bringing the tale of Ken Swift and Jimi Lee to the page.

You can find me at ericjeromedickey.com. From there you can link to me on social media. Follow or add, but don't mute! LOL.

April 2, 2018, 09:27 P.M.
57 degrees, mostly cloudy,
chance of rain 10%
Gray Adidas T, beat-up fitted cap,
joggers, trainers
Latitude: 33.988543
Longitude: -118.3340814
Carolyn's son.
Miss Virginia's grandson.
Mrs. Gause's godchild.
That dude from Carver High
and U of M in the 901.

Eric Jerome Dickey, 06

ABOUT THE AUTHOR

Eric Jerome Dickey is the *New York Times* bestselling author of twenty-four novels and is also the author of a six-issue miniseries of graphic novels for Marvel Entertainment, featuring Storm (*X-Men*) and the Black Panther. He also penned the original story for the film *Cappuccino,* directed by Craig Ross Jr. Originally from Memphis, Tennessee, Dickey is a graduate of the University of Memphis, where he pledged Alpha Phi Alpha, and also attended UCLA. Dickey now lives on the road and rests in whatever hotel will have him.

The employees of Thorndike Press hope you have enjoyed this Large Print book. All our Thorndike, Wheeler, and Kennebec Large Print titles are designed for easy reading, and all our books are made to last. Other Thorndike Press Large Print books are available at your library, through selected bookstores, or directly from us.

For information about titles, please call:
  (800) 223-1244

or visit our website at:
  gale.com/thorndike

To share your comments, please write:
  Publisher
  Thorndike Press
  10 Water St., Suite 310
  Waterville, ME 04901